THE CRYING GIRLS

BOOKS BY WENDY DRANFIELD

WENDY DRANFIELD

THE
CRYING
GIRLS

bookouture

Published by Bookouture in 2024

An imprint of Storyfire Ltd.
Carmelite House
50 Victoria Embankment
London EC4Y 0DZ

Storyfire Ltd's authorised representative in the EEA is Hachette Ireland
8 Castlecourt Centre
Castleknock Road
Castleknock
Dublin 15 D15 YF6A
Ireland

www.bookouture.com

ISBN: 978-1-83525-976-4
eBook ISBN: 978-1-83525-975-7

For Joey, my first cat, who sadly passed away at almost sixteen during the writing of this novel. I never thought I'd say this, but I actually miss the 4 a.m. wake-up calls.

PROLOGUE

The grainy camcorder footage begins. An overweight man appears on the TV screen. He's seated in a dirty brown armchair, surrounded by an unkempt, dimly lit living room. The picture has interference, making it difficult to see the man's features.

He takes a deep breath before raising a whiskey glass to his mouth. The ice rattles inside. He swallows before exhaling loudly.

Minutes pass, and the only sound is his soft crying, which halts each time he sips his drink. His face is a blur of beige. The VHS tape has degraded over the years and the dated VCR struggles to play it properly. The absence of daylight in the house doesn't help the picture quality, causing shadows to creep in the space behind him.

Suddenly, a voice. "I'm so sorry!" he whimpers. "I never meant for that to happen, sweetheart." He leans his head back and groans at the ceiling as if in physical pain. After another sip of his drink, he mutters, "Why did you have to ruin everything?"

He gets up and disappears off camera. While he's gone, the empty armchair keeps the outline of his shape, or perhaps it's his soul left behind. The tape churns as the camcorder records the chair. Ripples in the picture quality cause the illusion of a paranormal entity moving back and forth nearby.

When the man returns, he collapses into the seat, bottle in one hand, glass in the other, full now. Irritating white lines of interference roll over the image, making it difficult to see any detail other than the color of his skin. He's white. A gold bracelet hangs loose at his wrist. His hair is brown.

"You've left me so lonely, and it's only been a few hours," he says. He raises the glass to his lips again and downs it all, ice included. He wipes his mouth with his sleeve. "Women are good at making friends—hell, you'd talk to anyone—but it's not like that for us. Loneliness can kill a man. You *knew* that. You knew that's why I needed you here."

He breaks down again. The sobbing comes from somewhere deep. His grief is so raw that it seems incomprehensible he'd want to capture it on camera. Is he hoping to watch it back one day to relive his darkest moments? Perhaps he's not in his right mind.

"I should've known this would happen." His words slur into each other. "I read in a newspaper once that women are more likely to try to escape their situation when they're pregnant. It's thought the baby gives them an incentive. They realize they have something to live for." He scoffs. "Like you had nothing to live for already." He suddenly yells, "You had *me*, dammit!"

A snowstorm attacks the picture, making it difficult to see the man for a few seconds.

"Is that what happened, sweetie?" His tone is sympathetic now. "You thought the baby needed a better life than I could provide?"

He listens for a response. When there isn't one, he downs

the liquor directly from the bottle and wipes his eyes with his spare hand. "I should be angry that you tried to take my first-born child away from me before I even met them, but I'm not. I could never get angry with you, as you well know. Hell, I let you walk all over me." He snorts affectionately at some memory the camcorder can't capture. "You know what I'm most upset about?" He doesn't wait for a response this time. "The loneliness that's waiting for me now. The long, drawn-out nights will close in on me again. The silence will scare me to the point of wanting to blow my brains out."

He suddenly jumps out of his seat, dropping the half-empty liquor bottle. It doesn't smash. It rolls toward his feet and hovers, a potential safety hazard. "I can't do it again. I can't go through that again!"

He paces back and forth, narrowly missing the bottle each time until he kicks it out of the way so hard it smashes against the wall, spraying liquid everywhere. With his head and shoulders out of frame, only his brown pants and bloodstained sneakers are visible.

He lets out a deep, sorrowful groan as the tape goes black for a second, leaving nothing except the rolling white lines. It's clear that this tape will soon be useless. Due to the years of degradation, his inadvertent confession will be lost forever.

He can be heard sniffing the air. "Man, you're starting to stink already." With a deep sigh, he adds, "How do I even begin cleaning you up? I don't know where you keep the mops."

Seemingly out of energy, the man flops down and rests his head in his hands. He has a full head of hair, which he grabs by the handful as he stares at his feet. "I don't get it," he mutters. "I was so good to you."

Several minutes pass as he remains motionless. The only sound is the irritating ticking of a large clock.

Finally, he sits back and inhales deeply. His emotions

appear to have gone full circle as he becomes more aware of his surroundings. Once again, he gets out of his seat. This time, he approaches the camcorder and leans over it to find the off switch, muttering, "I guess I need to go out and find a replacement."

CHAPTER ONE

Lost Creek, Colorado

Detective Madison Harper wakes to the sound of a dog barking. Unwilling to believe it's Monday morning already, she pulls the comforter farther over her head. "Sort your dog out, Nate."

She tries to fall back to sleep without waiting for a response. But Brody is persistent. He barks again, causing the cat to jump down from the bed.

She sighs. Now he's woken Bandit, there's no hope.

As if on cue, the cat begins loudly protesting at the closed bedroom door. Nate must have shut it by mistake when he came up last night.

"Nate," she mumbles. "Open the door."

When he doesn't respond, Madison turns over to nudge him, rolling onto the bullet wound she received to her upper arm last month. She winces. Although it's healing nicely, it's still sore when she puts too much weight on it.

She finds his side of the bed empty. Confused, she looks at the clock on her nightstand. It's almost 6 a.m. on a dark January morning. Her alarm is about to go off. She switches on a lamp. It takes a few seconds for her eyes to adjust to the soft orange glow. When they do, she realizes Nate's not here.

"Where is he?" she asks the cat.

Bandit meows. He doesn't care where Nate is. He wants breakfast.

She figures Nate must have fallen asleep downstairs. They only recently moved in together, so Madison's not used to his routine yet. She switches off her alarm before it comes on and yawns. It dawns on her that if Nate were downstairs, Brody wouldn't be trying to claw his way into the bedroom. Alarmed, she flips back the covers and gets out of bed. She crosses the room to open the door and finds the large German shepherd/husky mix pacing back and forth in the hallway, agitated.

Madison's heart drops into her stomach. Brody's a former cadaver dog. And Nate hasn't been himself for weeks. Not since he shot a man dead right before Christmas. As someone who wanted to become a priest before he was wrongfully incarcerated on death row for almost two decades, taking someone's life has caused him untold trauma that he vowed to fight.

A lump comes to her throat. What if he's lost the fight?

Images of Nate's lifeless body flood her mind as she considers the worst-case scenario. Her experience in law enforcement means her imagined scenarios are graphic. She sees the people she's discovered over the years: hanging from the rafters, slumped in their armchairs with gunshot wounds to the head, sprawled on concrete after jumping off tall buildings in a bid to escape law enforcement...

Brody barks impatiently in his bid to get her to follow him downstairs.

Madison swallows. "Where's your dad, Brody?"

He runs downstairs. The cat follows.

Madison forces her shaky legs to walk her to the top of the stairs. She can't smell anything. If Nate's taken his own life, he's done it within the last few hours. She'd left him reading downstairs when she went to bed last night. It had been a long day at work, and she had fallen asleep within minutes, failing to notice he hadn't followed her up.

She shudders. Hadn't she known this was a possibility the minute he fired the weapon he never wanted to own in the first place? Hadn't she known his mood was going downhill and his smile no longer reached his eyes? The minute he killed the Grave Mountain Stalker, he changed. And despite Owen, her son, returning from college for Christmas, Nate still hadn't been himself. Not really. He was distracted. He sought more alone time. He seemed less affectionate.

Now, she wonders whether that was because he blamed her for what happened. Not only had she urged him to carry a weapon for protection against the serial killer she was hunting, but she had also inadvertently put them both in a situation where he'd had no choice but to use it in order to save her life. Nate isn't a cop. He isn't trained to deal with the repercussions of killing someone.

Her legs are frozen in place.

A sound in the distance distracts her. Sirens. More than one. Blue and red flashing lights illuminate the street outside the window. "Oh no."

Did Nate have second thoughts and call for an ambulance to save himself? But what if they're too late?

She flies down the stairs to search for him, ready to administer first aid. "Nate!" she shouts. Her voice sounds like someone else's. It's too high-pitched.

He's not in the kitchen. She runs to the living room, but it's empty.

The sirens retreat as they race past the house to an accident or a crime scene.

Brody scratches at the front door as though he needs to get outside urgently. Could Nate be in his vehicle? Madison's hands are like ice as she considers whether he killed himself outside in an attempt to lessen her pain.

She opens the front door and peers into the darkness. The icy temperature sends chills through her pajamaed body. The porch light illuminates the driveway. Nate's Chevy is gone.

She takes a deep breath as relief swamps her. Maybe he couldn't sleep, so he went to fetch breakfast. But the tightness in her chest doesn't disappear. Her gut tells her something's still wrong. Nate's absence is palpable. Brody runs back inside. After closing the door, Madison heads through the kitchen to fetch her cell phone from upstairs. Something catches her eye on the way, stopping her in her tracks.

A note is pinned to the fridge. It has her name on it.

She stops breathing as she approaches it. It's Nate's handwriting.

If they hadn't recently gone through the Grave Mountain Stalker ordeal, she would assume it was a note saying he'd gone to fetch coffee or left early for work. But Madison feels in her bones that something's wrong. The air around her feels empty without him here. This is *his* house.

That's when she spots his cell phone on the counter. She frowns. Why would he leave that behind? How is she supposed to get hold of him? His firearm sits next to it, discarded. She already knows he'll never touch that again.

With growing trepidation, she opens the piece of paper and reads the message.

I'm struggling to exist right now. I need space or I'll die. I'm sorry.

Madison blinks back tears. He's left her. He's at his most vulnerable, and he's left to deal with his guilt alone. But what if he can't? What if this new guilt he carries—and not the seventeen years he spent on death row—is his breaking point?

Restless, Brody searches the house for his dad. The seriousness of the situation hits her with the realization that Nate left the dog behind. The pair have been inseparable since they met during a missing child case. It can only mean one thing: Nate's not thinking straight. He's going backward, into the pits of depression.

Madison is overcome with disappointment. She thought they had a chance at a good life together and that the worst was finally behind them. Instead, her world has changed in a heartbeat.

She drops the note. It gently floats to the floor and disappears under the refrigerator.

She touches the ring on her engagement finger. The ring he presented her with just five weeks ago. Angry that life continually wants to tease her with happiness before yanking it out from under her, she pulls the ring off and throws it across the room.

Upstairs, her cell phone rings. She considers ignoring it. She's not in the mood to talk to anyone. But it could be work. She forces herself upstairs and grabs it from the nightstand. "Hello?"

"Sorry to bother you so early," says Dina Blake from dispatch. "But I need you to attend the scene of a homicide."

Her heart flutters as she considers Nate's disappearance. He could still be dead in a ditch somewhere. "Homicide or unattended death?"

"Well, the guy's missing his head," says Dina, "so we're calling it a homicide."

Alarmed, Madison swallows. "Text me the location. I'm on my way."

CHAPTER TWO

Madison uses the flashing blue and red lights from the stationary police cruisers to lead her to the crime scene. She raced through red lights to get here, but all she can think about is Nate's absence and whether she'll ever see him again. Disturbed by not seeing his dad this morning, Brody barks from the backseat. Madison has to take care of him now, and she's unsure how the dog feels about it.

She makes a left into the Aspen View Mobile Home Park. The only information dispatch could give her about the crime scene was that the headless body of a white male has been found in the water just north of the park.

She's still unsettled by the thought that it could be Nate. He could've gotten drunk or high and picked a fight with the wrong person. The knot in her stomach tightens. Surely not? His note made it sound like he's left town. She tries to push the thought away, but her hands tremble regardless.

Her vehicle crawls past darkened trailers. Most residents are still sleeping, although she passes a couple of people getting into their cars, leaving for work. A tabby cat lazily watches her from behind someone's front window. When she reaches the creek at the end of the park, she switches the car's engine off and turns in her seat to look at Brody. "I know you miss your dad, but I need your help this morning. Think you can focus for me, buddy?"

Brody tilts his head as he tries to understand her. She didn't use any of his favorite words. His huge ears stand erect as saliva drips from his long tongue onto the black and ruby-red leather interior of her Dodge Demon. The car was a generous gift from Nate, which he could only afford due to his wrongful conviction compensation.

The shepsky eventually looks beyond her and through the windshield to the flashing lights and busy uniformed officers. As a former K9, Brody feels most at home around other cops. He barks forcefully. Maybe he thinks Nate's out there.

Madison smiles sadly. "Okay. Let's go."

She gets out of the car and opens the back door. Brody jumps out and races ahead of her to see his friends. Once he's made the uniformed officers aware of his presence and accepted their greetings, he gets to work sniffing the long grass that runs along the banks of the water.

The morning is frosty, making Madison shiver as she zips up her thick coat. Her shoulders sag when she realizes she left her gloves and hat at home due to her earlier distraction and the urgency of the dispatch call. Her shoulder-length blonde hair, which is well overdue a trim, quickly becomes wild in the wind.

As the sun is yet to appear over the distant snow-topped mountains that circle the town, Alex Parker, the Lost Creek PD's forensic technician, is setting up scene lighting. When she passes his car, she notices a tan-colored chihuahua in a knitted sweater contently curled up on a blanket on the front passenger seat. Mrs. Pebbles. Madison had temporarily homed her after the tiny dog's owner died last month. But Mrs. Pebbles is a diva, and she refused to cohabit with Brody and Bandit. Although, truth be told, she tolerated them better than she did Madison.

In the end, Alex offered to take her in, and Madison thinks it's a good pairing.

Her boots crunch over frost-tinged grass as she ducks under the yellow tape and hesitantly approaches the crime scene. Her new detective partner and former sergeant, Steve Tanner, is already here. Tall, dark-haired and always clean-shaven, Steve is the kind of guy most women look twice at in the street. Previously single for as long as she'd known him, he started dating the town's medical examiner last year. Although he's hinted to Madison that things were easier when he could concentrate on his two favorite things: working hard and keeping fit. Being a workaholic makes him an indispensable member of the department.

As he's a private guy, Madison doesn't know much about him outside of what he's like at work, but he was one hell of a sergeant until he swapped roles with her last partner. She's been working closely with Steve for the past week, and so far they're getting along great.

He slowly approaches her, wrapped up in a thick parka. "Morning."

"Morning." She narrows her eyes. The crime-scene lights highlight a dark circle under his left eye. "Is that a bruise?" He's the last person she would expect to get into a fight.

He laughs. "Yeah. My bathroom bulb blew as I was getting out of the shower. I walked straight into the door."

Madison snorts. "I'd come up with something better than that if you don't want to ruin your reputation." She turns to look at Alex, who's wearing waders over his pants and hovering over something on the side of the bank, taking photographs. "Who called it in?" she asks.

"Elaine Brown." Steve points to a single-wide trailer behind them. "One of the nearest residents. Her little girl was out here last night looking for their cat, but she ran home bawling her eyes out. Her mom says she wouldn't tell her what the problem was, but she knew it wasn't related to the cat as that turned up fine shortly after. Her daughter just kept pointing to the creek and crying."

"Her mom phoned this in last night?" Madison says, thinking of Nate again. Dread pulses through her. Presumably Nate left the house shortly after she went to bed.

"No," says Steve. "She waited until this morning to take a look for herself. She didn't want to come out here in the dark as she was afraid there was some weirdo about. While she was looking around, she discovered this poor guy." He leads her over to the body, pulling his collar up against the chill. "He's missing his hands and head. Ms. Brown called dispatch right away. She's keeping her daughter out of school today, so you can question them both when you're ready."

Madison shudders at the sight of the headless corpse, but relief sweeps through her as she realizes this isn't Nate. He doesn't share Nate's athletic physique. He's taller and heavier, with his bulk concentrated around his midriff.

A gust of wind fans the stench of decomposition right into her face. "Someone didn't want him identified," she mutters. It seems killers these days are convinced that if they remove the victim's identity by way of fingerprints and teeth, they don't need to dispose of the whole body. They're getting lazy. Which is good for Madison and the team, because it means the medical examiner has something to work with.

She sighs. It's hard to imagine how someone could dismember another human being. This man would have had loved ones: family, friends and possibly children. They'll be devastated to learn not only of his death, but that his body was mutilated.

Alex Parker looks up from his position in the creek and smiles widely. "Ah, Detective Harper. How are you today?" The cold air mists in front of him as he speaks.

His British accent makes him sound so polite that Madison

can't help but smile, despite the fact her fiancé has gone AWOL, the bitter cold air is biting at her gloveless fingers and there's a dismembered corpse at her feet. "Good. You?"

"Well, I'm knee-deep in icy water photographing a grisly crime scene," he says. "What more could I want on a Monday morning?"

She snorts. "You're one of a kind, Alex."

He smiles. Single, with short black hair, glasses and pale skin, he looks younger than his mid-thirties. He uses dark humor not to minimize what happened to the person in front of them, but to help keep spirits up during their investigation. Because if you don't find a way to deal with these things, you can easily end up a victim of the job.

"How's Mrs. Pebbles settling in?" Madison asks, nodding to his car.

"You mean Deanna," he says.

"You changed her name?" She always thought Mrs. Pebbles was a strange name for a dog, but that was the name she came with.

He nods. "I did. I chose Deanna after one of my favorite characters from *Star Trek*, but also because if you say it fast enough, it sounds like my favorite three letters of the alphabet."

Madison and Steve share a puzzled look.

"DNA," says Alex with a grin.

Madison laughs. "And you wonder why Adams calls you a geek." Sergeant Adams doesn't get Alex's dry sense of humor.

She kneels to get a closer look at the mottled gray body, which lies at the edge of the murky water, surrounded by stones and weeds. A cluster of fat flies is buzzing around it, with some laying eggs in the exposed flesh. The corpse is naked and drained of blood, but she doesn't see any blood in the water, or on the bank. "Do you think he was killed elsewhere?"

"Very observant, Detective," says Alex. "It looks that way,

but I'll need to check the entire creek in case he simply floated away from somewhere nearby."

Looking at the victim in the icy water makes Madison shiver. She shoves her hands into her pockets. She can't see any identifying scars, tattoos or markings from here, but the medical examiner will concentrate on the details. What *is* certain is that his death was gruesome, and she needs to find out why someone wanted him dead.

"How were his hands and head removed?" she asks.

Alex lowers his camera and points to the lacerations around the neck. "A hacksaw would be my guess. The sawing is clumsy and obviously rushed. I'd guess our killer wasn't experienced with tools, but I'll leave it to Dr. Scott to confirm," he says. "After all, I'm no medical examiner."

Perhaps not, but Madison trusts his judgment. "Think he was dismembered while alive?"

"I highly doubt it, because he would've fought for his life. We'd see obvious defense wounds. Perhaps he was drugged first, or tied up."

She looks up and down the water, but it's still too dark to see much outside the harsh circle of light coming from Alex's light source. "We need to find the hands, head and clothes."

"I've already asked the rookies to start looking," says Steve. "I'm about to bang on doors to see if the residents saw or heard anything."

Madison can imagine the greeting he'll get this early on a Monday. She looks around. "I don't like this, Steve. I mean, shooting someone is one thing, but *decapitating* a person?" She shakes her head.

He nods. "I know. Whoever did this is one angry son of a bitch."

Madison looks up at the sky, which is beginning to pale with the promise of daylight. "Let's hope someone has security cameras. I'll see if Brody can get a scent and help us find the rest of the body."

Bright flashes go off as Alex resumes photographing the scene.

As they walk away, Steve asks, "Is Nate on his way?"

Madison looks at him, unsure how to respond.

He senses her hesitation. "Sorry. Are you guys not—"

"It's fine. I just don't know what to tell you." She decides to confide in him since he'll find out soon enough anyway. "Nate's gone. I don't know where, and I don't know if he'll be back."

Steve stops walking and glances at her ringless hand. "Shit. I'm sorry. I thought you two were good."

With a deep breath, she says, "So did I. I mean, I just moved in with the guy, right?" She sighs. "I don't know what's going on in that head of his. He left a note saying he needed some space."

Steve rubs his jaw. "Think it's down to him shooting the Grave Mountain Stalker? Because he strikes me as the kind of guy who would dwell on taking another person's life."

Madison's alarmed to feel warm tears accumulating. Right now, she could vomit. She trusted in a future with Nate Monroe. But by making him carry a weapon, did she cause him to lose himself? She blinks back tears. "Could be. Or maybe I snore." She forces a laugh. "I'm not the easiest person to be around."

Steve's expression softens. "Please. You're the most easy-going person I know."

She scoffs. "Yeah, right."

He fixes his eyes on hers. "I'm serious, Madison. With everything you went through, you have every right to be mad at the world. If I'd spent six years in prison for a murder I didn't commit, and lost all that time with my child because of it, there's no way I would've had any fight left in me to clear my name and get my old job back. I'd be stewing in a pit of anger and resentment."

Madison lowers her eyes. There's no denying she's been through hell, but getting Owen back was the start of her healing. And now her job keeps her too busy to dwell on the injustice, especially as it wasn't half as bad as what Nate went through on death row.

"So if Nate's left you," says Steve, "you're better off without him, because he clearly didn't know what he had. It's unfair to treat you like this, no matter what he's going through."

Surprised that he cares, Madison looks up at him. He eventually lowers his eyes, and the silence becomes awkward.

"Detective Tanner?" shouts one of the rookie officers from behind them.

Steve turns, then walks away when Officer Fuller waves him over.

Madison watches him go, trying to figure out why he cares so much about her relationship with Nate.

CHAPTER THREE

The trailer park slowly comes to life around them as Brody and the officers search the creek and tape off the crime scene in all directions. Alex processes the scene in minute detail while Steve goes door-to-door to question residents and try to locate security footage.

The winter sun peeks over the tips of the mountainous skyline as Madison approaches the trailer of the mother and daughter who discovered the remains. As mobile home parks go, this is a good one. With a mixture of single- and double-wide trailers, the residents take care of their small patches of land. The homes are well maintained, and some have small gardens with evergreen shrubs or planters containing bare soil, probably housing dormant plants awaiting spring's arrival.

There are some exceptions. A couple of trailers have porches littered with broken A/C units and old kitchen appliances that have seen better days, but overall, it doesn't look like an unpleasant place to live, especially with the creek running alongside it and the pine and aspen trees from the nearby woods shielding the park from the worst of the winter gusts.

Madison climbs the steps and knocks on the door of one of the smarter-looking homes. All the lights are on inside. It doesn't take long for the door to open. A woman around her own age—late thirties—appears. Her long black hair has been straightened and she's dressed in jeans and a crumpled gray sweatshirt.

Madison flashes her gold badge. "Hi, I'm Detective Madison Harper. Can I come in?"

The woman steps aside for her. The heat from inside hits Madison's face, bringing instant relief. She tries to untangle her hair with one hand, so she doesn't look so windswept, but it's a lost cause. The home is clean and cozy, with a cartoon playing low on the TV.

"You can sit here." The woman moves a pile of clean laundry from a seat next to the couch. Her young daughter is sleeping on her side with a blanket pulled over her. She's sucking her thumb. Her mother gently rouses her and slips the girl onto her lap as she sits.

Madison smiles. "How old is she?"

"Five. She should be getting ready for school, but I thought it best to keep her home today."

"Sure," says Madison. She pulls out her pocket notebook and pen. "Could you confirm your names for me?"

"Elaine Brown. This is Willow."

She makes a note. Her phone suddenly rings. Usually Madison wouldn't interrupt questioning an eyewitness to answer it, but she checks the caller ID in case it's Nate. Then she remembers he left his cell phone behind, so even if he does get in touch, she won't know it's him. Disappointed, she sees Sergeant Adams's name and declines the call. He can get in touch with Steve instead. "What time did Willow go looking for her cat?" she asks.

Elaine looks at her sleepy daughter. "Just after dinner, wasn't it? Around seven thirty, I think."

The dark-haired girl removes her thumb from her mouth. "I couldn't find Minnie anywhere."

"That's our cat," explains Elaine. "Damn thing's always going missing. I swear one of the older residents is enticing her over there with food, trying to claim her for herself. That cat's brought nothing but trouble."

Madison smiles as she says to Willow, "I have a cat. He's naughty too."

The young girl's eyes light up. "Can I see a picture?"

"Sure." Madison pulls out her phone and selects a photo of Bandit asleep on Owen's lap. She shows it to Willow. "He's my son's cat really."

Willow leans over to look. "He's bigger than Minnie."

"That's because his brother is that big dog outside, and Bandit thinks he can eat as much as him."

The girl leans back into her mom's chest and giggles.

Madison slips her phone away. "Did you see anyone outside last night when you were looking for Minnie?"

Willow's face darkens. "Someone was in the water."

"I know, sweetie," says Madison. "But aside from him, did you see or hear anyone else? Anyone running away from the creek? It's okay if you didn't."

Willow doesn't need to think about it. She shakes her head, resolute that no one else was there. Not that she noticed anyway.

Madison looks at Elaine. "I understand she came home upset and you chose not to investigate until this morning."

"Right," says Elaine. "My daughter's not someone who gets upset easily, so I thought it would be stupid to go out there on my own and leave her vulnerable inside. I looked out of my windows, but I didn't see or hear a thing. Neither did my two closest neighbors. I called them right away to tell them to lock their doors, just in case. You can't be too careful these days. It feels like half the population is a predator of some kind."

From the lack of blood and the color of the man's body, Madison thinks he was probably dumped there hours before Willow discovered him, so it's not surprising there were no yells or raised voices. "If you'd called us last night, we might have had a better chance of catching whoever put that man in the water. The killer could've hung around to watch him get discovered."

Elaine looks away. "I don't like inviting trouble into my home, Detective. No offense, but it's difficult to trust the police these days. I mean, I know *you* were in prison not so long ago, so it leaves me wondering..."

Although she doesn't finish her sentence, Madison knows the woman is questioning her integrity. It hurts that despite having proven herself as someone the community can trust, some locals remain unconvinced about her character.

She stands. "Well, thanks for your time. Get in touch if you or your neighbors remember anything else or hear credible rumors about what might've happened to the person we found. It might take time to identify him, so we could use the community's help with that." She hands Elaine a card with her contact details on. "Bye, Willow. It was nice meeting you."

The girl turns shy, covering her mouth with her blanket.

Madison smiles. Once back outside in the bitter cold, Brody runs over to her. Instead of wanting some fuss, he stares behind her at the closed door, as if expecting someone to follow her out. She rubs his thick fur, a mix of browns and creams. "He's not in there either, buddy."

Her phone rings with an unidentified caller ID. She answers it as Steve approaches. "Hello?"

"Detective Harper, it's Doug Draper."

Madison frowns. Doug and his wife, Nancy, live in the ranch her sister used to own in Gold Rock before Angie was incarcerated on various drug charges. "What can I do for you, Doug?"

"You can remove your sister from outside my property.

She's been sitting there for a half hour already and it's upsetting Nancy."

Madison's blood runs cold. Her sister is supposed to be in prison. "What did you just say?"

Steve notices her tone. He lowers his phone to look at her.

"Your sister. She's outside my property. I've asked her to leave twice already," says Doug. "But she's parked on the street and says she has a right to be there. This is harassment, Detective, and Nancy isn't well enough to deal with it."

Madison knows his wife is recovering from some heart issues and has been in and out of the hospital over the last month. She swallows. "I'll be right there." She ends the call and pockets her phone, her heart pounding hard.

"What's wrong?" asks Steve.

She looks at him. "It's my sister, Angie. She's back."

CHAPTER FOUR

Brody sits in the cramped backseat of Madison's vehicle, eagerly peering between the front seats and out of the windshield to see what new adventure awaits as they drive to Gold Rock. She brought him with her in the hope that his presence will deter Angie from trying anything stupid. Her sister could be armed and looking for revenge.

The drive takes thirty minutes on a good day but is longer this morning, thanks to traffic. It gives her time to think about all the ways her sister has betrayed her over the years. Angie is her only sibling, and at almost forty-four is older than Madison. They never got along well as kids. Angie accused their father of favoring Madison, but the only reason he spent more time with her was because of her interest in his job. He was a detective at the LCPD too, before he joined the FBI.

Later, Angie married the first person to ask her, as she always threatened she would. Unfortunately, Wyatt McCoy was one of the worst people she could have chosen. A boorish criminal who took whatever he could get from people, including Madison, he ultimately destroyed his and Angie's lives. He didn't make it out alive, and Angie was arrested for their criminal activities and has been in prison ever since.

Early in December, Madison got word from the penitentiary that Angie had agreed to a plea deal for the only crimes the DA could make stick, which were drug charges. The DA's office knew they couldn't secure convictions for the couple's more serious crimes because crucial witnesses died before Angie was caught and Wyatt was killed, meaning those charges were never brought. So, in return for Angie naming several high-profile drug dealers, all running drugs through America's Four Corners, her annoyingly excellent lawyer has secured her release. But no one gave Madison a heads-up about how fast that would happen, and she intends to make her feelings about that known to the prison warden as soon as she gets a chance.

Her stomach is heavy with dread as she wonders why her sister has returned to the home she lost while incarcerated. Is she hoping to pick up where she left off? Buy it back from Doug Draper and hire new employees to run the scrapyard and auto repair shop that comes with the land? If so, she's dreaming. The dealers she snitched on will likely send someone after her for revenge. Would she really risk her life just to cause Madison more misery by coming home?

Probably. Because Angie McCoy holds a grudge. Always has and always will. And she's always viewed Madison—not Wyatt—as the cause of all her problems.

As Madison crosses into Gold Rock, she slows her car and creeps toward Doug Draper's ranch. Brody whines softly behind her, sensing her anxiety. She dreads facing her sister again, and wishes Nate were here for moral support. She finds herself resenting him for leaving her in this position, since he also knew Angie's release was imminent.

The first thing she sees is an old Ford Taurus parked outside the ranch. Standing beside it is a woman with long graying hair dressed in faded blue jeans and a plaid shirt under a thick jacket. Angie never bothered with hair dye or makeup. She's gloveless and hatless. The sun has appeared, but it's still deceptively cold. She's probably freezing.

Madison prepares herself before getting out of the car and letting Brody out. "Stay back for now, boy."

The dog finds a spot to relieve himself and then looks toward the scrapyard with his ears raised at the sound of Doug Draper's employees banging on metal out of sight. The car crusher rumbles ominously in the background.

Madison approaches her sister, who's facing the house. "Why are you here, Angie?" She suddenly wonders if she's come to mourn her dead husband.

Angie takes a deep breath before turning to face her. Her face is heavily lined, too heavily for her age. "All I ever wanted was kids. A family of my own."

Madison bristles. "You can't see Owen. He's away at college." She will never let her sister see him again.

Angie nods sadly. "Is he happy?"

Madison tenses. Angie has no right to ask her that. "Happier than when he lived with you and Wyatt."

Her sister's eyes narrow for a second, reminding Madison of her mean streak, but she quickly disguises her expression by turning away to look at her old home. "I took good care of him for you. You make it sound like he was beaten every night or something."

Angie and her husband may not have physically hurt Owen, but they kept him from Madison, and for that, she doesn't know how to forgive her sister. "This isn't your home anymore, Angie. You should make the most of this opportunity you've been given and start fresh elsewhere. Somewhere no one knows what you're capable of, and where those drug dealers you snitched on won't find you. There's nothing for you here, or in Lost Creek."

Angie lowers her eyes. Madison's taken aback when she

sees tears filling them. Has her sister softened in prison? Has she had time to reflect on the damage she and her husband caused?

No. Madison knows from experience that prison doesn't soften anyone. It brings out your worst qualities and wraps them in a layer of anger and resentment, making them harsher than ever. "Don't come back here again. It's not fair to the current owners. They have no beef with you, so leave them alone."

Angie doesn't respond.

"I wish you well, but I have to get back to work." Madison turns to leave.

"Do you really?" says Angie. "Wish me well."

Madison stops in her tracks, unsure how to answer. She's not certain why she said that. Family is complicated. You put up with more from them than you would from anyone else, which is stupid when you stop to think about it. But the pull of family is difficult to ignore, no matter how awful they can be. If it was up to her, Angie would still be in prison, but she also wants the sister she never had. The one who didn't marry Wyatt McCoy. She wants a relationship with *that* woman. Perhaps Angie will be different now he's dead and she's out from under his control. Madison's intrigued to find out. But not at any personal cost to herself or her son. She needs to protect Owen from this woman.

"Because it doesn't have to be like this," says Angie. "We're blood, Madison. We have no family left but each other. Seems to me the smart thing to do would be to stick together."

Madison swallows. She's always felt the absence of her parents, and she'd like nothing more than a loyal sister in her life. Someone to have her back. Especially now Nate's gone and she's all alone again. But how can she trust Angie of all people?

She's often wondered whether it was purely Wyatt's influence on her sister that made her evil. And whether Angie is also a victim of everything that happened. That's the problem with men like Wyatt, they ruin every life they touch. She's seen it happen time and again.

She turns. "You're the one who always hated me. I never had a problem with you. And I didn't cause any of this, Angie. You did."

"Would it help if I apologized?"

She's never heard her sister apologize for anything. "Depends. Are you actually sorry? Can you see now that Wyatt was a monster? That what he did to me..." She swallows the lump in her throat. Angie never believed Madison when she told her that Wyatt sexually assaulted her when she was a young woman. Instead, her sister chose to believe Madison had lusted after her disgusting husband and offered herself to him on a plate.

Angie steps forward and rests a hand on her arm. Madison flinches. Out of habit, her eyes search for a weapon.

Behind them, Brody emits a low growl and takes a few steps forward.

Angie laughs as she withdraws her hand. "Relax, would you? I'm not here to hurt you, sis. I'm not going to hurt anyone. God knows I want an easy life now. I know Wyatt abused you. I know because I experienced emotional abuse every day I was with the asshole. You wouldn't believe half the things he put *me* through. Half the things he made me do. I'm not the woman I should've been, and I wish I'd never met him."

"So why'd you stick up for him all the time? Why did you choose him over me and Owen? Why didn't you reply when I sent you word of Dad's death?"

Angie seems to consider it before replying. "Dad left us and Mom for another woman, so I guess I still had resentment for that. Besides, he'd been gone so long I always assumed he was already dead, so when I heard he'd been killed, I didn't need to grieve."

Family estrangement causes not just a physical distance, but an emotional one too. After their father left them to join the FBI in Alaska, he kept in touch for a while, but contact dwindled as he chose hunting serial killers over visiting his daughters. He recently returned to reunite with them. At least, that's what he told Madison. Things didn't turn out how she had hoped.

"As for the rest," says Angie, "all I can do is apologize, because I don't have a time machine, Madison. The sad truth is that I can't change a damn thing. Neither of us can."

"Would you if you could?" Madison asks.

Angie looks her in the eye. "I'd change everything."

Madison is surprised to find she believes her. Her phone rings, breaking the tension. "I need to go."

Angie nods. "I'm leasing a trailer in Lost Creek for a few weeks while I consider my options. Maybe we'll see each other around?"

Madison's feelings confuse her. She feels a spark of hope in her chest at the thought that she and Angie could tentatively build a relationship. That she could one day talk about her sister with pride instead of shame. But it's mixed with dread at the thought of how easily Angie could destroy her again. Unsure which instinct to trust, for now, she leaves without answering.

CHAPTER FIVE

Not a single part of the girl's body is free from pain, despite the bed of soft grass beneath her. The early-morning sun peeks out from behind the mountains, promising a hot summer's day full of potential, but it's out of her reach because she can't move. Her ankle is throbbing and her bones are bruised. All she can do is lie still where she was dumped, in the hope that the pain will eventually subside or she'll slip into a blissful unconsciousness, whichever happens first.

She shouldn't have snuck out last night and gone to her friend's house. She should have stayed home. But she and Emma had a project they needed to finish for school, and besides, she was heading home by midnight, speeding down the dark streets on her bike. Some kids her age stay out all night, not to study but to party.

When a pickup truck appeared behind her, she hadn't thought much of it until it drew closer to her. Too late, she sensed the driver's intention. Before she could react, he pulled up alongside her and shoved her off the bike with his car door. He'd grabbed her off the ground in seconds and duct-taped her mouth after zip-tying her wrists together.

The swift attack left her in shock. She hadn't said a word. She hadn't fought. Part of her believed she was immune from other people's depravity, so she held on to the hope that this was a prank orchestrated by her father to show her what could happen if she didn't pay attention.

Once the shock wore off, her brain kicked in. It quickly brought home the seriousness of her situation, but by then, she was helpless as the driver sped to the woods, where he dragged her from the car and spent the next five hours...

She pushes the thought away to avoid a panic attack. Her chest is already constricted, her breathing shallow. She'll need medical assistance. She can feel blood down there. He left her shorts around her ankles.

Her dad will blame her for this. He'll blame her stupid fifteen-year-old brain. He tells her all the time it's not developed yet and that she needs to listen to him more. He insists he only has her best interests at heart, but it doesn't always feel that way.

She suddenly remembers that at midnight, she turned sixteen. Today is her birthday.

She blinks. A blackbird with a bright yellow beak arrives out of nowhere and perches on the tip of her sneaker. It looks as though it's trying to figure out whether she's edible. She's interrupting the bird's familiar landscape.

Its presence brings home how this could be her final resting place if no one finds her. If she gives up. The thought makes her choke back a sob. If she hadn't left her cell phone in her bedroom, she could've called her dad to collect her. She'd prefer to see her mom right now, but that's impossible. Her cheeks burn with shame. Everything her mom tried to teach her went in one ear and out the other, just like she said it would.

The sound of an engine approaching from the distance rouses her. She lifts her head, wincing at the pain in her neck. Her swollen eyes struggle to focus. One won't even fully open.

It's a vehicle. She tries to lick her dry lips, but she has no spare saliva. Sensing this is her best shot of getting out of here before her attacker returns, she raises her arm and cautiously waves from the long grass in the hope the driver will see her.

As the vehicle slows, her heart suddenly races with fear.

What if it's him?

Has she just made a deadly mistake?

She holds her breath, desperately hoping it's not the same vehicle that brought her here. She decides that if it *is* her attacker, she won't fight. She'll let him kill her. It's better than living with the shame of what he did to her.

Her heart thuds too hard as the pickup truck comes to a stop.

She doesn't recognize the driver as he slips out, but she hadn't seen her attacker's face once during the ordeal. He'd worn a ski mask and hadn't said a word.

"Holy crap." The stranger kneels beside her and gently pushes her shoulder to get a good view of her face. Through her good eye, she sees concern. "We need to get you fixed up."

Relief floods her, causing her eyes to relax enough to release the tears she's been fighting. Finally, her ordeal is over.

The man crouches and gently lifts her to his chest. His hands are warm and strong as he cradles her. He smells of fresh coffee, and the aroma takes her back to memories of breakfast at home, surrounded by her mom and dad. She curses herself for not being grateful for how comfortable her life was pre-trauma.

She feels each and every muscle slowly relax into the stranger's grip as he carefully stands. No one else is out here at this time. It's still early. She's lucky to be found so soon. It's an isolated spot.

"Grab the handle, honey."

She does what he says and opens the door. He gently rests her on the backseat. It hurts too much to sit up, so once she's inside the truck, she lies on her back, looking up at the brown ceiling. Exhaustion envelops her, and she can't keep her eyes open as he squeezes her hands, trying to provide comfort.

She just needs to sleep. Then she can wake up at home and start the day as if nothing happened. Perhaps no one needs to know anything. She doesn't want to risk angering her dad. She'll bury it deep within her mind, where she buries other things unsuitable to dwell on.

She hears the sound of a camera clicking, and a flash goes off. The man shuts the door and slips into the driver's seat. He starts the engine and lets out a strange whoop.

The girl looks up and meets his eyes in the rearview mirror, her gaze questioning.

He slips his phone into his pants pocket. "It's a good day for both of us, wouldn't you say?"

She frowns.

Her confusion appears to amuse him. "You got saved from death, and, well, when I saw you lying there like that, I could hardly believe my luck."

His words don't make much sense to her. "Why?" she croaks.

He grins. "Because someone else has done all the hard work for me." He pulls away at speed.

Goosebumps break out over her entire body. In a weak voice, she says, "You're taking me home, right?"

He laughs. "Of course I'm taking you home, honey!"

But he hasn't asked for her address. He hasn't even asked for her name. She winces in pain as her bruised body tenses with fear. Something terrible is happening. Again.

"Hell, I'll even carry you over the threshold if you like!"

She locks eyes with him again in the mirror. Against her better judgment, she asks, "Why would I want you to do that?"

He snorts as if she's playing with him. "Because that's what newlyweds do, silly."

The doors lock in unison.

The girl breaks eye contact and rests her head on the seat. Adrenaline floods her body so fast that her hands twitch. She looks down at them and gasps. He wasn't comforting her earlier. He was binding her hands together. A tear escapes her eye. This man was supposed to help her, not abduct her.

A scream builds from the pit of her stomach as she realizes her ordeal is nowhere near over.

Time captive: Day 1

CHAPTER SIX

Madison drops Brody at the Aspen View Mobile Home Park on her way back from Gold Rock. She knows the officers will take good care of him as they scour this morning's crime scene, and he could help them reach parts of the creek they can't get to. She tries to put all thoughts of her newly released sister out of her head, as she has enough to deal with already.

The clock on her dash tells her she has just enough time for a quick stop at Ruby's Diner for an early lunch before meeting Steve at the medical examiner's office. During a homicide investigation, mealtimes are taken whenever you pass a diner or a drive-thru.

A blast of warm air hits her when she enters the diner, along with the comforting smell of fried food. Out of habit, she glances around for Nate. He isn't here, but it occurs to her that the owner of this establishment, Vince Rader, might have heard from him, given how close they've grown over the last year or so. With a nervous flutter in her stomach, she heads straight to the counter, where Vince is stacking dirty dishes into a bowl. Tall, with cropped hair and a lean build, he looks younger than sixty-one. He keeps active by helping the LCPD with search and rescue when required.

He smiles widely when he sees her, but that falters when he notices the expression on her face. "Everything okay?" he asks.

She's surprised to find his concern sparks emotion in her. "I think so." She quickly checks over her shoulder to see if anyone's listening. It's busy already, despite not being noon yet. The waitresses go back and forth between the kitchen and the tables, with one noticeably absent due to the Grave Mountain Stalker's rampage. "Have you heard from Nate today?"

Vince pulls his phone from his back pocket and checks for notifications. When he finds none, he says, "No. Why? What's going on?"

She leans her elbows on the counter, unsure whether to tell him what's happened. For all she knows, Nate could come to his senses and be home by the end of the day. She decides not to worry him. He's been through a lot lately, having recently buried Carla Hitchins, the absent waitress and a close friend of his. "Nothing. It's okay. He left his phone at home and I'm not sure whether he's working today."

Vince looks relieved. "Is that all?" He laughs as he rests a hand on his heart in relief. "Jeez, Madison. From the look on your face, I thought you were going to tell me he's run off to join the church or something."

Despite her worry, Madison laughs. Given Nate's history, that's the last thing he should do.

"Why don't you ask Richie?" He gestures to a booth in the far corner. "He'll know where Nate is."

She briefly glances at Richie Hope, attorney-at-law and Nate's boss. "Good idea. Can I get my usual lunch order to go?"

Vince nods. "Sure."

Madison meanders through the packed tables to approach Richie's booth. Although Nate works for himself as a PI on special cases, he also works part-time for Richie's small law firm as an investigator. Papers and files are spread out on the table before the older gentleman, plus two full boxes sit on the seat opposite him while his briefcase rests at his feet. His thick white hair looks like it hasn't been combed today, and his dark suit is crumpled.

When he notices Madison, he beams up at her. "Detective Harper! Here for a coffee fix?"

"Lunch, actually." She gestures to the mess. "What's all this?"

Richie removes his glasses and leans back. "This is my new office."

She frowns. "What do you mean?"

"Well, I've given up my old office in favor of a partnership with Mr. Rader."

Madison moves a box out of the way and slides into the booth to sit opposite him. "You've *downsized*?" She knew business was bad, but not this bad.

"I prefer to say I've optimized," he says. "Vince wanted to mix things up around here since the sale of his business... fell through last month." He's being cautious. Madison tries not to think about the couple who were in the process of purchasing the diner from Vince. They both died before that could happen. "So we're investing in each other," Richie continues. "I'll lease this booth as an office space, and he'll get more business through the door as a result."

Madison smiles. He may well bring in customers, but she thinks Richie will spend more money here than all his clients combined, thanks to his love of fried food. "That's actually a great idea. The diner could become a community hub where people go for different things." Vince already offers the space to missing person support groups and the occasional paranormal society meet-up.

"That's the plan," says Richie.

"So you two get along okay?" she asks.

"Oh sure," he says. "We're of a similar age, both currently without romantic partners and like-minded in our views on idiots. Although there are two bones of contention."

"Oh yeah? What are those?"

"Well, first of all, I'd like a jukebox so I can listen to music while I work."

She smiles.

"And secondly, I think the diner needs a name change, so I suggested we use something that epitomizes everything it now offers. But it's fair to say Vince doesn't like my idea."

Madison can't imagine what he's come up with. "Which is?"

"You've Been Served." He grins. "You can be served food while sorting your legal affairs. It's genius!"

Madison snorts. "I like it. I can't see why Vince doesn't." She wonders what Richie's office manager will do for a job now he's downsized. "What about Janine?"

Richie removes his glasses and rubs his eyes. "Janine's decided to retire early. When I told her about this new setup, she told me that her latest lover is a wealthy gentleman who wants to take care of her into old age." He shrugs. "I think it's madness, but she's never listened to me."

"You never know, it might work out," she says diplomatically. Changing the subject, she says, "Is Nate working today?"

He checks his watch. "You tell me. I'm waiting to send him on a mission."

Her heart sinks. If Nate hasn't been in touch with Vince or Richie, he really has left town. She decides to confide in Richie. "Nate's disappeared."

He frowns. "What do you mean?"

With a deep breath, she says, "He hasn't been himself since everything that went down before Christmas. He was gone when I woke this morning. He left a note saying he needs space or he'll die. He even left Brody behind."

Richie visibly pales. "Oh dear."

"I know. I'm worried for him. He left his phone behind too, but took his car. If I don't hear from him within the next forty-eight hours, I'll see if I can track his license plate." She's suddenly filled with self-doubt. Will he be mad at her if she does that? Is it *her* he's fleeing from?

"Maybe we should take it at face value," says Richie. "Perhaps he really does just need some space to think about his next move in life. He's a smart man. He knows we'll be ready and waiting for him when he feels able to return."

Madison takes a deep breath. "You think I should leave him be?"

He nods. "I do. Let him miss us. He'll soon come to his senses."

Madison isn't sure whether the state of his mental health will allow him to do that, but she's willing to give him some time. "You're probably right. Thanks, Richie. Not a word to anyone. You're the only person who knows besides my partner."

"You're not going to tell young Owen?"

Nate isn't Owen's father, but he might as well be considering how close the pair are. With Owen away at Arizona State University studying law, Madison doesn't want to worry him. The last thing he needs is a distraction from his studies. "Not yet." She stands. "He's had enough upset to last him a lifetime."

Richie nods sympathetically. "I think all three of you have."

She fixes a smile on her face as she turns to collect her lunch order.

CHAPTER SEVEN

Nate Monroe sits on a concrete bench in the grounds of the Fairview Cemetery in western Kansas. A vast space filled with hundreds of headstones, the cemetery is almost empty of visitors despite it being lunchtime on a weekday. A downpour has soaked his clothes. The air is bitter, sending a chill through his wet open jacket. He can't even find the energy to zip it up, and not even the cold distracts him from the overwhelming certainty that he's a complete failure as a human being.

He tries to figure out why he's still alive when so many of his loved ones have perished over the years. He hasn't done anything good with his life, not really, and he doesn't have kids to give him a reason to keep fighting, so he's struggling to think of a single reason not to give up on what has been a life filled with grief and tragedy. His mood has declined so severely over the last few days that he keeps imagining himself jumping in front of a speeding train. It would be a relief not to feel this way any longer. Not to feel anything. He doesn't necessarily want to kill himself. He just doesn't want to exist anymore.

He's convinced he doesn't deserve to. Not after taking someone's life. Madison would be better off without him dragging her down. She'd be free to date someone who comes without baggage. Someone the media and the true-crime community aren't obsessed with.

Ever since he was released from death row three and a half years ago, he's been inundated with requests for interviews on TV, podcasts and in print. He's declined them all. His life isn't for other people's entertainment. But it means they've gone ahead and published whatever they want about him, most of it inaccuracies or outright lies. He let it go. He didn't pay any attention. He was too busy helping Madison find her son and get her job back after *her* release from prison.

The last year and a half of his life has been good. Great, even. He proposed to Madison because he loves her and wanted her to know how much. But the truth is, she pushed him into carrying a firearm, something he explained time and again he wasn't comfortable with. He knew it could only end in trouble. Now, he really is a killer, and the media have gone wild, dragging up the case that saw him locked up all those years ago. They're claiming he probably killed that woman too. But he didn't. He loved Stacey Connor. Just as he loves Madison.

Some sections of the media are capable of seeing what happened before Christmas for what it was: a man protecting himself and his fiancée against an armed serial killer. Protecting the whole town even, as the perpetrator's actions had already led to eleven deaths by that point. But the truth doesn't sell as many papers or get as many clicks on websites. So Nate followed his instinct and left home in the middle of the night to escape the headlines, the phone calls and the guilt. He needed to drown out the noise around him or he would've given up. He might yet anyway. He can't live with the constant speculation. He just wants a quiet life, free from drama. He wants the life he was supposed to have before he left Kansas as a young man.

He looks at the headstone in front of him.

CLINT ALAN MONROE
LOVING HUSBAND AND DOTING FATHER OF
THREE
1950–2003

Nate's hometown of Fairview is even smaller than Lost Creek, and no one ever leaves. It's like the residents can't get through the invisible forcefield that holds them here. Nate was considered strange when he told his friends and family that he was leaving at eighteen to study philosophy at the University of Texas at Austin with a dream of eventually becoming a priest. He's never returned since, and Austin is where he met Father Connor, the man responsible for his time on death row. Nate's mother passed away before it all happened, and his father, Clint, was the only person who stood by him when he was arrested for murder at twenty years old. Both his siblings disowned him immediately, and he's never heard from them since. He had hoped they might reach out once his conviction was finally overturned. It would have been easy to locate him, since the press followed him to Lost Creek. But he's heard nothing. And he feels their absence keenly.

He doesn't blame them, because his incarceration ruined their lives. But if his own family can't stand to be around him, it's a sign there's something wrong with him.

He looks up, expecting to see Brody sniffing the ground in the distance. He misses the dog, but the truth is Brody was never truly his. He was a stray he and Madison unofficially adopted during their first case together. Or maybe Brody adopted them. He's unsure. He just knows the animal kept him alive when he wanted to give up. Madison will take care of him now.

He looks up at the gray sky. More rain is coming. His hands are numb now, and his lower back aches from where he was stabbed with a shallow knife last month. But still, he can't bring himself to find a coffee shop to warm up in, or to go sit in his car. He can't bring himself to move. Everything takes so much effort now he's arrived home. The drive here was straightforward given he left Lost Creek at midnight, but he suspects it was a one-way journey.

He sighs heavily. He came home with just two things in mind: to visit his father's grave for the first time and to see whether his siblings still consider him family. If they reject him, his decision will be made for him. He's tried to live a good life, but it's time to stop trying, because no matter what he does, it just isn't working.

CHAPTER EIGHT

When Madison arrives at the medical examiner's building, Steve is waiting on the plastic chairs in the office lobby. She spots him through the glass. He stands and opens the door for her as she approaches the building.

"I've already spoken to Lena," he says once she's inside. "She's taking a call in her office, but she'll join us in the morgue shortly. We can go straight in."

Madison follows him to the clinical room at the end of a long corridor. It's lit with harsh fluorescent lights, and is kept cool, making her shiver despite the layers she wore in preparation. The air has a grim underlying aroma that, while bearable during brief visits, causes relief when it's time to leave.

Skylar and Jeff, Lena's assistants, are suited in protective gear and masks. Jeff has the kind of pale skin that burns after five minutes in the sun, and with a buzz cut to disguise hair loss on his crown, he's done what many balding men do and resorted to facial hair. He's opted for a well-trimmed goatee. He's in his late thirties and has worked here for years. He yawns before nodding to Madison and Steve and removing his mask. "Hey.

You can use those." He gestures to the counter, where boxes of disposable aprons and masks are readily available.

"Thanks," says Madison as she slips an apron over her head.

Jeff yawns again, loudly this time. When Madison looks at him questioningly, he says, "Busy weekend. I need to start going to bed earlier. Aging sucks."

She laughs. "I hear ya."

"Morning, Detectives," says Skylar. Younger than Jeff, she wears her long black hair in braids under a surgical cap. Her tattoo sleeves are visible before she pulls on some long latex gloves. She helps Madison tie up her apron at the back before assisting Jeff to pull a body out from the refrigerator and onto a trolley.

Steve has difficulties tying his own apron, so he approaches Madison and turns his back. "Give me a hand, would you?"

Amused, she shakes her head as she ties it.

Dr. Lena Scott enters. Lena has perfect skin and shoulder-length brown hair, which she keeps tied back in a ponytail while she works. Unusually, her hair looks a little disheveled today, with some strands hanging loose in her face. "You can't tie your own apron?" she says to Steve, a little too harshly. "What are you, five?"

Madison has sensed an undercurrent of hostility from Lena for a while now. Something's off with her, and she's taking it out on everyone around her.

Jeff and Skylar share a look. They've obviously noticed it too.

"How are you today?" asks Madison, attempting to break the tension.

With a sigh, the medical examiner says, "Overworked and underpaid."

Perhaps she's tired of her job and that's contributing to her negativity. She could be forgiven, since so many bodies passed through here last month. They'd had to bring in a forensic anthropologist to help spread the workload.

Lena instructs her assistants to bring the body to her as she pulls her mask up over her nose.

Jeff wheels John Doe to the mortuary table, and Skylar helps him lift the headless body out of the body bag and into position in front of Lena, who moves the overhead light to give her the best view of the dismembered corpse.

"He's five foot nine without his head," says Jeff. "And weighs two hundred and fourteen pounds."

Lena jots it down on her draft autopsy report.

On the opposite side of the table, Madison pulls a mask over her nose and leans in to get a good look. Steve stays at the foot end. The assistants busy themselves with paperwork for other bodies.

Madison wonders whether their victim is from Lost Creek. Just because he was found here doesn't mean he wasn't dumped here from elsewhere. "Alex thought a hacksaw might've been used to remove the head and hands," she says, peering at the ragged tearing at the neck. The thin pipe of the esophagus protrudes next to the stump of white spinal cord. The thought of someone hacking through all that makes her wince.

"We'll test the pattern with a range of saws and see what matches," says Lena. "The lack of blood in his body means we have no lividity to give us clues, and the lack of blood at the dumping site suggests he bled out before he was moved to the creek. You need to find the scene of the murder."

Steve scoffs. "Easier said than done."

Lena doesn't respond. She checks the handless wrists. "Identifying his cause of death may be difficult since there's no obvious external cause on what's left of him. I can't even see any lacerations or bruises."

Madison turns to Steve. "So he didn't defend himself."

Steve nods. "Must've been taken unaware or drugged first."

"I'll send tissue samples to the lab so they can run toxicology to check for drugs and poisonous substances," says Lena. "But it could be that his head holds the answers we need, if it was trauma to that area that caused his death." She leans over the torso before picking up one of his arms. "Huh."

"What is it?" says Steve.

She pulls the overhead light closer to the man's torso. "See this red mark here?"

Madison and Steve lean in. "Looks like something chafed him," says Madison. "Maybe he carried a weapon in a shoulder holster."

Lena moves around the table, making Madison step out of her way. She checks the opposite area and finds the same chafing. "These marks are consistent with ligature marks. He could've been tied up."

Madison pulls out her pocket notebook and pen to make a note of it. "It would make sense since he didn't defend himself. Perhaps it was a home invasion gone wrong. He could've died of a heart attack while tied up."

"I don't know," says Steve. "Why would the intruder go to the effort of hiding his identity and dumping the body if the guy died of natural causes?"

She chews her lip as she thinks. "Maybe they were related to the victim and thought they'd be easily traced for the robbery. I don't know." She turns to Lena. "How old do you think he was?"

Lena examines the body before grabbing a layer of loose fat from the man's side, where his love handles rest. "His skin was beginning to sag, his chest and pubic hair is sprinkled with gray... I'd age him between forty-five and fifty-five. I'll be able to give you a more accurate age once I've opened him up and assessed the condition of his organs and tissue. Want to stay for that?"

"I don't think that's necessary, do you?" Madison glances at Steve.

"No," he says. "We'll wait for your report. Oh, and we need samples for DNA analysis. Our priority is identifying him."

Lena lowers her mask and smiles at him. "Of course. This isn't my first autopsy." Her sour mood appears to have lifted. "With no distinguishable features such as tattoos, birthmarks or operation scars, and with no teeth or fingerprints, you have quite the task ahead of you."

Steve takes a deep breath. "You can say that again."

"He has some moles," says Madison, pointing to the man's arms. "If all else fails, might they be useful?"

"Maybe," says Lena. "But only if you find someone who knew he had moles there. And if you find someone who knew him, he probably won't need to be identified by his moles. I'll email you my report as soon as it's ready."

Madison removes her protective gear and bundles it into the biowaste trash at the same time as Steve. Before she leaves, she turns and says, "Thanks, guys. Catch you later."

Skylar and Jeff say goodbye. Lena's already focused on opening the victim.

Outside the building, Steve inhales the fresh air. "I hate that place. I don't know how Lena can stand it."

"You never say that about Alex. He deals with dead bodies all day too," she says.

"Yeah, but I don't have to kiss Alex." He sighs. "You know, I can smell that place on her after work. Even after she's showered."

Madison grimaces. It doesn't surprise her, as the aroma of decomposition lingers, but she'd never considered it before. She wonders whether Lena's ever lost partners over it.

Steve checks his phone. "Adams has messaged me. He says Gina Clark's arrived early."

Madison checks the time. It's twelve thirty. She'd arranged

to meet Gina at the station at one. She takes a deep breath. "I'll head there now."

When she makes no moves to leave, Steve frowns. "Everything okay?"

She nods, but she's dreading this meeting. Gina's baby went missing eighteen months ago, and despite no new leads, she's expecting Madison to find the poor boy alive.

CHAPTER NINE

The station is filled with the aroma of fresh coffee, but instead of heading to the kitchen to pour herself a cup right away, Madison approaches Sergeant Marcus Adams. He's seated at the desk opposite hers, buried in paperwork. She hasn't gotten used to seeing him in uniform yet, and black could be his color since it matches his hair, which she's convinced he secretly dyes to hide the fact he's in his early forties.

Adams joined the department from a large PD in Denver to fill the vacant detective role. But moving down here to southwestern Colorado unsettled him, especially as he had plenty of issues in his home life that distracted his attention. He recently separated from his wife, moving out of the home he shared with her and their twin ten-year-old daughters. He has his strengths, but even Adams admits he wasn't right for the role of detective, and decided he was better suited to being the department's only sergeant, which is why Chief Mendes agreed he and Steve could switch roles.

He looks up as Madison approaches. "Hey. I took Ms. Clark to interview room one. I made her coffee."

Madison looks at her coffee-less desk. "Thanks," she says,

trying not to roll her eyes. No one could ever accuse Adams of being considerate.

Chief Carmen Mendes joins them. The chief is an attractive woman in her mid-late forties with long black hair she keeps slicked back in a ponytail at work. They think she's single, but as she's so private, they're not really sure, and none of them would dare ask. Although she's a fair, hardworking and trusting boss, Madison knows the chief is a little worried about Adams's recent role change, since the sergeant role is arguably one of the most important in a police department like theirs, and Steve was so good at it.

Adams lost his head a few times while detective, and investigating didn't come naturally to him, so Chief Mendes is hoping he does better in a supporting role. He's in charge of supervising the rookies, which is a little awkward since he recently locked lips with one of them in a drunken stupor. But only Madison knows about that. She may have had her differences with Adams in the past, but loyalty among the team is essential, so she'll never tell a soul what happened between him and Officer Kent.

"Stella's already fielding calls from the press," says the chief, referring to one of their long-term dispatchers. "My guess is a resident from the trailer park contacted them about this morning's homicide victim."

Madison nods. "I don't have much to tell them yet, so they'll have to wait." She looks at Adams. "Steve's returned to the scene and Nate's dog is helping the officers search for evidence."

Adams nods. "Find the poor guy's head and hands yet?"

She shakes her head. "Nope. We don't think he was killed where he was found, so it's unlikely we'll locate them today. Lena's about to perform an autopsy. Fingers crossed she can find a cause of death on the body parts we *do* have."

Chief Mendes rests her hands on her hips. "We've had no

other reported homicides overnight, so let's pray this is a one-off. I don't think I could handle another serial killer anytime soon."

The town is still reeling from the Grave Mountain Stalker case. It exhausted the entire department. Madison thinks of Nate. Did that case ruin their relationship too? Will she ever see him again? She forces him out of her head. He's a grown man. He'll be fine. She needs to focus on finding their killer and helping Gina Clark find her missing child.

She collects a notepad from her desk. "I better go see Ms. Clark."

Passing the dispatcher's cubicle, she heads to the interview room. Inside, Gina Clark is seated at the table, lost in thought. Not yet thirty, she appears older, with pale skin and dark circles under her eyes that she doesn't bother disguising with makeup. The trauma of having a missing infant is evident. Her long dark hair is as limp as her expression.

She looks up when Madison closes the door. The aroma of cigarette smoke hangs in the air.

Madison chooses a seat across from her. "Morning." She smiles. "Sorry to keep you waiting. I was called to an emergency."

Gina nods. "I wish Toby's disappearance was considered an emergency."

Madison ignores the dig. It probably wasn't intentional. She pulls out a photograph of baby Toby at six months old. Two tiny front teeth are beginning to emerge from his bottom gumline, and his hair is fine and blond, like Owen's at that age. Gina gave her this photo last month, as a reminder that her son is a real person who needs to be found.

"I wasn't a detective at the time Toby disappeared," Madison says, "so I don't know any details yet." She had only just returned to Lost Creek having recently been released from prison. It wasn't until later—once her conviction was overturned —that she rejoined the LCPD. Which means her predecessors,

Don Douglas and Mike Bowers, would have investigated Toby's disappearance. But as they're both now deceased, she can't ask them for their thoughts on the case. "And I haven't had an opportunity to locate Toby's case file yet," she adds. "I intended to do so this morning, but I was called straight to a crime scene and then to the morgue. I'm sorry about that. As soon as we're done here, I'll get right on it."

Gina straightens in her seat.

"So, unfortunately, I need you to start at the beginning," Madison continues. She pulls out a pen, ready to make notes, before looking at Gina. To ease her in gently, she asks, "What was Toby like as a baby?"

A smile hovers on Gina's lips. "He was the best baby I could've hoped for. That's not to say he slept through the night right away or never cried, but he was fun, you know? He loved to play. He started smiling young, and his laugh was adorable. It made my whole day when he'd laugh." Her smile falters as she returns to reality, where Toby is missing. "We were a little family. We didn't need anyone else."

"Were you and Toby living with anyone at the time of his disappearance?" asks Madison. "Was his father in the picture?"

Gina shakes her head. "Toby's father is unaware of him. He was the result of a one-night stand." She quickly adds, "That doesn't mean I love my son any less."

"Of course," says Madison. Sensing the woman feels uneasy, she adds, "You're not on trial here, Gina. Whoever took your baby is responsible for what happened, not you. My questions might seem intrusive, but I'm trying to build a picture that leads me to your son and the person who took him."

Before agreeing to look into this case, Madison had to ask Chief Mendes for permission. The chief takes a harsh stance on cold cases. She believes the department doesn't have the resources available to allocate to them unless new information or evidence arises. She's right, of course, but to get around that,

Madison intends to find new information, maybe a new lead. Still, the chief made it clear that all current cases should be prioritized over this one, which will leave Madison little time to delve into it.

Gina takes a sip from her coffee cup, and Madison notices her hands trembling. She gets up to turn the heat higher. It's not unusual for this room to get cold. Once back in her seat, she says, "Tell me what happened on the day Toby vanished."

Gina lowers her eyes. "This is the part where you start judging me."

Madison frowns. "Why?"

With a deep breath, Gina says, "Because I was drinking at the time. I can barely remember a thing from that week, never mind that day."

Madison lowers her pen. She knew this case wouldn't be easy to crack given the time that's elapsed, but she wonders whether this is why Douglas and Bowers never found the child.

Before she can speak, Gina adds, "Also, I..." She closes her eyes as if she dreads saying it aloud. "I never reported him missing." She meets Madison's eyes. "Your department didn't find him because they didn't know to look for him."

Madison leans back, dumbfounded. With so many questions springing to mind, she realizes she may have been too quick to agree to help in a case that could be unsolvable.

CHAPTER TEN

"First of all," says Madison, "what do you mean you never reported your baby missing?" She's trying not to judge, but she's astounded Gina wouldn't get the police involved. They could have issued an Amber alert and perhaps notified the FBI, which would have given them a better chance of finding Toby within hours of his disappearance.

Gina swallows, clearly upset. She knows she made the wrong decision. It's written all over her face. "Please don't look at me like that," she whispers. "I can't bear it. And this is partly why I never approached the police in the first place."

Madison realizes she's intimidating the young woman with her reaction. She leans back in her chair to appear less confrontational. "I'm sorry. It's just... You took me by surprise." With a deep breath, she says, "I take it you've had a bad experience with law enforcement in the past?"

"Not me," says Gina. "My parents. My dad hated cops. He put the fear of God into my mom before he died, and believed asking a stranger for help was safer than turning to anyone who works in law enforcement. So my mom always told me not to involve the police in anything."

Madison raises her eyebrows. It's disheartening to hear, but not surprising. Many Americans have a poor opinion of the police, and with various high-profile corruption cases making headlines across the U.S., it's understandable. She realizes she'll have to work hard to break down that barrier with Gina in order to find out what happened to the woman's baby.

"I was afraid they'd accuse me of harming my son if I reported him missing." Gina lowers her eyes as she speaks. "I've seen enough crime documentaries to know how *that* goes. They'd have taken one look at the vodka bottles, smelled the liquor on my breath and seen I hadn't done any housework in a couple of weeks, and they'd point the finger of blame at *me*." A tear falls from her eye, which she quickly wipes away. "And I was terrified that when they found Toby, they'd give him straight to child services and never let me see him again. If that happened, I'd be no better off than if he were never found!"

Madison would like to say her fears were unfounded, but her own brush with child services taught her a harsh reality. *Sometimes* they take children from the wrong people. That's not to say they get it wrong every time, or that they set out to cause emotional harm to families, but thanks to a dishonest social worker, Madison wasn't even allowed to communicate with ten-year-old Owen by letter while she was incarcerated. She wasn't allowed to know who he was placed with and whether she'd ever see him again. And that was far worse than serving six years in prison for a murder she didn't commit. So she understands this woman's fears, especially if they've grown from decades of living within a family that doesn't trust anyone in a position of power. All she can do is try to focus on finding Toby. She hands her a tissue.

"I did cross paths with a detective once," says Gina, dabbing her eyes. "By that point I was desperate, and I thought he might help, but although he seemed interested in the case, I never heard from him again. It was just before you arrived back in town and he started investigating your ex-girlfriend's murder."

Madison swallows. A pang of guilt runs through her. She hasn't thought about Stephanie Garcia in a while. So much has changed since they were together. "Was it Detective Mike Bowers?"

Gina nods. "He was too distracted to help me. And since he took his own life shortly after, it's clear he had demons."

That's an understatement. Madison still misses Mike, despite what he did to her, and she wishes he'd found another way to deal with his guilty conscience. But Gina's right. He was more than distracted at that time trying to cover up his own illegal activities, so she can believe he didn't make an effort to win the woman's confidence and persuade her to file a missing person complaint.

"It put me off pursuing it any further with the cops until now." Gina's eyes lock onto Madison's. "You're my last attempt to find Toby. I thought that since you know what it's like to not know where your son is, you might be more compassionate than Detective Bowers."

The expectation weighs heavily on Madison. "Let's start with the day Toby vanished. What happened?"

Gina wipes her face and sniffs back tears before responding. "I passed out. Slept for twenty-four hours straight, which is unheard of for me. I've never used drugs. Alcohol is my poison. I'd kept a handle on it for a long time, and it didn't consume me. I suffer from severe anxiety, and I need something to take the edge off. On that night, I drank way too much vodka. I was feeling melancholy, so it went down quickly. I polished off a large bottle in under an hour, along with some sleeping pills." The shame is evident on her face. No one chooses to be an alcoholic. It's a complicated disease that destroys lives, and if alcohol were outlawed tomorrow, their holding cells would be a lot emptier than usual. But the addition of sleeping pills makes Madison wonder whether it was a suicide attempt.

"I lost consciousness. I could've died." Gina fixes her eyes on the table. "Maybe it would've been better if I had, because coming round the following evening was like finding I was stuck in a nightmare I couldn't wake from." Her voice breaks as she adds, "It's been eighteen months since I last saw my baby. Sleep is the only time I get any respite from the horror."

Madison is concerned by the pain on this woman's face. She's been through a hellish experience that few can appreciate. "Were you at home?" she asks gently.

Gina nods. "Toby and I lived alone. I wasn't blessed with family. My mom was widowed when I was young and never remarried. She was deeply religious. She disapproved of my pregnancy and soon gave me the cold shoulder, eventually moving away. I don't know where to. I didn't have any friends or siblings. I was on welfare when Toby disappeared. I didn't want to be, but trying to get a sitter for your baby so you can earn money when you have absolutely no one to help you is impossible."

It must've been tough. And Madison isn't here to condemn the woman. She's already suffered the worst consequences imaginable. "What time did you start drinking that day?"

"Around seven at night. I always waited until Toby was asleep in his crib before I took a drink. When I eventually came to at around seven the following evening, he was gone."

Madison grabs her pen. "What was he wearing?"

"A pale blue jumpsuit with a bunny rabbit embroidered across the front in a dark blue thread. He had a diaper on but no socks. It was a warm summer's evening, so I didn't want him to overheat. I didn't find it anywhere afterward, so he must've still been wearing it."

It sounds like Gina was trying to care for him as best she could. Madison writes it all down. "Could he have climbed out of his crib?" Some babies are more adventurous than others. Owen was barely crawling when he discovered how to escape his crib, meaning she spent many sleepless nights worried he'd harm himself.

"No, he was only just learning to crawl," says Gina. "And besides, all the doors and windows in the house were closed. There's no way he could've gotten out by himself."

"Were they also locked?"

She hesitates. "I thought they were, but when I checked, I found the back door unlocked."

So the perp entered and exited through the back door. If she'd contacted the police, they could've dusted for prints and searched for trace evidence. They could've obtained local security footage and canvassed the neighborhood.

"I approached my two nearest neighbors, but no one saw anything." With a frustrated shake of her head, Gina adds, "They didn't even offer to help me search. It was like they didn't want to get involved. Probably because I'd kept to myself for so long. They weren't willing to help a stranger."

"Didn't they offer to call the police?"

"One told me I should, so I got scared and lied. I pretended Toby's father was in the picture. I said he probably collected him early without telling me. Like I already said, I didn't want anyone calling the cops."

Madison takes a deep breath. "Did you do anything else to find him?"

Gina lowers her eyes. "After an agonizing few days searching the entire area by myself, I approached a PI. He was expensive, and I don't think he was a hundred percent legit, but I knew him from school so I thought I could trust him, and he understood why I didn't want the cops involved."

Madison tries to keep her expression neutral. It worked in the PI's favor for Gina to rely on him instead of the police since he was making money from her. The internet is full of people calling themselves private investigators. Many of them are unlicensed. Some, like Nate, can't get a license for legitimate reasons. Others, not so. "What's his name?"

"Scott Richards. But he's dead now."

"He's *dead*?"

Gina nods. "He had cancer for five or six years on and off."

Madison's shoulders sink. Just when she thinks the story can't get any worse, Gina surprises her.

CHAPTER ELEVEN

Madison looks at her notes, but the page is almost empty. "Did Scott offer any leads at all? Have there been any sightings of Toby since that day?"

Gina straightens in her seat. "During our last phone conversation before he died, he told me he'd learned something from one of his acquaintances, another PI he would swap information with. Apparently, this guy—I never knew his name—saw a blonde girl in a drugstore downtown in the week after Toby's disappearance. She was carrying a baby dressed in blue who matched Toby's description. The baby wouldn't settle for her and was crying while wriggling to get out of her grip, like he was mad about being carried by a stranger. It made the girl flustered because people were starting to notice. When Scott's friend approached her to get a closer look at the boy, she backed away. So the guy called Toby's name to see if either of them would react, and that made the girl run from the store. By the time he got outside, they were gone." She takes a deep, steadying breath. "That's why I think my son's still here somewhere. I think he was sold to someone who couldn't have their own kids." Tears spring to her eyes as she adds, "I think he's being raised by another woman, completely oblivious that his real mommy misses him with all her heart."

Madison briefly rests a hand on the woman's. It's a big assumption based on one possible sighting, and if he was sold to an infertile couple, he would likely have been taken out of Lost Creek immediately. But she has to agree it's their only lead. Plus, the girl reacted to Toby's name. "Did your PI ask to see the store's security footage?"

"Yeah, but they wouldn't let him since he couldn't produce a PI license. They were probably worried he was stalking the girl. And the store went bust a few months later. It's a coffee shop now."

Frustrated, Madison asks, "Did Scott tell you anything else? And are you sure you don't know his acquaintance's name?"

"I'm sure. Scott died a few days later."

Madison's confused about something. "If he died of cancer a few days later, how was he well enough to be working?"

"When he knew he was getting close to being housebound, he shot himself. I guess he wanted to go out on his own terms and before he was bedridden." Gina is so used to suffering that she says it matter-of-factly, as if it's not deeply tragic. "The only description I have of the girl is that she was around nineteen or twenty, and had shoulder-length blonde hair like you."

Madison writes it down. "With Scott being gone, I'm assuming you don't know of any other sightings of the girl or Toby in the last eighteen months?"

Gina shakes her head. "No. But I think I see him all the time."

Madison says softly, "That's not unusual. I imagine what you've gone through feels a lot like grief, where your brain tricks you into thinking you're seeing him in a crowd full of people." When Madison's father died, she saw him for months afterward. It was never him, of course, just people who looked similar.

"I don't think it's just that, though," says Gina. "Sometimes, I'm convinced it's really him to the point where I approach the family and question them." She wipes her eyes. "It gets me into a lot of trouble, but I can't risk missing him. Because what if his new family doesn't know he was abducted? They might think they legitimately adopted him. Human trafficking is so common now, right?"

Madison's unsure how to respond. While there *is* a chance Toby could still be alive, the chances of him being trafficked are small. It's more likely he'd be living with the person who took him. Or he was killed soon after his abduction.

She slides her notebook and pen across the table to the woman. "I need the names of everyone who visited you and Toby at home. I know you said you didn't have any friends or family, but anyone else you can think of. Construction workers, your landlord, neighbors, acquaintances. I need the names of anyone who knew you had a baby, especially if they ever took a special interest in him."

Gina looks horrified. "What do you mean, *special interest?*"

"I mean anyone who insisted on holding him, or who stared at him a little too hard in the grocery store. Anyone who ever gave you a bad feeling, no matter how brief."

Lowering her eyes to the paper, Gina says, "I don't think you get it. I'm an introvert, Detective Harper. Some might call me reclusive. I didn't grow up with a big family or a circle of friends, and I *never* let anyone into my home. I sure as hell never let anyone hold my son."

Madison frowns. "You must've interacted with someone. Your landlord, maybe?"

"Not really. I never asked him for repairs, and like I told you, I didn't know my neighbors. All our homes were flattened to be turned into offices last year. I live in a small apartment now. Although I still have room for Toby. I still have his clothes and his favorite toys." She holds back a sob with a hand over her mouth.

The unanswered questions are clearly torturing her, and Madison isn't sure how much longer she'll hold on to find them. She gets the sense that this woman is close to giving up not just on her missing boy, but on her own life. She's one of those people society is blind to. The kind of person who dies alone in their apartment and isn't found for months. Her existence is deeply depressing to Madison. This woman probably has so much to offer, but her low self-esteem doesn't allow it. It's heart-wrenching. Madison wants to help her.

Gina inhales deeply, trying to remain in control of her emotions. "I know I'm asking for a miracle and you have an impossible task. But miracles *do* happen, don't they? Why can't it happen for Toby? He's got to be somewhere."

When she breaks down, she comes across as especially vulnerable. It makes Madison want to protect her. Gina's had a raw deal in life, and she has no one looking out for her or Toby. It's tough to improve your situation when you have no support network. "The problem we have," says Madison gently, "is that the answer to this kind of mystery usually lies in the family's inner circle."

Frustrated, Gina wipes her eyes. "That's not relevant in our case, which means whoever took my baby was opportunistic. I don't believe it was planned. I think they were looking for someone to rob, or perhaps assault, but instead, they found my baby boy, and they knew Toby would be worth money to one of those rich women who can't conceive."

Madison feels the weight of expectation on her. So much time has passed that finding leads will be almost impossible. She pulls the notebook back toward her. "Gina, you're asking me to find your son with no clues whatsoever."

Gina leans forward, tears brimming her lower eyelids.

"Look for the blonde girl from the drugstore," she pleads. "I guarantee she'll lead us to my son."

CHAPTER TWELVE

Driving through town in the dark with Brody in the back, Madison wonders whether she should stay at her house or Nate's. Most of her belongings are at Nate's now, and Sergeant Adams is leasing her house. He moved in after he and his wife separated. But Madison doesn't want to be around Nate's belongings if he's not there too. It'll feel weird, like he's died or something.

Brody snores from the backseat. He's had a busy day. He may not have found any evidence at the crime scene, but he tried his hardest, which is tiring work for a dog. His food and bowls are at Nate's house, which decides it for her. She may as well try to keep things normal for him and the cat.

When she pulls into Nate's driveway, the house is in darkness and the front door is ajar. They usually keep the porch light on. Her arms break out in goosebumps. "What the hell?"

Brody immediately perks up and scratches at the window to be let out.

She switches the engine off and retrieves her service weapon before exiting the car. As she lets Brody out, she tells him to stay quiet. Somehow, the dog always knows what she and Nate mean when they give him orders. Before she can stop him, he silently races straight into the house. Madison winces. What if she gets Brody killed while Nate's away? There really would be no hope for their relationship if he came back to find *that* had happened.

She races in after him, shouting, "Who's here?"

She switches the light on, but nothing happens. Moonlight seeps in through a window, illuminating the kitchen. Everything looks as she left it this morning, with no evidence of a stranger present. Brody is already searching upstairs, but a scratching sound to her left makes her tighten her grip on her weapon. She hears it again and frowns. It sounds like it's coming from outside.

She runs out of the house and turns left. A figure is walking away, behind the house. "Stop or I'll shoot!" she yells.

The person stops and holds their hands up.

"Turn around. *Now.*"

When the figure turns, she sees a tall white man in his thirties. He smiles broadly. "Sorry to scare you, ma'am. I'm not an intruder."

Irritated, she says, "Then what were you doing in my house?"

He steps forward, so she keeps her weapon raised. "The name's Kyle Davenport. I'm here to install a home security system. Nate Monroe hired me a week ago. He left the spare key for me to find in case he was out."

Nate wanted to make the house secure so no one could target them during an investigation, a hazard of the job. Embarrassed, Madison lowers her weapon. "Sorry. I had no idea you were coming today." She frowns. "Wait, why's the house in darkness, and where's your truck?"

He approaches her, a stupid grin fixed in place. "I accidentally tripped the electrics, so I was about to fetch a flashlight from my truck. I parked at the wrong house. Over there." He points east, but she can't see a truck from here as the house is in the way.

Madison leads him to her own vehicle. "I have a flashlight in the trunk."

Brody comes bounding out of the house, barking as he approaches the stranger.

Kyle Davenport appears to be afraid of dogs. He steps behind Madison. "Whoa! Who's this fine beast?"

"This is Officer Brody. So if you have any drugs or blood on you, say your prayers, my friend."

Kyle looks at her. "You guys are *cops*?"

"Nate's a PI, but he's away right now. I'm Detective Madison Harper." She holds her hand out while Brody sniffs the stranger. "That's not a problem, is it?"

He shakes it. "No. Not at all." He takes a nervous step back from Brody. "He's not going to bite me, is he? It's just that, well, I have a little recreational cannabis in my back pocket."

Madison scoffs. "I think we can overlook that. But only if you get the lights back on."

He nods. "Sure thing."

She follows him into the garage, where he quickly works on fixing the electricity. Untrusting of strangers in his house, Brody stays to keep an eye on him. He sits a few feet behind Kyle, and Madison knows he won't let the man out of his sight.

She smiles faintly as she enters the house to feed Bandit. The white cat rubs himself all over her legs when she crouches down to pour food into the small bowl he eats from.

"Hey, cutie. Have you had a good day?"

He meows before giving her the cold shoulder the minute his food hits the bowl.

"Charming." When she rises, the lights flicker on and a few electrical items beep, wanting their digital displays reset.

Kyle appears. "I just have one more camera to install out

back, then I'm done. I'll show you how to control everything from your phone before I leave."

She nods. "Thanks."

He heads outside with Brody close behind. She smiles. It's comforting to know the dog is making sure she's safe. Grabbing a bottle of cold white wine from the refrigerator, she pours herself a glass and sits at the dining table with a sigh. She's exhausted. It's been a strange day. Not long after she realized Nate had vanished, her sister reentered her life as if nothing ever happened between them. She's still unsure how to deal with either situation. The Feds called her this afternoon to update her on Angie's release. Better late than never. They apparently advised the prison warden to give her plenty of notice before letting Angie out, but that obviously didn't happen. Nervous she might reoffend, they've promised to stay in touch.

Her phone rings. It's Owen. She smiles as she answers. "Hey, stranger."

"Hey, Mom. Where's Nate? He's not answering his phone."

She glances at the breakfast bar, where his phone sits. She doesn't want to tell Owen that Nate's left her as she doesn't want to distract him from his studies. He'll be devastated if Nate doesn't return, so she decides to delay hurting him for as long as possible, in the hope that her fiancé comes to his senses in the meantime.

She takes a deep breath and tries to sound offended. "So you're not calling to speak to me?"

He sighs in that way teenage boys do. "I guess, but Nate never misses my calls. You miss them all the time."

She's hit with a pang of guilt. "Hey! Only *sometimes*, and only because of my job. If you ever call twice in a row, I answer."

"I know. Sorry," he says, "I wasn't trying to make you feel guilty. So where's Nate?"

She shakes her head with a patient smile. "He's lost his phone. Can I help?"

"No, definitely not."

Her eyebrows raise. "What does that mean? Oh, wait. Is it girl problems? Because Nate's not very good at that kind of thing."

He laughs. "No. I just wanted to run something by him, but it can wait if he's not home. So, how's things with you?" He says it as an afterthought, but that's okay. She understands moms are boring to their sons.

She considers telling him about Angie being freed but decides against it. She doesn't think she could handle it if he showed interest in a reunion with her. Angie is both his aunt and his stepmother. A shiver goes through her at the thought. "Nothing new. I'm just working a lot, as usual."

"This is why I never ask you what's up, because all you do is work!"

She smiles. "I'm boring, aren't I? Maybe if you visited me more often, I'd have something else to do with my time."

Kyle starts banging something outside. The noise is loud enough for Owen to hear. "What's going on?"

"We're finally installing security cameras," she says. "Brody's helping." She hears other voices at the end of the line. Someone's talking to Owen.

"Mom, I've gotta go," he says. "Tell Nate to call me, okay?"

Her shoulders sag. "Sure. Love you."

"Bye."

When he hangs up, the house feels empty. She wishes he were here to help her deal with Nate's sudden departure and whatever Angie has in store for her. But he's safer in Arizona.

"Okay, all done." Kyle enters, followed by Brody. "I need you to download our app." He sits next to her at the dining table without being invited. She raises an eyebrow at his easy familiarity.

"Do you know Nate?"

"Nope. I dropped a flier in your mailbox, and he called me the same day to book the job. Never met him, though." He holds his phone up so she can see which app she needs to download. It takes a minute or so to create a username and password, then he takes her phone from her. "Okay, let's get your settings optimized."

She watches as he zooms through the options. He's an attractive guy, with light brown hair and a ready smile. "You should install cameras at my place too." She figures Adams would probably appreciate it, especially as his girls sleep over some weekends. She pulls out her spare key and slides it across the table. "A friend of mine lives there."

He nods. "Sure. What's the address?"

She tells him the street name and house number, and watches as he puts the details in a text message, which he sends from her phone to his.

"I'll stop by later this week," he says.

"Thanks." Something occurs to her. "Can these cameras or the app be hacked?"

He smiles. "Well, technically, anything can be hacked."

That doesn't fill her with confidence. "Did you put any cameras *inside* the property?"

He nods to one in the corner of the kitchen ceiling. "That covers the entire open-plan kitchen diner and the entrance. It's the only internal camera. There are four outside, on each corner of the house. Oh, and one in the garage too. None are pointed at your neighbors' properties, as that's illegal depending on which state you live in." He smiles. "Although people still do it. My ex loved watching true-crime documentaries, especially when a neighbor's home security footage would catch a killer taking a dead body to their car. I tried telling her it was super shady to watch the neighbors on camera, and pointed out how she'd hate it if someone was recording *her* comings and goings. Know what she said?"

Madison shakes her head.

"That those cameras were providing her with hours of entertainment."

She smiles politely, but it's sad how many people find entertainment from other people's misfortune. Although that's not the only reason so many people are sucked into those shows. They show you how *not* to become a victim, and what to do if you are. They raise awareness of red flags to be aware of in partners and other people in your life. She'd still hate to be the subject of one herself, though. Imagine all those viewers watching the intimate footage and text messages that make up your life, and then judging you for it. Imagine them sipping wine and eating potato chips as they and their friends gasp at the gory details of your final few moments alive.

That's why Nate's always refused to give any interviews. But she can't help thinking he could have kept media speculation at bay if he'd done just one to set the record straight. Vince Rader wanted to do a sympathetic piece for his *Crime and Dine* podcast, but Nate couldn't be swayed.

Installation complete, Kyle stands. Before he leaves, she joins him at the door. "Do you or your co-workers have access to this footage from our house?"

He shakes his head emphatically. "No, ma'am. It would be illegal for us to access customers' cameras remotely. We'd be fired immediately."

"But it *is* possible to look?" she presses.

"I personally don't have access, but I guess the bosses would." He gently nudges her arm in an attempt to reassure her. "Listen, I appreciate you're a cop who has to see the worst in everyone, but these cameras are here to *protect* you. And believe it or not, we don't have time to sit around watching you guys all day. I mean, unless you and your friend Nate are making out on that counter ten times a day, you're probably pretty boring to watch."

She laughs. "Yeah, well, you have a point there."

He opens the door and is about to pet Brody but decides against it. Instead, he says, "Bye, Officer Brody." He turns to her and nods. "Detective Harper."

"Thanks for coming." She closes the door behind him, and the house suddenly seems unbearably quiet.

CHAPTER THIRTEEN

Time captive: 2 weeks

The man who pretended to be her hero is called Eugene. He doesn't like her name, so he's given her another in an attempt to detach her from her real identity, but she refuses to utter it. She refuses all his attempts at normalizing what he's doing to her, determined that her previous identity and her new, enforced one will never merge before she escapes. Because she *will* escape.

Her ordeal has caused something to awaken inside her. The only way she can explain it is that it feels as though she's been forced into an early maturity. She's discovered a bloody-minded streak that makes her want to survive the horror she finds herself in. She refuses to let him get the better of her. She won't whimper around him or submit to his every whim. She's going to beat him at his own game until she finds a way out of here and back to her real life.

There are rules here. She's not allowed in the locked basement. Not because he has other girls down there, apparently, but he says it's the only part of the house where he gets complete privacy. For what, she can't imagine. She is in charge of all of the housework. She isn't locked up for the entire day. She has some freedom as long as she follows him around. If he wants to sit in the kitchen, she has to go with him. The only time she can be alone is when locked in her bedroom, which has a comfortable single bed, a nightstand, and a dresser for her clothes. It's better than being locked in a darkened basement, so for that, she *is* grateful.

His house is grimy without being obscenely so. She can tell he doesn't like mess but is unable to help himself for some reason. Perhaps his mother always cleaned up after him. He set her to work immediately, dusting the furniture, vacuuming the floors, cleaning the dishes and washing his clothes. He doesn't beat her, and he hasn't spoken harshly to her. He's making good on his promise and treating her as his wife. One who had no say in the union. One who is just sixteen years old and, despite the lack of violence, fearful for her life.

On her fifth day here, he presented her with a simple gold wedding band. He filmed the occasion, to complement the random photos he takes of her, like on that first day in the back-seat of his truck. When he slipped the ring on her finger, he spoke into the lens of an ancient video camera—a camcorder—and explained how it was one of the best days of his life. Once he stopped recording, he told her she didn't have to consummate their marriage until she felt comfortable around him, as if he were being reasonable. Until her recent assault, she'd never even kissed anyone before, and the thought of letting this over-weight, unkempt man who smells of whiskey see her naked and then touch her brings bile to her throat.

She's allowed to wash her clothes when she washes his. Not just the ones she was wearing when he took her, but the pile he already had for her. They look used and must've been purchased from a thrift store. The bra cup sizes are too big for her, but she wears them anyway as an extra layer of protection over her nakedness. If she can delay his touch on her skin for even a second longer while he unclasps her bra, she'll take it as a win. The secondhand jeans and pants need a belt to stay up, and she has to roll up the legs. The T-shirts are oversized, and one smells of perfume. It can't have been washed before it was donated, and the flowery smell reminds her of her mother.

"You missed a spot," he says from his armchair behind her.

She realizes she'd been in a daze and had stopped dusting.

Eugene points to the TV cabinet and a thick layer of dust, which stands out now the other surfaces in the room have been polished.

She wipes it with the duster, then sprays polish. She's thought about spraying the aerosol into his eyes, but it wouldn't do her any good. The detached property only has one door, at the front of the house. It's secured with three locks, and only Eugene has the keys. All knives and forks are locked in a drawer, and the windows are sealed with paint. Some are nailed shut, and there are bars on the upstairs windows at the back of the house, including her room. She prays a fire never breaks out on one of the few occasions he leaves the house to fetch groceries, because he locks her in her bedroom before leaving.

The blinds on the windows are always pulled low, although long-term sun damage means they still let in light through the cracks and tears. She could remove them, stand in the window and bang and wave, but he has no neighbors. They're in the middle of nowhere and surrounded by trees, so she doesn't know how close or far away the nearest help is. It was difficult to tell anything from the drive here. She'd blacked out with panic and wasn't sure how long she was unconscious, so she couldn't measure the distance or direction they'd traveled in.

Eugene gets out of his chair. She watches his reflection on the TV screen and tenses when he approaches her from behind. She doesn't turn. He pulls her long blonde hair to one side and leans in to kiss her bare neck. She grimaces as her body freezes.

"You're so warm," he says, going in for another. "And you taste sweet. Must be your age."

Her bladder threatens to let go. He only allows her a small number of bathroom breaks each day, and she mustn't close the door. The bathroom window is tiny, but perhaps he thinks she'll smash the glass and use it as a weapon. Dread consumes her when she thinks about how limited her options are for escape.

Why on earth did she leave the comfort of her own home to go to Emma's place that night? She silently curses herself for being so naïve. It's been *fourteen* days. Is anyone even looking for her?

Eugene recently broke the news that he brought her here because her father paid him to take her off his hands. Her dad didn't want her anymore as she was too much of a handful. It broke her heart. She wasn't sure whether to believe him at first, but it would explain why no one has rescued her yet. Maybe, given more time, her father will miss her. He might come to his senses before it gets out of hand. She's learned her lesson. Don't go out alone at night. Don't forget how dangerous strangers are. Don't be a female.

"I wasn't going to tell you this," Eugene says behind her, "but your daddy actually paid me to *kill* you."

Her eyes widen but she doesn't turn.

"But if you're good, I won't kill you. I'll take good care of you. Better than your daddy ever did. Better than my little brother would if he'd bought you." He laughs as if the situation has humor to it. "Man alive, if he got his grubby paws on you, you'd think this place was heaven in comparison." He strokes her greasy hair while pressing his body closer to hers. "Lucky for you, he and I don't get along, so there's no reason you should meet him. Not unless you're *bad*."

He's not comforting her, he's threatening her. He's trying to scare her to control her. She may be naïve but she's not stupid. She's seen women on social media talking about their abusive partners. She knows all about narcissists, controlling partners and emotional abuse. It comes as a surprise that Eugene has the intelligence necessary for mind games, but now she knows he does, she needs to stay even more alert around him.

She smells his foul breath as he whispers into her ear, "I'll look out for you, sweetheart. I'll give you the world if you'll love me." With a final kiss of her neck, he leaves her to go down to his basement for privacy.

When he's out of sight, her muscles relax and she shakily inhales. Her knees almost give way with relief that he's gone. This is the kind of stuff horror movies are made of. She can't survive in this situation. No one could. She'd rather be dead.

She doesn't dare to move as the floorboards will creak, giving her away. He expects her to wait here for him until he's done doing whatever he feels he needs to do in private.

The setting sun seeps through the cracks in the blinds, casting shadows over the living room as she stands frozen to the spot. It'll be dark soon. Nighttime is the most bearable part of her day. It's when she's locked up in her own room. There are three bedrooms upstairs. Eugene's is next to hers. He says he locks her in to keep her safe, but once they fall in love, she'll share his bedroom. If the day ever comes when he forces her into his bed, she'll act. She won't let him violate her.

She'll make sure one of them dies before that can happen.

CHAPTER FOURTEEN

The morning starts with downpours, and Madison can barely keep her eyes open. Brody spent the night doing something he's never done before. Howling. He's half husky, but she's never heard him howl once in all the time she's known him. She can only conclude he's unsettled by Nate's absence. And thanks to Nate, she'll need multiple coffees in succession if she's to stay awake this morning.

She enters the bright police station and nods at the officer behind the front desk. Officer Shelley Vickers smiles as Brody follows Madison inside, as if it's perfectly normal for a dog to be present at the station. He shakes off rainwater all over the tiled floor.

Madison goes straight to the kitchen to fetch her second coffee of the day and a bowl of water for Brody. The break room smells of spilled coffee and heated oats. Alex is at the sink. He's holding Deanna against his chest, and the chihuahua immediately growls as they enter. Madison suspects the animal's disdain is aimed more at her than Brody.

"Morning, Detective," says Alex, turning from the sink. He pats the chihuahua's head. "Now, now, Mrs. Pebbles. Be nice."

Madison keeps her distance as she pours coffee. "I thought you renamed her?"

He sighs. "I tried, but she won't play ball. She just ignores her new name, so I've let her win this battle."

It doesn't surprise her one bit. "And the chief finally gave in and let you bring her to work?"

He nods. "As long as Mrs. Pebbles remains primarily in my office and doesn't attack anyone, Chief Mendes says she's welcome."

Madison smiles. "Good. That means she can't complain about Brody being here."

Unconvinced, Alex says, "But Brody's about ten times the size of this little one." He gives his tiny dog a squeeze, and she lovingly licks his face before turning back to look at Madison, her beady eyes narrowed and untrusting.

It's unnerving. "I wish I knew why she dislikes me so much. I mean, I saved her from the pound!" When the dog's previous owner died, Adams was going to take her straight to a shelter, where she would probably have ended up on a kill list. Madison hadn't let that happen.

"It's a female thing," says Alex. "She's fine with men. Don't take it personally."

She notices Brody keeps his distance too.

"How come you're on doggy daycare duty?" Alex asks.

"Nate's busy today." She doesn't elaborate.

"I see. Well, I'll just get this little lady settled in her crate, then I'll join you and Detective Tanner."

"Sure." Madison follows him out of the kitchen and leads Brody to her desk, wondering if she needs to purchase him a crate or a bed to sleep in beside her chair. She hopes he doesn't start howling here, as the chief won't stand for it.

Steve glances up as she passes. His bruised eye doesn't look any better today. If he's anything like her, it will take weeks to fade.

"Morning." He calls Brody over and lavishes him with attention. "Hey, boy. Are you joining us again today?" Brody pants heavily, his tail whipping Steve's desk in excitement. Steve looks up at Madison. "No word from Nate overnight?"

She shakes her head. "No, and I haven't told anyone but you and Nate's boss that he's gone, so if you hear me lying to anyone, go with it."

"Sure, but I don't know why you don't want anyone else to find out. Nate's actions don't reflect poorly on you."

She doubts that's true. Besides, they were recently engaged. It's embarrassing that her fiancé has gone AWOL so soon after popping the question. She rubs her ring finger, suddenly remembering she threw the engagement ring across the room in frustration. She should probably retrieve it at some point. She might need to sell it to cover the bills for the two houses.

Steve's cell phone rings. He checks the caller ID. "It's Lena's office."

Madison switches her computer on while he talks to his girlfriend. Brody settles next to her desk as she looks around the station to see who's in. The office is slowly beginning to fill as the morning shift arrives to replace the evening crew. Dina is packing her purse, ready to leave. She works the night shift on dispatch. Stella is just arriving, and they're already swapping stories about drunk callers. Chief Mendes is on the phone in her office. Various uniformed officers nod in greeting as they pass Madison. Officers Corey Fuller and Lisa Kent—the department's most recent recruits, fresh from the academy—arrive at the same time as Sergeant Adams. He's usually at least ten to twenty minutes late but can be forgiven since he has to get his daughters ready for school. Some days, it's the only time he sees them, thanks to the separation.

Sergeant Adams and Chief Mendes approach. The chief is eyeing Brody disapprovingly, but before she can say anything,

Steve turns to look at Madison, phone to his ear, saying, "Are you serious?"

Madison frowns. It must be news of their victim's autopsy.

"That's messed up. Send me the photos. Okay, bye." He ends the call. "Lena found something odd inside our victim's body."

Chief Mendes steps closer while Adams goes to his desk and removes his coat. He pulls out a granola bar for breakfast, muttering, "Damn, I wish this was something fattening and greasy."

"She's emailing me the photos." Steve opens his emails and waits.

"What did she find?" asks the chief. She's wearing a thick sweater over her blouse. It feels cold in here today. Heavy rain suddenly lashes against the windows, swept up in a gust of wind.

Alex approaches them without his dog. He's carrying a hot drink instead. "What have I missed?"

"Lena's performed the autopsy," says Madison. "Apparently, she found something inside the guy's body."

An email appears on Steve's screen. He opens the attached images. Adams hovers behind Madison as they all peer at the screen. The first image shows the victim's shiny pink stomach, which is sliced open, revealing the contents.

Adams groans in disgust. "Suddenly, breakfast doesn't seem so appealing anymore."

Steve points to a gray mass on the screen. "Lena says this is the remains of a sandwich."

What's also visible is something Madison would never expect to see inside a human body. Red rose petals. They've been hastily chewed in an effort to swallow them. It's bizarre.

"Why would anyone eat a rose?" says Adams.

Steve scrolls down to the next photo, which is worse. It's the guy's esophagus, still in place in the torso. Lena has delicately sliced it open to reveal its shocking contents. The long stem of a rose is wedged there. Its large thorns have crudely torn the esophagus in several places as it traveled down the victim's throat. It looks painful, and Madison can imagine it felt like a thousand papercuts as it made its way through the delicate tissue.

Chief Mendes steps back and takes a breath. "Either this guy was mentally unwell, or someone forced that down his throat."

"Since he was found decapitated," says Steve, "I'd say someone forced him to eat it before they killed him."

Alex leans in for a closer look. "He didn't even chew the stem. For it to enter the esophagus intact like that means his head would've been tilted all the way back to create a straight entry point. Fascinating..."

Adams gives the forensic tech a sideways glance before returning to his desk and dropping the granola bar.

"Or," continues Alex, "his head was already removed at this point, giving the killer easy access."

"I think whoever killed him wanted him to suffer," says Madison. "He was more likely alive while ingesting it."

Steve looks up at her from his seat. "Lena said that this alone wasn't enough to kill him, as it didn't block his windpipe, and the internal lacerations wouldn't have caused significant blood loss. She's still finalizing her report but wanted to give us a heads-up about what to expect." He looks at Alex. "Did you manage to get anything useful from his body to help the investigation?"

Alex straightens. "Afraid not. We obviously don't have his hands to take his palm or fingerprints, or to know which was his dominant hand, which is sometimes helpful in identification, and we also don't have his head to compare dental records, or to take ear prints."

"*Ear* prints?" says Steve, incredulous.

Alex nods. "Ear prints can be used to assist in identifying remains when all else fails. Unfortunately, I found no trace evidence or stranger's fingerprints on his body because the water washed away anything useful. His killer knew what they were doing by dumping him in the creek. Lena's taking blood and tissue samples that we can send to Nora at the crime lab. She can then look for a direct or familial match on the CODIS database in a bid to identify him, assuming he or one of his relatives has a criminal past."

"Could we pull the killer's fingerprints or DNA from the rose?" asks Madison.

"Well, all contact leaves a trace," he says. "But it's likely that any evidence would've been destroyed by the victim's body fluids. I'll check once Lena's retrieved the items for me."

She nods. "I guess our best bet for a fast identification is if someone who knows him reports him missing."

"Or a member of the public discovers his head or hands somewhere and calls it in," says Steve.

Chief Mendes crosses her arms. "In that case, we need to hold a press conference sooner rather than later. We need this man's identity asap so we can figure out who wanted him dead."

"Agreed," says Madison. "I'll organize it right away." She hesitates, before adding, "Can I also broach the subject of Toby Clark at the press conference?" She quickly explains the case to those present who don't know anything about it.

Adams is horrified that Gina never reported her baby missing. "Who does that?"

Steve is more compassionate. "Fear of law enforcement is a real thing that we need to respect," he says. "Add to that fear of her baby being taken by child services and I can understand why she was too afraid to come to us."

Exasperated, Adams crosses his arms. "Why are people so afraid of us when all we do is risk our lives to protect them?"

"A negative experience for one family member can allow

bad blood to fester through generations," says the chief. "The only way to limit that is through education. If we had more officers, we could visit the local schools and educate them on what we do and how we're here for the community's benefit."

Madison couldn't agree more. It's something they've done in the past, but they don't have time for it right now. "So I can make the press aware of Gina's son?"

The chief nods. "Do it. But remember—"

Madison cuts her off. "I know. It's a cold case. Yesterday's homicide is more important."

Mendes shoots her a hard stare. "I know you're annoyed with me and think I'm being unduly harsh, Madison, but we're stretched as it is."

"I'm not annoyed at *you*," Madison says. "Just at the lack of resources and how it affects victims like Gina Clark. She's never had any help in her entire life, and then someone goes and kidnaps her baby. It's frustrating that we can't throw everything at it to find out what happened to him, that's all."

"I know," says the chief quietly. "Just do what you can." She returns to her office.

"If I can help with that case in any way," says Alex, sympathetic to Gina's situation, "just let me know."

Madison smiles. "Thanks." She's frustrated because if Nate were around, she could give him Gina's case to work on. She sighs as everyone disperses. All she can do is concentrate on the press conference for now, and do what she can to raise awareness of the little boy's disappearance.

CHAPTER FIFTEEN

Nate purchased breakfast from a drive-thru, but he's struggling to eat it. His appetite has vanished in the last week or so. He's more thirsty than usual, though. Perhaps his body is trying to keep him alive by forcing him to drink fluids. He stuffs the leftover takeout food into the paper bag it came in and throws it onto the floor on the passenger side.

His reflection in the rearview mirror would be worrying if he cared enough. He spent the night in his car to avoid interacting with anyone who might recognize him. It was uncomfortable in the backseat, not least because Brody has caused so much damage to the upholstery. He rubs his eyes, but it doesn't make him feel any more awake.

He wishes he'd brought his cell phone with him so he could check on news from Lost Creek. He imagines Madison is keeping track of him using traffic cameras, capturing his journey through license plate recognition. She may even turn up here at some point today. He hopes not. He meant it when he said he needs space. He doesn't think he could face her in his current state.

After a sip of weak coffee, he starts the car and heads to his sister's address. The drive takes him through his old neighbor-hood, and he sees the ghosts of his childhood friends every-where. The movie theater he'd go to with his brother most weekends is long gone and replaced with a parking lot. His high school is still standing but looks ready for demolition. The entire area has gone downhill. Green spaces and children's parks are showing signs of neglect. The toy stores are all gone, replaced with coffee shops. The mall looks abandoned. Fast-food chains now outnumber independent stores.

He sighs heavily. It's depressing to destroy what happy memories you have left. Maybe he shouldn't have returned. But he has to see his siblings once more before he decides what's next for him.

The house that Dawn shares with her husband and kids is in a nice part of town. She must have done well for herself. Nate doesn't know what she does for a living. He's tried to keep tabs on his siblings over the years, but they're both surprisingly private on social media. Perhaps because of the drama that surrounds him. He parks outside her house and turns the engine off. She might not even be home.

His gut tells him not to go any further. To keep this door closed forever to avoid more pain. But there's a tiny spark of hope that she might want to let him in, share a cup of coffee with him and welcome him back into the fold. He needs to know once and for all whether he can still consider her and his brother family.

As he tries to force himself out of the car, her garage door rattles open and a white SUV pulls forward into the driveway. A woman gets out and leaves the car unattended as it warms up, white smoke billowing into the cold morning air. She dips back into the garage to grab something. When she steps out again, the door closes automatically behind her.

Nate's stomach flips with nerves. Dawn has aged, obvi-ously, but he wasn't prepared for how much she looks like their mother when she was in her mid-forties. No longer slim and athletic, his sister looks her age, probably exhausted from being a working mother. Her blonde hair is brassy and in need of a root touch-up, and her round face is lined. He watches, transfixed, as she wrestles with her purse, a briefcase and a large thermos on her way to her car. She's heading to work.

He knows it's now or never. He gets out of the car and slowly approaches the end of her driveway.

When Dawn notices him standing there, she steps behind her open car door as if readying herself for a quick getaway should this stranger attack her. "Help you?" she says, her eyes unfriendly.

She hasn't recognized him. Nate swallows. Before he can say anything, she gasps. They silently assess each other for what seems like ten minutes but can only be a few seconds.

"What the hell are *you* doing here?" she says bitterly.

His heart sinks. His father was his only visitor during his murder trial, and he'd told Nate how Dawn had taken a harsh stance on his situation. She didn't want to be associated with him, and his dad thought she might even believe the charges. Nate never thought she'd welcome him home with open arms, but he'd hoped her views had softened over the years. Especially since his conviction was overturned.

"Sorry for turning up unannounced."

She looks around at the neighboring houses with concern in case anyone's watching them. "Come here." She leads him around the side of the house to the landscaped backyard. Kids' toys sit discarded on the deck. The lawn is impeccably trimmed. Dawn stands several feet away from him as if afraid he could lash out at any time. "You shouldn't have come." Her anger is evident. She hates him.

"I'm sorry," he murmurs. He realizes he's messed up. He's overcome with the urge to flee, to save himself from the pain of rejection. How could he have been so stupid as to come here? "I'll go." He turns.

"Wait!" She rests her hands on her hips. "So, you did it again, huh? You killed someone else. I knew I was right all along, and Dad was wrong."

Nate finally makes eye contact with her. "How can you say that? You know me, Dawn. I'm your *brother*."

"And I'm your sister, but that didn't stop you from ruining my life!" she snaps back. "You don't even care what you put us through, do you?" He's shocked by the venom behind her words. She used to be so caring when they were kids.

"Of course I care what you went through," he says quietly. "But I didn't kill Stacey Connor. I loved her. We were getting married. It was Father—"

She cuts him off. "Your conviction put the spotlight on me, Dad and Kurt. We went through *hell* because of you. Whether you killed that woman or not, the outcome was the same. I had a brother on death row. Do you think anyone cares that we weren't guilty? No! Because it was all about you, and we were tainted by it. Do you know how hard that made it for me and Kurt to find work? To have a relationship with anyone? They all looked at us like we were just as bad as you. We had to work harder than everyone else to prove ourselves as good people. I mean, *my God*, Nathaniel. My church even asked me to leave! Do you know how humiliating that was?"

Nate lets her rant, because she's right. They all suffered because he had a relationship with a woman who had a sociopathic relative. But he couldn't have foreseen that. No one could. Hearing that her church didn't support her makes him angry. "I'm truly sorry for what you went through."

"And what about Dad?" She continues as if he never spoke. "He *died* because of you. The stress of defending you gave him cancer. I'm sure of it."

Nate already carries guilt for his father's death, so she can't make him feel any worse about that. "I'll go."

"No, you won't!" she hisses. "I've wanted to say this to you for a long time, so I'm going to get it all out. God knows it might save me from spending more money on therapy." She takes a deep breath. "Whether you killed that woman or not, you made the situation worse by fighting to get out of prison. Every single time you appealed, the media came knocking at our doors again, asking whether we supported your appeal or whether we wanted to see you die on that gurney as if you were a worthless piece of shit." She unexpectedly lets out a sob and covers her mouth to take a second.

He lowers his watery eyes. If he was in any doubt about whether to end things, his sister just helped him decide. Every day he's alive, he's causing her and Kurt unnecessary pain.

Dawn sniffs back her tears and approaches him. She pulls him into an embrace that takes him by surprise. As she hugs him, Nate puts his arms around her and squeezes. Tears escape his eyes. He wishes he could go back in time and change the course of history. He should never have left Kansas. He wouldn't have met Stacey Connor. She'd still be alive, and he'd still be part of this family. But equally, if none of that had happened, he would never have met Madison and Owen.

Dawn pulls away first. Her eye makeup runs down her cheeks. "A big part of me hates you, Nate. Like, *really* hates you. But an even bigger part of me misses you with every bone in my body. At least, the boy you were when we were kids. You were so kind and caring toward us. That made it so much worse when I heard you'd turned into a predator. I guess I'm just so damn disappointed in you. Disappointed that you were hiding a dark streak all that time, just like all the other sick bastards out there."

He wipes his eyes. "Dawn, I'm not a predator. I was cleared." He opens his mouth to say more, but has no fight left in him. How long is he expected to answer for something he didn't do?

"But you killed a man last month," she says. "I read the headlines. I got calls from the press asking whether I was surprised you'd reoffended. It makes me vomit to know Dad wasted his last years defending you."

He suddenly feels overwhelmingly exhausted. His life goes around in circles. The drama never ends. He thinks of Madison, and how she's the only person who's ever accepted him for who he is, even with all his issues and baggage. He questions why he left the safety of their relationship to come here and expose himself to more pain. Does he seek it out? Is *he* the problem?

It dawns on him that he's put himself through this painful showdown because he feels he deserves to suffer for taking a man's life. He's punishing himself. He looks at his sister. "It's all going to stop. You don't need to worry anymore." As he turns to leave, he murmurs, "I have a way of making it all stop."

CHAPTER SIXTEEN

Before Madison heads to the conference room, where reporters are noisily arriving for an update, Steve approaches her. "Officers are still questioning residents at the trailer park to see if anyone saw or heard anything with regards to our John Doe murder," he says. "But the ones I spoke to hadn't seen a thing. Some residents are freaking out at the thought the killer might target one of them next."

Madison sips her third coffee before responding. "And we can't even reassure them that won't happen until we have a motive for the murder. Find any cameras on site?"

He takes a seat next to her, ignoring Adams, who's drowning in paperwork at his desk. "No, but that doesn't surprise me. Security cameras are expensive, and a lot of the residents will be short on money."

She's reminded of Kyle Davenport. "We had cameras installed yesterday. Nate booked it before he left. Hopefully he'll still pay the guy." She can't afford to. Especially if she's now solely responsible for all the bills.

Steve leans back in his seat. "It's smart. I've had them at my place for years. I've got a door cam now too. Lena hates them, though."

"Why?"

He shrugs. "Thinks it's an invasion of privacy. She's weird like that. I have to turn them off when she comes over."

"To tell you the truth," Madison says, "I can see her point. They're hackable, apparently."

He shakes his head in disgust. "Some people have way too much time on their hands."

Madison looks at her computer screen. "I've double-checked, but we don't have any recent missing person reports that could match our John Doe. We need to check with the surrounding PDs in case they have someone who matches his description, limited though it is."

He nods. "I can do that."

They watch as an officer leads more reporters to the conference room. Madison recognizes a few faces. She suddenly frowns as a woman breaks from the crowd to come her way.

"Hey, stranger!" says the attractive blue-eyed brunette.

Kate Flynn and Madison were at high school together. They've remained friends ever since, despite some bumps in the road over the years. Kate was a seasoned local TV reporter, who sensationally quit after the Snow Storm Killer abducted her and her little boy. The experience shook her so badly she hasn't worked since. She and her husband took their two children out of school to travel the world while they recovered. It's a wonder they survived the ordeal unscathed.

Madison stands. She had no idea Kate was home from her travels. "What are you doing here?" She hugs her friend. "You know Steve, right?"

Kate nods at Steve. "Of course, but you were a sergeant last time I was here, not Madison's partner." She looks at Madison. "Did the new guy not work out? I remember you said he was a douche."

Sergeant Adams looks up from his desk.

Madison cringes. "Kate, this is Marcus Adams. He decided investigating wasn't for him, so he recently swapped roles with Steve."

"Pleasure," says Adams, with a look that suggests it's anything but. He immediately goes back to what he was doing, clearly unimpressed.

Steve stifles a laugh as he returns to his own desk.

Kate winces. To Madison, she mouths, "Sorry!"

Madison smiles as she leads Kate to the conference room, where they linger outside. "So how come you're here? Last I heard, you were cruising around Barbados, or was it the Mediterranean?"

"Both!" says Kate. "But I figured it was time to return to doing what I love. I was bored without chasing the news. And my therapist told me it was time to get over what happened."

Madison snorts. "Man, these therapists... They're full of good ideas, aren't they?"

"I know, right? I wonder if they ever take their own advice."

"I doubt it. I've heard they're more messed up than the rest of us."

"Anyway, enough about me," says Kate. "A little birdy tells me you're finally with Nate Monroe now. *Congratulations!* I'm so pleased for you, and I cannot wait to help you plan the wedding. So, have you set a date?"

Madison straightens. "Oh boy. That's a conversation for another day. We need to catch up over a glass of wine."

"Sure, I'd love that."

A reporter makes eye contact with Madison and taps his watch, suggesting he has places to be, so she heads into the room. Kate chooses a seat in the middle row behind a couple of journalists from the local paper.

The small room is a little cramped as well as freezing cold. Chief Mendes makes them turn the heat off in rooms they don't use often to save money, which is fine, but no one remembers to preheat the rooms before meetings, so they're always cold in winter.

A cameraman approaches Madison at the front of the room and whispers, "You're live on Channel Nine right now. Do me a favor: no potty mouth."

She laughs. "I'll try."

A hush falls over the crowd. Madison has five cameras and several smartphones aimed at her. Right before she starts, Gina Clark enters. She stands alone at the back of the room. Madison had asked her to attend. The public likes to see the face of a missing child's mother. They're more likely to help if they can witness raw grief on display. It doesn't seem right, but that's just how it is. To find a missing child, you have to play the game.

Gina had worried that she wasn't smartly dressed or well-spoken enough to go on TV and talk about Toby. She thinks the viewers and reporters will judge her for wearing cheap clothes and no makeup. It's a valid concern when you see how some victims' families are treated these days. Madison assured her that they'll want to help find Toby and that all publicity will bring them closer to getting answers about what happened to him.

"Hi, everyone," she says to the room. "Thanks for coming at short notice. I'll keep this brief as I'm sure you're all busy." Their hungry eyes bore into her. "First, I need to explain why we were called to the Aspen View Mobile Home Park early yesterday morning. We were responding to reports of a deceased Caucasian male in the creek. It's clear from the condition of the victim's body that he was murdered, and we need help identifying him, so consider this an appeal for information."

She's interrupted by a young man in jeans and a dark jacket. "How was it clear? And will there be an autopsy?"

"The medical examiner is currently conducting an autopsy," she says. "But Dr. Scott has already provided some details to aid identification. She believes the male is between forty-five and fifty-five years old, and weighs approximately two hundred and fourteen pounds." She doesn't say *without his head*. She also doesn't give his height since they can't give an accurate measurement until they find his head. "He has no tattoos or distinguishing features on his body." She pauses as some reporters scribble handwritten notes despite also recording her. She decides against telling them the victim's head and hands were removed, as she doesn't want to scare the community unless she really has to. "No weapon has been located, and we have no suspects at this time."

"I assume you've already checked his prints and haven't found a match in the system?" asks another man. "Are dental records next?"

Madison chooses her words carefully. "We've been unable to identify him."

They turn to each other with a ripple of excitement. They're intelligent enough to read between the lines. Before they can probe her further on this, she says, "He was naked, so we don't have his wallet or driver's license, which means we don't know if he's local. If anyone watching this hasn't heard from their husband, son, father, brother or male friend in the last two or three days, then please check on them. If you can't reach them, contact us so we can investigate further. If a co-worker has failed to arrive for work yesterday or today and they haven't been in touch with a reason, we can perform a welfare check if you're unable to get hold of them."

"Detective?" Kate stands. "Could you explain why you've been unable to identify him through prints or dental records? Did you mean your attempts failed to identify him or that those identification methods aren't an option because you don't have his prints or teeth?"

Madison almost smiles. Trust Kate to probe further. "We're

exploring every avenue open to us. Our priority is to identify this person and find the crime scene, as we don't believe he was killed at the creek."

"Is there a risk the killer will strike again?" asks the first guy.

Madison shifts her weight from one foot to the other. "That's impossible to know without learning the motive behind the murder. Therefore, identifying our victim is essential."

"How worried are you that Lost Creek has a third serial killer in just over a year?" asks an older woman Madison recognizes from the local TV station.

Madison's gaze flickers to Kate's face. She sees fear in her friend's eyes, making her wonder whether Kate really is ready to return to this line of work. It was Kate's job that made her a target for the Snow Storm Killer. She gives the woman who asked the question a hard stare and says firmly, "There is absolutely no reason to believe the perpetrator of this crime is a serial killer. *None whatsoever.* So I'd ask you not to suggest that in your reporting."

The woman looks away.

"While we're here," Madison continues, "I want to appeal for information about a missing infant too. Gina?" She looks at Toby's mother. "Would you join me?"

The crowd straightens in unison. Several flashes go off as Gina self-consciously walks to the front of the room. She stands beside and a little behind Madison, who catches a whiff of cigarette smoke. Dressed in faded black jeans, a thick jacket and a clean white top, Gina looks like someone with no money who's tried to dress nice for a special occasion, knowing the audience of mostly females will be judging her.

Her hesitant eyes peer through straight dark hair at the crowd before her. She stands sideways, concentrating her gaze on Madison instead of the reporters, and trying to stop her hands from shaking by clutching them together. People don't realize how nerve-racking it is to stand in front of a bunch of reporters, especially for an introvert like Gina. Once you've exposed yourself to media attention, there's no going back. Your image remains online forever. Along with strangers' opinions of you, good or bad.

"I want to introduce you to Gina Clark," says Madison. "The department would like to appeal for information about an older case. Eighteen months ago, Gina's six-month-old son, Toby Clark, was abducted from his home on Brook Street, and there have been no confirmed sightings of him since."

She doesn't want to lose the community's sympathy for Gina by admitting the young woman didn't file a missing person report at the time, so she omits that for now. But she's aware these reporters will figure it out sooner or later, and she's concerned about how judgmental they'll be in their reporting. "We currently have very little to go on other than a description of Toby and the time frame during which he was taken."

She clicks on a nearby laptop, which makes the baby's face appear on the wall behind her. "As you can see, Toby is white, blond-haired and blue-eyed. He was last seen wearing a pale blue jumpsuit with a bunny rabbit embroidered across the front in dark blue. He had a diaper on but no socks. He was taken from his home sometime after seven or eight p.m. on July seventh, 2019, and before seven p.m. the next day. Ms. Clark understandably wants to find her child, so I'd appreciate it if anyone who lived in the area at that time and sighted someone carrying a baby boy would get in touch. It could be that someone you know introduced a baby to their family unexpectedly, or you heard a child crying in the neighborhood, maybe in a residence where there shouldn't have been a child. Please contact us immediately if you can think of anything useful, no matter how insignificant it might seem."

She's already decided against sharing the information that Gina's PI obtained about a blonde girl in a drugstore, as she doesn't want to muddy the waters. At this stage, she wants genuine sightings of the baby first.

Kate stands. "Ms. Clark, you must be devastated," she says with genuine compassion. "I'm so sorry for what you're going through. How hopeful are you that your son can be found after all this time?"

Madison is grateful she didn't ask how hopeful Gina was that her son would be found *alive*. Some reporters would.

Gina looks like a rabbit in the headlights. "I've spoken to Detective Harper about my son, and I know she has the best intentions, so I'm hopeful."

"Who investigated the case at the time?" Kate probes. "Do we know why your son was never found? Were there ever any suspects?"

A tear escapes Gina's eye as she becomes flustered. "I'm sorry. I'm not good at this kind of thing. I only came because I want my baby back more than anything in the world." The room is silent as she takes a breath. "Waking up is hell. Going to sleep is hell. I'd do anything to hold him again. I never got to hear his voice. You see, he wasn't yet talking the last time I saw him. I just want to hear my son say *Momma*." She turns away and sobs into her hands.

Madison decides that's enough for now. Gina's not used to this kind of attention.

A man raises his hand. "Can I ask—"

She cuts him off. "I'm sorry, but that's all we have time for right now. I'm sure you understand that we're extremely busy. Thanks for coming. I appreciate it." She leads Gina away and they quickly exit the room before anyone can stop them.

Madison doesn't like keeping her cards close to her chest, but there are some things that should be withheld from the press and the public if it increases the chances of finding Toby alive.

CHAPTER SEVENTEEN

Madison pulls over at the gated entrance to an office development. The building is large and gray. It must house fifty or more separate offices. The midafternoon sky is overcast with rain clouds, which means some offices are lit from within, but the majority appear to be empty, with no movement behind the windows. A sign at the parking lot entrance tells her four companies house their office workers here, and several units are still available to lease.

This is where Gina Clark lived at the time Toby vanished. All the residential homes were demolished to make way for this prisonlike building. It's no wonder people prefer remote working when this is the alternative. Madison sighs as she looks around. None of the original homes remain, so she can't speak with any of Gina's neighbors from that time. She's hoping that if any of them saw anything the night Toby was kidnapped, they'll come forward once they see the press conference, but from what Gina said about their willingness to help her search for him, she's not holding her breath.

She takes a missing person poster from the stack on the passenger seat and leaves the car. She created the posters herself and distributed copies to patrol to spread around town. She pulls some tape from her coat pocket and approaches a street light. The wind tries to tear the poster out of her hand as she holds it against the metal while winding the tape around the top and the bottom of the paper, all under the watchful eyes of cute baby Toby.

When she's done, she pulls a cigarette from a pack she bought at a gas station on the way here. She lights it and inhales deeply while closing her eyes. The smoke warms her from within, and she gets a slight buzz from the nicotine. It's the first cigarette she's had since she quit months ago. It was a bad habit she picked up in prison as a way to pass the time and calm herself down during stressful moments. But it feels good to fill her lungs with smoke. She figures she has no one to smell nice for now Nate's gone, so why not start up again? As long as Owen doesn't find out.

She inhales another puff and stares at the poster. Ever since her first meeting with Gina Clark, she's struggled to get her and Toby out of her head. She feels sorry for the woman. Gina is one of those people who exists with no support. No family or friends to ease her financial and emotional burdens. Madison didn't exactly have a tough upbringing—her mom raised her and Angie alone for part of it, after their dad took off to Alaska—but she lost her mother young, so she knows what it's like not to have any family support as an adult. It makes existing harder. She also has some idea of the strain Gina's under due to her own experience with Owen being taken from her during her trial and subsequent incarceration. It's only thanks to Nate that she was eventually reunited with Owen, which is why, if she can help Gina find Toby, she's determined to do so, despite Chief Mendes's reservations about cold cases.

She stubs the cigarette out against the street light before slipping back into her car, where she pulls open her laptop and clicks on Facebook. Social media can be a pain in the ass where missing people are concerned, thanks to wannabe detectives and trolls, but she thinks it's worth setting up a Facebook page for Toby. Some witnesses prefer to provide information anonymously through messages. It's less scary than calling the police.

She sets up an account and is about to upload some of the last photos taken of him as a six-month-old baby when she gets a notification from her new security app that someone is inside her house.

Her heart skips a beat. Has Nate returned? She quickly opens the camera app and spots Bandit chasing Brody around the kitchen. She rolls her eyes with a smile. For the most part, they get on, but the cat definitely rules the roost.

Putting her phone down, she returns her attention to Facebook and enters all the relevant facts about Toby's case, followed by her name and the station's contact number. If she gives her cell number, she'll be swamped with hoax callers, whereas the dispatch ladies are good at weeding out assholes and timewasters.

The heavens suddenly open, and a heavy downpour bounces off the car's windshield. She switches the wipers on and glances in her rearview mirror. She notices a car making a dangerous U-turn in the narrow road behind her, which is odd because there's plenty of room ahead of her to turn around. Her arms break out in goosebumps as the temperature lowers. Was someone following her? The combination of rain and bright headlights makes it impossible to see the make or model of the car or the license plate.

The only person who might want to follow her is her sister.

The FBI agent Madison spoke to gave her Angie's new address. As the driver of the vehicle has made a fast getaway, she decides to head to Angie's place to check whether she's up to no good.

. . .

Angie is leasing a mobile home in a trailer park that's nowhere near as nice as the one where their male victim was found in the creek. Various dogs are chained to patches of grass, barking nonstop at Madison's arrival.

She pulls up outside a run-down single-wide trailer that looks like it needs a good clean on the outside, so she can only imagine what the inside looks like. She notices a dark blue Ford parked nearby. Did Angie get here just before her? A couple of concrete blocks lead to the door, which opens before Madison has even exited her vehicle. Her sister appears.

Madison gets out of her car and touches the hood of the Ford as she passes. It's warm. She approaches the steps, slick with rainwater. Angie doesn't seem surprised to see her. She motions for Madison to go straight inside, out of the downpour, and then follows her in.

Angie has a slight limp, probably from where Officer Shelley Vickers shot her in the thigh before her arrest. She switches on a light and stands behind the kitchen counter. "I guess that's the end of daylight for today. Coffee?"

Madison glances at the jar of instant coffee, wondering if it's been laced with something. "I'm good."

Angie smirks. "Poison's not my style, sis. You should know that by now."

No, but murder is. Ignoring the comment, Madison takes a seat on the worn couch. The carpet is threadbare in places, and a musty smell fills the air. She'd have all the windows open if it were her place. Angie has few personal belongings, which makes sense. Madison herself left prison with very little, just the clothes she entered with and a few books. She had no one waiting for her on the outside to help rehome or clothe her. Once she was assigned a parole officer a few days later—delayed for unknown reasons, but she always suspected it was because she was a convicted cop killer—she was eventually offered a room in a seedy motel meant for former inmates to get back on their feet.

"Not exactly Buckingham Palace, is it?" Angie opens the fridge, which is empty except for a carton of milk and a loaf of bread.

Madison's hit with a rush of sympathy for her sister, and wonders if she's hungry for a good meal. She tries to decide whether she should give her some money to help her get by, but that might offend her. She watches as Angie pours hot water over a mug of instant coffee and stirs in some milk before joining her on the couch. "It's better than where I ended up when I was released," she says. "You can make a home anywhere if you have to."

"You're right about that," says her sister. "Even prison."

Madison frowns. "No. Not me. I never got used to being locked up." The never-ending noise and foul smells, the terrible food, the crippling depression... It was an anxiety-inducing environment.

"It wasn't so bad where I was." Angie sips her drink. "I got lucky with my cellmates. Remember Ashlee Stuart?"

How could Madison ever forget the young waitress who was followed by tragedy? She nods.

"I was like a big sister to her. She listened to me. She's intelligent, that one. The judge who locked her up wants their head examined. How can you be abused by so many men and *you're* the one who ends up inside?"

Madison refrains from comment. She wishes Angie had been a big sister to *her*. But she suspects her influence on the young woman won't have been good, which is a shame. "How is Ashlee?"

"She's doing pretty well. Misses her baby girl, of course, but she's convinced she'll get out soon and eventually get custody."

Alarmed, Madison says, "That's probably unlikely given she killed a man."

"She killed a *pedophile*," spits Angie. "There's a difference." Her mean streak didn't take long to show itself. It quickly dissipates. She must have learned how to control it better. Perhaps she attended anger management classes inside. It's something most inmates are encouraged to do.

"What are your plans now you're out?" asks Madison, changing the subject, something everyone with quick-tempered relatives learns to do early on in their lives.

Angie sits back and crosses her legs. "I'm gonna keep my options open. Maybe get a job so I can find a better place to live. Hit up a few old friends for favors."

Madison tries to gauge whether her sister plans to return to criminal activities to get by. "Do you have any friends left since you snitched on your associates?"

Another spark of anger crosses Angie's face. "They were Wyatt's friends, not mine. I don't need friends like that. I need family and an income. I'm a woman in her forties with no kids, no husband and no prospects. I've learned from my mistakes, Madison. I want a quiet life now. Maybe with a man who has his own kids and a little money. A widower would be good." She smiles wistfully. "Someone who knows what it's like to lose everything you ever cared about."

Madison can't understand why she still has feelings for Wyatt McCoy after everything he did. "Are you keeping Wyatt's last name? Because it seems to me you'd be better off as Angie Harper if you want a fresh start."

Angie takes a second to sip her coffee before responding. "What does Mason call himself these days?"

Madison bristles. Angie had renamed Owen while he was living with her and Wyatt. "Listen, Angie, *if* we stay in touch, Owen's off limits. I won't tell you anything about him. He's my only child. I need to protect him. You must understand that."

Her sister looks away, eyes filled with disappointment. She treated Owen as her son for the entire time Madison was in prison, and she didn't want to return him when the time came. "Fine. As long as he's doing well. That's all I ever wanted. He still fixated on becoming a lawyer?" She laughs. "Cause Wyatt was *not* keen on that career path!"

Wyatt would have been insulted that Owen didn't want to join him in his criminal endeavors. Madison stands, unwilling to share anything about her son. "I need to go. I'll keep an eye out for any vacancies that might be suitable." She pulls her card out of her wallet. "Here's my cell number. For emergencies."

Angie stands before taking it from her. She scribbles her own number on a napkin and hands it over with an embarrassed shrug. "I don't have a fancy card."

Madison feels another spark of sympathy as she takes it from her. She's hit by a wave of nostalgia for how things could have been had they made a deeper connection during childhood. Their lives could've turned out so different if only Angie hadn't married Wyatt McCoy.

CHAPTER EIGHTEEN

Sergeant Adams has invited the team for drinks after work in the spirit of team bonding, something that traditionally hasn't happened much in the department as they're always too exhausted to socialize at the end of a long workday. Entering Joe's Saloon downtown is like walking into the station. Most of the bar is taken up with Madison's co-workers, some still in uniform.

She spots Officer Lisa Kent chewing the ear off of her fellow rookie, Officer Corey Fuller, while sipping a glass of clear liquid, possibly vodka or maybe water. Both twenty-seven, they'd make a cute couple, but with Fuller being a work-focused introvert who blushes when addressed, and Kent being the complete opposite, it probably wouldn't work out. Plus, he's about seven inches taller than the petite redhead, who commands stares from most guys she passes, thanks to her generous bust.

Steve is seated alone at a round table in the corner, messaging someone on his phone. The pool table is occupied by Lena's assistants, Jeff and Skylar. Chief Mendes isn't here, but Madison doesn't know if that's because Adams didn't invite her.

Mendes is reluctant to let her hair down around her team, wanting to maintain a professional distance. It's probably for the best. Some of them might feel they can't relax around her.

At the bar, she orders a bottle of beer before approaching Steve. "Hey." Removing her jacket, she drops it on a spare seat and sits opposite him.

Steve looks up. "Hey. Adams is on his way."

She's tempted to ask him for an update on the John Doe case, as she was out of the office for a few hours, but she's tired and she wants to forget about work for now. She sips her cold beer. It tastes great.

"I know where Nate is," says Steve.

She slowly lowers her beer as she looks at him. "How? Where?"

"Watch." He shows her a video on his phone. It's from a TV news website. The male anchor talks to the camera in a studio while running footage behind him of a town she doesn't recognize.

"We have reliable information that the infamous death row exoneree, Nate Monroe, who recently killed a man in self-defense, has been unexpectedly spotted in his hometown of Fairview, Kansas," says the anchor. "He's rumored to be alone, without his detective fiancée and trusty K9 companion. His presence has unsettled locals as they wait with bated breath to see whether he's considering a permanent move back to the town. The residents we spoke to weren't keen on the idea, and understandably so. Because wherever Nate Monroe goes, trouble seems to follow."

Steve stops it there and pockets his phone. "Are you okay?"

Madison is both surprised and relieved. Relieved that Nate's still alive, but surprised at his destination. He never mentions his hometown. "He must be visiting his brother and sister," she says. "They're the only family he has left, as far as I know."

Steve nods. "It would make sense. His Chevy's been spotted, so he's not exactly going incognito."

"That's a bad thing," she says, dread weighing heavy on her chest.

"How so?"

"Because it means he doesn't care who finds him, including the press. He's not thinking straight."

Steve leans back. "Not necessarily. Why should he hide? He's done nothing wrong. I mean, sure, the media like to make out he has, but he knows the truth."

Madison lowers her eyes. "But *he* believes what he did was wrong." She wonders whether his siblings have been receptive to him. Her heart aches at the thought that they might turn him away. Can Nate handle rejection right now? She should be there with him. It's the kind of thing she could support him with, but he's chosen to do it alone. It makes her think he has no intention of coming home. "I don't want to talk about it. It's too depressing." She gets up. "Let's watch the guys play pool."

Steve's phone rings, but he rejects the call as they head over to join the others. The two rookies join them to watch Jeff and Skylar shooting pool. The medical examiner's assistants have some friendly rivalry going on, but it looks like Skylar's playing better than her co-worker.

Jeff looks at Madison. "Do you play?"

Steve's phone rings again. He switches it to silent without disclosing why he's not answering. It can't be work-related, as he'd answer immediately.

Madison shakes her head. "Put it this way, I've torn up more tables than pocketed balls."

Jeff laughs. "We can teach you if you like?"

She waves a dismissive hand just as Adams arrives. He grabs a beer before joining them, still in uniform.

Madison looks him up and down as he approaches. "Okay, guys." She looks around. "Who ordered the stripper?"

Everyone laughs. She likes teasing Adams.

He takes it well. "Hey, if you're willing to throw money at me, I'll strip right here. Daddy needs a new car, baby!"

Madison grimaces. "How about we pay you *not* to?"

He laughs. It's a relief to see him cracking jokes. The past few months have been rough on him.

"How are your girls, Sergeant?" asks Officer Kent. "Are they getting used to you not living with them anymore?"

Adams turns serious. "They've surprised me. I'm getting on a lot better with Summer since I left. She was becoming a nightmare before. I think she was afraid of me leaving, but now I've gone, she realizes not much has changed and she still gets to see both her parents. Although she's told me I'm not allowed to date anyone new until she's eighteen and leaving for college." He smiles. "And Lizzie loves staying at my place." He looks at Madison. "Or should I say your place?"

"That reminds me," says Madison. "I've arranged for security cameras to be installed. A guy named Kyle Davenport is coming by this week. I've given him the spare key since you're never home. He's already installed cameras at Nate's place."

Adams nods. "Is that so you can watch me walk around naked?"

"Yes, Adams," she says deadpan. "You got me. I can't wait to spend my evenings watching a middle-aged divorcé wander the house in the nude. In fact, I'm paying for the cameras with optical zoom just to make sure I capture your... assets."

He laughs loudly. "No zoom needed for me, Harper." He winks at her. "You'll see."

She rolls her eyes, amused. He's easier to like now he's no longer her detective partner.

She notices Officer Fuller blushing. Kent nudges him in the ribs to show he should join in. It makes Madison smile to know that Kent tries to help him lighten up. It's just what he needs. Luckily, his awkwardness doesn't extend to his job, just social situations. She wonders where he gets it from, as his father isn't like that. Mark Fuller is a volunteer search-and-rescue leader who helps them out when they need it.

Skylar suddenly leans over the pool table, a hand to her stomach. Jeff looks concerned. "What's up? Are you okay?"

She nods before straightening. Her face reddens. "I guess you guys might as well know. I'm pregnant."

Madison smiles. "That's great. Congratulations!" She's not sure who Skylar's other half is, as she doesn't know Lena's team outside of her trips to the morgue.

"Congratulations," says Steve. "Does Lena know?"

Skylar makes a face. "She does. And she didn't exactly hide the fact she's unimpressed."

"Why?" says Officer Fuller.

"Because it means she'll need to hire a replacement at some point."

"Man, she's cranky lately," says Jeff. "We can't do anything right."

Madison glances at Steve. "I feel like she's always mad at me too. What's going on with her?"

Steve holds his hands up in a surrender pose. "Hey, don't ask me. I guess she has a highly stressful job that gets to her sometimes."

Madison wants to point out that they all have stressful jobs and manage not to treat each other with contempt, but she doesn't want to talk about Lena behind her back, so she changes the subject. "Do you have kids, Jeff?"

"Hell, no!" He looks offended at the suggestion. "I can barely take care of myself. I don't need rugrats leeching what little spare time I have left. Besides, I'm not sure how much longer I'll be with my other half. She's too needy, as well as a little too... well, old and boring." He looks at Skylar, adding, "You do realize that once you have kids, you're stuck with Jason for at least the next eighteen years, right? That's what kids do to you: tie you to people you might not want in your life for that long."

Skylar punches his arm gently. "Stop putting me off. It's too late for that now!"

"Was it unplanned?" asks Kent.

Officer Fuller nudges her, shocked. "You can't ask a woman that!" He looks at Skylar. "Sorry about her. She has zero filter."

Skylar laughs. "It's fine. I can't say pregnancy and labor appeal to me, but the thought of having a baby does. It's just the baby's father I'm not too sure about. We haven't been together long. And, I don't know, but..." She takes a deep breath. "In our job," she glances at Jeff, "we see dead infants all the time, and it really brings home how vulnerable kids are to all the horrors of the world, right?"

"We could all say that," says Adams, "with the things we witness daily. Things that would traumatize most people. But you can't stop living your life because of it. That kid will be the best thing you ever did, trust me. My girls..." He chokes up and shakes his head. "They're amazing."

Madison thinks of Owen, and how he has always been a light in her life during terrible times. She hates him being away at school, becoming a young man in her absence. And it's gut-wrenching to know he'll probably never live with her again. Not full-time. She's going to be lonely without both Owen *and* Nate.

Skylar smiles sympathetically at Adams. "Thanks, Marcus. I needed to hear that after working with this guy all day."

Jeff laughs. "I'm just messing with you. One day I'll sort my own life out and stop scaring you with everything I'm afraid of.

Madison suddenly gets the urge to go home, call her son and check on Brody. After all, the shepsky is missing Nate as much as she is.

CHAPTER NINETEEN

Time captive: 5 months

Eugene wants a baby. Despite their best efforts, she's not pregnant yet. He thinks it should happen soon, and he's increased the number of times she has to sleep with him to boost their chances. She's worried she can't get pregnant. What he'll do to her. But she's also worried she *can* get pregnant. What will happen.

How can she have a baby? Eugene won't take her to the hospital to deliver it. She'd have to give birth here using weak drugstore pain meds. If she doesn't get pregnant, she fears she'll be of no use to him. She can't decide whether she should make herself useful in a bid to stay alive until she's found, or let him kill her to end her suffering.

He's never hurt her physically. He genuinely believes they're a loving married couple. He's patient with her when the cracks show. When she can't stop herself from dwelling on her situation. He thinks she's suffering from depression, so he bought some pills online and made her take one at the same time every day. He set an alarm so they didn't forget. They hadn't helped, though. They caused debilitating panic attacks during the first few weeks of use, and last night, he threw them in the trash. He thinks they might be stopping her from getting pregnant. He lets her drink alcohol now, just a little, and nowhere near enough to psychologically distance herself from what he does to her, but she likes it all the same.

When she's compliant during sex, he rewards her afterward with things she likes. It helps her get through it but doesn't make up for her situation.

It appears that her family really did sell her to Eugene, because no one has come to save her, suggesting no one is looking for her. She thinks of her friend Emma. Didn't she ask questions about her whereabouts? Didn't their teachers wonder why she's not at school? Do people think she's run away? Does nobody *care*?

These thoughts circle her head every minute of every day. It's so exhausting trying to make sense of what's happening to her that it's a relief when Eugene gives her chores to do.

This morning, he unexpectedly cut her hair off. Not all of it. It was all the way down her back, but he cut it to shoulder length, like how her mom used to wear it. He did a good job—it's mostly straight—but she doesn't recognize herself anymore, especially as her tan has faded from a lack of sunlight, along with her smile. It's better that way. She doesn't want to see her old self in the mirror. Not while she's here, living in these conditions. She'll let her hair grow long after she escapes. For now, seeing a stranger staring back at her helps her play this role. She's like an actor in a wig, playing the part of a helpless victim in a dark crime thriller.

"You don't know how special these last months have been," he says from beside her in his bed. She'll be allowed to return to her own room in fifteen minutes, after his semen has had a fighting chance to get where it needs to go. "I was so lonely after... Well, just so lonely. You've brought meaning back to my life. I feel like the part of me that's been missing for some time has been found and slotted straight back into place like a jigsaw puzzle." In her peripheral vision, she sees him wiping a tear from his face. "You don't know how special you are to me." He stares at the ceiling, and she isn't even sure he's talking to her. "You've driven away the demons."

She almost scoffs at the comment. She hasn't driven away the demons. She's lying right next to one.

His breathing becomes heavy. His eyes are closing. "And a baby will be the icing on the cake."

If she gives this man a baby, she'll be guilty of child abuse. The child would never see the light of day, and he or she would never have friends, or a family of their own. They'd be held captive with her.

She decides then that if she does get pregnant, she'll need to ensure it fails. Terminate it somehow. A tear escapes her eye and runs down the side of her face to the pillow. It would be the kindest thing she could do for her child.

After a few minutes pass in silence, she realizes Eugene has fallen asleep without tying her up. On the nights he doesn't lock her in her own bedroom and makes her share his bed, he ties her to the heavy wooden frame so she can't escape or harm him while he sleeps. But today, he's slipped up. She carefully cranes her neck to look past him to his nightstand, and gasps.

The keys to the front door are just sitting there, urging her to take them and flee.

She rests her head back on the pillow as her heart hammers in her chest. Is this the moment she's been waiting for? Should she risk her life to get out of here? If he catches her, he could shoot her. He has guns.

She closes her eyes and prays for guidance for as long as she can bear before she makes her move. Silently, she slides off the bed with as little movement as possible. On shaky legs, she walks hesitantly to his side of the bed and watches the steady rise and fall of his chest. Is he tricking her? Is this a test?

The keys taunt her. His truck key isn't there, but that doesn't matter, since she can't drive. Her hands tremble as she slowly reaches for them. The ring holds three keys. One for each lock. She hesitates just short of touching them as a thought occurs to her. Maybe she should kill him instead. She looks around the room, which is sparsely furnished. Having recently cleaned it for him, she knows there's nothing that she could use as a weapon in here. She could smother him with a pillow, but he outweighs her by at least a hundred pounds. Why risk her only chance of freedom unless she's certain it would work? He doesn't have a cell phone she can steal, just an old red landline phone, which he keeps on his nightstand. By the time she called the cops, he could be awake. He'd hear her talking to them. Even if she whispered, he might hear the dispatcher.

Sweat builds under her armpits as fear consumes her. She shouldn't have to make life-and-death decisions at her age. She's not equipped for it. She's only *sixteen*.

She considers his guns. Her heart thuds so loudly she fears it could wake him. Her breath comes in short, shallow bursts. She has to decide whether to waste precious time searching the house for a weapon or to take the keys and run.

His breath catches, making him move. He smacks his lips together as if thirsty. She stands deathly still.

He doesn't wake. But her time is limited. She thinks about all the stories she's heard of girls escaping their captors, and how it took just one act of bravery to change their lives. They go on to be reunited with their families. They go on TV and get book deals. They become famous. She'd hate that. She'd be too afraid Eugene would track her down. Show up at a book signing or wait outside a TV studio for her to appear so he could grab her again and bring her back here to this hell.

She swallows her fear. It's now or never.

She scoops the keys into one hand as slowly and silently as possible. They burn into her palm as she turns away from Eugene and crosses to the door. She's naked, but she doesn't care. Being naked in front of a stranger used to be her worst nightmare, but now she understands that it's only skin. It's not as important as her life.

She stops in her tracks as doubt niggles away at her. What if she goes outside and the same thing happens again? What if she's discovered and it turns out the people around here—assuming there are people nearby—know and like Eugene? Or what if they're no better than him? It was another man who dumped her where Eugene found her in the first place. Is *anyone* trustworthy?

Eugene snores behind her. She can't allow herself to believe that everyone is as evil as the two men who have ruined her life. She just can't.

Trying to restrain herself from running, she cautiously leaves his room and heads downstairs. She stops when a step beneath her foot creaks loudly. Wincing, she looks behind her and waits for her captor to appear. It's inevitable.

She thinks she hears him getting out of bed, but he must've just turned in his sleep, because he doesn't appear.

Eventually, she continues downstairs and makes a beeline for the front door. Her heart is hammering now, and her hands are slick with sweat. She tries one of the keys in the lock on the door handle. Unbelievably, she gets lucky first time. The handle turns. Next, she crouches and tries a key in the lock near the bottom of the door. It doesn't fit. She slips the third key in. It turns and releases.

She stops briefly to take a deep breath and glance behind her. Nothing.

As she reaches for the final lock at the top of the door, the keys slip through her sweaty grasp. They clatter to the wooden floor, too loudly not to wake her captor. Blood roars in her ears as the unmistakable sound of Eugene's heavy breathing stops. Not wanting to waste a second, she picks them up, forces the key into the lock and twists. It pops open.

She pulls the door wide to a blast of fresh, cold air. The winter sun hits her skin as she steps outside. It's the first time she's left the house since her capture five months ago. Freedom smells of her old life.

"Get back here, *now!*" yells Eugene behind her. He's bounding down the stairs, also naked.

She takes off through the woods to her right. She wants to follow the road off his property without being in full view of him. Thanks to his excess weight, she'll have a speed advantage.

Stones and twigs beneath her feet hurt her as she flees, but she doesn't care. She feels Eugene's semen running down her inner thigh as she escapes. Tears spring to her eyes. The baby he wanted won't come to fruition. It's safe to go to another family. A normal family.

Just as she reaches the treeline, something hits her right shoulder, making her swing off balance. She goes face-first into a tree. Winded, she falls to the cold ground but scrambles to get up immediately. The accidental slip only cost her a few seconds, but her shoulder throbs, and she can feel blood running down her bare back. Her breathing becomes labored. Looking ahead, she sees the main road. She just needs to make it that far to flag someone down.

So why is she stopping?

She's unable to take a breath. Forcing her feet to move, she stumbles onto her knees. She hears panting closing in behind her. "No!" she sobs. "Leave me alone!"

Within seconds, Eugene crouches beside her in the dirt, trying to steady his breathing. "Look at us!" he snorts. "Anyone would think we were nudists out here like this." He's holding his archery bow. He keeps it in the cubbyhole under the stairs. She thought he enjoyed archery as a hobby, but he shot her with an arrow. He hunted her like she were an animal.

Her eyes meet his. "I want to go home."

He uses his hands to wipe the tears from her face. "So why'd you leave, silly?" He thinks she means his house. Or he's deliberately acting stupid.

"Please take me home, Eugene. I promise I won't tell anyone about you."

He stands before pulling her up by her arm. "Come on. It's dinnertime. I'll make your favorite."

She lets him lead her back into the house she hoped never to see again. Because what choice does she have?

CHAPTER TWENTY

Brody howls for the entire night. At least that's what it feels like as Madison prepares for work bleary-eyed and craving sleep. It's the oddest thing, as he doesn't do it at any other time of day. Before she moved in, the dog slept beside Nate on the bed, but he never complained when her arrival meant he had to sleep on the floor instead. Yet now, he howls the house down. It's embarrassing, as it's just a matter of time before the neighbors complain.

Before she leaves for work, she quickly checks Facebook to see if anyone's gotten in touch about the missing infant. She has zero messages on the *Find Toby Clark* page she set up, but comments are starting to appear under her first post, which outlines the case. Most are caring, from people who want Toby found soon for his mother's sake. Others are from scammers trying to sell things, or from people already concocting their own warped theories about what happened to the baby. She sighs. Using social media is a double-edged sword that comes with exposure to timewasters.

She pockets her phone before crouching next to Brody to stroke his gorgeous face. "Howling won't bring him back, boy.

It'll just make me even more tired than I already am. *You're* lucky. You get to sleep all day. I have to be ready to pull a weapon on dangerous killers. And if I'm tired, I might hit Sergeant Adams by mistake."

Brody's brown eyes bore into her, as he desperately tries to understand what she's saying and whether it involves him seeing his dad anytime soon. It was cruel of Nate to leave the dog behind. She's hit with a pang of guilt for the thought, because actually, it brings home how desperate Nate must have been to leave without him.

She hugs Brody to her. "I'm sorry. I *am* trying to take care of you." She pulls away, adding, "How about you join me at work today? Would that distract you?"

His tail starts thumping the floor, sensing she's offering something fun.

"But only if you stop shedding in my car. I seriously *loathe* vacuuming my car. It's bad enough cleaning up after you in the house. Do we have a deal?"

He barks before bounding to the front door.

Madison grabs her purse and keys before letting Brody out of the house. She locks up. It's early, so it's still dark out, despite the porch light. A light drizzle clings to her hair and clothes. As she nears her car, she sees a soaked white envelope under the windshield wipers. She lets Brody into the back before grabbing it. Her heart beats faster. The last note she received was from Nate.

As she opens it, she realizes it's not a note. It's a photograph. She gets into the car and leaves her door ajar, using the overhead light to see. She shivers as the damp air cools her wet skin. She distractedly pulls out the photo and gasps. The image shows a female tied to a bed in near darkness. A thin rope is secured around her wrists and her arms are above her head. She's trying to avoid the camera by turning her face away. Her shoulder-length black hair obscures her features, and it's clear the photo is being taken against her will. That the entire situation is against her will. There's little else captured in the picture. No view of the room or reflection of whoever took the photo. She can't even tell if the woman is clothed, as the image is cropped at her neck.

A chill goes through her as she checks the back, which has something scribbled on it.

Sofia. Day 1.

Her blood runs cold. "What the hell is this?"

The envelope doesn't contain anything else. She wonders briefly if it was left on the wrong car by mistake, but she doesn't think so. She peers into the darkness at her neighborhood. Most people are only just waking up, with few lights on in the nearby houses. It's eerily quiet outside. Anyone could be standing out there, hiding in the shadows. She closes the car door and starts the engine. The headlights illuminate the street. She can't see anyone, but she senses someone's watching her. Thankfully, she has security cameras now, so she can check the footage as soon as she gets to work to see who slipped this under her wipers.

Brody peers out of the windshield. His panting stops as his ears rise. Madison tries to see what he's looking at.

Her phone suddenly rings, making her jump. The caller ID tells her it's dispatch. She hits accept. "Hey."

Dina's voice greets her. "Morning, Detective. I'm afraid I have a job for you already."

"No problem. What is it?" Holding her phone against her ear with her shoulder, Madison crams the photo back into the envelope and then into her pocket. She should have worn gloves to open it, but she thought it was from Nate, and besides, it's likely the rain had washed off any trace evidence before she got to it.

"Possible human remains have been found on a construction site on Cliff Road," says Dina. "Just past the drive-in theater where they're building the new homes."

Her heart sinks. Not another body. "Understood. What kind of remains?"

"Just bones, according to Officer Fuller," says Dina. "A construction worker called it in. Detective Tanner's already on his way."

Madison nods. "I'll head straight there." Fearing they have another homicide to add to their workload, she wonders how she'll find time to look into Toby Clark's disappearance. She glances at Brody in the rearview mirror. "I hope you're ready for a busy day."

He pants contentedly as she pulls out of the driveway and onto the street. Traffic is still light, as she's ahead of rush hour, so she makes it to the construction site in fifteen minutes. Two cruisers are already parked, and she spots Alex and Steve crouching over a patch of open concrete. Brody races ahead of her as she makes her way over to them, zipping her jacket on the way. The rain has stopped, but the wind whips her hair in a million different directions, so she pulls her woolen hat on.

"Morning," she says when she reaches them. They glance up and nod as she crouches next to Steve. "What am I looking at? Oh." She spots the unmistakable curve of a partially buried skull at Alex's feet, next to some bone fragments he's carefully unearthed.

Chief Mendes suddenly appears in her thick winter coat and stylish leather boots. "Please tell me we don't have another homicide victim."

Alex takes a deep breath. "I wish I could. Sadly, from what's evident so far, we have a skull, several bones and some hair. No tissue remains, and I can't see any garments yet, which suggests they may have been naked when they died."

"So they were dumped here," says Steve. "Probably after a sexual assault."

Madison nods. If they *are* naked, this person was likely murdered, but they won't know for sure until Lena examines the remains. She leans closer to get a better look as Steve shines his cell phone light at the ground. The yellowing skull is on its side, as if the person was placed in a fetal position. "The skull looks small to me," she says. "Not infant-sized, but not large enough for an adult either. What do you guys think?"

"Unfortunately, I suspect you're right," says Alex. "This could be an adolescent."

She takes a deep breath. "Damn."

Chief Mendes looks around. "Keep your fingers crossed that this isn't some kind of burial site." Mendes is braced for the worst because of the recent Grave Mountain Stalker case. But the town has already seen two serial killers in her time here, so it's doubtful they'll see another one anytime soon. It's well known that serial killers are more prominent in large towns or cities, where they can remain anonymous and go about their business in plain sight. That's more difficult in a small town like Lost Creek.

The chief pulls out her phone and wanders off to make a call.

Madison's left knee gives out as she tries to stand from a crouching position. She uses Steve's back to push herself up, but he flinches from her touch.

"Sorry," she says. "Did I hurt you?"

He stands too and rolls his left shoulder a couple of times. "Workout injury. I've pulled a muscle. Hurts like a bitch."

"Isn't aging great?" she jokes. "My knees are giving up already and I'm not even forty yet."

He smiles. "I guess you need to work out more and I need to work out less."

She snorts. "I'd say there's little chance of either happening." She rubs her sore knee as headlights illuminate them. A car approaches so fast she thinks it's not going to stop. Brody barks to warn them as Steve moves Madison aside.

Madison is blinded by the headlights and has to shield her eyes as the vehicle stops. "Why is she driving like a maniac?"

The car door opens. Lena gets out, but she doesn't turn the lights off. She walks up to them and stands between Madison and Steve. "Alex called me." She looks at the ground. "Another body?"

Madison's eyes water, and she blinks. "Turn your lights off, would you?"

Lena looks at her. "I'm trying to help."

"Not necessary, Doctor," says Alex. "I'm about to set up lighting." He's struggling to see in the headlights too.

Lena smiles. "Sorry, guys. Didn't mean to blind you! I'll get my team here to recover the remains." She slips back into her car and switches the engine off.

Relieved, Madison has to blink a few more times before she can see clearly again. "Who called it in?"

"This guy over here." Steve leads her away from the scene. "Rob Hammond. He works on-site as a laborer."

A large guy in dirty pants and a hi-vis vest looks self-conscious as they approach. He's sucking on a cigarette with shaky hands, igniting Madison's craving. She holds out her hand and introduces herself, adding, "Tell me what you were doing when you realized you'd found something."

He licks his lips. "Like I told your guy here, I'm paid to prepare the area for groundworks. The concrete over there was in bad condition, so I was going at it with my digger. It didn't take long for me to see something was in the way down there. I didn't think it was anything significant at first, maybe some trash, so I kept going. Then I thought I saw a skull, so I jumped down to take a closer look." He swallows. "Is it a body?"

"It is," says Steve. "So we'll need a statement from you, and the contact details for your boss or whoever owns the land."

"Sure," Hammond says, pulling out his phone. He looks a little upset at his discovery, pale-faced and somber. "This guy hires me." He hands the phone to Steve, who notes the name and number on the screen before handing it back. "He usually arrives on-site around ten." He scoffs. "Must be nice to be the boss, right?"

Madison looks around the large site. Various building materials and vehicles are lined up, along with employees in hard hats, all waiting for the cops to leave so they can start work. The construction will be meticulously scheduled to keep it on track. "What used to be here before?"

Hammond follows her gaze. "A large outdoor apparel store, but that went bust and nothing was done with the site for years. It was bought almost a year ago by my boss."

"What's he planning to build here?" she asks.

"Apartment complexes. Lucky SOB's gonna make a fortune."

He is, but they need more affordable housing options in Lost Creek, as there aren't enough apartment complexes here, so it should be a good thing for the town. "Okay," she says. "Thanks for your time. We'll need work to stop for the foreseeable while we excavate the remains."

Hammond looks disappointed. "Great. No pay for us this week then." He wanders off to the area where his co-workers have congregated. They gather around him, ready to hear what's happening.

Steve looks at Madison. "I'll check out the current owner and the last one, in case they're responsible for our victim."

"Sure." She sighs heavily and looks back at the open grave. "I really hope there's only one body down there."

CHAPTER TWENTY-ONE

As Steve and Lena hover over the remains, talking forensics with Alex, Madison calls Adams at the station. She looks around the site while she waits for him to pick up. Chief Mendes has left, and the uniforms are busy securing the scene and taking statements from the other construction workers present.

"Hey, what's happening?" says Adams in her ear. "Dina says you've been sent to some human remains."

"Right," she says. "Alex thinks they could belong to an adolescent. Do me a favor and look into our cold cases for missing teenagers. It could take a while to extract the remains and get them identified, so if we can narrow down potential names, it'll help."

"Sure. I'll get back to you."

"Thanks."

She slips her phone away, hoping there *is* a cold case for this victim. Some kids vanish without ever being reported missing, for a variety of reasons. For Gina, it was a fear of law enforcement and child services that kept her from reporting Toby's disappearance. But some parents just don't care enough to look for their kids, or they're hiding what they've done to them. It happens more often than the public would like to believe. Most of the children who run away from or are disowned by abusive families come to harm and are never found. Some are able to start fresh, away from everyone who ever knew them. Away from everyone who ever hurt them.

She glances over at the skull poking out of the ground, hopeful that this child has a family who fought hard to find them.

Steve approaches. "Officer Sanchez led Brody around the entire site, but it doesn't look like he's found anything of interest yet."

That's good. She doesn't want more bodies. With gloved hands, she pulls out the photograph that was left on her windshield and shows it to him. He snaps on some latex gloves and takes it from her. "What the hell is this?"

"Someone left it on my car overnight. Turn it over."

He reads the handwriting on the back. "Sofia. Day one." The blood visibly drains from his face.

She selects the surveillance app on her phone and opens the footage from her and Nate's driveway camera. "I'm hoping the new cameras captured who left it there."

He leans in to watch over her shoulder as she speeds through the early hours. "There!" He points to a blur on her screen.

She has to rewind a few minutes, but sure enough, a figure dressed in a dark coat with the hood up, plus dark pants and boots, approaches her vehicle at 4:56 a.m. They slide the envelope under the wiper and flee in the same direction they came from. Her shoulders sag. "Their face is obscured."

"Yeah, that doesn't help us identify them at all," he says. "But why leave the photo on your car and not just drop it at the station? Why play games?"

"I guess they don't want to get too involved. I'm assuming

the woman in the photo is being held against her will, and whoever gave me this wants her to be located. But we'll need more than an obscure photograph." It's frustrating. Although someone is trying to help them, they're wasting precious time not coming directly to her or the station. She doesn't have time for games. Every second they're trying to piece the puzzle together, this woman is suffering and her chances of being found alive significantly reduce.

Steve sighs as he looks at the photo again. "Humans never fail to disgust me." He runs a hand over his face. "I'm getting sick of this job."

Alarmed, Madison looks at him. "Hey, don't say that. I don't want to lose another detective partner already."

He pulls his collar up to block out the cold. "Sorry. I'm just growing tired of attending homicides and sexual assaults. As fast as we put away one perp, five more sick bastards pop up. Where does it end? There aren't enough of us in law enforcement to keep the predators in check."

"You're not wrong," she says. "But that's always been the case and it's not going to change anytime soon. Sounds to me like you need a vacation. A break from all the negativity. I'm sure Lena does too. Why don't you whisk her away for a romantic weekend somewhere?"

He looks away. "You know how hard it is to get time off. Especially during a homicide investigation."

She makes him look at her. "Steve? Everyone needs time off. I'm serious. When was the last time you got out of town and stopped thinking about work?"

He shrugs. "I can't even remember." He looks around to see if anyone's listening before saying, "I assume you haven't heard from Nate overnight?"

She shakes her head. It's hard not to think about him every minute of the day.

"We should go for a drink when you have a minute," he says. "There's something I want to tell you."

"About Nate?"

"No," he says. "Something about me."

"Sure." Intrigued, she adds, "Or you can tell me now?"

He shakes his head. "It can wait. It's stupid really. Don't mention it to anyone else."

She snorts. "I couldn't if I wanted to since I don't know what it is!" She wonders why he wants to tell her and not his girlfriend. Maybe he's already told Lena.

He stuffs his hands in his coat pockets as he surveys the construction site. "So who do we prioritize: our headless John Doe, Sofia, the sex slave from the photo, or these teenage remains?" He nods to the ground in the distance.

It's difficult not to feel overwhelmed at times like this, so she understands his frustration. She takes a deep breath. "You're forgetting Toby Clark, the missing baby."

"Right." He rolls his eyes.

Officer Luis Sanchez approaches them as Brody wanders off to see what Lena's doing. She's alone, crouching over the skull.

"I'm no K9 handler," says Sanchez, "but Brody didn't find anything. He didn't seem interested in any particular locations. Maybe if Nate were here guiding him, we'd have better luck."

Madison straightens. "That's not an option. Nate's out of town. But I'm sure Brody would've let you know if he thought more bodies were out here."

A scream from behind makes the three of them look around. Lena's holding her hand to her chest and backing away from Brody. "He *bit* me! Get that animal away from me!"

Steve runs over to her. "Let me see."

"No, get him away from me first!"

Madison approaches them, shocked. Brody looks confused

and moves to sit next to her. She can see blood on the exposed part of Lena's white shirt, where she's pressing her hand to her chest. "Oh my God."

Steve looks at her. "Brody doesn't bite. Right?"

Madison's mouth goes dry. "No, of course not!"

"Are you calling me a liar?" yells Lena, clearly upset.

Madison looks at Brody. "I mean, he's been acting out of character lately, but..."

Looking indignant, Lena says, "Oh great, and you didn't think to tell anyone about his behavioral changes? A dog that size should be euthanized for biting someone. He's dangerous."

Madison can't believe what she's hearing. They can't euthanize Brody. If he did lash out, it's because he's stressed, or maybe Lena scared him. She wishes Nate was here to get Brody away before something terrible happens. If Lena wanted to, she could have the dog taken away by animal control.

"Lena, let me see." Steve tries to touch his girlfriend's hand again, but she pulls back. Frustrated, he says, "He probably caught you by accident. I'm sure he didn't mean it."

Lena backs away. "Of course you'd take *her* side over mine. You know what, Steve? Screw you." She turns to her car. "I'm going to the hospital. I probably need stitches."

No one dares move. The whole situation is shocking.

"Well, are you coming?" she barks.

Steve jumps into action. "Sure. Get in the other side, I'll drive."

Madison and Sanchez watch in horror as he drives her away from the construction site.

"What the hell just happened?" she says.

"That was wild." Sanchez leans down to stroke the dog, who looks like he knows he's in trouble. "You wouldn't hurt a fly, right, buddy?" Brody's tail hits the floor, but not with his usual enthusiasm. Sanchez glances over his shoulder. "The press are starting to arrive. What do you want me to tell them?"

"Nothing," says Madison. "Tape off an exclusion zone and keep them at bay. They can wait until we know what we're dealing with. And they definitely shouldn't hear about what happened to Lena."

"Got it." Sanchez walks away, leaving Madison stunned.

She looks at the dog. "I need to get you out of here."

CHAPTER TWENTY-TWO

Madison approaches the turning for the Aspen View Mobile Home Park. The weather has turned stormy, with high winds and a downpour making driving conditions difficult. It's just a matter of time before someone crashes their vehicle.

She makes a left and enters the park. Before leaving the construction site she'd taken a call from Officer Shelley Vickers. Shelley found a resident who saw someone taking photographs of John Doe's body after little Willow ran home in tears and before her mom called the cops the next morning. Madison needs to find out if it was the killer.

As she drives past homes, a car approaching hers slows. Madison lowers her window when she recognizes the driver. It's Willow's mom, Elaine. "Hi, Ms. Brown."

Elaine looks a little on edge at bumping into her. She glances at Brody in the backseat, who's keeping unusually quiet. "You're not here to see me, are you? I'm already late for work."

"No, don't worry," says Madison. "That's not why I'm here. How's Willow?"

"Fine," says the woman. "Back at school. She hasn't

mentioned what happened since you left our place the other morning."

Madison smiles. "Glad to hear it. Have there been any rumors about who the victim might be, or who might've put him there?"

"Not really. Everyone's talking about it, but no names have been mentioned."

That's disappointing. Rumors sometimes have a shred of truth in them that can provide a direction for the investigation when all else fails. "Okay. Well, have a good day."

Elaine nods. She raises her window before continuing toward the exit as Madison pulls up outside the witness's home and exits her car. The slim elderly woman—Paige Harding—is already waiting for her with her door wide open, despite the rain. She's holding a thick cardigan closed against the increasing wind. Her long gray hair is coming loose from its clips.

"Hello, Detective. I recognize you from the news."

Madison smiles. "Hi. Thanks for talking to me."

"Of course." The woman doesn't move aside to let her in. Some people dislike the thought of a cop in their home. It doesn't necessarily mean they're hiding something. They might just be private people. Madison prefers those types of people compared to the ones who just won't shut up and try to waste her time.

She pulls her hat on, trapping her hair in a tangled mess. "I understand from Officer Vickers that you saw a man near the crime scene before the body was removed by police. Is that correct?"

"Uh-huh, yes," says Ms. Harding, nodding emphatically. "And I know who he was."

Madison raises her eyebrows. "Oh?" She hadn't told Shelley that.

Movement behind the older woman surprises her. Two men step out of the trailer dressed in blue uniforms. Madison recognizes them both. One is Kyle Davenport, the guy who installed her security cameras. He smiles broadly when he sees her. "Hey, Detective! We're going to your place next to fit those cameras you wanted."

She smiles. "Thanks. I'll let Sergeant Adams know."

Kyle frowns. "Who?"

"The guy who leases the house from me."

He glances at his companion, saying, "More cops. Looks like we can't rob that place either, right?" He turns back to her with a mischievous glint in his eye. "I'm just messing with you."

She nods at the guy standing next to him. "Jerry. Long time no see."

Jerry Clark has messy shoulder-length bleached-blond hair, like a surfer from California. He's in his early thirties and always reeks of weed, but he's charming in a *Bill & Ted* kind of way. She first met him when investigating the murder of two adults and two children in a house he had cleared for someone. Back then, he ran his own business making money from other people's unwanted junk.

He grins at her. "Hey, Detective Harper. I knew you couldn't stay away from me for long."

She rolls her eyes good-naturedly. "I take it you're no longer in the house clearance business?"

He pushes his unruly hair behind his ears. "I still dabble. I like to do a little bit of this, a little bit of that... You know how it is."

She wonders if he's declaring all his side hustles to the IRS. "Hey, Jerry, you're not related to a Gina Clark, are you?"

He shakes his head. "Nope, can't say I am."

The rain suddenly stops.

She looks at Kyle. "I take it you two have installed cameras for Ms. Harding?"

"They've been ever so good," says the older woman. "They've managed to explain to an old dinosaur like me how to watch my new cameras on this." She pulls a smartphone from her pocket. "They were so patient. Jerry even fixed my shower while he was here."

Jerry hands the woman a card. "If you have any other odd jobs around the place, including yard work, just call me."

She beams at him, delighted with the two young men. "Oh, I will. And I'll make some more of that cake you both love."

The young men say their goodbyes and Madison watches them get into an unmarked truck. She wonders why they don't brand it with the company logo. Brody is watching them too, from inside her car, and she sees Jerry wave to the dog.

"Kyle is Elaine's partner," says Ms. Harding. "She recommended him to me. You know Elaine, right?"

"Your neighbor?"

"That's right."

She hadn't known that. It gets her thinking. "Does he live with Elaine and Willow?"

"No," says the woman. "I think it's still fairly new. A few months or so."

When their truck has vanished out of the park, Madison changes the subject. "You were going to tell me who you saw at the crime scene?"

Ms. Harding leans in and lowers her voice. "Now, my eyesight isn't what it was, and I must admit it was dark out, but the flashes drew my attention to the window. When I got up to look outside, I saw someone taking photos."

Madison waits, but the woman doesn't offer the name. "And that was?"

The older woman leans in even closer as she says, "Ralph from number forty-seven." She straightens. "Now, I'm not saying he murdered anyone, and I don't know what the man's character is given I rarely speak to him except to say hi in passing, but I'm seventy-five percent sure that's who was out here that night."

With a raised eyebrow, Madison smiles. "Seventy-five percent?"

Ms. Harding nods. "Of course, I had no idea until the next morning what he was taking photos of. The minute I learned about the body, I knew I needed to get security cameras installed. It frightened me to think I'm living among murderers and perverts! I might even get a guard dog."

Madison tries to reassure her. "It's unlikely the killer will strike twice in the same location, but you did the right thing. And if your cameras ever capture anything suspicious, don't hesitate to call me." She pulls out her card and hands it over. "In the meantime, I'll go speak with Ralph. Do you know his last name?"

"No. Sorry. This place has expanded in recent years. Most of us are strangers to each other now. It's not like when I first moved here and we were all one big happy family, with the exception of Sharon Carter and her inbred relatives."

Madison tries to remain expressionless.

"But Ralph's retired, so I'm sure he's home at this time on a weekday."

"Well, thanks for your time." Madison leaves to find Ralph's trailer. It's behind Ms. Harding's and farther from the creek. It lacks personal touches on the outside. No plants or vehicles. The windows are covered with brown drapes that are drawn closed. Maybe he's napping. She climbs his porch steps and knocks on the door.

No answer. And no sounds from inside. She tries to peer in the nearest window but sees only her reflection. She pulls out her phone and is about to call Adams to see if he can find the guy's phone number when she notices a couple of large flies trying to get out of a closed window. On closer inspection, she spots a maggot crawling along the base of the window.

Her stomach flips. "Shit."

She calls dispatch. Stella answers immediately. "Yes, Detective?"

"I'm at the Aspen View Mobile Home Park at the residence of a guy named Ralph who was spotted taking photos of our male victim." She pauses. "I think he may be deceased. I'm about to force entry. Would you ask Steve to join me? I'll let you know what I find."

"Will do."

"Thanks." She pockets her phone and takes a deep breath, possibly the last fresh air she'll get for the next hour or so. She tries the door handle. It's locked, but the door is flimsy. It takes just two hard shoves with her shoulder to open it. She's rewarded with the rancid smell of a decaying body, followed by a flurry of flies rushing past her to freedom.

CHAPTER TWENTY-THREE

Time captive: 1 year

She wakes to an unfamiliar noise in the room next to hers. Before she can figure out what it is, Eugene bursts in holding his camcorder in one hand and a plate with a slice of cake in the other. He's recording her.

"Happy anniversary!"

The broad smile across his face is infectious. She finds herself almost smiling back at him. "Has it been a year already?" A year since she was knocked off her bike by another man. A year since Eugene then found her. A year since she became his wife.

She tries to think of the day he first took her, how she was a child twelve months ago. Naïve and immature. So much has happened in the last twelve months, but also nothing has happened. She's matured, certainly, and she doesn't look the same anymore, but her everyday routine is monotonous and similar to that first day.

Memories of her family try to flood her mind, but she won't let them. Eugene is her family now. Once she accepted that, things became easier. That doesn't mean she doesn't miss her parents terribly, or dream of a police officer one day knocking down the front door and rescuing her, but she's come to accept her current reality. She's hopeful it's temporary, but if it's not, then it's better that she learns to live with what's happening to her as best she can. She gets more freedom that way.

To help her, she often thinks about a prison documentary she once watched with her dad where an inmate who was sentenced to life in prison without the possibility of parole was asked how he coped with the certainty of knowing he'd never get out. Knowing he'd never hug his family again or go to the beach. Never make himself a meal or have control over his life ever again. He had shrugged and told the interviewer that even in prison you could create a life for yourself.

She hadn't fully grasped how that was possible at the time, but now she realizes what he meant. The prisoner's world became a whole lot smaller once incarcerated, but he was still alive. He could still work out, socialize with other inmates and take up hobbies. Keeping his mind active and forming meaningful relationships would keep him alive. So that's what she's trying to do. Her world may be even smaller than the prisoner's, but when the alternative is death, she can't complain too much.

She suspects she'd have a different perspective had Eugene been mean to her. But it's not like he beats her. He doesn't have a temper like her dad, so she doesn't walk on eggshells around him. He buys her favorite foods, keeps her busy and watches the shows she likes so they have something to talk about. It almost feels normal, like it's her and her mom discussing the people on TV together. Except, he likes reality shows about guys with more than one wife, but she finds them creepy. On those shows, it's like the men are all Eugenes but openly so, which is gross to her. Eugene keeps what he does to himself. He doesn't invite neighbors or family over to meet her. To show off.

It occurs to her then that the women in those shows aren't

being held captive. They're with these men by choice. The thought makes her grimace.

Eugene has promised that one day he'll make an enclosed extension to the house out of wire and wood, so she can be outside like one of those patios that crazy cat ladies have for their pets. Once they've reached that level of trust, she's hoping he'll then agree to take her out for a drive. Even if she's handcuffed to the seat, she wants to get out of this house. To feel the sun or the wind or the rain on her skin. To expose herself to crucial vitamins. Small goals like this are vital when she has no control over her life. It will take some time to convince him about the drive, but she thinks she can get him there. Then, who knows what could happen? If she proves herself to him, he might take her out regularly. She could live a more normal life.

"It sure has!" he replies. "Time flies when you're having fun." He sets the camcorder on her dresser, aimed at her, and approaches the bed so they're both in shot.

She no longer winces when he nears. He allows her privacy by letting her keep her own bedroom, which she deeply appreciates. She needs alone time. Without it, she might lose her mind. It would be even better if he didn't come and go as he liked, never knocking, just appearing. It sets her on edge.

"Here. Have some cake." He perches beside her on the single bed. "It's from a box, but I mixed it together and baked it myself. Red velvet."

The sponge is black, not red, but that's okay. He tried. He used to lace her food with drugs to keep her compliant, but she doesn't think he's done that for a while, as she doesn't get as sleepy anymore. She takes the plate and fork and tries a bite. The sugar has clumped together in places, but it tastes fine. Sweet. "Thanks." It's not ideal for breakfast, but she forces it all down to keep him happy.

Something occurs to her. She can't believe she hadn't

remembered until now. In her surprise, she says it aloud. "Today's my birthday."

Eugene's eyes widen in surprise. He wouldn't have known. Aside from some tentative questions about her mother and the rest of her family, he's never asked her anything about the girl she was before he found her. Perhaps that helps ease his guilty conscience. Assuming he has one.

"You don't say?"

She nods slowly. "I'm seventeen." She doesn't allow the tears she can feel building behind her eyes to show. She quickly blinks them away. She can't understand why turning seventeen has upset her. Not until her old life flashes before her eyes. Is anyone doubling their efforts to find her on her birthday? Are they marking the occasion? Will there be a televised vigil?

A bang from the wall next door makes her drop her plate in surprise. The fork clatters to the floor. "What was that?"

Eugene laughs. "That's our anniversary gift."

She frowns. Another bang is followed by crying. She gasps and looks at her husband. "What's going on?" For some reason, she covers her pajamaed chest with the blanket, not wanting to be seen in bed by a visitor. Then she realizes someone might have come to *save* her. She feels her heart swell with hope as she straightens. Did Eugene want to keep her for only one year? Is this her release day? "Who's here?" she gulps.

He gets up and goes to the door. "Wait there."

He pulls out a set of keys attached to his belt—he's learned from his earlier mistake—and unlocks the door to the spare bedroom. A female voice whimpers before yelling, "Let go of me!"

It's followed by what sounds like a hard slap, then silence.

She tenses as Eugene appears. He's pulling the arm of a dark-haired girl. She's younger than seventeen. The girl looks her in the eye. "Please help me get out of here. I want my mom."

Eugene scoffs. "Now, don't be like that. You'll get used to us eventually, Sofia."

Disappointed, and a little jealous that Eugene needs another girl, she looks at him. "What do you want with her?"

He smiles. "Well, you're clearly infertile, so she's going to have our baby."

Anger builds in her chest. She won't be special anymore. She'll be one of two. She looks at Sofia, who lets out a blood-curdling scream at the thought of giving them a child. It annoys her so much that she jumps out of bed, crosses the room and slaps the girl hard across the face.

CHAPTER TWENTY-FOUR

"Ralph Smith. He was seventy-two years old," says Steve as he and Madison look at the short guy hanging from the rail in his closet. "I banged on his door the morning we were called to John Doe, but got no answer. He was on my list of people to return to." He sighs. "He was probably already dead."

Ralph is naked. His dark eyes bulge from their sockets, staring into space. His lips are blue, and his skin is turning black. Dark fluid leaks from his anus onto the rug beneath his feet, which rest awkwardly atop a crate of clothes. If he took his life when he saw them investigating the body almost two and a half days ago, it would explain his current state. It doesn't help that the heat is on in the trailer, hastening his decomposition.

"Why *naked?*" she asks. "Think this could be a case of auto-erotic asphyxiation gone wrong?"

Steve shrugs. "Beats me."

The smell makes her throat randomly close up, and the flies are unrelenting. They're in the air, as well as bashing against every window, desperate to find an escape despite the door being wide open. Madison doesn't blame them. She'd like to escape too. "It looks more like he's deliberately taken his own life," she says. "Maybe he knew it was just a matter of time before someone told us he was seen photographing the body." She sighs. "Think he's our killer?"

Steve rests his hands on his hips, trying not to take deep breaths. "Well, he lives close to the crime scene, he wanted to document it and when the cops were called, he turns up dead. I'd say he makes a good suspect."

She nods. That's something, at least. Maybe once they've searched his home, they'll find a clue to John Doe's identity.

Officer Vickers appears with a stash of well-thumbed magazines in her hand. "I found these under his bed."

Steve takes them from her and looks at the covers before opening one of them and flipping through it. "Looks like he was turned on by necrophilia and sexual violence." They're old porn mags. The naked men and women featured in them are staged to look dead or in the middle of a physical assault. Some are being sexually assaulted in their death positions.

"Sick bastard," says Officer Kent behind them.

Kent and Officer Fuller are from a generation that can access porn for free online whenever they want to. They'll never know the embarrassment of taking a dirty magazine to the counter and watching as it's slipped inside a brown paper bag while the salesclerk eyes the customer with concealed disgust.

Madison would love to see the statistics on whether free online porn has resulted in an increase in sex crimes. Maybe it hasn't. Maybe better access to porn stops some people from acting out their fantasies in real life. She'll probably never know. But she knows one thing. Porn *addiction* has increased, and it's being accessed by youngsters and skewing their view of what a sexual relationship should be like. And when online images no longer satisfy the viewer, some will seek a bigger thrill. A real experience. Something that isn't staged by paid actors. That's why the dark web is full of snuff movies and child abuse images. People like Ralph Smith can no longer get off to the image of a naked man or woman. Their desires have escalated. They want to experience the scenarios depicted in porn for themselves.

She glances at Kent. "Don't take this the wrong way, but you might want to keep your opinions to yourself at a crime scene. You never know when a reporter or family member could overhear you and take offense. We aim to be nonjudgmental."

Kent nods. "Sure. Sorry. I'm just sick of perverts."

Madison raises her eyebrows. "Then I hate to break it to you, but you might've chosen the wrong profession."

The young rookie leaves the trailer to get some fresh air. Officer Fuller is already outside, trying his hardest not to vomit. Madison remembers the first few times she smelled a rotting corpse. It stays with you. As a new officer, it leaves you wondering how it can be acceptable to be exposed to such a horrendous ordeal as part of your job when other people get to work in comfortable offices all day surrounded by the aromas of fresh coffee and printer ink. Because the smell can be worse than witnessing the body itself, and all you want to do is go home and shower it off you.

Madison had struggled to cope when she first joined law enforcement. She'd had an overwhelming realization that she didn't want this to be her daily life. But then the wins started happening. Helping to apprehend killers. Locking up assholes who'd battered their partners to the brink of death. Removing drugs from the street. And helping children escape abusive parents. Those wins kept her in law enforcement when the bad days stacked up. It doesn't mean she ever grew accustomed to this smell or to seeing mutilated bodies, but she's learned to focus on finding the people responsible to stop them from harming anyone else.

"Adams hated gory crime scenes like this," she says. "He

didn't have the stomach for it. I'm convinced that's what made him want to return to being a sergeant."

"I don't blame him," says Steve. "I'm starting to wonder why I was in a rush to accept his job."

She looks at him. He seems tired. "How's Lena?" She hadn't wanted to ask right away, as he didn't appear to want to talk about it.

He shrugs. "She wouldn't let me go inside the hospital. Told me to return to work since that's all I care about." His tone suggests their relationship is on the rocks.

Madison wants to ask whether Lena will pursue punishment for Brody, but it doesn't feel like the right time. "It's almost lunchtime," she says brightly. "Let me fetch some coffee. Caffeine will help."

He snorts. "Sure, if you lace it with vodka."

Before she can leave, a man appears at the door with Officer Fuller close behind, trying to stop him. "Sir, I said do *not* enter!"

Madison blinks. He's the spitting image of Ralph Smith.

Steve steps forward to join her. "Are you related to the person who lives here?"

The man grimaces as he covers his nose and mouth. He nods and says through his hand, "Ralph's my brother. What the hell happened here?"

Madison leads him outside and is relieved to breathe fresh air. Steve stays on the top step of the porch, magazines in his hand. "I'm sorry," she says gently, "but we found your brother deceased inside about an hour ago."

The man's lower lip quivers. "Someone killed him?"

"We don't know the details yet. We'll know more once we've consulted with the medical examiner."

His face screws up but no tears fall. He's in shock. Many people feel they have to show emotion after receiving a death notification from the police, but Madison knows that in real life, your body sometimes conspires against you as it absorbs the news. Gently, she asks, "Can I get your name?"

"Stanley Smith. We're twins. I'm eleven minutes younger than him." He lowers his eyes. His face has turned pale. "I guess I'm older than him now. I never thought that would happen. *I'm* the one with the health problems, not him."

She glances at Steve, who looks sorry for the guy. It has to be more difficult for a twin to lose their sibling. Especially if they're close. Looks-wise, Stanley reminds her of Truman Capote in his older years.

Stanley peers beyond Steve, into the trailer. "Is he still in there?"

"He is. He'll be taken to the medical examiner's office shortly. We'll let you know as soon as he can be released to a funeral home of your choice."

Stanley's eyes fall on what Steve is holding. Madison can make out naked bodies from their position, so she steps in front of the older man to block his view of the magazines, but Stanley suddenly seems desperate to leave. "I didn't really see him much over the past few years, so if anyone else wants to sort through his belongings, let them. I'm not responsible for whatever my brother was getting up to." He walks away.

Madison frowns. His shift in behavior seems odd. Does he know what his brother was capable of? Did he know he favored violent pornography? "Mr. Smith, I need your contact number," she shouts.

He stops but doesn't turn to face them. "I'm in the book."

She slowly approaches him but pauses when his hand reaches into his pocket. "I'm sure you are, but with a last name of Smith, it would be easier if you give it to me now. I'd prefer a cell number, and I need your address too."

Steve has also noticed the man is acting strange. He approaches Madison. "Sir? Do we have a problem?"

Stanley turns with a broad smile fixed in place. It's creepy, given he's just learned of his brother's death. "Not at all." He gives them his personal details. "I'm sorry I can't stay longer. I need to start letting people know."

Madison nods. "We'll be in touch."

They watch as he walks away.

CHAPTER TWENTY-FIVE

Madison leaves Steve at the scene and goes to fetch coffee. Ralph's neighbors had quickly started showing up full of concern, suggesting to Madison they didn't really know the guy that well. Although he makes a good suspect for John Doe's killer, he could just be an oddball who stumbled across the body and decided to photograph it out of morbid fascination. It happens. Or perhaps for sexual gratification. That happens too, but less often, thankfully.

She slows as she approaches the diner's parking lot. It's almost empty, and the steamed-up windows obscure her view of the inside. She turns to look at Brody. "I won't be long. And I might have something tasty from Uncle Vince when I return. Okay?"

Brody leans in to lick her face. He's never done that before. It brings tears to her eyes. "We're going to be okay, boy. With or without Nate, we'll be okay."

She readies herself before forcing the door open against the wind. Racing from her car to the entrance with her hood up, she still manages to get soaked in the short distance.

Inside, a couple of old-timers are seated at the counter,

watching the small TV above them. Madison lowers her wet hood and sees herself at yesterday's press conference, repeated by the local news station. Gina looks nervous as reporters address her.

"Poor woman," says one guy. "Imagine not knowing where your baby is. What could be worse, right?"

The other guy waves a dismissive hand as if he disagrees. "I bet she was high, drunk or screwing around when the poor kid was taken. If they find him, he should be handed straight to CPS, not back to her."

Madison rolls her eyes behind them. Vince appears from the kitchen and slides their food across the counter. Madison couldn't eat anything. Not with the smell of Ralph Smith's decaying body still in her nostrils. She keeps deodorant in the car for spraying herself after attending a scene like that. Otherwise she gets funny looks from anyone she goes near.

Vince smiles at her. "You smell nice." He suddenly catches on to why the flowery scent is more potent than usual. "Oh. Bad morning?"

She smiles faintly. "You could say that."

"Then I'll bet you need coffee. How many?"

She tries to remember the other officers' orders. "Two cappuccinos, two flat whites and two lattes. All to go."

He nods. "Sure. Is Nate with you?"

She looks around. Nate isn't here, not that she expected him to be. Richie Hope's booth is empty too. Perhaps he's in court. "No."

"I sent him a couple of texts over the last day or two, but he hasn't responded." Vince frowns. "Come to think of it, I haven't seen him in here either. Is he okay?"

The old guys at the counter appear to be listening in, so she motions for Vince to join her in an empty booth. She can't lie to him. When he's seated opposite her with his dishcloth flung over his shoulder, she says, "Nate's gone."

Vince makes a puzzled face. "What do you mean he's *gone*? Gone where?"

She swallows. "He left me a note on Sunday night to say he's struggling and he needs some space or he'll die."

Alarmed, Vince says, "He'll *die*?"

"Right. So I spoke to Richie about it, and he thinks Nate just needs some time alone after what happened. He feels guilty for taking a life, Vince, and there's not a damn thing you or I can do to help him with that."

He seems surprised by her attitude. "Of course there is. We keep him close and don't let him out of our sight!"

She leans on her elbows. "Vince, he's a grown man. He knows how to seek help. He's done this too many times now."

"Madison, you're not thinking clearly. He needs you right now."

"Then why isn't he here?" Her voice rises, making people glance at them. She can't help it and realizes she's angry with Nate. Does he even care how his leaving has made *her* feel? How it makes Brody feel? She lowers her voice. "I could've helped him if he stayed and talked to me, but he left in the middle of the night. I thought he was dead." Her throat clamps shut.

Vince rests a hand on hers. "He's his own worst enemy, that's for sure. Do you know where he went?"

She clears her throat. "A Kansas TV station has reported he's been spotted in his hometown of Fairview. I'm assuming he's gone to see his brother and sister."

Vince rolls his eyes as if annoyed. "That's the last place he should go if he's seeking comfort. Those assholes didn't stand by him when the shit hit the fan."

"I know," she says sadly. "He's probably craving their rejection right now because he's punishing himself. It's what he does best. He didn't even take Brody with him."

"Wait," he says. "He left Brody behind?"

"Yeah. The poor thing is unsettled, to say the least. He keeps me awake all night howling." She pauses. "In fact, he's just been involved in an altercation with Dr. Scott."

Vince shakes his head, confused. "What do you mean?"

"Lena says he bit her."

"*What?* That's ludicrous. That dog wouldn't hurt a fly."

Madison shrugs. "That's what I thought, but I saw the blood. She was pissed too. Talked about Brody being dangerous. I need to keep him away from her in case anything else happens."

"Let me take care of him. I have a plan." Vince pulls his phone out.

"What are you doing?" she asks.

"I'm organizing cover for this place so we can go track Nate down."

She shakes her head. "I wish I could. Seriously. But I'm in the middle of too many cases, including a homicide investigation. There's no way Chief Mendes will let me take time off just to look for Nate."

"Fine," says Vince. "But *I* can go. With Brody. We'll find him and bring him home. He shouldn't be alone right now."

Madison feels bad for not acting sooner. But she knows Nate doesn't listen to her when he's like this. She thought he was on the mend, and the disappointment at knowing that even their engagement can't keep him here made her hesitant to follow him. Because the reality is that her love for him isn't enough to get him through difficult times, and that sucks. He needs specialist support, which neither she nor Vince can provide or make him agree to.

"You'll let him come home, right?" says Vince, locking his eyes on hers.

She takes a deep breath and looks out of the large window that overlooks the parking lot and the road beyond. She wipes away some steam for a clearer view. "I'm so tired, Vince. Tired of bad news and dashed hopes. I love him, you know I do, but something's got to give. He needs professional help."

"Of course he needs help. But you're going to stick by him, right? I don't want to bring him back here if you're going to call off the engagement and move out of his place."

Madison knows her future lies with Nate because she misses him so badly. She just wishes he'd find a different coping mechanism than taking off when times get hard. "Of course. I want him home. Brody wants him home. And once Owen realizes he's gone, he'll want him home too."

Vince appears to decide something. "I have an idea to ease the pressure on him. I think I can help him put his past behind him once and for all."

Madison feels a flurry of hope in her chest. "I really hope so, Vince. Because I love him so damn much." She blinks back tears as he squeezes her hand.

CHAPTER TWENTY-SIX

Nate spent the night in a cheap motel by the highway. He couldn't stand another cold night alone in his car. He'd had nightmares. Seeing other people's faces in place of the person he shot dead. He tried to stay in bed all morning to satisfy his exhaustion, but he couldn't drift off for long and grudgingly got up to take a long-overdue shower. That had cleared his head a little and forced him to change his clothes. Sitting on the bed afterward, he'd looked around the dirty room and wondered why he was putting himself through any of this. He almost got in his car and drove home, but he just couldn't summon enough motivation. He's already ruined things with Madison, so it's unlikely she'll want him back.

The truth is, he's struggling to care about anything. He feels like he's drifting from one lousy mistake to another, and he can't find the willpower to stop. He wishes he could call his dad to ask for advice. Vince Rader crossed his mind, but Vince would drive straight out here, and Nate couldn't bear the shame that would come from disappointing his friends.

After his sister had delivered her devasting verdict on him yesterday, she must've worried he was going to harm himself, because she followed him out of her yard and insisted he come back today so she can talk to him some more. Maybe she has more to get off her chest.

Nate was in two minds about returning. There's only so much hostility he can take. The motel was uncomfortable and loud, with sex workers arguing with johns outside his window. He was surprised to find his Chevy still outside when he'd left an hour ago.

After a couple of tasteless takeout coffees, he's on his way to Dawn's house. She's warned him her husband will be there this time, as if she needs moral support to continue berating him. It occurs to him that she might not want to be alone with him again in case he tries to harm her. She'd certainly kept her distance yesterday. The thought squeezes his chest in a vicelike grip. As if he'd ever hurt his sister. He never wants to hurt anyone.

He glances at his rearview mirror as he drives, expecting to see Brody sitting there, panting in anticipation of the next crime scene. He keeps forgetting he left the dog behind and may never see him again. His broken dreams were filled with Madison and Owen, making sleep difficult. Part of him wants to race home to see them. But a bigger part warns him he's ruining their lives, and they'll flourish without him.

He pushes his conflicting thoughts away as he pulls to the curb outside Dawn's house. She told him she's taking a vacation day for this. So is her husband. He briefly wonders whether the nieces and nephews he's never met will be present, but quickly realizes that's a stupid thought. If she doesn't want to be alone with him, it's unlikely she wants him to meet her kids.

He forces himself out of the car and slowly approaches the house. The door opens before he gets there. A tall overweight man dressed in smart jeans and a blue shirt stares at him.

"I'm Ted. Dawn's husband. You better come in." He doesn't

hold out his hand or refer to himself as Nate's brother-in-law. That tells Nate everything he needs to know.

He nods at the guy before stepping into the house. It's a typical suburban detached home. The layout is open-plan, the rooms extremely tidy considering they have kids. Dawn would hate having Brody in her home. She'd be forever sweeping up his fur and mopping the water he drips when drinking from his water bowl. Nate smiles faintly at the thought.

The hallway wall is covered with family photos, including a couple of Nate's dad when he was younger and Dawn and Kurt hugging each other as children on some long-since-forgotten summer day. Not a single photo includes Nate. Shame burns his face as his eyes continue along the hallway. Several photos show Dawn and Ted with their own kids. It seems they have two boys and a girl, the girl being the youngest at around eight or nine when the photograph was taken. She's cute. There are hints of their mother in her eyes and the color of her hair: golden brown. The boys look more like their dad, with short dark hair and serious expressions.

It's clear from the stylish decor that they have money. Ted strikes Nate as some kind of banker, or perhaps a politician. He looks like he'd happily talk bullshit all day.

He finds Dawn waiting behind the breakfast bar in the large kitchen diner. The white marble counter matches the kitchen units. She has an herbal tea in front of her. She doesn't offer him a drink. "Where did you stay last night?" she asks without smiling. Her eyes are swollen and red. Maybe she didn't sleep well either.

He stands opposite her, not daring to pull a stool from the breakfast bar since he hasn't been offered a seat. "At the Alexander Motel."

She raises an eyebrow. "With *your* money? You could've stayed anywhere. Unless you've squandered it all on drugs and women."

He doesn't know how to respond. Is she going to condemn him for accepting the compensation he earned? "You can have the money. You and Kurt can share it. I don't even want it."

She crosses her arms over her chest. "You can't buy us back, Nathaniel. We don't want your blood money."

Disappointed that he can't say anything right, Nate realizes he shouldn't have come.

Ted clears his throat and goes to stand next to his wife. "Why did you return to Fairview, Nate? Do you want something from us? Is that it?"

Nate looks him in the eye. "I don't want anything from anyone. Dawn's my sister. I thought..." He stops. Truth is, he doesn't know what he thought or why he came. He was at his lowest when he left Lost Creek in the middle of the night, and his internal compass brought him here. "How's Kurt?"

Dawn takes a deep breath. "Leave Kurt alone. He's not in a good place. He has his own demons." She swallows. "He hasn't messed up his life as much as you have, but I tell new people I meet that I don't have any siblings. It's the only way to avoid awkward conversations."

It hurts to think his little brother isn't thriving. "Is he okay?"

"Not really. Let's just say he favors money over morals. He's constantly in trouble with law enforcement, but nothing serious like your charges. Still, Sheriff Rainer would sure be happy to see the back of him."

Her heartless words annoy him. "Did you ever consider he's going through something and could do with your help?"

Her eyes narrow. "Of course he's *going through something*. Because of *you*, and what happened. Didn't I make that clear enough yesterday? Once Dad died, I was the only person who was around to help Kurt cope. *I'm* the one he calls from jail. *I'm* the one who constantly has to bail him out of whatever mess he's gotten himself into."

Nate lowers his eyes and takes a deep breath. "You're saying my incarceration messed up his whole life."

"*Yes*. That's what I'm trying to get you to understand. As much as I loved you as a brother and missed you when you left home to study in Texas, we're strangers now, and it should stay that way. Too much has happened, and if I'm honest..." A sob escapes her, causing Ted to rest a hand on her back. "If I'm really, truly honest with you, Nate," she says tearfully, "I *wanted* you to be executed."

He closes his eyes against the horror of her words. Despite everything he's been through, and all the people who've deliberately hurt him over the years, no one has ever said anything that cuts so deep.

"I wanted to stop suffering!" she weeps. "And the part of me that still loved you wanted *you* to stop suffering too. I hate you for what you've put us through. Whether you killed that woman or not, the end result was the same. I can't offer you any comfort. I just can't. I'm sorry."

"Don't apologize to him," says Ted quietly, with a judgmental stare that needs wiping off his face.

"I didn't kill Stacey Connor," says Nate for what feels like the hundredth time. "I don't know how else I can make you understand."

"I don't know whether you did or not," she says, "but you killed that guy last month, and that's brought more trouble to my door. Reporters want to know what it's like to have a killer for a brother. They're dragging everything up again, making my friends and neighbors look at me differently. With suspicion. As if *I'm* the criminal!"

Quietly, Nate says, "I'm sorry for that. I shot a serial killer. If I hadn't, he would've killed me and my fiancée. I don't feel good about it."

Ted scoffs. "*Fiancée*. From what I've read, she's just as bad as you, except she's a *cop* killer. But I guess it would take a killer to love a killer."

Nate loses it. He lunges across the kitchen and lands a punch on Ted's jaw. Pain radiates up his wrist.

The asshole stumbles backward, his hand to his mouth and his eyes wide with shock. "You can't do that!"

Nate looks him in the eye. "Keep your mouth shut. You don't know anything about Madison. She's a better person than you could ever hope to be." His throat seizes.

"Stop it!" yells Dawn, getting between them. Her face has turned bright red with anger. "I gave you the benefit of the doubt by letting you into my home, but you haven't convinced me of anything. It's clear to me now that it would cause me more harm to try to rebuild our relationship than to pretend you never existed. And unlike you, I have children to worry about. I'd never be able to relax if you were around them. You must understand that? I'd be worried in case you lashed out at them."

Nate might hate himself right now, but not enough to stick around for ignorant comments like that. "You won't see me again." He turns to leave.

They don't stop him or follow him to the door.

As he pulls the front door open, desperate to escape their gaze, he comes face-to-face with a younger man with thick sandy-colored hair and blue eyes. At first, Nate sees his father's features in the man, and is overcome with a pang of shock that turns into happiness when he realizes it's his younger brother.

Kurt is equally surprised. His eyes widen. "Dawn said you were coming. Jeez, you look like crap."

Nate swallows a lump in his throat. It's been twenty-three years since he saw Kurt. His little brother was just fifteen when he left for Texas. "Good to see you."

Kurt breaks out in a wide grin. "Come here." He pulls Nate in for a hug.

An embrace from a family member feels different. It's more comforting than that of a friend's embrace. There's a connection that makes Nate feel whole again, which is understandable since they shared childhoods. He feels warm tears run down his face.

Kurt pulls away. "How about we get out of here, just you and me?"

Nate nods. His brother's arrival might have just saved his life.

CHAPTER TWENTY-SEVEN

Madison puts thoughts of Nate aside so she can concentrate on work. She's asked the team to meet her in the briefing room for an update. With so many developments happening, she wants to know where everyone is at with the various investigations.

Chief Mendes approaches her at the front of the room while they wait for the others to arrive. She has someone with her. Madison smiles at Dr. Conrad Stevens, a forensic anthropologist from out of town who helped them with an earlier case. His daughter, Nora, works at the crime lab up north and helps them with their DNA analysis.

"Conrad!" she says, stepping forward. "Lovely to see you."

Dressed in a crumpled beige suit that looks more suitable for a safari vacation, he shakes her hand. "Lovely to be here again, Detective. I do enjoy visiting Lost Creek. It strikes me as a nice place to retire."

Madison refrains from comment. Most people dream about moving away from the town the minute they finish high school. Few return. "Are you just visiting?"

"No, actually. Chief Mendes has asked me to help age the bones found on the construction site earlier today."

She glances at the chief. Her keenness to call Conrad for support confirms the attraction between the pair that formed during the Grave Mountain Stalker investigation, which is odd as they're so different from each other in many ways. "Great! We need all the help we can get. I hope Lena doesn't mind."

"Why should she?" says Mendes. "It's our call, not hers."

Madison explains what happened earlier with the dog bite, and Chief Mendes is as surprised as the rest of them. "How bizarre. Has Brody ever shown signs of aggression before?"

"None," says Madison. She doesn't explain that the shepsky is unsettled right now because that would mean revealing that Nate has taken off. "He's going to stay with Vince Rader for the time being. Vince will keep an eye on him."

A crowd forms as Alex approaches Conrad, hand outstretched. "You should've told me you were in town," he says. "I would've taken you for lunch."

Madison doesn't know how Alex managed to eat after this morning's gruesome discovery at Ralph Smith's trailer. All she could eat was a couple of dry crackers with coffee. Steve had passed on lunch completely.

Alex looks around the room. "Is Nora with you?"

"Afraid not," says Conrad. "As much as she would've loved to visit, she's too busy at the lab."

The two men quickly launch into a discussion about bone fragments and advances in aging skeletons. Officers Sanchez, Kent and Fuller chat among themselves as they wait for the briefing to begin.

Steve is the next to arrive. He downs the last of his coffee before tossing the empty cup in the nearest trash can, shutting the door behind him.

Just as Madison's about to start, Sergeant Adams rushes into the room. He can always be counted on to be late. "I looked into our cold cases," he says, not waiting to be asked, "and we don't have any missing teenagers. So I contacted Prospect Springs PD to see if they have any. They sent me a list of seven kids. I could do with something to try to narrow them down to look for a match for our victim. Age range and gender of the remains found at the construction site, for example."

"I hope to be able to help with that," says Conrad.

Adams nods before looking at Alex. "Was anything found with the body?"

Alex shakes his head. "No clothing, but some hair was still intact. I've sent it to the lab. Nora should be able to extract DNA from it, so if the Prospect Springs PD took DNA samples from their missing children's belongings as part of their investigations, we can cross-reference our DNA with theirs."

Adams nods. "Sounds time-consuming."

"I'm sure Nora will prioritize it for us," says Alex. "So let's hope the PSPD will too. The fact the body wasn't clothed or wrapped in something suggests the killer didn't want any of his hairs, fibers or DNA on it." The forensic technician is holding something. He looks at Madison. "I've downloaded images from Ralph Smith's phone as we were told he was photographing the John Doe crime scene." He walks to the whiteboard and uses tape to secure his printed images. "As you can see, he did indeed take photographs. Just four." Two of the photos capture the male victim's entire headless body in long shots. The other two are close-ups. One of the severed neck, and one of a severed wrist.

"What's interesting," he continues, "is that Mr. Smith's photos captured something I missed." He picks up a pen and circles something on the bank of the creek that doesn't look like anything at all from Madison's position. "A shoe print," he explains. "I did already capture a partial print, but this is better, so I'm heading there again after this to see if I can take a cast of it."

"Won't it be Ralph's print, though?" says Officer Kent. "And if it is, does that mean he was the killer?"

Alex smiles. "I have Ralph's shoes to compare it to, and his sexual interests certainly suggest he might've killed the victim for sexual gratification. But if it's not his print, then we can look elsewhere."

Madison nods. "Well spotted, Alex." She pauses. "I asked Skylar at the morgue to pass a message to Lena earlier. I want her to check for signs of sexual assault during John Doe's autopsy. Hopefully her hand has healed enough for her to return to work."

Adams looks confused, so Steve fills him on what Brody did. When he's finished, Adams shakes his head. "No way that happened."

Steve bristles. "What do you mean? Are you calling her a liar?"

"No comment," says Adams, suggesting that's exactly what he's doing. He's never been the medical examiner's biggest fan.

Steve glares at him before looking away.

Madison's surprised Steve is defending his girlfriend, since she treated him with contempt earlier. Perhaps they haven't ended things after all.

Chief Mendes's cell phone beeps with a notification. She glances at it. "Lena's just sent me the autopsy report for John Doe."

Madison shares a look with Steve. Lena would usually send it to them.

The chief reads it through before informing them of the pertinent points. "She ages our victim at around fifty and believes he was forced to ingest the rose while alive. He was dismembered *after* death with a type of saw, but she can't figure out which kind due to the skin being water-damaged."

Alex nods as if he was expecting that.

"He wasn't killed where he was found," continues Mendes, "but Lena believes he died within the twenty-four hours before the little girl stumbled across his body. He didn't defend himself during the attack, and his body showed signs of physical restraint. She thinks he was bound with some type of rope around his torso. She can't give us a precise cause of death and says it's imperative we find his head, as without it, she can't rule out trauma to the skull." She looks up. "Perhaps he was shot or bludgeoned to death." She continues reading. "I doubt this is relevant, but she says his liver showed signs of cirrhosis. Maybe he was a drinker. Toxicology results will take a while longer, so we don't yet know whether he was poisoned or under the influence when he died."

"If he was drunk or high," says Steve, "it could explain why he didn't defend himself."

The chief nods. "And as he was physically restrained and tortured, it's likely his killer was someone he knew."

"Exactly," says Madison. "Which makes identifying him vital."

The chief finishes reading the report. "Looks like Lena got your message, Madison. She says there are no signs of sexual assault."

Madison shifts position. That's something, at least, and it could help rule out Ralph Smith as his killer. But overall, the autopsy hasn't helped their investigation much. "If he wasn't sexually assaulted, then we still don't have a motive."

"Officers are still searching Ralph's trailer," says Steve. "And Alex will check his social media history and phone activity, right?"

Alex nods. "Perhaps we'll still find a link to the victim. But if Mr. Smith did kill him, he didn't do it in his home, as I didn't find any traces of blood or a clean-up."

"Okay," says Madison. "Did we receive any leads about John Doe from the press conference?"

Adams shakes his head. "Stella said she and Dina took a few crank calls but nothing credible enough to pass on, and no males have been reported missing yet."

The dispatchers are highly qualified and trusted team members, so if they didn't think the information was worth passing on, Madison believes them. "I can't believe no one's reported him missing. Surely someone's noticed their neighbor, brother or friend is out of circulation?"

"Perhaps he was a recluse," says Alex. "Not everyone enjoys spending time with people."

That reminds Madison of Gina Clark. "So, no calls about Toby Clark either?"

Adams shakes his head.

"Tell them about the photograph that was left on your car," says Steve.

The photo is in an evidence bag now, along with the envelope it came in, so Madison passes it around the room. "We need to locate this woman. All we have is her first name, Sofia. I don't know who left this for me."

The chief passes it to Officer Fuller to look at as she says, "As distressing as this photograph appears, we don't know that it's real, or recent, so unless we get any more information about it, we can't waste precious time pursuing it."

As much as it pains her to think the female in the photograph could be suffering, Madison knows the chief is right. It could be a hoax designed to waste their time and draw attention away from their other cases. That doesn't mean she can't have Alex test the photo for prints and possible trace evidence, though. She's got to at least try to see if she can locate this poor woman.

CHAPTER TWENTY-EIGHT

Time captive: 4 years 7 months

Sofia's second baby was stillborn, just like the first. It was a traumatic day for all of them. Having tried to nurse the young girl through a difficult premature labor, she'd had to break the news to her that her child wasn't breathing. Eugene cried the hardest out of the three of them. He locked himself in the basement for hours to grieve privately, after securing them in their rooms.

She had tried to comfort Sofia through their shared wall, but the girl wanted to die. Sofia has never acclimated to living here. She fights Eugene every step of the way, and she can't be convinced to play the game until they might one day be rescued. And because of that, she's ruined things for all three of them.

Eugene has confided in her that he thinks Sofia's hatred of them killed the babies.

Now, he's drunk at the kitchen table, and Sofia is huddled on the couch under a blanket. Her eyes are distant. She's pale from blood loss, but together the two of them have to bury the baby, as Eugene needs closure.

"It's time," she says.

Sofia looks up at her. "I can't."

She holds out her hand. "Just come with me. I'll do the digging." Secretly, she's excited at the opportunity to leave the house for the first time since her only escape attempt, four years ago. Like many of Eugene's promises, the human "catio" extension never materialized, so she only has a distant memory of how it feels to have the sun on her skin.

She plans to bury the baby in the yard. Eugene won't let them go far, and he has his shotgun ready in case one of them should attempt something stupid, but it's still time outside the house, which should be cherished, regardless of the reason for it.

Eugene stands and picks up the weapon. He's put away so much whiskey it's doubtful whether he'd be a good shot. Sofia eyes him with hatred, but she dutifully stands and follows them to the front door, wincing at the pain in her lower abdomen.

Before unlocking it, Eugene looks back at them. "Don't make this more upsetting than it already is, understood?"

She nods, but Sofia doesn't, so she gently nudges the girl in the ribs. That makes her nod too. She worries Sofia will make a run for it, which would be stupid since she's still shaky on her feet. The house reeks of her blood, no matter how much she cleans.

"Good," he says. "Get the baby."

Sofia shakes her head. It's clear she doesn't want anything to do with Eugene's child, and not just because the little girl is dead and she's afraid to handle a corpse.

Anger flashes in Eugene's eyes.

Realizing Sofia won't do it, she goes to the refrigerator herself and gently pulls the swaddled baby out, cradling her head with her elbow. The baby just looks like she's asleep and could wake up at any minute. If only she would.

Tears fill her eyes. She had been eagerly awaiting this birth, but the baby didn't even manage one breath in this world. She finds herself wishing *she* could get pregnant, but it's impossible, no matter how often they try.

"Let's get this over with," says Eugene as he opens the front door.

A blast of fresh air hits them as they step onto the porch. It's a cold day, and the ground is soft from recent rainfall. Eugene waits on the porch, his legs unsteady and his gun aimed at them as she takes the lead with the baby in her arms. She savors every step in the daylight as she leads Sofia to a spot near the treeline, where she was once shot with an arrow. She can't imagine running now. She knows it would do no good.

The sun cruelly hides behind rain clouds. The disappointment at not experiencing the warmth on her face threatens to bring tears to her eyes. Or maybe it's the dead baby in her arms. She turns to Sofia. "Take her while I dig."

Sofia swaps the shovel for her baby, not daring to look at her. She holds her like a football, with no maternal instinct at all. Maybe it's her age. Or perhaps it's because living here has traumatized her. Everyone has different levels of resilience. It's no one's fault that some can handle less trauma than others.

Thankfully, the ground is soft enough to dig, and Eugene shouts instructions from the porch. "It needs to be deep enough not to attract animals. And not obvious enough for any visitors to notice."

She scoffs. They don't get visitors. Eugene collects his mail from town, and no neighbors or uninvited callers have ever stopped by in the time she's been here. But it is possible that one day someone may turn up unannounced, so his caution is understandable. She knows it's a cause of pain for him that he can't have a headstone for his daughter. They can't risk it being seen. Eugene buried the boy behind the house less than a year ago. He spends time out there when he's melancholy. She watches him through a crack in the blinds.

She digs for fifteen minutes, but her arms are weak from a lack of exercise, so she eventually sets the shovel down and takes the baby from her mother.

Eugene silently approaches. He says a prayer as she lays his daughter in the grave. It's a lovely prayer. It feels fitting for the occasion. Surprised to learn he believes in God, she glances at him. Tears run down his face. It's clear he's in pain. He wants a child so bad. She reaches out to squeeze his hand.

Sofia's expression suggests she's scheming. She doesn't look at the grave, or at them. She's looking at the road that leads out of Eugene's property. Her hands are twitchy. She wants to run.

Eugene turns to the young girl. "I'm sorry for your loss, Sofia. For *our* loss. So is your sister."

Her face turns red. "That's *not* my name! And *she* is not my sister! She's a stranger, just like you! I'm meant to live in Prospect Springs with my parents. Not *here* with *you!*"

He sighs. "I'm sorry you hate it here. I truly am. I want you to be happy."

With hate in her eyes, seventeen-year-old Sofia spits, "So let me go."

He takes a deep breath. "Is that really what you want?"

Tension fills the air. Sofia glances at her, surprised. But all she can do is lower her eyes, because she can't help the young woman. They each have their own choices to make, and she's already made hers. If Sofia doesn't want to be here, she has to decide whether the alternative is better. That's one thing she has some control over if she's clever enough.

"Of course it is. I want to go home. I never wanted to be here." Sofia's voice rises as she adds, "I gave you two children. I did my part. It's not my fault they died. They probably didn't want to be born into this life. They didn't want *you* as a father!"

She's gone too far. That was hurtful. It's not Sofia's fault.

She's too young to know how to handle this situation. But she wishes she could help the girl all the same. The problem is, unlike Sofia, she's lost all her fight. She doesn't have the energy to get herself out of here. She's not even sure she wants to leave anymore. How could she survive alone? Where would she even go? Unlike Sofia, she has no one eagerly awaiting her return.

She looks at Eugene and wonders how he'll react.

He surprises them both by stepping forward and pulling Sofia in for a hug. The girl cries in his embrace.

"Thank you for spending time with us," he whispers into her ear. When he pulls away, he adds, "None of us knew whether it would work out, so all we could do was try. But now we know you can't settle with us, I think it's best that you leave."

Sofia's eyes widen. She doesn't trust him. "Are you for real?"

He nods. "Say goodbye to your sister first."

Stunned, Sofia approaches her and offers a limp hug. The brief embrace shows she never felt anything for her, which is disappointing.

After pulling away, Sofia looks at Eugene. "I won't tell anyone anything. I just want to see my mom." She backs away at first, not trusting that he won't shoot her in the back. She stumbles on some branches and falls down.

Eugene smiles. "You'd get a lot farther if you look where you're going and stick to the road. You could get lost in the woods, and I'm assuming you don't want to end up back here."

Sofia scrambles to her feet and turns. She runs toward the road.

She doesn't get far before Eugene raises his weapon and fires a shot. The blast echoes through the woods, startling the birds in the trees around them, which take off in unison. The shot hits her between her shoulder blades, and she goes face-first into the gravel, where she lies still.

After almost four years with them, Sofia has finally found peace.

Eugene holds out his spare hand. "Don't cry, sweetie. It's the kindest thing we could do for her. If she wasn't able to live with us, how could she cope with the memories after she got home to her parents? She's too delicate to put her time here behind her and live a prosperous life elsewhere. She's not like you."

She takes his hand and slowly nods. He's right, of course. Sofia would've needed decades of therapy, and there's no guarantee that would have helped. Her life effectively ended the day Eugene took her.

But what does it say about *her* that she can handle this life?

As they approach Sofia's lifeless body, she finds herself wondering whether her resilience is a blessing or a curse.

CHAPTER TWENTY-NINE

Madison stares at the photograph propped up against her desk phone. Not the one of the mysterious Sofia, but the one of Toby Clark's smiling face. She keeps it out to make sure she dedicates some time to his case, but with everything else that's going on, she can't prioritize it right now, and she can't even ask Nate to investigate. So looking at the photo just leaves her feeling guilty.

She wonders how Nate's reunion with his siblings went and whether he's missing her and Brody yet. The thought stresses her out in case he's not. Vince has texted to say he's planning to drive to Kansas first thing tomorrow. Brody's being spoiled by Vince's young grandson, Oliver, so he's happy for now.

She sighs. It's midafternoon already and her energy levels have dipped due to skipping lunch. As she leans back in her creaky office chair, intending to see if Adams has anything in his drawer that she can steal for a snack, Stella approaches with her unhooked headset lowered at her neck.

"Hey," says the dispatcher. "Gina Clark's here to see you. She's out front."

Madison's heart sinks. She has no updates for the woman. "Thanks, Stella."

Adams offers a sympathetic look from his desk as she walks away. She heads through the open-plan office and lets herself into the front desk area with a passcode for the secure door. Gina spots her immediately and stands. Her dark circles appear worse every time Madison sees the woman. She's wearing a jacket too thin for the weather they're having, and her long dark hair has been battered by the wind and rain.

"Come on through," says Madison, holding the door for her.

Gina smiles briefly as she passes. Not wanting to make the woman any colder by taking her to one of the interview rooms, Madison leads her to the kitchen to pour them both a hot drink. Alex is in there with Mrs. Pebbles, topping up her water bowl.

"Hey, Alex," says Madison. "This is Ms. Clark." To Gina, she says, "Alex is our forensic technician."

"Pleasure," says Alex. The chihuahua starts trembling uncontrollably and looks like she wants to get to Gina.

Madison frowns. "Is she okay?"

Gina steps forward to pet the dog, all misty-eyed. "She's *adorable*! My mom loved chihuahuas."

It's the first time Madison has seen her face light up.

Alex hands the dog to her, saying, "She's trembling because she's happy. She does it when afraid and angry too. I think it's a chihuahua thing." He shrugs. "They just tremble!"

"It's definitely a chihuahua thing," says Gina, who lets Mrs. Pebbles lick her face. "They're so special." She coos over the dog as Madison pours coffee.

"Do you take milk and sugar?"

"Both," says Gina. "Two sugars." She hands the dog back to Alex with a wide smile.

"Hang on a second." Madison looks at him, puzzled. "I thought the dog only liked men?"

He shrugs with a smile. "That's what I thought too."

She sighs. "I guess it's just me she's not keen on then."

"I'm sure she'll get used to you eventually," says Alex diplomatically. "I better get back to work." As he turns with the dog in one hand and the water bowl in the other, he accidentally drops the bowl, splashing liquid everywhere.

"I've got it," says Gina. She picks it up, refills it and hands it to him while Madison wipes up the water with a mop.

"Thanks," says Alex before leaving.

When the room is empty, Madison gestures for Gina to take a seat at a small round table and then joins her with their drinks. "How have you been?" she asks.

Gina takes a deep breath. "I never know how to answer that question. I guess I'm just existing. I eat and wash because I have to, and because it fills the time."

Madison wishes she had some good news. "I'm afraid I don't have any significant updates. I've added Toby's details to important systems such as the National Crime Information Center and NamUs, the National Missing and Unidentified Persons System. And our officers know to be extra vigilant around anyone who has a toddler matching Toby's description, but to tell you the truth, the likelihood of finding him around town isn't realistic this long after he disappeared, as officers can't stop every person who has a blond boy with them." She pauses, trying to think, "Oh, and I've set up a Facebook page for people to get in touch about sightings, so I'm hopeful that will result in some leads."

Gina's eyes light up. "Can I have the password so I can check the messages?"

"Afraid not, sorry. Social media is useful for spreading awareness but also as a medium for people to get in touch as witnesses. The department needs to protect the identity of anyone who contacts us through those channels. I'm sure you understand."

Disappointed, Gina nods. "I guess." She sips her coffee, using the mug to heat her cold hands.

"I've also visited where you were living when he disappeared and produced a missing person poster for him, which patrol has spread around town. We haven't received any tips from the press conference yet, but hopefully it's just a matter of time. Has anyone approached you after your appearance on TV?"

Gina shakes her head. "A woman recognized me in the grocery store and said she'd pray for me, but that's all. Everyone probably assumes Toby's already dead."

Madison wishes Gina had an inner circle of people around her who she could question. A thought occurs to her. "Could Toby's father have taken him?"

"No, because he never knew our one-night stand resulted in pregnancy."

"How do you know that, though?" she asks. "Was he local? Could he have seen you pregnant without you knowing?"

Tears spring to the young woman's eyes.

Alarmed, Madison says, "I'm sorry. I'm not trying to upset you."

"It's okay. It's not Toby's father I'm crying over. It's the time when I was pregnant. My mom was so horrible to me." Gina wipes her eyes with her hands. "I met him at a club in Prospect Springs. We were strangers and I've never seen him again since. As far as I know, he lived there. I never told him I was from Lost Creek, so I don't see how he could've seen me pregnant."

Madison nods. "Fine. And you mentioned you didn't speak to your neighbors back then, but could any of them have wanted to take him? Was there anything strange about them?"

Gina gives it some thought. "I don't think so. One side was an elderly couple who barely left their house, and the other was a couple of young women."

"Do you know if they were in a relationship?" Madison is considering whether the women were desperate for a child.

"No, they were just roommates who'd bring boys home all the time. They were friendly enough, but I wasn't interested in getting to know them. People always want too much. It starts with a friendly wave, then stopping to say good morning, then the next thing you know, they're stopping by every day to snoop into your private life, and because you live next door to them, you can't get rid of them without moving." Gina offers an apologetic smile. "Sorry. Like I told you, I'm not a people person. In my experience, the more people you have in your life, the more trouble comes from it."

Madison agrees to some extent, but she'd find it difficult not to have friends around her. "Were you the same at school?"

"Not as bad. You have to have friends at school to survive the experience."

"What about workmen?" she presses, determined to find someone to question. "Did you have any repairs done at your home in the weeks and months leading up to Toby's disappearance?"

Gina scoffs. "My landlord never did repairs. The house was in a bad state, like me, I guess. I never saw him once I moved in. He never checked on the condition of the place and just accepted my money into his account. He had other properties and didn't even live in town. He had a Denver address."

Madison knows some landlords don't care about their property or tenants as long as they get paid on time. Perhaps the condition of Gina's house contributed to her problems. Who wants to invite visitors over when your home is run-down? "And you hadn't seen or spoken to anyone on the day or the day before Toby vanished?"

"Right. I'm sorry. I wish there was someone I could point the finger at, an overfriendly neighbor or a creepy mailman, but if it were that easy, he wouldn't still be missing."

That's true. Madison tries a different angle. "How was Toby's health? Did he have any medical conditions or appointments?"

"None. He was a healthy baby. The midwife told me he'd

probably be a football star when he was older." Gina smiles at the memory, but it quickly falters. Her hand flies to her chest as she tries to breathe deeply. "Oh God."

"What's the matter?"

She suddenly becomes overwhelmed. She pushes her chair out from the table with her legs and bends forward at the waist. She must be dizzy. Her breathing becomes short and shallow, and she looks panicked. Madison stands and approaches her. "It's okay. You're fine. Nothing's going to happen to you. You're safe here. Just breathe through it. I'll stay with you."

Gina reaches for her hand, which Madison grips while rubbing the woman's back. "Nice deep breaths. In through your nose, out through your mouth." She might need to call an ambulance if this escalates.

Stella appears at the door with an empty cup in her hand. She looks at Gina. Trained in first aid, she knows not to react with alarm. "How can I help?"

"Water would be good," says Madison. She doesn't let go of Gina's hand. "You're doing great. It's passing. Just keep breathing."

Stella gives the young woman space but stands nearby with a cup of water ready.

When Gina's breathing eventually returns to normal, she leans back, her face flushed with embarrassment and panic. "I'm so sorry. I never know when I'm going to have a panic attack." She takes the cup from Stella and sips the water.

"Don't apologize," says Madison. "We know how unpredictable they are, right, Stella?"

"And more common than you'd think too," says the dispatcher. "Anyway, I'm glad you're feeling better." She discreetly slips out of the room and closes the door to stop anyone from interrupting.

"It doesn't help that I haven't eaten anything today."

Concerned, Madison says, "Nothing at all?"

Gina shakes her head. "Since I came to you about Toby, I've felt sick a lot of the time. My appetite has vanished. I guess I'm constantly alert for bad news."

"You need to eat. So do I. I skipped lunch." Madison glances at the clock, wondering if she can get away with taking a late lunch break. "How about we head to my place and I'll make something for us?" She doesn't want to take Gina to the diner, as it might be too busy for her, but she feels like the young woman is holding back from truly opening up about her life. There could be something she's reluctant to admit about Toby's disappearance because she still has that fear of being completely honest with law enforcement.

Gina looks surprised. "Oh, no, that's okay. I don't expect you to do that. I have food at home."

Madison insists. "It's no problem. If I don't cook for two, I'll just eat something unhealthy. You'd be doing me a favor."

Gina smiles gratefully. "It would be nice not to have to stare at my own four walls for a little while longer."

Madison stands. "Great. Let's get out of here."

CHAPTER THIRTY

Madison makes pasta since it's quick and easy, while Gina peers closely at the family photos on the sideboard in the dining room. They mostly consist of pictures of Owen up to ten years old, and then from seventeen onward. Madison wonders if they make her uncomfortable, since she may not get to photograph her own son ever again. But if Gina's uncomfortable, she doesn't show it.

"He looks just like you."

Madison leans over to see which photo she's looking at. It's one that was taken last summer. In it, Owen's grinning at the camera. His blond hair covers his blue eyes, and she can see the similarity herself. She's glad he looks more like her than his father. "Everyone says that. He's a freshman in college. Wants to be a lawyer."

"Wow. You must be so proud."

She is. He overcame so much to get there.

"I often wonder what Toby will look like as a teenager," says Gina, "and then as a young man. Will he marry? Will he want kids? Will he prefer men or women?" She smiles shyly. "I have strange thoughts like that. I even wonder if he'll be unkind or turn into a criminal."

Madison smiles sympathetically. She can see that his disappearance consumes her every waking thought.

Gina approaches the breakfast bar. "Do you ever think about how unfair life is to good people? Seems to me that life favors the bold. Those people willing to take what they want from those lacking the confidence to stop them." She sighs heavily. "Sorry to be morose. It's just that I don't know why I was born. What I'm here for. It can't be to have a child who goes missing. It just can't. Why was I allowed to meet my son if I wasn't allowed to keep him? That seems like an unnecessary cruelty to me." She wipes her eyes with her sleeve.

Madison doesn't know what to say but suspects it was a rhetorical question anyway.

"Do you believe in God?" asks Gina suddenly.

Madison inhales. "Oh boy. That's a big question!" She thinks before answering. "I guess, in my own way, yes, I do. I don't go to church or discuss my faith, but I'm quietly confident in a higher power. That might not be the same God we're supposed to believe in, but it's something bigger than me."

Gina seems intrigued. "So how do you explain what happened to me? Toby's abduction?" Her eyes are filled with tears.

Madison drops the fork she's holding to reach out and place a hand on the other woman's. "What happened to you was simply the result of another human being making an evil, selfish decision. It had nothing to do with God and everything to do with who the abductor is. I think the question isn't why God let this happen, it's who in this perpetrator's life turned a blind eye to the warning signs along the way that enabled him to feel confident enough to enter your home and take what he wanted." She pulls her hand away and straightens.

"What if the people in his life weren't strong enough to stop him or speak out?" asks Gina.

"Then society is to blame," says Madison. "We're creating these monsters by making it acceptable to ignore what our neighbors or family members are doing. Perhaps if people were less afraid of law enforcement, more would come forward with their concerns."

Gina doesn't seem convinced. "You're approachable, which is why I built up the courage to ask for your help, but some cops don't want the extra workload. And some just don't care." She takes a deep breath. "If only I hadn't drunk anything the night he vanished. Maybe that's why my baby was taken from me. God judged me."

"Or someone around you did," says Madison. Her gut tells her that someone who knew the young mother took him. It's more likely than a stranger entering the house at random.

"Perhaps you're right." Gina nods. "Someone thought he deserved better. And they were right, weren't they? I didn't deserve Toby, and I sure as hell don't deserve to get him back. But he's all I have. I have no identity without him. I'm supposed to be a mother. I know that sentiment makes some people cringe, but it's true in my case."

Madison hates hearing her talk this way. "Come eat." She takes two bowls of pasta to the dining table and hands over cutlery and pepper. "I don't have any Parmesan, sorry." She goes back to fetch the garlic bread from the stove.

Gina sits at the table and sniffs her bowl. "I haven't eaten a hot meal all week. Just sandwiches and cookies. This smells amazing." She tucks in, and Madison gives her time to eat in silence, her own stomach grateful to be fed.

Bandit suddenly appears. He must've smelled the food. He jumps up on the table. Madison gives him a quick fuss before planting him back on the floor. "Not while we're eating, buddy. I'll feed you in a second."

He meows in protest, then sits licking the areas she touched, as if he's offended she had the nerve to manhandle him.

As she eats her food, she notices the camera in the corner of the kitchen ceiling flashing red, as if someone's accessing it. She lowers her fork and frowns. Is someone watching them? It stops flashing, making her think she imagined it. She'll check the app when Gina's gone to see if it has a fault, but it makes her uneasy, as Kyle told her the cameras are hackable. It reminds her of Elaine Brown, and how she and Kyle are dating. It just seems odd that the first time she met Kyle was the day a dead body showed up near his girlfriend's home. She should ask Adams whether Kyle and Jerry have installed cameras at his place yet. If Adams met the guy, she can get his opinion of him.

She wonders if she's being paranoid. Ralph and Stanley Smith make better suspects for John Doe's murder, given what was found on Ralph's phone and his brother's strange behavior after his twin's suicide.

With the pasta finished, Gina starts on the garlic bread, using it to mop up the leftover sauce from her bowl. "Do you have a partner?" she asks.

"Yeah, but he's away at the moment." To deflect attention away from her own sorry situation, Madison asks, "How about you?"

Gina looks thoughtful as she says, "Kind of, but he probably won't stick around for long. I'm difficult to love because of my anxiety about finding Toby. Men don't like drama, so I'm more of a burden than most women."

Listening to the way she talks about herself is gut-wrenching. It's as if she doesn't believe she deserves to be loved. Perhaps that's why she steers clear of people and doesn't let herself trust anyone. It's not just that she's an introvert, she has zero self-esteem because of her mother's rejection. She's the kind of person who looks apologetic that their very existence is taking up space.

Madison has lost her appetite, vaguely aware that she's beginning to feel protective toward the younger woman. She wishes she could do more for her. Leaning back in her seat, she gently asks, "Have you told your mom that Toby's missing? I know she disowned you during your pregnancy, but I just wondered if she knew and if she'd be willing to offer a reward for information, since he's her grandson."

Gina stops chewing and looks at her. "I don't even know if she's still alive, and if she is, where she lives. But it doesn't matter, she would never give me money. Not just because it's highly likely she has none, but because the church has her well and truly in its grasp. Her preacher told her I was evil for having sex outside of marriage, so that's what Mom will go to her grave believing."

It's clearly a difficult subject, so Madison doesn't pursue it. "Okay. But I do think a reward is the fastest way to get witnesses to come forward with information. As bad as it seems, money's a great motivator."

With a shrug, Gina says, "I don't have any money."

Madison thinks of Nate's compensation money. If he were here, she'd ask how he'd feel about offering a small reward. Say five thousand dollars to start. It would speed things up while potentially providing answers about what happened to Toby. "Leave it with me," she says. "I'll see if I can raise some funds."

"No, please don't. I'd be too ashamed to take other people's money."

"But it could *help*," presses Madison.

Gina eyes her with confusion. "Why are you doing this for me?"

Madison almost says, *Because no one deserves to be* this *alone, especially when their child is missing*. But she doesn't want to upset her.

The sound of a key in the front door behind her makes Madison start. Her heart is in her mouth, as she assumes Nate's come home. She quickly stands and turns as the door opens wide. It's not Nate. It's Owen.

He grins at her. "Hey, Mom." His eyes flicker to Gina. "Oh, sorry. Didn't mean to interrupt."

Madison's shocked to see him. "What are you doing here? You should be in Arizona."

Gina stands too. "I should go. Thanks for lunch. I appreciate it."

"Are you sure?" says Madison. "I'm sorry. I'll keep you updated on the case." She walks her to the door and holds it open as Gina leaves, watching as she gets into her vehicle and drives away. She can't help but feel guilty that her son has come home when Gina might never see hers again.

CHAPTER THIRTY-ONE

Madison hugs her son tightly. "It's so good to see you!" As she pulls away, she looks him over to check he's intact. You never know with boys. "Why didn't you say you were coming?"

He shrugs and heads straight to the refrigerator. "I've been trying to get hold of Nate, but he won't return my calls, so I thought I'd just come. You're always telling me to visit more."

Madison joins him in the kitchen. "I have leftover pasta and garlic bread?"

His eyes light up. "Hit me." He grabs a fork and sits on a stool at the breakfast bar as Madison plates the food. Bandit suddenly appears. He jumps onto the counter and meows loudly at his favorite person. Owen pulls him in for a hug and lets the cat rub its face all over his jaw. "Hey, buddy! Did you miss me?"

Madison's never heard the cat purr so loudly. He starts making biscuits against Owen's shirt. "He never does that to me."

"That's because you never give him any attention," says Owen. He fusses over the cat until Bandit's had enough. Bandit jumps down and disappears through the flap in the door to enjoy the wilderness outside.

With the cat gone, Madison realizes she should address the elephant in the room. "Nate's gone home to Kansas to see his brother and sister. He accidentally left his phone at home."

He frowns. "He went without you?"

"I can't get away because work's so busy right now."

He looks around the kitchen diner. "He took Brody with him?"

She slides the bowl across the counter, and he launches his fork straight into the pasta. "No, I need Brody here to help with searches," she lies.

"So where is he?" His mouth is full as he talks.

"He's with Vince right now."

"How come?"

Madison smiles. "He's searching a crime scene." Another lie.

"So when's he coming home?"

She rests her hands on her hips. "Close your mouth while you eat, please. And jeez, what is this, an interrogation? Want me to sit under a bright light in a dimly lit room so you can pressure me for information?"

He laughs. "Are you saying I'd make a good cop?"

"I'm saying eat your food without showing me you're eating your food. That's gross." She uses a sponge to wipe up the mess he's made from the tomato sauce hitting the counter as he talks. You wouldn't think he was almost nineteen years old. Or maybe you would. It's difficult to tell when you only have one child.

He puts his fork down and turns serious. "I guess I may as well come clean and tell you why I really came home."

A flutter of dread runs through her. "Oh Lord. What have you done?"

He slowly looks her in the eye with a serious expression.

"Don't be mad. But... I got a girl pregnant. And I wanted to tell you in person."

Madison's mouth drops. Her son's going to have a *baby?* "Say that again?"

"You're gonna be a grandma," he says gravely.

She swallows, her mind whirring with questions and flashes of Owen's new future. "Are you in love with this—"

He bursts out laughing. "I'm sorry. I couldn't keep a straight face. You're so gullible!"

Madison's confused.

"I'm just messing with you, Mom! I couldn't resist. Sorry."

She takes a deep breath and tries to slow her heart rate. In retaliation, she grabs his bowl of food away from him.

"No, wait! I'm not done!"

"You almost gave me a heart attack!" she says, trying not to laugh. "Your entire life flashed before my eyes and it wasn't good, Owen." When he stops laughing, she asks, "So why are you *really* here?"

He takes a deep breath, and she has a horrible feeling that what he's going to say will be even worse. "Well, I've decided on a new career path," he says slowly. "I don't want to be a lawyer anymore."

She shakes her head, confused again. "Wait, *what?* But you're studying law." Nate's paying his tuition fees, as long as he keeps getting good grades. "Owen..."

"Relax." He stretches his arms over his head like this isn't a big deal. "I think you'll approve."

Dread squeezes her chest. He's making a life-changing decision and being flippant about it. It suggests his mind is already made up and nothing she says will stop him. This must be what he wanted to discuss with Nate. Maybe he hoped Nate would smooth the waters with her before the announcement. But what is he going to do instead? "What's the new plan?" she says quietly, dreading the answer.

He swallows nervously. "I've given this a lot of thought, so just know it's not a hasty decision, okay?"

She nods.

"Basically," he continues, "Instead of being a lawyer, I want to be a cop."

"*What?*" Her eyes well up immediately. That's the last thing she expected to hear. He wants to follow in her and her father's footsteps. She should probably be touched, but the dread gripping her lungs tightens. If he becomes a police officer, his life will be in danger every single day. He'll be a target for any criminals mad at *her*. He'll attend armed robberies and physical assaults. He could get shot while on duty or stabbed while breaking up a bar fight. Tears run down her face. She's both proud of him and afraid for him at the same time.

He slips off the stool to walk around the counter and embrace her. "Don't cry, Mom. It means I'll be home sooner. You'll get to clean my laundry again."

She nudges him hard in the ribs.

"What?" he exclaims. "When I left for college, you said you'd miss washing my dirty laundry! I'm literally doing you a favor."

She laughs as she pulls away and tries to stop crying. "You realize that if you join the Lost Creek PD as an officer, I'll never sleep again, right?"

He grins at her. "I'm sure I could procure a substance or two from the evidence lockup that would solve that problem."

"Owen!" Despite the shock, she laughs. "Corrupt already? Great. You've not even started yet and you're going to get us both fired." She sighs shakily, coming to terms with the thought of her son as a police officer. "Wait until Nate finds out."

"He should be glad. I'll be saving him thousands of bucks in law school tuition fees. When's he getting home?"

Madison inhales. "I have no idea."

A knock at the door makes her jump. She frowns. "I'm suddenly popular today."

"I'll get it." Owen heads to the door and opens it. He doesn't greet their visitor. Instead, he goes deadly still.

As Madison approaches him with trepidation, he turns to look at her. The expression on his face reminds her of when he would get scared as a little boy. He's frozen. She realizes he doesn't know how to react. "What's the matter?" She looks past him and sees her sister standing there. Her gut tells her to slam the door shut. Owen hasn't seen Angie since he lived with her and Wyatt while Madison was incarcerated. Being his biological father, Wyatt was able to claim his son should live with him during her absence, something Madison would have fought tooth and nail over had she known. Because Owen's conception was the result of a sexual assault. She would never have voluntarily had sex with that monster.

Owen's never fully opened up to her about what it was like to live with them, but she knows they weren't physically abusive. Wyatt was mentally controlling and verbally abusive, and he despised Madison. Owen was fed lies about her for the entire seven years they were apart. He was told she didn't want him back, and that was why she hadn't come to see him after her release. The truth was that no one would tell her who he was living with, so it took time to track him down.

She steps in front of her son. "Go finish your dinner. I'll deal with this."

Owen turns, shoulders slumped. He must be remembering that time. How he had to survive without his mother while believing she didn't want a relationship with him. And how Angie was responsible for his vulnerable girlfriend's death. It breaks her heart to see how, in a split second, he's gone from a happy, confident young man who wants to become a police officer to that scared little ten-year-old boy who'd watched her get driven away from their home in the back of a police car.

When he's out of earshot, she steps onto the porch to join her sister, closing the door behind her. "How dare you come here unannounced. Have you been following me?"

Angie's eyes are watery. She claims she cared for Owen and treated him like the son she can never have. "Sorry, okay? I didn't know he was here. I came to see you." She looks up at the house. "I heard through the rumor mill that you'd moved in with your boyfriend. Got engaged even. I'm going to guess I'm not invited to the wedding." Before Madison can reply, she adds, "That's okay. I get it. We're taking things slowly." She turns to leave. "Sorry to bother you."

The pain in her sister's face is evident. It makes Madison's anger dissipate until she remembers how the woman once wanted her dead. "Now's not a good time," she says bluntly. "I hadn't had a chance to warn Owen you were out yet."

Angie turns to look back at her. "*Warn* him? Like I'm some kind of threat to him?" She shakes her head and continues down the steps.

The brief interaction leaves Madison feeling guilty. Her conflicting emotions over her sister are exhausting, and she's aware she needs to either cut her out of her life for good or commit to trying to help her with her fresh start. She wishes she could let go of her one remaining family member. It would be easier than the alternative. But equally, she can't help feeling it would be safer to keep Angie close, as the old saying about enemies goes.

Torn over what to do, she heads back inside. Owen is on the couch in the living room. She sinks into the seat beside him. "I'm sorry. I would've told you sooner that she was out, but I wasn't expecting you home anytime soon and I guess I hoped she'd leave town before you could bump into her."

He shrugs. "It's fine. It just took me by surprise, that's all. It could've been worse. It could've been *him*."

Madison swallows the lump in her throat. "Angie took a

plea deal and says she wants nothing to do with her old life. She said everything that happened was Wyatt's fault. You lived with them, what do *you* think? Should I trust her?"

Owen looks at his hands in his lap. "Some people are open about who they are," he says quietly. "Like Dad. He was mean, and he let everyone know it. But at least I knew where I stood with him. How to set him off, and when to avoid him. But with Angie..." He takes a deep breath. "I felt more on edge around her. Because she knew what Dad was like and she never did anything to stop him."

Madison's reminded of her earlier conversation with Gina, when she'd tried to explain that she believes people who enable criminals can be just as bad as the criminals themselves. If Angie hadn't turned a blind eye to what Wyatt was capable of, Owen wouldn't have suffered as much as he did.

"Have you forgotten how much she hated you?" says Owen. "How she literally plotted your downfall?"

Madison has to concede she's been too quick to overlook their past. Her need for family blinded her to Angie's toxic traits. "I guess I just needed you here to remind me." She takes his hand in hers. "You have excellent timing."

He squeezes her hand. "I don't want anything to do with her, and I don't want her to hurt you again. I'm sure Nate would say the same thing."

Madison smiles reassuringly, but she suspects it's Nate's absence that made her consider giving her sister another chance in the first place.

CHAPTER THIRTY-TWO

Nate's drunk. Kurt brought him to a dive bar, the kind where you can't tell what time of day it is as the place has no windows and probably breaks all fire regulations. His younger brother has been filling him in on Dawn's secrets while ordering rounds. Nate will need a cab to take him somewhere later this evening. For now, he decides he's drunk enough and pushes the latest beer away from him.

He ignores the hostile glances from other drinkers. There's no hiding who he is. And he can see he's not wanted here. People are talking about him. A football game is playing on the TV above the bar, but it's just a matter of time before someone switches it to the local news station, where his arrival will undoubtedly have made headlines. Nate knows how these things work.

Against his better judgment, he takes a slug of beer, ignoring the pain in his knuckles, hopeful that Ted's jaw hurts more than his hand. Kurt talks a mile a minute and Nate has trouble keeping up. He's managed to work out that his brother isn't keen on their sister. According to him, Dawn tries to control him. To mother him. But it sounds like she's just trying to have Kurt's back and stop him from repeating his mistakes. Nate now knows all about her marriage issues and her debt problems, both of which weren't evident while he was at her house.

None of it matters. He doesn't want to know these things. It's private, and he won't rejoice in his sister's pain no matter how much Kurt gets off on running his mouth. It's sad to see his brother acting this way, because it's clear he's not an honest person anymore. Even with the hug and the fake breeziness, Nate senses a simmering hostility from him, making him feel as though their drinking session isn't about two estranged brothers catching up, but an act designed to manipulate him. He may be drunk and depressed, but he's not stupid.

"I wanted to come to your trial," says Kurt, wiping his nose. "But Dawn made me stay away. She said we should wait for the outcome, because if you were convicted, it would reflect poorly on us."

Nate figured as much. "Didn't you ask Dad what he thought?"

His brother bats the comment aside. "You were always Dad's favorite, so he was bound to take your side. He had blinkers on. Even if you'd killed that woman, he would've defended you until the day he died."

Nate is hit with a wave of grief for his father. Wanting to change the subject, he asks, "So what do you do for work?"

After a long slug of his beer, Kurt says, "I buy and sell vehicles, do a little high-stakes gambling, that kind of thing. I prefer fast money over a nine-to-five job."

Nate raises his eyebrows but keeps his opinion of Kurt's so-called job to himself.

"But now I can give all that up."

He frowns. "How do you figure?"

His brother leans forward with an alarming grin. "Because you're gonna help me out, right? I know you were awarded a generous sum of compensation, and me and Dawn deserve some of it too, don't you think? We suffered just as much as you did."

Nate bristles at the comment. He looks his brother in the eye. "Ever been incarcerated?"

Kurt shrugs. "Sure, here and there. Not long stretches. It was bearable."

"Yeah? Well, death row wasn't *bearable*." Nate sighs. He doesn't have the energy to get angry. Mainly because he's disappointed. He had high hopes for Kurt. Maybe Dawn's right and their brother was on a straight path until Nate's arrest. Guilt makes him want to give his siblings all his money and be done with it. Be done with them. Dawn made it clear she doesn't want a relationship with him, and Kurt just wants his money. But he suspects Kurt would let the money fall through his hands faster than Nate can get out of Kansas. And if he ever manages to pull himself out of this depression without killing himself, he wants the money to do some good. The thought of it paying off his brother's gambling debts and God knows what else makes him angry.

Before he can say anything, Kurt jumps up and heads to the bar with Nate's bank card to buy another round.

In his absence, an attractive redhead slowly approaches the table and sits in Kurt's vacant seat. "Well, well, well. Nathaniel Monroe. You're a sight for sore eyes. Remember me?"

He doesn't. He barely glances at her.

"We went to high school together." She sips from Kurt's beer, trying to be seductive, but it doesn't work on him. "I saw you on the news. I think we should get out of here and have some fun."

He feels her hand on his thigh under the table and quickly

pulls his leg away. He doesn't want to offend her, but he also doesn't want to lead her on. "I'm engaged. And I'm not the kind of person you should be trying to sleep with."

Her eyes narrow. "If you're not careful, I can get you put back inside. All I'd have to do is tell Sheriff Rainer that you assaulted me. Maybe if you throw some money my way..."

Nate turns his back to her. He should leave, but his brother has found trouble at the bar. It didn't take long. The woman gets up and walks back to her friends, muttering obscenities under her breath. Nate needs to get out of this town in case she makes good on her threat. He runs a hand through his hair in frustration. Why won't everyone just leave him alone?

At the bar, two older guys in plaid shirts and dirty jeans gesture angrily. Kurt probably owes them money. Or maybe they're pissed that Nate dared to show up here. He scoffs. It's a weekday afternoon and they're in here drinking. Probably the same as every other weekday afternoon. And they think *they're* better than *him*?

The bartender steps in. "Listen, Leroy, as long as his money's good, I don't care that he's here. Mind your own business for a change, would you?"

Nate looks away, and within a minute or two, Kurt returns with a tray containing shots, more beer and a small pot of salted nuts meant for the bar. "What was that about?" asks Nate.

Kurt smiles as if he doesn't have a care in the world. "Not everyone's pleased to see the Monroe boys back together." He downs a clear shot and winces, saying, "They'll treat us differently once they realize we have money now. Hell, we could afford to buy their land and drive them and their inbred families out of town if we wanted to. It's about time they gave us some *respect*." He says the last word loudly, glancing at Leroy, who's stewing over by the pool table.

Nate realizes he doesn't like his little brother much

anymore. The fun, adventurous young boy he knew has been replaced with a selfish, greedy version. But no matter how uncomfortable he feels around him, he can't bring himself to leave, so he picks up a shot glass and downs the fiery liquid in the hope of finding some motivation at the bottom.

CHAPTER THIRTY-THREE

Madison left Owen at home while she returned to work for a couple of hours to focus on figuring out the motive for John Doe's death. Why someone stuffed a rose of all things down his throat.

It could suggest he was on a date that went wrong. Or that he was stalking someone. Or was someone stalking him? The dismemberment and dumping of his body suggests his killer was physically strong. Perhaps a male. That could mean John Doe received or gave unwanted attention to another man. It had made her think of Ralph Smith. Many of the skin magazines he had in his trailer contained more men than women. And he took photos of their murder victim. Was he infatuated with John Doe? Was his brother, Stanley? The two of them together could've killed him before panicking and dumping his body nearby.

Going around in circles gave her a headache, so she decided to call it a night.

Now, driving through town in the dark, her eyes keep checking the rearview mirror as she senses she's being followed again. She briefly thinks of her sister, but why would Angie follow her? She'd be more likely to turn up at the house while she's out, to try to talk to Owen alone. Maybe it's the person who put the photograph of Sofia on her car. Perhaps they're planning to leave her more evidence.

She's following Steve to his place. He wants to talk to her about something away from their co-workers. Madison's a little nervous about what he's going to say in case he wants to quit or asks for advice on how to end things with Lena. She doesn't want to get involved in their relationship and make Lena more inclined to report Brody for the attack. Lena could easily argue that the dog is unpredictable and needs to be destroyed. The thought sends a shiver through her. She still can't believe Brody would bite someone.

By the time Steve pulls into his driveway, the feeling of being followed has eased. Maybe she's paranoid. Or perhaps it's Nate, biding his time to return home. If it is, and he sees her here at Steve's place, he might get the wrong idea.

Steve lives in a small two-story home not far from Madison's old place. There's room for two cars in his driveway, so she pulls in next to him. The porch light is on, and he waits for her as she gets out of her car. "I hope you have alcohol," she says as she climbs the porch steps.

Inside, his home is exactly as she expected: tidy, sparse of belongings and clean. A home gym fills one side of his living room, a geeky wargaming table on the other. She glances at him. "Toy soldiers? Really?"

He shrugs. "My dad got me into it when I was a kid. It keeps me out of trouble."

The kitchen is a separate room, with the home not having been converted for open-plan living. Madison prefers these traditional layouts. The rooms are cozier as well as cheaper to heat. Steve's decor, although clean, is a little dark and dated for her liking. She can tell he's lived alone for years.

"Coffee?" he asks, dropping his keys on the large oak coffee table in front of a leather couch with recliners at both ends.

"No, I've had too many already today. I'm good."

He seems nervous as he gestures to the couch before sitting in the mismatched armchair. "I guess you want to know why you're here." It comes out as more of a statement than a question.

She laughs to break the tension. "What's going on?"

Steve appears to struggle to explain. He won't make eye contact. The atmosphere has turned tense.

"Steve, you're starting to freak me out. Are you okay?" She's never seen him this way. His face turns ashen, making the bruise under his eye more prominent. It dawns on her that he might be sick with something serious and he's struggling to accept it.

She swallows. What if he has a terminal diagnosis?

Unable to find the words, he stands and pulls his shirt out of the waistband of his jeans. He lifts the shirt, revealing his toned torso. But all she notices is the shocking blue and purple bruises spread across his skin.

She gasps. "What the hell happened to you?" She stands and pulls his shirt up farther, leaning in to check out his back. She vaguely remembers bruising being a symptom of some type of cancer, but she doesn't remember which one.

He takes a step back and drops his shirt, unable to respond.

Madison gently touches his arm. "Are you sick?"

He shakes his head in a way that suggests he's ashamed. His face flushes red.

Madison feels sick as she suddenly realizes she's missed something terrible that has been happening to him. "Steve? Who did this?" She thinks of his bruised eye. When she'd asked about it earlier this week, he'd told her he face-planted the bathroom door when stepping out of the shower after the power went out. If a woman had told her that story, she would've seen through it immediately. Her blood runs cold. "Lena?" she whispers cautiously.

He nods, still without speaking. His throat is holding back emotion, she can tell. She steps forward and embraces him, tears springing to her eyes. "Oh my God, Steve." She swallows. "I'm so sorry."

He squeezes her as he breaks down and lets the shame pour out of him.

Madison closes her eyes in frustration, hating the fact he's been suffering in silence. How many times has he winced from her touch, like earlier today at the construction site when she used him to push herself up? How many signs has she missed during his five months with Lena? Lena's attitude has steadily changed toward her over the past four or five months. She's been making barbed insults and acting hostile. Madison put it down to the fact that things were awkward between them once she and Nate became a couple because Lena had previously shown an interest in him. Then she thought Lena was stressed due to the pressure of the job, which has been particularly bad lately. But now that she knows the medical examiner has been physically abusing Steve, it all makes sense. Lena's afraid Steve might confide in someone. In *her*. Because if he does that, he might get away from her.

Relieved that he's been brave enough to disclose what's happening to him, Madison can't help wishing he'd said something sooner. Before it got this bad.

"This is why she makes you switch your security cameras off when she's over, isn't it?"

He pulls away and nods before dropping onto the couch and wiping his face with his hands. Madison goes to his fridge and finds a six-pack of beer. She grabs two and joins him on the couch, handing him a bottle. "When did it start?"

He twists the lid off and takes a slug before replying. "Within the second or third month of dating. She became unpredictable, with mood swings that left me dizzy. I thought I was an asshole who pressed her buttons. I wanted out of the relationship, but she wouldn't let me go."

"She lashes out when she's pissed?" she probes.

He nods. "It's ridiculous that I just sit back and take it, right? Am I a pushover? I should've done something the first time she swung at me, but to say I was shocked into silence is an understatement. I literally convinced myself I imagined it."

Madison has no idea how he should've handled the situation, but she knows it's harder for him because he's a man. He can't defend himself by hitting back without serious consequences, including the end of his career in law enforcement. And who knows? Maybe that's what Lena's hoping for. Because then she could file assault charges against him. Is that her ultimate aim?

"Does she apologize after?"

"Not really. She'll sometimes be extra loving, though, making me think I've overreacted."

"So you *do* react?" She feels bad for pressing him, but she can't help him until she knows the full facts. And she fully intends to help him. Lena won't get away with this.

He drinks some beer and nods. "I try to keep it light, but I've told her I don't like it and suggested we end things because I clearly make her mad. She wasn't happy with that. Hence this." He points to his eye.

Madison shakes her head. "Did she do that with her fist, or does she use weapons?"

He murmurs something she can't hear. It's clear he can barely bring himself to talk about it, so she decides to leave the details until he's at the station, providing a recorded interview. In the meantime, she needs to go slow and give him time to come to terms with what he has to do next. It's rare for victims of abuse—whether domestic, sexual or any other kind—to want to go straight from confiding in someone to getting the police involved. Because once that happens, the situation takes on a life of its own. The victim is no longer in control of how they deal with it. It begins the process of giving countless statements while the abuser is investigated, sometimes arrested and held, but more likely released on bail during the investigation. And in a town like this, it would be difficult not to come face-to-face with your abuser.

"I'm trying to recall what I know about her," she says. "She arrived in Lost Creek before I was released from prison. When I rejoined the PD and first met her, she told me she was from somewhere in New Hampshire." She tries to think back. "I'm sure she told me she had sworn off men for a while because her last relationship ended in violence."

Steve seems surprised. "Wait. *She* was the victim in that relationship?"

Madison tilts her head as she thinks. "No, that's not what she said, just that it was violent. She probably knew I'd assume that she was the victim." She pauses. "What if she's done this to previous partners and that's why she left New Hampshire?"

Headlights illuminate the front window. A vehicle pulls up outside. Alarmed, Steve looks at the window, saying, "What if it's her? She can't know you're here. She already thinks we're having an affair now we're partners."

Madison's shocked. Everything's becoming clearer now. This is why Lena hates her. She's convinced herself that Madison wants to take Steve from her, the way she supposedly took Nate, which is ridiculous since Nate only ever went for one coffee with the woman. They were never dating. Lena practically threw herself at him, and Nate still wasn't interested.

Steve rushes to the window and closes the drapes, even though his blinds are already shut. Before long, a loud bang at the door makes them both jump.

"Steve?" Lena's voice. "I know you're in there with her! I *knew* you were cheating on me. And some friend you are, Madison! Is this why you let your dog bite me?" She bangs the door hard again.

Madison jumps out of her seat, but Steve steps in front of her, blocking her way.

"Please don't."

She holds his arm. "Steve, I need to arrest her. You're a victim of domestic violence and she should be locked up for what she's done."

"No, Madison." He keeps his voice low. "I don't want anyone else to know. You're the only person I've told." His eyes implore her to keep his secret, but in doing that, she'd be keeping Lena's too.

"Listen," she says. "If Nate was beating me, what would you do about it?" She wants him to see sense, but he's too caught up to think straight. He lowers his eyes.

"I trusted you to love me, Steve!" yells Lena. "When you've been cheating on me this entire time. You make me *sick*."

Steve shakes his head. "She knows that's not true. She *knows* it."

Madison's fists ball in anger. "She's making sure the neighbors hear what she wants them to hear. She wants people to think we're having an affair, so that when we arrest her, it will look like you're the one who mistreated her."

"You two can have each other!" shouts Lena. "Let's see if he hits you like he did me."

Steve gasps. "I never touched her."

"Of course you didn't," says Madison. "Don't rise to the bait."

Lena stomps away so loudly that they hear her retreat all the way to her car, where she slams the door after getting in. As a parting shot, she loudly revs her engine before pulling away, leaving the neighborhood dogs barking at the commotion.

"This is insane." Steve sits on the couch. "I need time to figure things out."

Madison's buzzing with anger. She wants to see Lena locked up for what she's done, but if Steve won't file charges, they have no evidence. Maybe she could find Lena's ex in New Hampshire. People like her usually leave a trail of victims behind.

She watches as Steve runs a hand through his hair. "What the hell do I do? I don't want to see her again. I don't want her in my home, and I don't want to work with her." His voice falters. "Maybe I should move away? I have a brother in—"

"No!" says Madison, a little too harshly. She hates the thought of him leaving his life and his job behind because of this woman. She takes a deep breath before sitting beside him and gently resting her hand on his back. "We'll figure it out. We can go to Chief Mendes or a domestic violence support organization. If you let me take photos of the bruises in case you decide to file a complaint..."

He's shaking his head. "I'd never be able to show my face at work again if the team finds out. I'd be the butt of all Adams's jokes."

Her heart breaks for him. "Adams wouldn't dare say a word. You shouldn't feel ashamed, Steve. Lena's good at what she does if she makes you feel this way. She's a criminal. She needs to be fired from her job. And you need to put this into perspective as soon as you can. Imagine it was me or someone else who was being assaulted. What would you advise them to do?"

"I don't know. It's always easier to give advice than to take it." He runs a hand down his face. He appears exhausted. "Let me sleep on it. Maybe things will be clearer in the morning."

Madison senses he's done talking about this. But she doesn't want to leave him alone. What if Lena returns? Things have escalated tonight, and she's worked up. She could bring a weapon next time. Leaving an abusive relationship is the most dangerous time for the victim.

Steve stands, signaling he wants to be alone. Madison

follows his lead. "If she comes back tonight, do *not* let her in. Promise?"

He nods.

"You can call me. I'll come right away. I'm glad you told me all this. I'll help you as much as I can."

He nods. "Our next trip to the morgue will be interesting."

Madison shakes her head. They can't work with the woman now. "You won't be setting foot in that place until she's gone."

He seems unconvinced. "I can't avoid her forever. Not without moving away or..." He tails off.

She frowns. "Or what? You're not thinking of doing anything stupid, are you?" The thought makes her shudder. "Steve, this is all fixable. As soon as you're ready to file charges. I'll testify in court if I have to, and her assistants have noticed she's been a bitch to them lately too, so I'm certain they'll back us up about her hot temper. We have your bruises—"

"Okay, okay, I get it." He ushers her to the front door. She's pushing him too much. She can't help it. But he needs to come to the decision himself. As hard as it is for her to walk away tonight, knowing Lena is free and a genuine threat, she can't force him to face the problem head-on.

She turns before leaving. "Sorry. I hope I haven't come on too strong. I don't want to make you feel bad." She leans in for a quick hug. He doesn't seem to want to let her go, which brings more tears to her eyes. When she pulls away, she smiles sadly before heading to her car. He waves her off before closing the door.

Pulling her phone out, Madison texts him.

Lock it. Lock all doors and windows. And keep your cameras switched ON! We need evidence.

He doesn't reply.

CHAPTER THIRTY-FOUR

If Steve thought Madison would leave him vulnerable to another attack, he was wrong. She raced home, showered, changed and grabbed some food and drink from the fridge. She summoned Owen downstairs and told him he was going to get his first taste of what it's like to be a police officer on a stakeout.

With Owen stationed near Steve's house, instructed to be on the lookout for Lena's vehicle, Madison had gone to the medical examiner's house to check whether her car was there. It wasn't, so she'd returned to Steve's place and joined Owen in his car. They'd spent the entire night outside. Owen's dedication had surprised her. She thought he might use the opportunity to gorge on junk food and watch stupid videos, and not focus on the shadows around them, but he had taken the assignment seriously. It gave her hope that he might make a good cop.

Lena hadn't showed up. Perhaps she'd had time to cool down and think about handing herself in for what she'd done to Steve. Or maybe she was too ashamed to show her face.

Now, Madison has arrived at work early to see if Lena contacted anyone overnight. "Hey, Dina."

Dina looks surprised and glances at the clock. It's not yet 7 a.m. Owen's lucky he gets to sleep all morning to make up for last night, but Madison has to push on, although he did allow her a few short naps in the car.

"What are you doing here this early?" says Dina.

"I need to see the chief about something. Is she in?" Madison glances at Mendes's office, which is lit from within.

"Yeah, she arrived a few minutes ago."

The rest of the station is quiet, with just a few patrol officers coming and going. Madison was worried Steve would get here early too, but there's no sign of him yet. She and Owen left his house at five thirty. Madison had gone home to get changed, brush her teeth and grab some breakfast before heading here. "Have you seen or heard from Lena Scott overnight?" she asks.

"No," says the dispatcher. "Why? Was she supposed to contact us?"

"No, I just wondered."

Stella Myers arrives for the day shift. After greeting her, Madison leaves the pair to it and heads to Chief Mendes's office. She knocks on the door.

Mendes looks up. "What's wrong?"

Madison smiles. Like her, the chief is always on edge, waiting for the next piece of bad news. She steps into the office and closes the door behind her, then quickly updates the chief on what happened at Steve's place last night. Mendes's face drains of color as she listens. When Madison's finished, she picks up her desk phone.

"What are you doing?" asks Madison, alarmed.

"I'm calling her boss and getting her suspended, then ordering a unit to pick her up and bring her in."

Madison shakes her head. "Steve will leave town if we get ahead of him. He's not ready for any of that yet. I have a better idea." Mendes puts the receiver back in the cradle as Madison says, "I'm going to talk to Lena's assistants today. I want their opinion on her behavior at work, because they implied she'd been cranky lately. We need to meticulously build our case against her and get as many witness statements as possible. Otherwise, it's Steve's word against hers, and juries may not believe someone like Steve could be a victim of DV. I'll try to track down her ex-boyfriend in New Hampshire. I'll need a little help locating where she was living and working, to narrow down my search."

"What about Steve?" says Mendes. "What if she continues abusing him in the meantime?"

"It's a worry, I'm not going to lie." Madison sighs. "But we can keep them separated as much as possible. Steve can stay with me if he has to."

Mendes gives her a look. "That's a terrible idea and will just fuel her suspicion that you two are having an affair." She frowns. "You're not, are you? Because I have noticed Steve's loyalty to you since you rejoined the department."

"*What?*" says Madison, offended. Steve's loyal to his job, not to her. Although she can't ignore the fact he's always made her feel safe and respected at work. He also thinks Nate's an idiot for leaving her. Has she missed something? "No, we're not," she says. "I'm engaged to Nate, remember?"

The chief nods. "Sorry. My previous place of employment was rife with co-worker affairs, so I had to check before we take this any further." She takes a deep breath. "Could Steve stay with Sergeant Adams?"

"That would mean telling Adams what's going on."

"I think the team around him has to know," says Mendes. "In order to keep him safe and to be prepared in case they're caught in the crossfire. I'll make it clear to Adams that this is a sensitive situation."

Madison isn't sure Adams is the best person to have around in sensitive situations, but they don't have much choice. "Fine. As long as he can persuade Steve to stay with him for a reason other than he's a target. Steve might not go if he thinks we're all plotting behind his back." She takes a deep breath, wishing more than anything that he wasn't in this predicament. "I'll attend morgue visits alone."

"I think it's best that I go in your place," says Mendes. "And that I liaise with Lena for any autopsy updates. Conrad will be a good buffer if she gets suspicious. I can pretend I'm visiting him."

Madison's relieved the chief is on board with going slow.

Stella appears at the glass-paneled wall and knocks on the door before opening it. "Sorry to butt in. I just took a tip about the body found at the construction site."

Madison's eyes widen.

Steve suddenly appears behind Stella, having just arrived for work. He takes his jacket off. If he's wondering why Madison's in with the chief, he doesn't show it. "What was the tip?" he asks.

Stella turns to look at him. "The caller gave me a name for the body. Bianca Marsh, from Prospect Springs. That's all she said before she hung up."

Excited, Madison stands. "Was the caller young or old?"

"She sounded young, under twenty-five. She called from a withheld number."

"Okay. Thanks, Stella. If she calls back, try to get more details. Tell her we'd be happy to talk to her and we'd keep her name out of the investigation."

Stella nods. "Will do." She leaves them to return to her desk.

Sergeant Adams arrives and hovers beside Steve at the chief's door. He slips out of his jacket. "What's going on?"

Steve turns to him. "Are any of those missing kids from Prospect Springs called Bianca Marsh?"

He doesn't even need to check. "Yeah. How'd you know?" He makes a thinking face. "If I remember correctly, she was fourteen when she vanished from her yard while cleaning her dad's car."

Madison closes her eyes briefly as she thinks of the poor girl's parents. "Get Alex to check whether the Prospect Springs PD took a DNA sample from her belongings after she vanished. The lab can compare it with our remains to see if it's a match. Also, let me see her case file." She heads to Adams's desk with Steve.

Adams switches his computer on before dumping his jacket on the spare desk next to him and taking a seat. He locates the email the PSPD sent him containing details and photos of their seven missing teenagers. "Here she is." He double-clicks on Bianca's photo.

A young white female with thick black hair smiles at the camera. A couple of what look like younger siblings clutch onto her legs, grinning up at her. Madison can't help but wonder how they coped with their big sister's disappearance. She looks at Steve. "If Alex confirms our remains belong to Bianca, we'll break the news to her parents in person."

He nods.

"Detectives?" shouts Stella from her cubicle. She has her headset on.

"Yeah?" says Steve.

"Kate Flynn wants an update on John Doe and Toby Clark. Do either of you want to talk to her?"

Madison doesn't. There's not much they can disclose to reporters at this stage, and Kate's good at reading between the lines of anything Madison does say.

"I will," says Steve. He looks at Madison. "She probably won't push me as hard for information."

She nods. While he's distracted talking to Kate, she can visit Lena's assistants. "I have to run an errand. I won't be long." She grabs her keys from her desk and heads out.

CHAPTER THIRTY-FIVE

Lena's car is noticeably absent from her dedicated space in the parking lot outside the medical examiner's building. Madison takes her chance to speak to the assistants alone and hurries inside the building. The male receptionist greets her, and before she can ask for Jeff or Skylar, he says, "If you're looking for Dr. Scott, she hasn't arrived yet, and we're not sure when to expect her. We assume she has a personal appointment she forgot to tell us about."

"Actually," she says, "I'd like to speak to her assistants. Are they in the morgue?"

He nods. "Go right ahead."

Madison makes her way along the familiar corridor adjacent to the reception desk. She enters the cool morgue and finds Jeff mopping the floor. Skylar is checking her phone. They look up when they hear the door creak. Madison smiles. "Hey, guys. Do you have a minute?"

"Sure," says Skylar. "What's up?"

"Come with me." Knowing that Lena could arrive at any minute, Madison turns and leads them out of the building's rear exit to where she knows Jeff likes to smoke during his breaks.

Outside, the early-morning air is damp thanks to the overnight showers, and the ground is littered with crushed cigarette butts. Once the door is closed behind them, she says, "Sorry for the cloak and dagger, but I wanted to ask you something about Dr. Scott."

"I told you something weird was going on," Jeff says to Skylar as he lights up a cigarette. "She usually tells us when she's going to be late."

"Is she okay?" asks Skylar, concerned.

Madison zips her jacket up against the cold and stuffs her hands in her pockets to avoid accepting a cigarette from Jeff. "Yes, as far as I know. I just wanted to pick up on something you guys said at the bar the other night. You said Lena has been a little cranky lately. What did you mean by that, and have you noticed her behavior change in any other ways?"

"Well, she threw something at me recently," says Jeff. He sucks on the cigarette. "Does that count?"

"*What?*" Madison's shocked.

"Yeah, a dead guy's boot." He exhales smoke. "I was so mad I almost threw it back at her, but I quickly saw sense. I can't afford to lose my job. Instead, I left the room and took a few minutes to calm down."

If Lena had thrown anything at *her*, Madison would've gone straight to the woman's boss. "Did you know about this?" she asks Skylar.

"I entered the room during the stand-off," she says. "It was awkward, to say the least. I knew something had happened, but not what until Jeff told me afterward. I was shocked. Lena was so nice when she started here, but she's definitely more intense lately."

Jeff nods. "I put it down to that condition everyone's talking about. Peromenopause?"

"*Peri*menopause," says Skylar. "She's probably not old enough for that. Maybe it's really bad PMS, or she's realized her life isn't going how she thought it would." She sighs and rubs her small baby bump, suggesting Lena isn't the only one.

"Well, whatever's causing it," says Madison, "there's no excuse to treat your employees or any other human being that way. Just be careful around her in case she lashes out again." Her eyes flicker to Skylar's stomach. Is Lena capable of hurting a pregnant woman? "And I'd make someone else here aware of anything she does that makes you uncomfortable. It's good to keep a log of this kind of thing, as it sometimes escalates." She's trying not to say too much, but any evidence these two can provide once Steve's filed a complaint—*if* he files one—could really help his case in court.

Skylar laughs nervously. "You make it sound like she's dangerous."

She doesn't want to scare them, but she also doesn't want to be responsible for not preparing them should Lena's behavior worsen. "I prefer the term *unpredictable*. If she's lashed out at Jeff, she could lash out again. If you sense her mood changing, give her some space and tell someone, preferably me."

The assistants share a look. "I don't like the sound of this," says Jeff. "I won't put up with it twice. Just so you know."

"And nor should you," says Madison. "Look, I can't say much, but this situation won't last long. Don't tell her what we've discussed. I intend to speak to her about it myself at some point."

"Sure," says Jeff. He finishes his cigarette and stamps on it.

Skylar eyes her with a worried expression. Madison thanks them for their time and leaves. Outside, she hovers at her car while she thinks about the best course of action. It sucks that she can't arrest Lena, and now she knows about the boot-throwing incident, she thinks it's best Chief Mendes makes Lena's boss aware of the situation after all. She pulls her phone out and types a quick text.

*Lena's assistants have witnessed threatening behavior at work.
I think we need to make her boss aware of the situation.*

She takes a deep breath and looks around. Lena's parking space is still empty. When her phone beeps with a notification, she sees the chief has replied.

I'll call him now.

Satisfied, she slips her phone away, but it rings before she can get into her car. It's Steve. "Hey," she says.

"Hey. Where are you?"

"On my way back. I'll be five minutes."

"Don't bother. We need to go to Prospect Springs."

Her shoulders tense. "Why?"

"Because the DNA from the hair found with our body matches that of missing fourteen-year-old Bianca Marsh."

She rubs her closed eyes and takes a deep breath. "So we need to tell her family."

"Right. Want me to ask someone from the Prospect Springs PD to meet us at their place?"

"No," she says. "We found her, not them. We can fill them in afterward. Her family should be the first to know."

"Got it. I'll text you the address and meet you there."

Prospect Springs is a two-hour drive on a bad day. Madison's too busy for a four-hour round trip, so she intends to get there faster than that. "Make sure you're quick."

He laughs. "Got it."

She slips into her car and speeds out of the parking lot.

CHAPTER THIRTY-SIX

Time captive: 8 years 10 months

She has a headache. Tumultuous times have returned to the house after a quiet break. A long break, while Eugene fought cancer. Now he's better and they have company again. A young girl called Macy has come to live with them.

Macy is different from Sofia. She has a feisty streak, making all kinds of threats to harm them. Over time, she should settle down enough to accept her role in the house. The age gap between the two females is just eight years, but Macy ranks lower in all respects.

After all, Macy isn't married to Eugene like *she* is.

She smiles as she washes dishes. She effectively runs the house these days. Eugene gives her more freedom than ever. She shares his bedroom full-time without being tied up, and she's to make sure Macy stays in line. That doesn't mean she won't be kind to the young woman. But if she's honest, she does feel some hostility, since Macy was brought in to fill a gap she can't perform herself. She hates that Eugene has sex with other girls. Jealousy rears its head all too frequently, but he tells her it's nothing like what they have. They love each other. He didn't love Sofia, and he won't love Macy. They're here to fulfill their purpose, that's all.

She often wonders what Eugene will do with Macy once she's given them a child or two. He's not a violent man. Sofia died because she wanted to, and because it was the kindest thing for her. Perhaps Macy will mature in time and stop making everything so difficult.

As she scrubs a dirty plate, Eugene slips behind her and kisses her neck. His belly fits in the arch of her lower back. "I love coming home to you." He's been out grocery shopping. They needed more vitamins. Macy is locked in her room.

She smiles. "Good. I love having you home."

"I love this shirt on you too." He turns her to face him. "And your hair that way. Shoulder-length. It was long when you first came here. This suits you better."

She once asked him where he got her clothes from, and he'd said from thrift stores, mostly. He brazenly tells the salesclerks his wife is housebound. She's surprised it's never raised any red flags with anyone, but she supposes people are too self-obsessed to notice these things.

He strokes her cheek. His breath smells of coffee, but she likes coffee now. She drinks a lot of it herself. It's nice with whiskey in.

"You know you're here because I just want to be normal, right?" he says.

She looks into his eyes. Eugene was sick for some time. Bladder cancer. His doctor says they caught it all, so he's not expected to die from it. He's been having treatment at the hospital. He sold some of his possessions to help with the cost, but she suspects he's in debt now.

"I brought you here because I wanted what everyone else has," he says. "Company. Love. A family. Macy could never replace you."

She's relieved to hear it. "I should hope not."

"You're more special than you'll ever know."

She studies his eyes, wondering what he means.

"I don't like the crying girls," he says. "I prefer girls like you who adapt. You hardly ever cried. Not in front of me, anyway. I'm glad. I don't want to see that. I always hated self-pity." He runs a hand over her hair. "I know you love me now. It took a while, but I knew you'd come around."

He's right, it took a long time. But she's glad to be here now. Most days. She still has conflicting emotions. They'll probably never go, given the way she was brought here. She still has nightmares too. And she dreams about her parents. Especially her mom. Her face is blurred these days, as her memory fades. She'd give anything to have one final conversation with her mother. She was so loving and fun. They had a great relationship, and her dad was never happier than when the three of them were together. But her mom would've hated Eugene. The state of his house, the way he looks, the way he kisses. She would've gone out of her mind in this house.

"I'm so glad your daddy sold you to me."

She tries not to bristle. For some reason, the statement irritates her.

"I never told you this," he says, "but a month or so after you came here, your family moved away as if you never existed. They must never think about you." He shakes his head in disgust. "I don't know how they can live with themselves. I think about you all the time."

A tear escapes her eye. She's so, *so* lucky. "Thank you for taking care of me."

A bang on the ceiling tells them Macy wants something. Eugene steps back and sighs as he undoes his belt and the button on his pants, acting like what he's about to do is a chore. "Dinner can wait until afterward. Then we'll all eat together. I bought her some chocolate ice cream for dessert to cheer her up and help her settle in."

She watches him leave before slipping some earbuds in. As she returns to the dirty dishes, she switches on a track at random. She doesn't want to listen to them together. She prefers to pretend she's not sharing her husband with other girls.

CHAPTER THIRTY-SEVEN

Bianca Marsh's parents live in a small one-story home that needs some attention. The front yard is overgrown, and the rain gutters running along the roof aren't secured properly, causing gaps where rain runs straight through onto the wall below. A large damp spot is evident from the outside, so Madison can only imagine what the inside is like. A quick look around tells her this is the worst house on the street. The neighbors probably gossip about the Marshes, exchanging comments about how their house brings the whole neighborhood down. Or maybe they're sympathetic to the couple's situation. It must be difficult to concentrate on keeping your house in good condition when your heart is broken and your daughter is missing.

She waits in her car until Steve's vehicle appears, slowly coming to a stop behind hers. She beat him by ten minutes, but she'd get more satisfaction from that if he were Sergeant Adams. She climbs out as he approaches. "The car in the driveway suggests someone's home," she says.

Steve hasn't mentioned what happened with Lena last night, so Madison thinks it's best not to raise it. He knows she'll help him when he's ready. He follows the path to the front door with Madison close behind him. The dated wooden door looks like one hard shove would open it. He knocks loudly, then takes a step back to stand next to her.

"You can lead this," she says.

"Gee, thanks," he murmurs.

She smiles sympathetically. This will be his first death notification as a detective. He has to start somewhere.

The door opens halfway, and a guy around fifty years old pokes his head out. His face is heavily lined for his age, and his receding hair is a mixture of brown and gray.

"Sorry to bother you, sir. I'm Detective Tanner and this is Detective Harper. We're from the Lost Creek Police Department. We're looking to speak with George Marsh. Is that you?"

The man nods. "It's about Bianca, isn't it?"

Steve takes a deep breath. "It is. Mind if we come inside?"

George turns and walks away from them, so Madison follows Steve inside and closes the door behind her. They've passed the point of no return. The last moment a loved one has of thinking their missing person is still alive. She and Steve are about to shatter that illusion, which will change this couple's life forever.

George takes a seat in the living room, which is nicer than she expected based on the condition of the home's exterior. The carpet is clean, and the furniture, although old and worn, is cozy. He doesn't offer them a seat, so they remain standing.

"Is your wife home?" asks Steve.

The older man shakes his head. "She left nine years ago and took the kids with her."

He must be referring to the children Madison saw in the photograph of Bianca before she vanished. They'll be young adults now. The disappearance of their big sister would have cast a shadow over their entire lives, but George lost all three of his children, as well as his wife. His weary expression tells her he's been to hell and back.

"We couldn't make it work without Bianca," he says. "Without knowing where she was and what happened to her." He clears his throat. "My wife lives in California now, but I can call her when you're gone and tell her what you've come to say. We agreed we'd stay in touch for that very reason."

Madison wishes he had someone with him to hear the news. Perhaps they can call someone to come sit with him once they're done. He clearly has family, because several family photos line his oak sideboard. She looks a little closer at one of them and frowns.

"We have an update about your daughter," says Steve, "and I'm afraid it's not good."

George appears to brace himself. He straightens in his seat and inhales. "Go ahead and tell me. I need to know what happened to her."

Steve clears his throat. "Yesterday morning, remains were found at a construction site in Lost Creek. I'm afraid that DNA comparisons have confirmed they belong to your daughter." He pauses. "We're very sorry for your loss, Mr. Marsh."

The man sucks in a gasp of air. His face scrunches up as he nods, trying to hold back a sob. He takes a minute to compose himself, pulling out a handkerchief from his pocket and placing it in his lap, unused. "How did she get there?" he whispers. "Was she murdered?"

"We believe so," says Steve. "But we don't yet know how or why. Finding who abducted her will be our priority, and we'll work closely with your local detectives."

George wipes his watery eyes, focusing on the coffee table before him. "She was washing my car when she was taken, twelve years ago. If I hadn't been so cheap and had taken it to a damn car wash, she wouldn't have been an easy target. I've blamed myself every day since." He scoffs. "And so has her mother."

Madison knows words won't console him. They could tell him that might not be the case and he shouldn't be so hard on himself, but that's not what people want to hear. They want to hear about what happens next. How they can get justice for their loved ones. "We'll find the person responsible, sir." She discreetly moves to the sideboard and peers at the photo again. Something about the image makes goosebumps break out over her arms. She picks the frame up before leaning into Steve's ear. "I need to head outside for a second."

He nods.

George doesn't notice. He's lost in his memories of Bianca.

Once outside, she turns her back to the rain and calls Adams. He answers right away. "What's going on?" he asks.

"I'm at George Marsh's home in Prospect Springs. I need a copy of the photo that was placed on my car. Would you send it to me?

"Sure," he says. "Hang on."

It doesn't take long before her phone buzzes with a new message.

"Got it?" he asks.

"Yeah." She opens the image and looks closely at the restrained woman's neck before comparing it to the framed photo of Bianca in her hand. Her heart sinks. "Shit."

"What is it?" he asks.

"The female in the photo—Sofia—has black hair, pierced ears and two moles on the left side of her neck."

"And?"

Madison sighs. "She shares those characteristics with Bianca Marsh."

"No way?" says Adams, shocked. "You think Sofia is Bianca Marsh?"

"Right. The moles match perfectly. There's no doubt. It's Bianca who's tied to that bed."

Madison's heart sinks as she comes to terms with the realization that the woman in the photo is already dead. She can't help her now. And it's likely she was sexually assaulted or tortured before she died. She looks at the front door behind her and exhales. She'll need to break the news to the girl's father.

CHAPTER THIRTY-EIGHT

"We need Conrad's approximation of age as soon as possible," says Madison into the phone. "So we can figure out whether Bianca was killed shortly after her abduction."

"I'll call him," says Adams. "I know he's with her remains now, so I'll text you as soon as he lets me know."

"Thanks. Her father's devastated. Her mother left years ago with their other kids. He's all alone."

"Is he devastated, or did he do it?" says Adams. "It might be worth checking with the local police to see if he was ever a suspect."

He's not wrong. Perhaps Bianca's remains will lead them to her father. "God, I hope not, because I really feel for the guy."

"Maybe you don't need to tell him everything. Spare him the worst of it."

She's thinking the same herself. "I can't tell him much until we know the facts ourselves."

"By the way," says Adams, "Alex found something in the envelope that came with the photo. An eyelash."

Her heart rate quickens. "So we might be able to trace who put it on my car, right?"

"Unless it's yours and you contaminated it."

Her shoulders sag. It's a possibility. "He can ask Nora to compare it to my DNA, but let's hope it's not mine." She looks at the house, wishing she didn't have to go back inside and break more bad news.

"Oh, and I know about Steve and the medical examiner," says Adams with a long sigh. "It's crazy, right? I always knew there was something about Lena I didn't like. She has zero personality if you ask me, and a bad attitude. Anyway, she hasn't turned up to work today."

"Did Chief Mendes tell you?" she asks.

"Yeah. Me and Alex. No one else knows except Lena's boss. The chief told him, but she doesn't think there's much he can do unless Steve files a complaint. At the moment, it's his word against hers."

He's right. Even though Madison and Lena's assistants have experienced her escalating hostility, none of them have witnessed Lena assaulting anyone. Not unless Jeff wants to file a complaint for the boot-throwing incident, but he probably wouldn't because it means risking his job while Lena's still his boss. "It's so frustrating," she says. "We have to keep Steve and Lena apart without either of them realizing we're doing it. We'll find something to nail her. We just have to be clever about it."

"Being clever is your department," says Adams. "I'm better at taking him for beer and making sure he doesn't harm himself."

She groans. It doesn't bear thinking about. "By the way, has Kyle Davenport installed cameras at the house yet?"

"Yeah, he was there last night when I got home from work."

"What do you think of him?"

"To tell you the truth, he barely said a word. From what I could hear, he was on the phone with his girlfriend most of the time."

That's odd, as Kyle was so friendly with Madison. "Did he install the app on your phone for you?"

"No, he told me to google how to download it and work it. I got the feeling he had somewhere more important to be."

She frowns, wondering why he installed it on her phone *and* took the time to show her how to use it. Did he do something with her phone while she wasn't looking? Perhaps she should revisit Elaine Brown and ask whether Kyle was at her place the night John Doe was dumped in the creek. But not yet. "I better go tell Mr. Marsh we have a photo of his daughter tied to a bed."

"Sure," says Adams. "Good luck."

She pockets her phone before reentering the house. Inside, she replaces the framed photo and takes a deep breath before turning to look at George. He appears to have made them coffee, as Steve is holding a cup and there's a second on the coffee table waiting for her. "Mr. Marsh, we have reason to believe that a photo we recently received through an anonymous source is of your daughter."

George frowns as he leans forward. "Taken when? After she died?"

"No, not after. While she was alive. But in the photo, she's... tied to a bed."

He slumps back. "Oh, good Lord." His throat constricts as if he's swallowing back bile. "So the son of a bitch who took her forced himself on her before dumping her like a piece of garbage?" He breaks down. Steve sits beside him, carefully taking the man's coffee cup from his trembling hand and placing it on the table.

George's anguish is palpable. His daughter being murdered is bad enough, but finding out she was likely assaulted before her death makes the situation even harder to bear. Madison can't imagine he's acting right now, but she won't know until she gets the investigating detective's case file. If they'll allow her access. They might be pissed she didn't tell them Bianca's been found before coming here.

"I'm so sorry," she says. "Can we call someone to come sit with you? A friend or neighbor?"

He nods and points to his cell phone on a sideboard. "Call Shirley. She'll come over and help me break the news to Bianca's mom."

Steve gets up to retrieve the phone and heads into the kitchen to make the call. Madison hears his voice. Her phone buzzes with another text from Adams.

> *Conrad believes the remains are approx. seventeen or eighteen years old.*

Madison's arms break out in goosebumps. Bianca was fourteen when she was abducted. Was she really held captive for three or four years? Her mouth goes dry. She sends a thumbs-up emoji and pockets her phone. This situation goes from bad to worse.

"Shirley's on her way," says Steve as he reenters. He places the phone in front of George. "Said she'd be only two or three minutes."

George nods. "She's my sister. Works at the convenience store on the corner. She'll be devastated. She's the only person who thought Bianca would return to us alive one day." He sighs shakily. "I guess I need to think about a funeral."

Madison's chest tightens with dread as she says, "Our medical examiner will try to find a cause of death, and then we'll release Bianca to a funeral home of your choice. Bear with us. It sometimes takes a little while during a homicide investigation."

He nods. "I just hope she didn't suffer for long. That she

died the same day. That's all I can hope for in this terrible situation, right?" He looks up at her for answers.

She shifts position, not wanting to tell him what she knows. But she has no choice. "We have a forensic anthropologist helping us. His job is to age the remains." She swallows. "I'm afraid I've just learned that his preliminary report suggests Bianca was around seventeen or eighteen years old when she died."

George's red-rimmed eyes widen. His mouth drops open. She sees the strength go out of him as he slumps back even farther into his seat. She senses Steve looking at her in shock at the news. "I'm so sorry, Mr. Marsh. I wish I didn't have to tell you these things." She crouches in front of him and takes his cold hands in hers. "There's no way to prepare you for any of this, but support is available. We can put you in touch with bereavement services, who can make a big difference over the coming days and weeks. They're specially trained. Now's the time to look after yourself. You've had a massive shock."

The front door bursts open behind them and a woman in her late fifties appears. Mascara runs down her flushed face. She heads straight to George, so Madison stands and moves out of the way as his sister embraces him.

"Not our beautiful Bianca!" she sobs.

Madison has to blink back tears.

Sensing they should leave, Steve places a business card on the coffee table. "If you need anything, call me. We'll be in touch over the coming days."

The grieving siblings ignore him, so he leads Madison out of the house. She closes the door behind her. With a deep breath, she says, "Whoever put that photo on my car is either responsible for abducting Bianca and wanted to brag about it, or they know who took her but don't want to be implicated in his crimes."

He nods. "I think you're right."

"Alex found an eyelash in the envelope. If it's not mine, it could lead us to that person." She walks to her car. "Finding them now takes priority over everything else." She gets in and races back to Lost Creek.

CHAPTER THIRTY-NINE

Nate wakes in pain. His back is screaming for him to change position, and his head feels like it's been hit with a sledgehammer. He tries to swallow, but his mouth is too dry from the booze. Vague memories of drinking with Kurt late into the night flood his dazed mind. He hasn't physically felt this bad in a long time, but then he hasn't been drunk in a long time.

"Coffee or water?" says a man. "I brought both." The voice is unfamiliar.

Nate sits up and squints into the light. The spacious room he's in is too bright. When his vision clears, he realizes he's in a church and has spent the night passed out on a hard wooden pew. He looks up at the guy in front of him, and his heart sinks. He's had enough of priests to last him a lifetime.

When he extends his hand to take the coffee—after all, beggars can't be choosers—he drops something. The rosary Madison gave him falls to the floor. He must have been holding it all night. Seeing it sprawled at his feet makes him want to cry. It looks shattered, like his faith.

The priest sits next to him and picks up the rosary, placing it and the cup of water next to him on the pew. "Your brother told me before he sped away in your car that I needed to take care of you."

Nate feels for his wallet. It's still in his jacket, but when he pulls it out and opens it, he realizes his bank cards are missing. Kurt's going to bleed him dry and probably kill himself in the process. Disappointed, Nate slips the wallet back into his pocket.

"He said the church owes you big-time."

Nate looks at the young man. He's probably in his mid-thirties, with a clean-shaven face and kind eyes. He's not jaded yet. He still believes that being a priest helps people. A priest used to symbolize wisdom and respect for Nate, but not anymore. "Was it you who banished my sister from this place?"

The young man sighs. "No. She did that herself. She knows she's welcome here anytime. But she can't bear the shame she feels, so she stays away."

Nate scoffs. "Shame plagues my family." He drinks the lukewarm coffee down in one go. It's bitter, but he needed it.

"I imagine returning home to a town and family who don't want you here is disheartening," says the priest. "But you shouldn't take it personally. You know in your heart that you're not who the press makes you out to be. If you can't find inner strength, perhaps you could lean on God for comfort. He'll never abandon you."

Nate could cry. Years ago, maybe decades, that statement would have comforted him. Which is why he doesn't have a problem with anyone else having faith. If it keeps them strong and gets them through tough times, then it has a valuable place in society. What pisses him off is men like this who imply that leaning on God can solve all his problems. It won't stop the press from lying about him. It won't give him back the decades he spent locked up awaiting execution, and it won't make his brother and sister love him. Sometimes, all a person wants is some practical help. And in his experience, people are less likely to provide that because it costs money.

"No offense, but I'd like to be alone," he says, eyes lowered. "I won't stay long."

The priest doesn't move, probably wishing he could convert him back to Catholicism. Or maybe he's just after a good quote to give the local newspaper as soon as Nate leaves. Nate knows his cynicism is a result of everything he's been through and a sign he's finally done with God and churches. This place feels cold and soulless. The only comfort he finds these days comes from his friends in Lost Creek. And he's ruined his relationship with all of them.

The priest eventually gets up and takes both cups away with him, disappearing into a room at the far end of the building.

Several thoughts occur to Nate all at once. He should cancel his bank cards. He has no way of getting out of here without his car or money. He should call Richie Hope and apologize for missing work. And he should check in on Madison, Owen and Brody. But he can't bring himself to do any of those things.

Minutes tick by silently as he sits alone with his thoughts, until a strange sound behind him makes him frown. He recognizes it, but he can't place it. Not here.

After a few seconds, a dog barks. Nate freezes. The sound he recognized was a dog's toenails hitting a wooden floor. Tears spring to his eyes. He slowly turns around in his seat.

Brody is standing well away from him, eyeing him reproachfully. Nate's never been so happy to see someone he knows. He has to choke back a sob. "Hey, boy. How did you get here?"

Brody won't come any closer. He offers a belligerent grunt and shake of the head. Then Nate notices Vince Rader slowly making his way down the center aisle. He takes a deep breath, touched that Vince came to find him. He has a second of disappointment that it's not Madison, but it's probably for the best. He has no idea what he would say to her. How to explain the black hole he's in.

When Vince nears, Nate silently stands. His friend pulls him in for a long hug. When he finally lets go, Vince says, "Of all the places you could've gone to, it had to be a damn church, didn't it?" He smiles. "Haven't you had enough of these places?"

Nate smiles with relief as he wipes his damp eyes. "I'm nothing if not predictable." He sits down and motions for Vince to join him on the pew. When he glances back at Brody, the dog hasn't moved. He's glaring at Nate.

"He's mad at you," says Vince, looking over his shoulder. "And rightfully so. What were you *thinking*, Nate?"

Shame burns his face. "I wasn't. All I knew was that I had to exit my life immediately. I almost..." He can't finish the thought.

Vince places a hand on his back briefly. "Well, I'm glad you didn't. Your damn dog's eating me out of house and home, so it's time for you to come back and face your responsibilities."

Nate doesn't know what to say. Somehow, disappointing the dog feels as bad as disappointing Madison. He hopes he hasn't broken Brody's trust in him.

When Nate makes no attempt to get up, Vince says, "You know, I've been to this part of town before."

Nate looks at him. "Fairview? How come?"

"Well, not here exactly, but to nearby Holcomb. When I was younger. I wanted to see where the Clutters were murdered. I visited their graves and even took a photo of them." He slowly shakes his head. "Seems disrespectful now. But I get it. I understand the public and media interest in shocking crimes and people like you. I know why people watch documentaries and follow breaking news. It's the same reason I host my *Crime and Dine* podcast. People want to understand what makes these killers tick, and they want to protect themselves from becoming victims. I understand why you, as a death row exoneree, would appeal to that audience. Especially as you've never given a single interview since your release. No one knows what you're thinking, who you blame and how you coped." He inhales. "But it's all gotten out of hand over the last five or ten years. Social media is full of assholes who make money from exploiting the victims. They point the finger of suspicion at whoever they want, which ruins that person's life as well as that of the victim's family."

Nate listens.

"I came across a woman online the other day who calls herself a *spiritual detective*," says Vince, spitting the title. "She has no law enforcement background or qualifications. She tells her followers she's communicating with the victims of a horrific quadruple murder, and that the young children who died have told her how it felt, and who struck the fatal blows. She even names someone as the killer. The damn woman's derailed the entire criminal investigation with her lies. The detectives on the case were forced to issue denials of everything she claimed, but it was too late for the man she pointed the finger at. He was hounded by some of her forty-five thousand followers until he killed himself."

Nate's shocked. He's never used social media for himself, although he has some fake accounts to access information. He needs them as a PI. "People follow that crap?"

Vince looks at him. "They don't just follow it; they believe every word these armchair detectives spew as if it's gospel. And the entire time this woman is making thousands of dollars from the platform. She's earning money from the children's murders."

It's unthinkable. Nate wonders how many people are profiting from his own misfortune by lying about him and claiming to have inside information about his case.

"I was so horrified by her that I've decided to end the podcast."

Nate's surprised. "Seriously?" He knows Vince set it up in response to his wife and grandson going missing. They were gone for six years until Madison, with Nate's help, found them. Vince's enthusiasm for the podcast waned after he buried Ruby.

Vince nods. "But not before one last interview." He turns to Nate. "I have a way of getting the media off your back. You and me in conversation. The interview they've all been waiting for. How about it? Give them something that will stop the speculation and the lies. The *truth* behind the salacious headlines. It doesn't have to be long, and you don't have to go into any detail. Just something to stop the harassment. Then I can end the podcast for good, and you can start fresh.'

Nate lowers his eyes. The thought of talking about the last twenty years fills him with dread. He's a deeply private person. He hates attention. But he accepts he's in the spotlight either way. "But how can I go home? Madison won't want me back. I've let her down too many times."

Vince waves a dismissive hand. "Oh, please. We all know you two are meant to be together, so just get out of this place and into your damn car. Fate will take care of the rest."

Nate smiles. He feels a tiny shred of hope for the first time in weeks. Could he still reverse his terrible decision to walk out on his life? "My brother stole my car and bank cards."

Vince surprises him by laughing. "My God, Monroe. You've got the worst luck in the world. With a family like yours, who needs enemies, right?"

Nate scoffs. "Wait till I tell you about my sister."

They laugh together, which feels strange but good, as if a weight has lifted from his shoulders and a darkness from his soul.

Standing, Vince says, "We'll call your bank and cancel your

cards, then get out of Kansas and maybe do the interview at a hotel on the way home. I have my equipment with me. You need to sober up and shower before you see Madison. If she sees you like this, she'd be well within her rights to call off the engagement." He smiles. "Let's get out of here. You must be starving."

He is. And Vince is offering him a way out of his black hole, so how could he not give him an interview? It makes sense. It might make people finally lose interest in him when they realize how boring he is. He probably should've agreed to it when Vince first asked, back when he first arrived in Lost Creek with Madison to look for Owen. But he and Vince weren't friends then, so Nate didn't trust him. Now he's trusting him with his life.

When Nate looks at Brody, the dog sits up straight. "Come here, boy." He wants Brody's approval, but the dog disobeys him. Instead, he turns and runs for the exit, glancing back at Nate all the way as if he wants him to follow.

"Why won't he come to me?" says Nate.

"He probably wants to get you far away from this place."

Vince walks ahead as Nate stops to glance back at the rosary on the pew. He thinks about taking it with him, but decides he no longer needs it.

He follows Brody outside. The daylight stings his eyes and his head throbs with every step. At Vince's pickup truck, Brody dodges his touch. Nate is bitterly disappointed the dog doesn't want petting. He opens the passenger door and slides inside. Brody eventually jumps in, and the minute Vince starts the engine, the big dog bounds onto Nate's lap and almost suffocates him with wet kisses and a mouthful of fur. His body wriggles with happiness. It makes Nate well up. He buries his face in Brody's fur and hugs him close.

"He wanted to make sure you agreed to come home with us

before he forgave you," says Vince. "He's a good boy." He pulls out of the church's parking lot.

Nate doesn't feel worthy of Brody's forgiveness. He keeps his wet face buried. "He's the *best* boy."

CHAPTER FORTY

Madison and Steve arrive back at the station a little over an hour after leaving George Marsh's house, having sped the entire way. Madison has a couple of missed texts from Kate Flynn. Her friend has concerns about Rob Hammond, the construction worker who found Bianca's remains.

Despite the site being closed for the investigation, he keeps returning to the open grave. That's weird, right?

The second text makes Madison frown.

OMG. He's brought flowers this time! Can you confirm whether he's a suspect?

His behavior does sound a little creepy, and she wonders if the flowers are roses. She tells Steve about it.

"That's interesting," he says, "because I had a message saying Hammond wants to talk to one of us about a theory he has. Maybe he's trying to insert himself into the investigation.

He could be the killer returning to the scene to relive the thrill of the crime."

"It's possible," she says. "But he didn't seem the type to me. Maybe he's traumatized by what he found. We should ask patrol to go along and clear him from the site. See how he responds to that. If he doesn't like it, we should speak with him."

"Sure. I'll ask dispatch to send someone over. They can check if the flowers are red roses."

She smiles. Great minds think alike.

Before leaving, he adds, "I checked out the site's former and present owners. Neither has a criminal background or anything that raises red flags. The current owner answered all my questions without hesitation and didn't appear to be hiding anything."

Madison nods, and when Steve leaves to talk to dispatch, she replies to Kate.

He's not a suspect right now but thanks for letting me know. We're sending officers to move him away.

She slips her phone away as Steve rejoins her.

"Stella's sending a couple of units over there," he says. "She'll let me know how Hammond reacts."

Chief Mendes greets them outside her office with a grim look. She leads them to the briefing room, where some of the team are waiting for them.

"What's wrong?" says Madison as Mendes closes the door behind them. "Not another body?"

"No," says the chief. "I've had Captain Henshaw from the Prospect Springs PD on my back. He's understandably annoyed that we didn't tell his department we'd identified Bianca Marsh before you visited her father."

"There wasn't time," says Madison, which isn't exactly true.

But she didn't want to wait for them before talking to Bianca's family. They might not have wanted her and Steve to break the news.

"Listen," says Mendes. "They're taking over that case."

"*What?*" Madison and Steve say in unison.

Mendes holds up a hand. "They're a larger PD than us, so they have the resources, plus the victim disappeared from their jurisdiction. We can offer help if they require it, but we need to focus on just two cases: John Doe and Toby Clark." She doesn't stop to give Madison time to react. "It's been four days since John Doe was discovered and we still haven't identified him, never mind got a lead on his killer. The press is making us look bad, so we need to put all our energy into that, and only follow credible leads on the Toby Clark case." She pauses. "In fact, Nate's good at cold cases; why don't you see if he'll share some of that workload?"

Madison bristles. Not only because no one but Steve knows Nate's taken off, but also because the chief has the audacity to imply Nate should help them without being on the payroll.

"Where's your engagement ring, Detective Harper?" asks Officer Kent. She's standing with Officer Sanchez.

Madison gives her a look that suggests it's none of her business. "It's with the jeweler to be resized."

Kent scoffs. "That's what celebrities say when they've split from their partner and don't want anyone to know."

Sanchez stifles a laugh.

Madison doesn't think Kent means anything by it, but it's irritating all the same. The young woman has a habit of speaking without thinking first.

Thankfully, Steve changes the subject for her. "How are we supposed to identify John Doe with no missing person report, no prints, no teeth and no crime scene?"

"With police work, Detective," replies Mendes sternly. "How else?"

"What about the photo of Bianca Marsh that was put on my car?" says Madison, not letting that case go. "We need to find the person who did that, as they're clearly involved somehow. Alex found an eyelash in the envelope. He's sent it for testing."

With a deep breath, the chief says, "Send the photo to the PSPD. And if the eyelash turns out to be useful, they can follow that lead." She crosses her arms over her chest, ready to change the subject before Madison can interrupt. "While I have you all here, you should know that Dr. Lena Scott has resigned from her post as medical examiner."

Madison glances at Steve. His face reddens.

"How come?" asks Officer Sanchez, surprised as the rest of them.

"We're not sure." Mendes won't meet Madison's gaze, as she doesn't want Steve to know they've discussed what Lena's done to him. "It appears she's decided to leave town at short notice. Her apartment has been emptied of personal belongings and she left rent behind for the landlord with a note saying she won't be returning. Perhaps she found a better job elsewhere. She's previously made it clear to some of us that she hasn't been happy for a while now."

Madison suspects Lena has fled town to avoid charges. Maybe her boss called her after Mendes told him about the allegations. The officers stare at Steve. They must wonder whether he knew she was going to leave. Maybe they'll assume the couple had a nasty breakup. Steve tries to keep his expression neutral, which must be difficult. He's probably relieved Lena's gone, but Madison would prefer to see the woman locked up for what she's done.

The door opens and Conrad appears. "Sorry to interrupt, folks. Is now a good time?"

"Yes. Come on in," says the chief. To the room, she says, "Dr. Stevens has agreed to cover Lena's job until a permanent replacement can be found."

"Thanks for stepping in at short notice," says Madison, relieved they don't have to wait for the position to be filled.

"Oh, not at all," he says. "It's an exciting town you have here. One day you're dealing with a terrifying serial killer, and the next, your medical examiner mysteriously takes off in the night without a word to anyone!"

Madison resists another glance at Steve.

"You know, I think I'd rather enjoy living here," Conrad continues. "It would probably test my skills no end. And Dr. Scott's assistants are professional while also being fun to work with."

"Me and Corey hang out with them sometimes," says Kent. "Skylar's cool, but I think Jeff irritates Corey."

Officer Sanchez smiles. "Corey thinks Jeff only hangs out with you both because he's interested in *you*."

Madison suspects Officer Fuller has feelings for her too, from the way he seems protective of her around other men.

"Well, duh," says Kent. "He's only human, right?" She laughs. No one can accuse her of having low self-esteem. It comes off as endearing rather than annoying, though, because of her bubbly personality.

Chief Mendes gets the conversation back on track by smiling at Conrad. "Well, the town obviously needs a full-time medical examiner, so how about I put in a good word for you? I'm sure I wouldn't be the only person here who would appreciate someone with your credentials and experience helping us with our homicide investigations."

Conrad beams at her. "How could I resist?"

Madison wonders if he's spent time living in the UK, as he reminds her of Alex in many ways. He has an American accent, but he's careful and precise with his words, almost imitating a British person. Perhaps he has British parents. Either way, he's clearly enamored with Chief Mendes.

"Now, on to more pressing matters," he says. "I've carefully examined Bianca Marsh's remains and found that her spine is shattered, which suggests she was shot, possibly from behind. And from studying the bone fractures, I'm almost certain she was moved *after* her death and not killed at the construction site."

"Apparently, we're not working that case anymore," says Steve.

Conrad looks at Mendes. "Oh. Should I send my report to the PSPD?"

"Please," says the chief. "Bianca's family can then have her remains moved to a funeral home."

"Will do," he says. "It may not be relevant to you anymore, but you should probably know that internal markings to her pubic bone suggest she gave birth during her short lifetime."

Madison closes her eyes briefly. Bianca's abductor must have impregnated her during her captivity. It doesn't bear thinking about. The PSPD will need to tell her poor father. She looks at Conrad. "Just once?"

"I wouldn't be able to tell how often, I'm afraid."

"I wonder what happened to the child," says Adams.

"Her killer could be raising them," says Madison.

"Assuming they're alive," says Steve. "Maybe Bianca's killer didn't want kids and that's why he murdered her. He could've killed the baby too. Buried it separately."

"We'll make sure the PSPD knows," says the chief, shooting Madison a look that suggests she shouldn't focus on that case.

Madison wonders whether Rob Hammond has any connections to Prospect Springs. He could've been Bianca's neighbor or a family friend. Since Mendes doesn't want them working the case, though, she can't question him. But she can pass his name to the detectives in charge of the case. Especially if he gives the officers any trouble when he's asked to move on.

"I also autopsied Ralph Smith in Dr. Scott's absence," says Conrad. "His cause of death was asphyxiation due to hanging.

The tox results will take some time, but he had an enlarged liver with signs of cirrhosis, suggesting he was a heavy drinker. I found nothing to suggest foul play from a third party."

Madison will need to call Smith's brother, Stanley, to confirm the cause of death. It's surprising he hasn't already gotten in touch for an update.

All of a sudden, the officers' radios come to life, making everyone freeze. Sanchez turns his up and they suddenly hear cries of "Officer down! Officer down!"

It's Officer Fuller's voice.

Madison's blood runs cold. She pulls the door open and races out of the room, heading straight to dispatch, with Steve close behind. "What's going on?" she says.

Stella's already standing. "Officer Fuller has reported shots fired at the construction site on Cliff Road. That's all I know so far. He beat Officer Vickers there and must've engaged the suspect alone." She swallows as the others join them. "I've asked for more details, but he's stopped responding."

Goosebumps break out across Madison's arms. "Get EMS there immediately!" she says.

Officers Kent and Sanchez are racing out of the station ahead of the rest of them, determined to reach their friend before something terrible happens.

Madison hopes they're not too late.

CHAPTER FORTY-ONE

Madison is the third person to arrive at the construction site after Officers Vickers and Sanchez. They're losing daylight now and the sky is overcast. The rain is holding off, but signs of the inevitable evening chill are already creeping in, with a low mist spreading over the ground. Her headlights illuminate the scene ahead of her. A bouquet of pink carnations sits atop Bianca Marsh's open grave. Nearby, twenty-seven-year-old Officer Corey Fuller is lying face-down in a pool of his own blood.

"Oh God. No." She forces herself out of the car just as Sanchez reaches Corey. She looks around with her weapon drawn. Rob Hammond appears to have fled the scene, but she keeps her weapon raised anyway. He could be lurking nearby. "Is he breathing?" she shouts to Sanchez.

"No. He's been shot in the armpit. Commencing CPR."

Madison takes a deep, steadying breath. He can't die. He's only been with the department for two and a half months, having arrived fresh from the academy. She blinks back tears as she imagines Owen lying in his place. An overwhelming urge to forbid her son to enroll in the police academy takes hold of her. She doesn't ever want to find him like this. It would kill her.

She turns to Shelley, who's visibly shaken. "He wasn't on a solo patrol, was he?"

"No, but he beat me here. I told him to hold back until I arrived." She joins Sanchez and helps him pull Fuller's bullet-proof vest off before applying pressure to his wound.

Madison leans into Sanchez's cruiser to use the radio. When she has Stella's attention, she says, "Officer Fuller has a gunshot wound under his arm and he's currently unresponsive. Sanchez is working on him. Where's the ambulance?"

"One minute away," says Stella. "I'll update them."

"Copy that." Madison drops the radio as Officer Kent arrives. Her cruiser skids to a halt nearby, and she jumps out of the car, racing toward Fuller. "Corey!" She kneels beside him but doesn't get in the way of Sanchez's compressions. "Corey, can you hear me?"

The ambulance arrives, but before the EMTs make it over to them, Rob Hammond appears from the shadows. Madison spots him first. He's holding his weapon out and aiming it at her. "Stop right there!" she yells at him. "Lower your weapon, *now*."

The EMTs, Jake Rubio and Rita Mellor, see him but ignore the danger. They approach Officer Fuller a little slower than they normally would, cautiously glancing between Fuller and Hammond. When they reach the young officer, they silently take over from Sanchez, who leans back on his heels, sweaty and tired. "He has a faint pulse now," he tells them.

Shelley stays still, her face drained of blood. If Fuller dies, she'll blame herself.

Madison takes a step toward Hammond. "Put the gun down, sir. We won't hurt you if you drop your weapon."

Hammond appears to be crying. "I'm sorry. I never meant to hurt him. He tried to make me leave but I don't want to go. Is he okay?"

"Not at the moment, no. Put your weapon down on the ground *immediately*."

"Oh God!" Hammond's hands fly to his head. He seems genuinely upset at what he's done. But he doesn't drop his weapon. He appears not to be in control of his emotions, which makes him a threat to all of them right now.

Madison uses the opportunity to fire at him. Her shot hits his arm, sending him flying backward. He screams in pain but doesn't go down completely. He holds his weapon up with his good arm. "Why did you do that?" he yells, on his knees. "I wasn't going to hurt anyone else!"

She grips her gun a little tighter. "Drop your weapon *now* or I'll fire again."

"But I want to talk about the girl you found."

Madison tenses. How does he know the remains were female? "Did you put her there?"

"No! I wanted to pay my respects, that's all. It *was* a girl, right? It always is. The story never changes."

She ignores him. "Why did you leave a message with dispatch to ask for a detective to call you?"

He winces at the pain in his arm. "Because I wanted to know who she was so I could send her family a card and some flowers."

Madison swallows. She has no way of knowing whether he's telling the truth. "Mr. Hammond? Do you know who killed her?"

Struggling to his feet, he gestures to Fuller with his weapon. "If he dies, I'll go to prison, right?"

"Detective?" says Jake Rubio behind her. "We need to get him to the hospital. Is it safe to leave?"

Madison doesn't dare look at Jake. She needs to keep her eyes on Hammond.

"What are you doing?" yells Hammond. "Keep your hands where I can see them."

He's shouting in Sanchez's direction. Madison risks a quick

glance behind her. Sanchez's hand rests on his holster, near his weapon. Officer Kent is leaning close to Corey and whispering reassurances into his ear.

Madison tries to figure out the best course of action to get everyone out of here alive. "Mr. Hammond, if you drop your weapon, one of the EMTs can get the injured officer to the hospital while the other one stays behind to fix your arm. Officer Fuller is less likely to die if you let them leave."

Hammond looks at Fuller lying still on the ground. "You're tricking me. He's already dead. I can tell. Which means I'm going to prison." Before Madison can say another word, he puts his gun to his temple and shoots himself.

"No!" yells Madison, sprinting toward him.

"Oh, shit," says Sanchez. He quickly gets up and joins her, but there's no point. Hammond is dead.

"We're leaving," shouts Jake over his shoulder as he and Rita slip a board under Officer Fuller and load him into the ambulance. "He has a pulse. I'll let you know what happens."

Rita stays behind to check on Hammond. Officer Kent slips into the driver's seat of the ambulance and Jake gets in the back with Fuller so he can keep working on him. The ambulance drives away, leaving Shelley standing alone, unsure what to do.

Madison looks at her and Sanchez. "Are you guys okay?"

Shelley nods uncertainly.

Sanchez wipes his bloody hands on his uniform. "Are you?" he asks.

She doesn't respond. Rob Hammond isn't the first person to take his own life in front of her, and no doubt he won't be the last. It's shocking for sure, and she wishes she could've stopped him, but what she can't help focusing on is how easily Hammond chose to shoot a police officer in an attempt to solve his problems. She can't get the image of her wounded son out of her head, even though it didn't happen to Owen. Because she knows that if he does become a cop, his life will be at the mercy of unpredictable and unstable people like Rob Hammond. And even though she does the same job, it's only now her son wants to follow in her footsteps that she realizes how terrifying that actually is.

CHAPTER FORTY-TWO

Time captive: 11 years 9 months

Eugene is sick again, and too afraid to go to the doctor this time because he can't afford more treatment. She's tried healing him using several holistic options based on information he researches online, but they don't seem to be working. It's distressing to watch him lose so much weight. She never expected to miss his protruding belly, but she does.

He tries to put on a brave face and focus on their son, but she watches him from the corner of her eye and regularly sees his mask slip. He's worried. Which means she is too.

While he naps, she goes to Macy's room and unlocks the door. Macy is sitting on the bed, cradling the baby. The positive pregnancy test sits beside her. She must've been dwelling on it. Dwelling on the next baby and wondering how many more Eugene wants from her. She'd announced the news last night. Eugene's delighted that Macy is pregnant again so soon. Their boy is only three months old. Once baby number two arrives, they're done with her. She's too belligerent. It's time she... leaves them.

She enters the room. It's raining out, and the gray clouds combined with the blinds on the window mean Macy has her light on. The bulb casts an orange hue over the room.

She forces a smile and sits next to the girl, who looks like she wants to move away. The baby is staring up at Macy like she's his entire world. A stab of jealousy hits her. "My turn." She takes the baby from her and cradles him in her arms. He's beautiful. His big blue eyes stare up at her now instead, and he flashes her his toothless gums. He knows who his real mother is, but they have to allow Macy time with him so he's well-adjusted. Plus, she's still breastfeeding, which is good for him.

He grasps her thumb in his tiny fingers while his inquisitive eyes search her face. She thinks he smiles, but it could be wishful thinking. She doesn't know much about child development and has to learn on the job, but she *does* know that her heart is full of love for the boy, and she can't wait for the day she and Eugene are alone with their children, to watch them grow up together.

A ball of dread weighs heavy in her stomach. When she pictures this baby's future, she gets a mental block. She can only visualize him as a baby, no older. Perhaps because she knows he won't be allowed outside to play. He won't go to school and make friends. He'll reach an age where he questions why they stay inside all day, every day. Unless Eugene allows him to go places with him. After all, just because he doesn't let the females out of the house doesn't mean he won't let his son out. Overwhelmed by a creeping sensation of fear for their future, she tries to focus on the here and now.

"Has he eaten?" she asks.

Macy nods. "He was hungry today. I'm wiped out."

She tries not to roll her eyes. Macy is always complaining. She has a negative outlook on everything. It's exhausting. "How's our girl?" She nods to Macy's stomach.

Macy bristles. "I don't know why you're so sure it's a girl."

She shrugs. "Just a sixth sense, I guess."

"Is Eugene sleeping?"

"Yeah."

Macy stands. She appears nervous, like she wants to say something that she knows won't go down well.

"What's the matter with you?"

Macy swallows before taking a deep breath. Quietly, she says, "Who *were* you? Do you remember your real name?"

She looks the girl in the eye. "You should make dinner. He'll be awake soon."

Macy returns to the bed. "Please," she whispers. "Please can we just have one real conversation? I need to tell someone what I'm thinking, or I'll go mad."

She doesn't want to hear what the young woman has to say. She looks at the baby in her arms. "He's getting so big. It won't be long before—"

"Stop it!" hisses Macy. "Please, stop it! I can't live here forever. I just can't. How can you let these babies grow up in this house? With that *monster!*"

She snaps her head up to look at the young upstart. "You better shut up or you'll be in trouble."

"I'm already in trouble, and so are you! How long have you been here? What's your real name? My name's *not* Macy, it's Claire! You may have gotten used to this life, but I never will." Her tone softens as she adds, "Let's help each other get out of here. We're smarter than him. We can go back to our families."

"Eugene *is* my family." She lowers her eyes to the baby. "So is this little one."

Macy grabs the child out of her arms in frustration. "No, he is not! He's *my* baby, not yours. Stop deluding yourself. You're as bad as *he* is."

She stands and slaps the girl hard across the face. "You're the delusional one."

Macy's face burns red. "He'll be dead soon anyway. Then

what? We'll need money to feed ourselves. You'll need to get a job. And while you're at work, I'll escape. I'll—"

Unable to listen to such terrible predictions, she pulls the baby away from Macy and rushes out the door, hastily locking it behind her before the girl can follow.

"What's going on?" Eugene's awake.

She enters his room with the baby, who's gurgling contently. She sets him on the bed next to his father and then slips in beside them. "He wanted to see you."

Eugene's face lights up. He pulls the baby to his chest and tenderly kisses his head. "Hey, you! How's my boy?"

The baby coos as his father tickles his neck.

She smiles. He's been an excellent father so far, and he's looking forward to the birth of their daughter. She ignores the sound of Macy's sobbing from next door. She has to. Because it stirs something in her that she doesn't want to acknowledge.

CHAPTER FORTY-THREE

After noticing several missed calls from Owen—reporters turned up at the construction site shortly after the shots were fired, and it's now headline news that an LCPD officer's life is in the balance—Madison called him to confirm she was safe before returning to the station to debrief the rest of the team about Rob Hammond's suicide. Rita was unable to do anything for him, as the gunshot wound to the head killed him instantly. He's now being transported to the morgue.

A somber mood has settled over the station as they wait for news from the hospital. Chief Mendes is on her way there to meet with Officer Fuller's family. They all know Fuller's dad from search-and-rescue operations, and there's not a single person on the team who isn't praying his son pulls through. Madison understands that Officer Kent hasn't left his side.

She collapses onto the seat at her desk and ignores the messages from reporters seeking information. That can wait. Chief Mendes can hold a press conference when she returns from the hospital.

Sergeant Adams has already left for the day, as has Officer Shelley Vickers, who wasn't fit to stay on duty. She's been told to expect a call from the department therapist, who'll offer specialist support over the coming days. Madison and Sanchez have been offered support too.

Steve joins her. "Hey. It's been a hell of a week. You should go home, get some sleep."

She smiles sadly. "You don't have to tell me twice." She wants to see Owen. To try to talk him out of becoming a cop. Before she gets up, she asks quietly, "How do you feel about Lena fleeing town?"

He perches on the corner of her desk and folds his arms. "Relieved, mostly. I just hope that's the end of it, and she isn't planning something stupid."

Madison tries to bite her tongue, but she can't. "I understand your relief at the thought of never seeing her again, but we can't let her get away with what she did to you, Steve. I can still look for her ex-boyfriend, and I think her assistants will provide statements to say how she—"

He's shaking his head. "No. Not right now. Give me some time to come to terms with everything that's happened. Maybe then I'll be angry. But right now, I can't. I don't even want to think about it." He lowers his eyes. "Sorry. I know I've gone about the whole situation wrong from start to finish. In some ways, it's given me a new appreciation of what our DV victims go through. I can see why they're so reluctant to file a report or to leave their partner. The whole experience has been humiliating and confusing."

She leans back in her seat to look at him. He doesn't want to be pressed, so she has to let it go. "Okay," she says softly. "Let's give it time. But the minute you—"

"I know." He smiles down at her and rests a hand on her shoulder. "Don't worry, I know. Thanks for your support. I didn't have anyone else to go to."

"Of course." His weary expression makes her want to cry. He knows what he should do about Lena, and he feels bad that he isn't up to it. Not yet. "At least Brody's safe now she's gone."

Steve removes his hand. "I don't believe he bit her. I think she was just trying to hurt you."

Madison shakes her head. If Lena faked the dog bite, there's something seriously wrong with her.

"She pursued me," he says quietly. "She must've known I was weak and that she could get away with it."

"No," says Madison. "It's got nothing to do with who you are. It's all about *her*. Don't blame yourself."

He nods, but he doesn't seem convinced. "I wish I'd never agreed to that first date." He pauses. "I wanted to ask you out instead."

Shocked, she laughs. "Yeah, right."

"I'm serious," he says. "I was planning to, but Nate beat me to it." He fixes his eyes on hers. "Who knows, maybe in the future, if he doesn't come back..." He doesn't finish the thought.

Madison feels herself blushing. She had no idea he was interested in her. It occurs to her then that if she'd never met Nate, she might have considered it. Steve's smart, attractive and easy-going. But she could never date someone she works so closely with. They'd have nothing but work to talk about. She attempts to lighten the mood and divert attention from her, saying, "Don't worry. I'll find you someone better than me and Lena." She smiles. "There's gotta be someone in Lost Creek who isn't as screwed up as us, right?"

He scoffs. "Nah, I'm good. I think I'm done with dating." He smiles, but she thinks he's embarrassed about opening up.

Alex suddenly appears, clutching Mrs. Pebbles in one hand and his cell phone in the other. "Detectives! I'm so glad you're still here." It's almost 8 p.m.

"What's wrong?" says Madison, eyeing the dog, who's looking at her suspiciously.

"I know we're not supposed to work on the Bianca Marsh

case," he says, "but the DNA results are back on the eyelash found with the photograph. I've found a match. But, well, the results are a little unexpected."

Madison's stomach lurches with dread. She has a feeling this latest development will complicate matters.

Steve stands. "What do you mean?" He absently strokes the tiny dog's head, making Mrs. Pebbles close her eyes with pleasure.

"The DNA from the eyelash matches that of a local girl, Claire Barlow," says Alex.

"Great," says Madison, standing. "Then let's go pay her a visit."

"That might be a problem," says Alex. "Because Claire was reported missing from her home four and a half years ago at the age of seventeen. She's not been seen since."

Madison sits back down. "*What?*"

"She was feared abducted. We have her DNA on record because it was taken from a hairbrush as part of the investigation into her disappearance. But she's no longer registered as missing because her father asked us to close the case. He believed she'd run away to live with a boy she met online."

She frowns. "That seems odd to me. He could've been lying. Maybe he tried to derail the investigation to divert attention from himself."

"Douglas and Bowers wouldn't have fallen for that," says Steve. "They would've looked into his claim, and for them to close the case, it must've been credible."

"True," she says, knowing that sometimes she's too quick to assume the worst of people. Detective Douglas especially would have immediately suspected Claire's father of wrongdoing, so the fact he agreed to close the missing person case suggests he exhausted all possible suspects.

"We need to pay her family a visit," says Steve. "See if she ever got in touch to tell them she was alive and well."

"Perhaps it wasn't Claire herself who put the photo on your car," says Alex. "Her eyelash could've been stuck to the photo if she was abducted by the same person as Bianca Marsh."

Madison takes a deep breath. He's right. "Huh. We can't exactly get in touch with her family until we know whether she's still alive. It's just going to upset them."

"Well, while you consider what to do," says Alex, "I have some more updates, but about our John Doe case this time."

Steve drags a chair over for Alex to sit in. Alex places the dog on his lap before continuing. "The shoe print found in the mud at the creek doesn't match any of Ralph Smith's shoes from his trailer. I took the liberty of asking Elaine Brown what size shoe she wears, and her feet are too small to be a match, as are her daughter's, obviously."

Madison wonders whether Kyle Davenport's shoes would match. She's yet to check whether Kyle was staying with Elaine and Willow the night the little girl discovered the headless body.

"As the print is a size ten," says Alex, "the person who discarded John Doe's corpse in the creek was probably male."

She nods. "Good to know. We can check Ralph's brother's shoe size." She cocks her head, thinking. "Or are twins' feet the same size?"

"Not necessarily," says Alex. "They can be different, the same as twins can be different heights too."

"Okay, well, I need to inform Stanley of Ralph's autopsy results anyway, so I can ask for his shoe size then. I also have someone else in mind." She explains about Kyle Davenport and how he's been installing cameras at the mobile home park, as well as being in a relationship with the witness who found the body.

"Sounds like a lot of coincidences to me," says Steve.

"I know, right? He has a co-worker I might approach before

speaking to Kyle. Jerry will tell me where Kyle was the night John Doe was dumped in the creek."

Steve looks at Alex. "Where are we at with the DNA samples taken from John Doe? Any closer to being able to check for comparisons to try to identify him?"

Alex strokes Mrs. Pebbles, who's contently curled up on his lap. "Nora's working on it, but I'll chase her for an update. As you know, that and the toxicology results take time, but with Conrad covering our autopsies now, I imagine she'll prioritize the results for us." Dr. Stevens is Nora's father.

"Let's hope so," says Madison. "Steve, could you locate the contact details for Claire Barlow's parents? We could visit them tomorrow." She glances at the clock. It's nearing nine. "It's getting late. They may as well get a full night's sleep before we break the news that their daughter may have been abducted by the same person who killed Bianca Marsh."

Steve nods, and he and Alex get up, leaving Madison to call Stanley Smith.

CHAPTER FORTY-FOUR

Stanley answers on the third ring. He sounds cautious. Perhaps he doesn't get a lot of calls. "Mr. Smith? It's Detective Harper. Do you have a minute?"

"Oh, hi, Detective. What's wrong?"

"I'm calling with your brother's autopsy results. Is now a good time to talk?" There's never a good time to receive this type of information, but hopefully he's somewhere private.

Stanley sighs heavily. "To tell you the truth, I don't know if I want to hear what you have to say."

It's not the first time someone's said that to Madison. A loved one's death is hard enough, but add to that an autopsy and a police investigation, and it pushes some people to the brink of their grief. They sometimes want to skip those parts and go straight to the funeral to try to end their nightmare sooner. Unfortunately, if they don't listen to the autopsy results, they'll find that later on in their grief they'll be hounded by unanswered questions about how their loved one died and whether it could've been prevented.

"I understand," she says. "And I'm sorry for your loss, but

hopefully, knowing how your brother died will bring some closure to the matter for you and your wider family."

He appears to consider it. "Fine. Let me sit down." She hears him exhale as he drops onto a chair. "Go ahead."

"Well, as suspected, the medical examiner has ruled your brother's death a suicide. He died of strangulation by ligature. I'm sorry."

Stanley's unconvinced. "He wouldn't have strangled himself. That's preposterous! How could anyone who wasn't present possibly know someone else didn't kill him?"

She understands the impulse to blame someone else, but he wouldn't question it if he'd seen how they found his brother. "We detected no evidence of foul play."

"Then it could've been that autoerotic thing. Maybe he was trying something new and died by accident."

She thinks about the porn mags found in Ralph's home. She has no idea whether Stanley knows about his brother's sexual fetishes. "I agree that might have been a possibility, but having seen how and where Ralph died, we believe he intentionally took his own life. You see, he'd taken photographs of a crime scene, and we think he was afraid he'd get into trouble for it."

"What crime scene?" Stanley sounds more guarded than confused.

"A body was found at the Aspen View Mobile Home Park shortly before Ralph died. You must've heard about it in the news? We found photos of the victim on your brother's cell phone, and a neighbor witnessed him taking them."

It takes a while for Stanley to respond. "Are you going to tell the media all the gory details so that my brother looks like some kind of sex freak? Or worse, a killer?"

"No," says Madison. "That's private. We can release his body to a funeral home now, so please get in touch with the medical examiner's office as soon as you're ready."

He scoffs. "I don't want anything to do with it."

She frowns. "I thought you were close to your twin?"

"I need to go. I'm busy. Bye."

Before he can hang up, she says, "Wait! I have more questions first, then you can go."

With a heavy sigh, he says, "Fine."

Taken aback by his attitude, she decides to ignore it in order to obtain information. "Do you know where your brother was during the weekend the victim was killed?"

"No."

"You didn't speak to him on the phone, or message with him, or—"

"I said no."

"Fine. Where were *you* during that time?"

He gasps. "How dare you! I'm nothing like my brother. I don't get off on seeing dead bodies, Detective, and I certainly did *not* kill that man."

"I didn't say you did," she says patiently. "But to rule you out as a person of interest, I need to know where you were. And what size shoe you wear."

He doesn't respond.

"If you don't tell me, I'll be forced to find out by other means."

He scoffs. "I'm a size eight. And that night I was with my boyfriend, Gary. We were at his place in Prospect Springs. We met online months ago, but that was our first physical meeting."

She writes it down, unsure whether she believes him. "Do you have any proof? Did anyone see you there?"

"How would I know?"

She's growing weary of his attitude. "I need Gary's number. I want to speak to him."

Stanley's tone changes. "Please don't call him. He might think I'm a criminal and leave me. It's all so new. I don't want to ruin things."

"Then find me someone else who can corroborate the fact

you were nowhere near your brother's place of residence the night our victim died. Think you can do that?"

"Yes," he says quickly. "Yes, I'm sure I can. I'll call you tomorrow."

"Fine."

Stanley ends the call before she can say goodbye, leaving Madison wondering whether she's just given him time to concoct a cover-up story.

CHAPTER FORTY-FIVE

When Madison finally arrives home from work, it's pitch black, and the house is lit from within. An unmarked truck is parked in the driveway next to Owen's car. She recognizes it as Kyle Davenport's. Her skin crawls as she wonders why he's come here without speaking to her first.

She gets out of her car and races inside, where Owen is pouring Kyle a cup of coffee.

"What's going on?" she asks.

"Hey, Mom." Owen comes in for a hug, something he wouldn't normally do upon her return from work. The news of Officer Fuller's brush with death must have scared him. "How's the officer?"

"He's at the hospital." She's reluctant to say more in front of their visitor. "Hi, Kyle. How come you're here?"

He points to the ceiling. "Your kitchen camera was faulty, so I've replaced it free of charge. It's still under warranty."

She doesn't move. How would he know it's faulty if he wasn't watching her? Maybe the camera automatically alerts him when it's broken. "I don't want it replaced."

Owen laughs. "Why not? You've paid for it."

She shrugs. "It made me uncomfortable knowing someone could watch us around the house." She drops her keys on the counter, suddenly wishing Brody were here with them.

"Sorry, I guess," says Kyle. "I can take it out completely if you want?" He doesn't seem to mind that she's reducing his opportunity to watch her.

She nods. "Thanks." It's plausible that he might already have other cameras elsewhere in the house. She wonders whether she's being paranoid again. Still, she wishes he'd phoned before turning up. Owen was too trusting to let him in. Looks like she needs to remind him about their increased risk of harm. How people may come to their house for nefarious reasons due to her job.

Movement behind her makes her turn. Jerry Clark emerges from the powder room, drying his hands on his pants. "Hey, Detective! Good to see you." He pulls out a pack of cigarettes. "Smoke?"

She finds herself nodding. It will give her a chance to speak to him. "Outside. I don't like smoke in the house." She glances at Kyle, who's climbing a footstool to reach the camera in the kitchen. Owen discreetly shrugs at her to indicate he's unsure why she's being weird about the cameras. She gives him a look to let him know she'll tell him later.

Outside, she takes a cigarette from Jerry and lets him light it for her before leaning against the porch railing. "How long have you known Kyle?"

He sucks on his cigarette before responding, his bleached-blond hair glowing under the overhead porch light. He's taller than her by at least five inches. "Only as long as I've worked for him, about four weeks."

"You like working with him?" She keeps her tone conversational.

"Oh, sure. I mean, I prefer being my own boss—who doesn't, right? But he's a cool guy."

"Were you two working on Sunday evening?" The night John Doe was dumped in the creek.

He gives her a look that says she's crazy to suggest it. "Detective, I do not work evenings. I need time to find a *Mrs. Jerry Clark*, and how would I do that if I'm working all hours?"

She laughs before sucking on the cigarette. The nicotine hit immediately helps her to relax her shoulders. "So how come you're here now at"—she checks the time on her phone—"nine thirty p.m.?"

"Well, that's different," he says. "First of all, it's a repair situation and we like to keep our customers happy, and secondly, it's you. *You* get special treatment."

She assumes he means because she's a cop. "But neither of you were working Sunday night?"

"Nope." He inhales on his cigarette. "Oh, by the way," he says, exhaling smoke. "I met your sister today!" He seems excited by it, but the thought fills her with dread.

"Oh yeah? How come?"

"We had a job at the trailer park where she lives. She came over to ask for a quote for a doorbell cam. Kyle told her we'd fixed your house up with cameras everywhere, and that's when I realized you two were related. I hope you don't mind me saying, but in my opinion, you got the looks in your family."

She raises a stern eyebrow.

"Well, er, and the intellect, of course," he says. "Which is just as attractive, if not more so."

She snorts at his compliment. He's a likable guy in a strange, innocent way that she's not used to. It occurs to her that if Jerry turns out to be a criminal mastermind, she'll never trust another person as long as she lives.

He leans in, resting a finger on his lips as he says, "Let me ask you a question if I may be so bold. Is there a *younger* Harper sister in town who might be looking for an eligible bachelor to wine and dine her?"

"Thankfully for me," she says, "no, there isn't."

Unfazed by her sarcasm, he grins. "You know, I'm feeling a little love-hate relationship vibe between us, Detective, similar to the famous enemies-to-lovers trope you girls love so much in your books. And I've gotta say, it's a yes from me."

Madison's surprised into laughter. She also finds herself inexplicably blushing. This guy must be seven or eight years younger than her, and although she would never go there, it's hilarious to think he's interested in her. Especially when she looks like she's been dragged through a hedge backward after a very long day at work. If Nate were here, she'd enjoy rehashing this conversation later over a glass of wine and teasing him that she has other options besides him. She thinks of what Steve said earlier tonight and realizes she wouldn't tell Nate about that. Somehow, that seems more serious. Jerry isn't a threat to Nate. Steve, on the other hand...

Kyle suddenly appears. "Stop sexually harassing the detective, Jerry."

"Yeah," she says with a smile. "Or I might lock you up."

Jerry winks at her. "Don't make promises you won't keep, Detective. Or can I call you Madison now? I feel like we're practically friends."

"Detective's good."

He laughs as he walks away. "You're so strict. I *love* it!"

She shakes her head as they get into Kyle's truck and leave. Now she knows that Kyle wasn't working on the night in question, *and* he somehow knew that she and Angie are related, he's worth looking into more closely.

She takes another puff of her cigarette and realizes she's been too busy to notice she hasn't heard from Vince since the early hours of this morning, when he'd texted to say he was leaving for Kansas. She pulls out her phone.

Have you found him yet?

She takes a few minutes to stare into the darkness, observing the quiet neighborhood as she waits for a reply. Is the person who put the photo on her car watching her now? Were they responsible for Bianca's death? Or is it Claire Barlow, the missing girl, who would be twenty-one years old now? She realizes tomorrow will be another tiring day as she searches for answers.

Her phone buzzes with a message from Vince.

We've got him. He's fine. We'll be home tomorrow.

A shiver goes through her. *Nate's coming home.* She becomes choked up as she imagines Brody's reaction to seeing his dad. It makes her worry about how *she'll* react. Work has been so busy that she hadn't let herself dwell on the outcome of Vince's journey to Kansas. The fact Nate is coming home suggests he might still want to be with her. Or it could mean he's coming back to say a proper goodbye and grab his belongings before moving on.

She blinks back tears as she considers what that would mean for her. She'd still have Owen, but what if she then loses him in the line of duty to a drunk driver or a violent encounter?

Exhaustion consumes her as she considers everything that could go wrong with their lives. Defeated, she stubs out the cigarette on the porch railing and heads inside.

CHAPTER FORTY-SIX

The next morning is bright and frosty, which lifts Madison's mood somewhat, especially as she has new leads to pursue in the John Doe case. But once she gets to her desk, her cell phone rings with a call from Gina Clark, immediately changing her mood. Now she feels guilty for not having the time to focus on finding Toby, because she has no updates for the poor woman.

Before answering, she nods in greeting at Adams, who arrives just after her.

"Any news on Fuller?" he asks, concerned.

She sighs. "He's stable, but he goes into surgery this morning." Chief Mendes texted her earlier with an update.

"Fingers crossed then." He shudders before removing his jacket. "Man, it's freezing out there." He heads for the kitchen.

She turns back to face her desk as she accepts Gina's call. "Hi, Gina."

"Hi. I saw you racing around town yesterday and then saw on the news about some guy killing himself where a body was found. Is it anything to do with Toby?"

She switches her computer on. "No, sorry. It was to do with a different case."

"Oh." She sounds disappointed. "Have you checked Facebook today for messages about Toby?"

"Not yet. But I can look now. Hold on a second." Madison feels bad. It must seem to Gina that she doesn't care about her missing son. She lowers her phone and opens the Facebook app. There are no messages, just several notifications about comments, which she'll read as soon as she's off the phone. Knowing that the comments are public and Gina would've alerted her to anything of interest, she assumes they're irrelevant. "No messages, I'm afraid. I'll post something today to try to get more interaction."

Gina's silent for a few seconds. "It's Toby's second birthday today," she says quietly. "Maybe you could post that?"

Madison's shoulders slump. She had no idea. Sure, she has Toby's date of birth on record, but she hadn't registered that his birthday was approaching. "It must be a difficult day for you. I'm sorry. We've had developments in another case that's eating into my time, so I hadn't realized he turns two today. I feel terrible."

"That's okay," says Gina. "I understand. I guess I've waited this long for answers, a little longer won't hurt."

Except Madison can tell it *is* hurting. Not for the first time, she wishes Nate were here to give the case the attention it deserves. That decides it for her. She's going to go ahead and offer a reward for information. Five thousand dollars. She can worry about securing the money if it ever comes to that. Once back in town, Nate will want to help. She's certain of it. Unless he's not staying.

"I'm going to offer a reward for information and see where that leads us." She glances at the clock. She needs to contact Claire Barlow's parents and update the Prospect Springs PD about what happened at Bianca Marsh's burial site yesterday. "I have to go, but I promise I'll keep you updated."

"Sure, sorry for bothering you."

Madison feels terrible. "Gina, you're not bothering me. You're keeping the pressure on me to look for your son, which is fine." She has an idea. "How about we hold a vigil for Toby later tonight? I'll invite the press and announce the reward for information. It could spark new leads." It would also mean Gina isn't alone on her son's birthday.

"That would be nice," says Gina, sniffing back tears.

Madison smiles sadly. "I'll be in touch later with a time and place. Take care of yourself, okay? Today's going to be extra tough for you."

Gina hangs up, too upset to say goodbye. Madison drops her phone on her desk and exhales loudly as she leans back in her seat. "This job sucks."

Adams approaches from behind and hands her a cup of coffee. "Here. This'll help."

She looks at him wide-eyed with disbelief as he sits at his desk. "Do you realize that this is the first time you've *ever* made me coffee?" They've worked together for thirteen months.

He grins at her. "Don't get any ideas. It doesn't mean we're dating or anything."

She laughs. "Thank God for that."

She opens Facebook on her computer and writes a new post explaining how Toby turns two today, and a vigil will be held later to mark the occasion. She decides against mentioning the reward yet, as she should probably run it by Chief Mendes first, plus she wants to make a poster to grab people's attention while they're scrolling through their feeds. It also gives her something to announce to the press at the vigil later.

She sips her coffee as she reads the comments on her earlier post. People are speculating about what happened to Toby, and tagging their friends when they recognize the street where Gina lived at the time, or if they think he looks like someone they know. It's good. Word is spreading.

Steve approaches. He looks more refreshed today, like he's finally managed the first good night's sleep in months.

She turns in her seat. "How did Rob Hammond's family take the news?" Steve drew the short straw and had gone to see them last night to inform them that Hammond was deceased.

"He had an ex-wife, but no kids or parents." He takes a seat next to her. "His ex said he was a loner who was hard to love. She wasn't surprised he'd killed himself, but she was shocked when I told her he shot Fuller beforehand. She didn't think he was capable of hurting anyone else. Sounds like he had self-esteem issues. He'd struggled with his mental health over the years, apparently."

"Did you run a background check on him?" she asks.

"Yeah, he was clean. That doesn't mean he didn't kill Bianca Marsh, though. It was odd how he took flowers to a stranger's grave."

"Are officers still searching his house?"

He nods. "It'll be interesting to see whether they find anything linking him to Bianca or Claire Barlow."

Madison updates him on Gina's call and shows him the Facebook account for Toby Clark.

"Do you have any leads at all?" he asks.

"Not really. I'm kind of at the mercy of someone getting in touch with information. It's weird that we've had no tips about the case at all, right? Normally, *someone* gets in touch to offer outlandish theories or to point the finger at someone they have a beef with."

"It's been eighteen months since his disappearance. Too much time has passed," he says. "People don't care as much about finding someone if they think they're already dead."

She nods. It's true, which is what makes cold cases so difficult to solve. "I feel so guilty whenever Gina calls that I've offered to organize a vigil for this evening." She sighs. "It's impossible to work on this case when we need to figure out who killed John Doe. Especially as the Bianca Marsh case distracted us. We still need to visit Claire Barlow's parents and update the Prospect Springs PD on everything. They need to know Rob Hammond makes a good person of interest."

"I can do that," says Steve. "Leave it with me."

She looks at him. "Are you sure?"

"Of course. Spend the morning working on leads for the Toby Clark case. I'll focus on John Doe and Bianca Marsh."

Swamped with relief, she says, "Great, thanks. I've been thinking about contacting the hospital where Toby was born. Gina's social circle was basically nonexistent, which means it's likely the only people she and Toby came into contact with were health workers. Maybe someone at the hospital remembers a visit they made, or someone creepy who used to work there. She could've unwittingly interacted with a sex offender."

Steve nods. "It's worth a shot." He heads to his desk, leaving her to call the hospital.

CHAPTER FORTY-SEVEN

Madison doesn't have any luck with the local hospital. The employee she talks to claims they don't have any records for Gina or Toby Clark. "That's impossible. Can you check again, please?"

"Fine. Hold on." The woman in patient records exudes attitude. Madison's already had to jump through hoops just to confirm who she is so that the hospital doesn't inadvertently provide confidential information illegally, which she fully supports, but the woman could've done it with less of a chip on her shoulder.

"I've rechecked." The employee sighs heavily down the line. "As expected, I was right. You must have the wrong hospital. Goodbye." The line goes dead.

"What the...?" Madison looks at her phone. "She hung up on me!"

Adams snorts behind his computer monitor. "She must be having a worse day than you."

Madison's tempted to call back and ask for the woman's manager, but she doesn't have time to be a bitch about it.

Besides, she must be right, which means Madison wrongly assumed Gina gave birth at the local hospital. It must've been elsewhere. She leans to one side to talk to Adams, who's stuffing his face with cookies dunked in coffee. "Do me a favor. Get me a copy of Toby Clark's birth certificate. He's two years old today. If he wasn't born in Lost Creek, try Prospect Springs."

"I'm busy!" he says, spitting crumbs.

"Yeah, I can see." She leans over and steals a cookie. "*Now*, please." Unease settles over her as she absently crunches on the cookie, but she's unsure why.

She texts Vince to ask if she can hold a vigil outside his diner tonight for Gina and Toby. He replies immediately.

Sure! What time?

She's uncertain, as she doesn't know when he'll be back.

What time are you three getting home?

Her stomach flips with a mix of excitement and dread at seeing Nate again. Vince replies quickly.

Probably by eight. Is that too late?

That gives her plenty of time to work beforehand.

That's perfect. See you soon.

Then she adds:

Tell Nate I can't wait to see him.

As he's without his cell phone, she hasn't been able to reassure Nate that she's happy he's coming home despite how he left her.

She receives just a thumbs-up from Vince. She was hoping he'd respond with a reply from Nate, something like *He can't wait to see you either* or *He's desperate to make it up to you.* Disappointed, she drops her phone on the desk. She wonders why they're still in Kansas. By her calculation, they won't be leaving until after lunchtime. What would keep them there that long? Perhaps they've stopped halfway for a break, or maybe Nate needed some persuading.

The pitter-patter of tiny feet nearby makes her look up. Mrs. Pebbles is doing zoomies around the office. After a few seconds, Alex appears, chasing her and glancing at Chief Mendes's office.

"Don't worry," says Madison, amused. "She's at the hospital."

Steve moves his chair back from his desk and picks the dog up. She circles his lap while licking his face excitedly.

"Good," says Alex, relieved. "This dog could give Houdini a run for his money. No cage can hold her." He catches his breath. "I'm assuming there's no update on Officer Fuller's condition yet?"

Madison shakes her head. "Not until he's out of surgery." Her cell phone rings. It's Gina. She frowns, wondering why she's calling again so soon. She turns back to her desk and accepts the call. "Hi, Gina. Is everything okay?"

"I'm too upset to attend a vigil." It's clear from the thickness of her voice that she's been crying. "I can't go. I'm sorry. I just want to be alone today."

Madison suspects she's going to drink. "I don't think that's the best thing for you. Not today."

"*Please.* I need to be alone."

She can't force the woman to attend, so she has no choice

but to agree. "Maybe tomorrow then. But before you go, I need to know where Toby was born. I thought it was the local hospital, but they couldn't find any records for you."

"It wasn't there."

Madison grabs a pen. "Where was it?"

"Why does it even matter? He's dead, isn't he? I should just accept it, right?" The young woman sobs hard down the phone. It's unsurprising that today would stir up more emotions.

"Gina?" Madison says softly. "Please don't give up hope. I hate to hear you like this." When she keeps crying, Madison tries to reassure her. "I'm spending all day on the case today. I promise I'll find somewhere to start. Which hospital did you give birth at? I want to check whether anyone there might've shown a special interest in the pair of you. Was there a particular person he would see regularly?"

"I can't do this," sobs Gina. "I wish I'd never come to you. It's making my anxiety worse. This is why I never told the police in the first place." The line goes dead.

Madison's shoulders slump. She rests her phone on the desk, unsure how to help her.

"Is she okay?" asks Steve.

"No." She stands and looks at Adams. "Any luck on that birth certificate?"

He looks up at her. "I can't find any record of a Toby Clark born in Lost Creek, Gold Rock or Prospect Springs two years ago today."

Madison frowns. "Gina said he wasn't born at the local hospital, but didn't say where she had him." Her sense of unease grows. Earlier, Gina said she'd seen Madison racing around town yesterday. She thinks of the car that's been following her this week. She'd assumed it was her sister, but what if it was Gina? "Why would *she* follow me?" she mutters.

Alex and Steve look puzzled.

Adams is typing fast on his computer. "What's Gina's DOB?"

Madison pulls open the case file. "April thirtieth, 1991."

Adams enters it on his screen before shaking his head. "I can't find a record of her birth either. Let me try the DMV." He takes a minute to check before shaking his head. "She's not registered with the DMV either, which means she doesn't have a driver's license."

"What?" Confused, Madison says, "But she drives a Honda. I've seen her in it. She drove to and from my house."

Adams shrugs. "She must be registered under a different name."

Madison tries to think. She might use a previous last name. Maybe she was once married, or renounced her family name after her mother disowned her. Another explanation occurs to her. One that doesn't bear thinking about. "Surely not."

"What?" say Adams and Steve in unison.

She sits down as she considers it. The fact they can't find a record of Gina and Toby's names. The lack of leads. The lack of witnesses coming forward to say they knew the young woman. Usually, someone comes out of the woodwork to provide information in a missing child case. Even just well-meaning do-gooders hoping to help the investigation in some small way. But this time, they've had nothing. It's unheard of.

"Oh God, no." All kinds of thoughts are running through her head. She looks up at Adams, Steve and Alex, who are staring at her, confused. Mrs. Pebbles jumps down and starts sniffing Adams's feet like she wants to urinate on him. "What if Gina's suffering from a psychological condition, and that's not her real name and date of birth? What if Toby doesn't even exist?"

Adams exhales, running a hand through his hair. "That would be, well, insane."

"That could be why no one has come forward to provide a

lead, she says. "Because if he's a figment of her imagination and never existed, he never vanished, right?"

Steve folds his arms over his chest. "Or perhaps he did exist, but he died as a baby, and she's never gotten over it."

Madison shakes her head. "That's probably more likely, but it would still be horrendous."

"We need to pay her a visit and ask what's going on," says Steve. "Because she's obviously been lying to you."

Madison's reluctant because of how upset Gina was on the phone. She doesn't want to push her too hard but agrees it's the only way to get answers in this sorry situation. "I don't know where she is right now." She thumbs through the case file she set up for Toby. "Shit!"

"What?" says Adams.

"I didn't ask for her address during our first meeting. I guess I got bogged down by the details of the case instead." And at that time, she was initially under the impression Gina had filed a missing person report back when Toby vanished, in which case all her personal details would already be on their system.

"Well, that sucks," he says, "because we have no birth certificate or driver's license for her either. You've never visited her at home?"

"No, she always came here." She's starting to feel anxious about Gina having been in *her* home. She even met Owen briefly. "You don't think she's dangerous, do you?" She looks at each of them in turn.

Only Alex offers a ray of hope. "If she has a mental health issue, she's probably just confused and needs help. Perhaps she's off her meds and in desperate need of a psychiatric evaluation. I'm sure if you called her and asked her to meet you here, she'd willingly turn up. Perhaps she'd even explain everything once you tell her we know her name isn't Gina."

She can't understand why the woman would use a false name. If she really isn't who she says she is, that's a problem, because it means she's lied to law enforcement, and not just once. But for what reason? "She ate lunch at my house." Looking at Alex, she says, "Had I known then that something was up, I could've brought her dirty dishes in for you to extract her prints. She might be using a fake name because she has a criminal record."

Alex looks like he's thinking about something. "Wait here a second." He disappears. Mrs. Pebbles watches him go with her ears raised before taking off in his direction as if they're playing hide-and-go-seek.

A surge of adrenaline makes Madison's hands shake. She feels like she's been fooled, and she's worried about how the young woman will react to being confronted. If Gina isn't well and Toby doesn't exist, Madison will try to get her help, but she's concerned that Toby *is* real, and if so, he might be in danger, but not from a stranger. From Gina herself.

She shoots Owen a quick text.

If that woman I was having lunch with when you arrived home comes to the house, do NOT open the door! She might be dangerous.

Stella from dispatch joins them. She's clutching the cross around her neck with one hand. "I've just spoken to the chief. She says Corey's out of surgery and in recovery, still unconscious. But they managed to remove the bullet."

"Thank goodness for that," says Madison. She gets a thumbs-up response from Owen on her phone. It makes her feel better to know he's seen it.

"Is Kent still at the hospital with him?" asks Adams.

"No," says Stella. "The chief sent her home. She'll be back on duty tomorrow morning. I imagine she's beside herself with worry."

He nods. He'll need to find cover for her night shift later.

Madison's phone rings. It's Kate Flynn. She hasn't spoken to her friend in a while and feels bad for declining her call again, but Kate will understand. There's no way Madison can comment on the Toby Clark case right now, and even if Kate's calling for an update on their other cases, she'll likely mention it at some point. She slips her phone away and says to Steve, "Kate Flynn's trying to get in touch. It could be about Fuller's condition, but I think it's best we don't speak to any press right now." She looks at Stella. "Just tell them we're busy, and we'll provide updates as soon as we have any developments."

Stella nods. "Got it." She returns to her cubicle as Alex comes racing back to them, out of breath. His office is on the other side of the building. One day, Madison will ask Chief Mendes to move him closer.

"I have Gina's prints," he pants. Mrs. Pebbles starts yapping as she approaches at speed behind him, tail high, her little legs working overtime. She's having the time of her life.

"What?" says Steve. "How the hell did you manage that?"

Madison gasps as she remembers. "The dog's water bowl!"

Alex nods, smiling, "Exactly. Gina picked up Mrs. Pebbles's water bowl after I dropped it in the kitchen. So I just ran the prints through the system and found a match."

Madison braces herself to learn she's been sympathizing with a criminal.

"Sergeant Adams is correct," Alex continues. "She's been lying to us, but it's not what you think." He looks at a sheet of paper in his hand. "She's not Gina Clark. Her name is Amber Nelson, and she was reported missing thirteen and a half years ago, on her sixteenth birthday. She was never found."

Goosebumps break out across Madison's arms.

"Amber Nelson?" Adams seems confused. "But I checked all our missing person cases for teenagers when Bianca Marsh's bones were discovered, and her name didn't come up." He grabs the piece of paper from Alex, and as he reads it, he turns pale. "Shit. I entered the wrong end date for the search by one year."

Madison bites her tongue. Just when Adams seems to be getting better at his job, this happens. Still, she knows it doesn't really matter, as they weren't looking for any other girls. They didn't know Gina was lying to them. Her heart hammers in her chest as she struggles to understand. "Just what the hell is going on?"

CHAPTER FORTY-EIGHT

Time captive: 11 years 11 months

She grips the landline and listens to Eugene wheeze down the line.

"I'm not coming home this time, sweetheart. The doc says I've got a week at best, maybe less. They're not letting me out. Truth be told, I wouldn't get very far even if they did." He sounds weak.

Blood roars in her ears as her world comes crashing down. When Eugene couldn't ignore his decline any longer, he got a cab to the hospital. That was three days ago. She barely slept as she waited to hear from him. She spent the entire time focusing on their son, with the help of vodka.

"Don't say that, Eugene. You need to fight."

"If it was a case of fighting, I'd be home in a heartbeat." He sighs wheezily. "We have to face facts, my love. I'm done for."

She breaks down so hard she has to put the baby on the bed. She can't remember a time when she felt so alone. So sad. When she pulls herself together, she picks up the phone. "What do I do without you?"

"I have a plan in place, don't worry. I called my brother. He's been to see me." He stops to catch his breath. "We've made amends, and he's settling some legal arrangements for me. I've explained everything."

Alarmed, she says, "*Everything?*"

"Everything," he replies. "I've given him the keys to the house. He knows he'll find you, Macy and our boy there. He's the boy's uncle. He can help you raise him."

She feels bile at the back of her throat. "But you always said he was bad. That if he ever got his hands on me—"

Eugene laughs softly. "Now, don't you worry about that. He likes them young, so he'll be more interested in Macy. You have my word on that. And his. I made him promise he wouldn't touch you. He knows he needs to take care of you and the babies. I've signed over the house as an incentive to do the right thing by you."

She tenses. What kind of man needs a financial incentive to stop him from harming women?

"I can't leave my house to you because you wouldn't know what to do with it," he continues. "And you'd need to get a job to support everyone, which is preposterous given all you're good for is cleaning and cooking. Besides, you have no ID or social security number. My brother can support you so that you're free to raise our children. He'll take good care of you as long as you do what he says. But be careful what you say around him. He doesn't have the same dark sense of humor that you and I do. He might take things personally."

Dread fills her stomach. She doesn't want to have to walk on eggshells around anyone. She had enough of that when she lived with her father. "Wasn't he shocked about me and Macy? Didn't he ask why you never told him you were married with a child?"

Eugene hesitates before gently saying, "I've never told you about my family, sweetheart, and with good reason. Our father... he wasn't a good person. My brother takes after him in a lot of ways. Let's just say that makes him unshockable."

She frowns. She doesn't understand what he's saying, but goosebumps run down her arms. "What will I do without you?"

"You'll mother our children the best you can. Don't you dare remarry, though. I'll haunt you from the grave." He attempts a laugh. It turns into a cough. "I'm tired, Macy. You need to let me go."

Funny, she remembers telling him the same thing once. A long time ago now. She ignores the name confusion. He can't help getting her and Macy confused in his current condition. "I'm scared," she says. "I don't like change, and Macy hates me."

"My brother will see to it that she falls in line, don't you worry about that." A strangled sob comes from him. "I just wish I could've lived to see my baby girl born."

Tears stream down her face. It's not fair. He's only forty-five. That's too young to die.

Pulling himself together, he says, "Just promise me you'll never go down to the basement, okay? *Promise* me. No good can come of you going down there."

She has no interest in the stupid basement. "I promise. But what if your brother goes down there?"

He takes a deep breath and releases it before replying. "Well, that's okay. He can. You can't. Got that?"

She nods, even though he can't see her.

"I'll call you again in the morning, okay, sweetheart? I want to keep calling until the end. There's so much I still need to tell you. I owe you an apology."

"You don't! I'm glad you brought me to live with you."

"Not for that," he says quietly. "For something else."

"Okay," she whispers. She doesn't understand but can tell he's too tired to explain now.

"I love you with all my heart."

She breaks down. "I love you too, Eugene." She puts the

phone down and stares into space while the baby cries uncontrollably.

"Is everything okay?" Macy's voice comes from next door.

She needs some time to herself, so she picks the baby up and goes to Macy's room, fumbling for the key in her pocket with her spare hand. The little boy's cries get louder, upsetting her. She can't deal with it right now. When the door opens, Macy is waiting. She takes the baby. "What's happening with Eugene?"

"He's dying. We'll never see him again."

"Oh my God." Macy's face drains of blood. "I'm so sorry." She steps forward and hugs her, squishing the baby between them.

It feels nice to be hugged, but the baby's crying is relentless. "Please make him stop."

Macy nods. "I'll put him in his playpen downstairs. Stay here and get some sleep. Can I fetch you anything? Water? Coffee?"

She should tell her about who's coming to take Eugene's place, but she's too exhausted. Numbness is spreading through her mind. She'd like nothing more than a stiff drink and some time alone in her marital bed before Eugene's brother gets here. "Bring me my drink. Then I'll nap. Please keep him quiet. He's making my brain ache."

"I will. Give me a second while I take him down and use the bathroom. I'll be right back."

Grabbing Macy's arm before she leaves, she says, "You won't get out. He took the house keys with him. I'll hear you if you try anything. I'm a light sleeper."

Macy looks her dead in the eye as she says, "I never needed to escape from *you*." She smiles reassuringly before taking the baby downstairs.

Unsure she believes her, but relieved at the fading noise, she goes to her bed and lies down. She hears the TV go on downstairs and a cartoon play. Macy turns it down so it's not too loud. Within a few minutes, she's back with a bottle of vodka and a glass already half full. She hands it over. "Yell if you need anything at all, okay?"

She nods. "Thanks." Before Macy can leave, she says, "It hasn't been that bad living with us, has it?"

Macy's expression softens. "I won't lie, it was scary at first. But I've gotten used to it. Having the baby helps. You're so good to him that I've grown to love you like a sister." She turns and leaves.

The first drink goes down too fast, so she pours another. That goes down equally fast. As she lies there looking up at the familiar cracks in the ceiling, she thinks of Eugene's frail body wasting away in an uncomfortable bed, surrounded by strangers.

Their beautiful baby boy is all she has left of him now.

CHAPTER FORTY-NINE

Madison peers closely at the photo on her computer screen of Amber Nelson, abducted the night before she turned sixteen. Her father reported her missing, which means Gina lied about her father dying when she was young and leaving her strictly religious mother a widow. In the photo, Amber has long blonde hair, a deep summer tan and a wide smile that shows her perfect white teeth, unstained by age. She looks nothing like Gina Clark at first glance. Gina is thirteen years older, with lank dark hair, a ghostly complexion, sunken under-eye circles and stained teeth. She also doesn't smile much. "So she's a missing person who never thought to tell us she wasn't missing anymore," says Madison, utterly confused.

"Just like Claire Barlow," says Steve. "Who, since we've never found a body, I think we can assume is alive and placed the photo of Bianca Marsh on your car. That's why it had her eyelash in the envelope."

Trying to piece everything together, Madison says, "So did they vanish together? Maybe they were friends who conspired to run away."

Adams is checking the notes on his computer. "Impossible.

They disappeared separately. Amber—or Gina—in July 2007, and Claire in June 2016."

"So there's no way they knew each other, right?" she says, puzzled.

Alex picks his dog up as she yawns. She's tired herself out. "It seems Gina *was* a victim of something," he says, "but not because her baby was abducted. Unless that really did happen, and the boy was born under a different name, like her."

A terrible thought occurs to Madison. "There are three of them."

"What do you mean?" asks Steve.

She looks at him. "What if all three girls were abducted by the same person and held captive in some kind of house of horrors? Amber Nelson, Claire Barlow and Bianca Marsh." She tries to piece together a theory. "Bianca was abducted from her home in July 2008. From Prospect Springs, not Lost Creek, but it's worth considering because she was found *here*, and if Conrad's correct, when she was killed she was three or four years older than when she was abducted, suggesting someone held her captive." A shudder goes through her at the thought. "And the photograph of Bianca had 'Sofia. Day 1' scribbled on the back. The asshole renamed her. He called Bianca *Sofia*." She gasps. "That could be why Gina doesn't call herself Amber. If she was also held captive, he could've renamed her too. Claire Barlow could also be living under a different name."

Alex considers it. "It's certainly possible, but how come two of them are free now? Because if you're right, their captor killed Bianca. Why not kill the other two as well?"

Madison crosses her arms as she thinks. "The obvious answer is that the asshole died, giving the girls a chance to escape. But I don't know why they wouldn't call the police as soon as they were free."

"Or go see their parents," says Steve.

"Perhaps they were afraid of something, or someone," says

Alex. "Maybe he instilled the fear of death into them and told them someone would look for them if they ever got out."

She nods. It's plausible. Being held captive would have made them vulnerable, and with no evidence that their captor was lying, they could have believed whatever he told them. She thinks about everything Gina's disclosed about her life. Most of it was lies. It must have been. That's the only logical explanation for the lack of leads in this case. She sighs. It's frustrating to think she's been working from false information. Wasting her time. But then why would Gina even approach her for help in the first place?

Perhaps some of her story is true. Either way, it's up to them to figure out which parts.

"Gina implied she was reclusive," she says, desperately trying to think. "Is that because she spent so long captive? I mean, it's been over a decade since she vanished. Did she grow accustomed to her isolation? To her captor?" It doesn't bear thinking about.

"We need proof," says Steve. "Where do we start?"

Her mind buzzes with different ways to approach this new, horrifying theory. "I don't want to spook Gina by telling her we know her real name. She might go into hiding and never get the help she needs. And for all we know, Toby could be real and in danger."

It occurs to her then that Toby might have been born out of rape. He probably wasn't the result of a one-night stand as Gina had made out. Her captor might have forced her into giving him a child. After all, there was evidence from Bianca's autopsy that she had carried at least one baby. Madison feels sick at the thought.

"I think Toby's real." She feels the blood drain from her face as she considers whether Gina is unstable enough to hurt the baby in response to what she must have experienced in captivity. "But I don't know why she no longer has him and why she wouldn't tell me who she really is."

"Her abductor could've had help," says Steve. "Claire and Gina could've been threatened with that person coming after them if they ever got away."

"Perhaps they killed their captor to escape," suggests Alex. "That would explain why they didn't come straight to the police or go home to their families. They're terrified of being arrested for murder."

"That would also explain why Gina never reported Toby's disappearance," Madison says.

Steve looks like he's thought of something else. "What if Toby was taken by the person sent to find her and Claire? That might explain why she's come to you now. She might be using us to get to that person and her baby."

Madison shakes her head in disbelief. "This entire situation is horrendous. We need to find that poor child. We should split up and visit the girls' parents. Gina told me her mother moved away and her father died when she was young, but as her father reported her missing, she was obviously lying. Presumably neither set of parents knows their daughter is still alive, because they've never gotten in touch to notify us of the fact. We need to tell them our theory about what happened and see if there's anyone they can think of who showed the girls a little too much attention before they vanished."

Steve stands. "I'll visit Claire Barlow's father. He was the one who told Detective Douglas to close the missing person case as he believed she'd run away."

"Take a uniform with you."

He frowns. "Why?"

"Because it could've been him who abducted these girls. It would explain why he told us to close the case. I'll track down Gina's parents and see what I can learn from them." The thought fills her with dread. On the one hand, they'll be ecstatic that their daughter is alive and well, and that they're now grand-parents. But on the other hand, they'll learn she might have been held against her will all this time, with terrible things done to her, *and* that their grandson is missing. On top of that, Gina chose not to return home to them the first opportunity she had. She's been brainwashed to believe she needs to isolate herself from her loved ones forever. She may have even committed murder to escape her ordeal.

Madison thinks of Nate's boss. Richie Hope could probably get Gina and Claire off a murder charge given the circum-stances. If there was ever a case for self-defense, this is it.

Adams hands her a piece of paper. "Gina's father is called Thomas Nelson. This is his address. Remember, her real name is Amber Nelson."

She grabs it. "Got it. Thanks. Update Chief Mendes for us."

She quickly follows Steve out of the station.

CHAPTER FIFTY

Time captive: 11 years 11 months

The sound of heavy footsteps on the stairs wakes her. She jumps, making the large vodka bottle roll off the bed and hit the floor. It's empty. She hadn't meant to drink the whole bottle. The side of her face feels wet. How long has she slept for? Her dry mouth makes it difficult to swallow.

Through blurry eyes, thick with sleep, the bedside clock tells her it's almost 7 p.m., but it was 7:15 p.m. when she came to lie down. Has she slept for *twenty-four hours*?

The footsteps reach her door. A man appears. Goosebumps break out over her arms. He's tall and slim, dressed in a black T-shirt with blue jeans. He has mean eyes. "You've gotta be kidding me."

"What's the matter?" she croaks.

He smiles strangely. "I didn't believe Eugene when he told me."

Annoyed, she sits up. "What do you mean?"

"Nothing. I recognize you, that's all. Amber Nelson, right? I always wondered what happened to you. How come you were never found." When she doesn't respond, he adds, "I saw you on the news, years ago. I heard you went missing, but I had no idea you were here all this time."

She frowns. "I was on the news?" Does that mean her dad *did* look for her? But why would he look for her if he paid Eugene to kill her? Her hungover brain won't work fast enough. This is only the fourth person she's spoken to in twelve years, and one of those was a baby.

Eugene's brother slowly enters the room, inquisitively peering at their belongings. He doesn't appear outraged or horrified that Eugene kept women locked up. But he also doesn't seem upset at his brother's imminent death.

"Will Eugene call me this evening?" she asks.

He turns to look at her, a little too fast. "He's dead. Happened this morning."

She gasps. "No."

He nods. "'Fraid so."

She feels dizzy, so she rests her head against the pillow. Her husband's dead. It's over. She's too dehydrated to cry, but her eyes prick all the same.

"Which means I'm responsible for you now." He approaches her. "Did Eugene tell you about me?"

She thinks he's trying to scare her, but she's past that emotion. Nothing scares her anymore. She wipes her dry eyes. "He told me he left the house to you, and that you're going to take good care of us."

He sits on the bed and rests a hand on her bare thigh. She hadn't even gotten under the covers before she blacked out yesterday. He strokes her skin gently, getting higher each time, his hand going back and forth until he's under her skirt.

She tenses. "Eugene said you're not to touch me. You're to have Macy. She's younger. Pretty, too. You'll like her." She frowns as she thinks. "Where is she?"

Eugene's brother stops stroking. "What do you mean?"

"Macy. She'll tell you her name is Claire, but ignore her." When he shrugs as if confused, she says, "Didn't you see her downstairs? With the baby?"

He stands. "No. I thought she was locked away somewhere. Are you telling me she's allowed to roam the house like a damn pet?"

She swings her legs off the bed, with dread squeezing her lungs. The house sounds too quiet. The baby isn't crying. It's been twenty-four hours since Macy took the baby downstairs. She hadn't thought to lock the girl away while she slept. She'd been upset from her last conversation with Eugene. She stands, going dizzy again from getting up too fast. "There's no way she got out of the house, because Eugene had those with him." She gestures to the keys in the guy's hand.

He leaves the room, so she follows him. Macy's not in her room, or the spare room. The bathroom door is wide open. It's empty. They rush downstairs. The living room is empty, and the TV is off.

Her heart hammers in her chest. "We have to find them." She runs into the kitchen. Nothing. The hallway is dark from a lack of windows, but even in the dim light she can tell the large oak bookcase on the far wall has been moved. Its contents have been neatly placed on the floor to make it lighter. "What the hell?"

Eugene's brother quickly squeezes by her and goes to the end of the hallway. He peers behind the bookcase. "There's a door."

Her stomach flips with dread. "No, there isn't. This house only has one door to the outside."

He opens it, and the hallway is flooded with evening sunshine.

She gasps. All this time, there was another exit. One not as well secured as the front door. The wood is flimsy. The oak bookcase was doing most of the work. She could've escaped years ago during one of Eugene's trips into town. Her heart almost stops as she realizes she didn't even try to search for a way out of here.

She rushes toward the stranger. "Macy's *gone*. And she's taken my baby!"

CHAPTER FIFTY-ONE

Amber Nelson's childhood home is a well-maintained two-story building surrounded by trees and a wide lawn. The neighbors are spaced far apart, so it would be easy to avoid getting to know them if you're that way inclined.

Madison gets out of her car and squints at the sun's reflection bouncing off the windows. It may be sunny, but it's bitterly cold. She shivers as she glances around the quiet neighborhood. The neighbors' driveways are empty, but there's an SUV parked on Thomas Nelson's, signaling someone is home. She crosses the sidewalk, approaches the front door and knocks hard. While she waits for a response, she imagines Gina as a child riding her bike up and down the street with her friends. Perhaps she played out front on the lawn while her parents attended to the rosebushes and shrubs.

She cranes her neck forward. She steps off the paving slab and onto the lawn, heading toward a dense row of leafless rosebushes. It's not the right season for blooms, unless you get your flowers from a florist, but it makes her think of their John Doe and the rose forced down his throat. Mainly because there are so many rosebushes in this garden. She spins around. They line every border.

A horrible feeling creeps over her. She returns to the stoop and knocks again. Still no answer. Moving to the large window, she peers inside and sees a spotless kitchen. The internal door is closed, so she can't see the rest of the house, but there are no signs of a struggle in this room. It makes her wonder whether Thomas is inside, hiding from her. Perhaps he already knows his daughter is alive and for some reason he doesn't want to discuss it with the police. Is that because *he* was the person who abducted her? Or is he helping Gina to avoid a murder charge?

Chills run through her as she reaches for her weapon. Something's wrong here. She heads around the house to the backyard. The rear of the property has mature shrubs and trees and a pleasant patio area with outdoor furniture covered for the winter. The only window she passes has heavy closed drapes obscuring her view of the inside. She goes to the windowless back door and tries the handle. It's unlocked. Something tells her to leave the door closed for now, so she removes her hand.

Backing away from the door while keeping her eyes on the property, she steps out of view and retrieves her cell phone. She calls dispatch, and when Stella answers, she keeps her voice low, saying, "I'm at Thomas Nelson's property. Send backup. I have a feeling something's wrong here, but I'm not sure what yet."

"Understood," says Stella. "Dispatching a unit now." Her voice is thick with emotion.

Madison's taken aback. "What's wrong?"

"Nothing. I'll tell you later."

Something's happened. Stella has maintained her composure in countless horrific situations, so whatever it is must be bad. Madison swallows. Her eyes brim with tears when it dawns on her. "He didn't die, did he?"

The other woman sniffs back tears, desperately trying to

remain professional. "Chief Mendes just called from the hospital to inform me that Officer Fuller has succumbed to his injuries." That's all she manages. The line goes quiet as she silently weeps.

Madison gasps. She slumps against the wall of the house. "Oh, Stella. I thought he was out of danger." Covering her mouth with one hand, she bites her tongue to stop from bawling.

Stella takes a deep breath to compose herself. "I know it's tough but concentrate on what you're doing. You need to remain alert. We'll give Corey a proper send-off in due course. I've dispatched Officer Sanchez to your location. He's already nearby."

Madison thinks of Fuller's first day in the department. He was brimming with excitement and nerves, and it was obvious he wanted to be a great cop. Her throat constricts with emotion. It's devastating that such a young officer was killed in the line of duty, and they can't even get justice for him because the asshole who shot him took his own life. One word keeps coming to her over and over. *Senseless*. His death was so senseless. He wasn't saving anyone at the time. He wasn't being a hero. He was simply responding to a callout. He asked Rob Hammond to move along. That's it. How are they supposed to make sense of the wasteful loss of one of their newest and youngest officers?

And what if it happens to Owen? What if that's how she loses her only child? She hasn't told anyone on the team yet that Owen wants to join them. Her eyes well up, so she squeezes them shut. She can't think about that now. Not here.

"Madison?" Stella's voice is stern now. "Keep it together. Now's not the time to lose focus. We haven't told the officers yet. Chief Mendes wants to do it when she returns from the hospital. Don't let Sanchez know. It'll distract him."

Madison nods. She wipes her eyes with her forearm. "I'm fine. Tell him I'm waiting around back."

"Understood," says Stella. "Be careful. We can't lose anyone else."

Madison ends the call, unable to speak. Normally, she would enter the house alone and face whatever danger awaited her, but not now. She's off her game. Instead, she listens for movement coming from inside as she waits for Sanchez to arrive. It's not long before his cruiser creeps up to the house. She takes a deep breath, preparing to act normal so the young officer doesn't know his friend has passed away.

"Hey," she says as he quietly approaches.

He smiles at her. "Hey. Stella says you requested backup."

"This is Amber Nelson's parents' house." She motions to the door. "We know her as Gina Clark. Did Stella fill you in on the background?"

He nods. "It's messed up. You came here to notify them their daughter is alive?"

"Right, but there's no answer, and the back door is unlocked. My gut tells me something's off, so I didn't enter alone."

He pulls his weapon. "Let's go."

She feels bad for withholding the information about Officer Fuller, but they have a job to do. She bangs on the back door. "This is the police! Make yourself known or we're coming in."

They wait a full minute. Nothing. The door is intact, and there are no signs of forced entry. She reaches for the handle and opens it slowly. They're immediately hit in the face with the foul smell of decomposition, followed by an escaping flurry of flies.

Madison turns her head, covering her nose. "Oh, man, that's bad."

Sanchez winces and digs a face mask out of his pocket. It won't do much good, but she understands the urge to cover his nose and mouth. Whoever is dead in here didn't die today, or even yesterday. The rancid odor has had time to infuse every soft furnishing in the house. They slip on some latex gloves, since they're probably entering a crime scene.

Sanchez radios dispatch and tells Stella to notify the medical examiner's office.

When he's done, Madison looks at him. "Ready?"

He nods, and she steps inside the house.

CHAPTER FIFTY-TWO

They tread carefully through the clean kitchen to reach the spacious, dimly lit living room. The TV is on but muted; the light from the screen casts flickering shadows around the room. Madison looks at the closed drapes. The table lamps are on, giving the room an orange hue. It suggests that whatever happened here occurred in the evening, while the victim was relaxing in front of the TV.

She looks around the room. The place hasn't been burglarized, as it appears at first glance that no items of value have been taken. The TV's still here, as well as a collection of guitars lined up against one wall and a cell phone and watch sitting on the coffee table. But there are clear signs of a disturbance. A side table has fallen against the couch, its contents spilled on the floor.

Sanchez goes to the hallway. "I'll check upstairs."

Her throat is heaving in reaction to the awful smell, so she goes to the drapes and pulls them open to reach the window. She disturbs a bunch of flies and has to swipe them away from her face, disgusted. They were likely born on whatever is rotting in this house. With one window open, there's a mad rush for an exit, but Madison knows that the smell will attract other flies *into* the house to lay their eggs on the flesh of the deceased.

When she turns back to face the living room, she gasps. What she had mistaken for a scatter cushion on an armchair in the corner of the room is a severed head and two crudely sawn-off hands. "Shit."

The head is shriveled up and pale from decomposition. The eyes have turned to mush and now house maggots. A bullet has opened the guy's forehead. She can tell it's a man, as the hair is short and receding. He has stubble on his jaw that will never grow any longer than it is now.

Madison swallows. The head belongs to their John Doe, which means they finally have a name for him. Since they're in Thomas Nelson's house, this is likely to be him. And now they know how he was killed.

Sanchez returns. "Nothing upstairs." He follows her gaze. "Whoa! What the hell?"

The mustard-colored rug under the armchair and coffee table is brown with dried blood, as is the wall behind the chair. Sanchez steps around it and pulls out a flashlight to get a better look at the head. With a gloved hand, he lifts the guy's top lip. "His teeth are intact. We should be able to confirm his identity easily enough."

"Radio Stella," she says. "Tell her to send Alex, and to let Steve know what we've found."

He nods before leaving, careful to avoid the blood on the ground. The armchair's fabric is saturated with it. A rope lies on the rug behind it, just poking out. They were right. This man was bound before being forced to ingest the rose found in his esophagus. Alex might be able to get trace evidence from the rope.

Madison looks at the floor for a shell casing but doesn't see anything. If it's here, Alex will find it. Her heart is heavy, because she needs to tell Gina her father is dead. The possibility that she killed him crosses her mind, but she doesn't understand what her motive would be. She tenses. Unless it was her father who held her captive, along with the other two girls. In which case, perhaps Gina wanted revenge. Perhaps Claire Barlow did too, and they did this together.

Overpowering a heavy six-foot-tall man and sawing his head and hands off before discarding his body miles away in a creek requires a lot of heavy lifting. She's never met Claire, but she doesn't think Gina is capable of that. Thoughts of Kyle Davenport cross her mind. He'd be physically capable of it. Does he even know Gina? Does his girlfriend, Elaine? The victim was dumped near Elaine's trailer. Does that mean anything? She thinks of Jerry Clark, Kyle's co-worker. He may share a last name with Gina, but he said he wasn't related, and she can't believe he'd be mixed up in something this bad. A chill goes through her at the thought.

Madison feels like she's missing the bigger picture. Something that only Gina can help her with. She's aware her feelings for the woman may be skewing her logic. She'd invited Gina into her home because she got under her skin. She wanted desperately to find her child. But if her name isn't even Gina, what else is she lying about?

Her cell phone rings, bringing her back to the violent scene before her. She turns away from the eyeless head and accepts the call without checking the caller ID.

"You've found him, haven't you?" It's Gina.

Madison's heart sinks. Gina already knows he's dead, which can only mean one thing. "Is it your father? Thomas Nelson? You're Amber Nelson, right?"

Gina clears her throat. "I don't like that name, so don't use it. *He* gave me that name. *He* ruined my life."

"Who, your father?" Madison is confused. "How did he ruin your life? Explain it to me. I want to help."

She's met with silence. She hears Sanchez on his radio outside. The house will soon be swarming with people trying to piece together what happened here.

"Did you kill your father?" she presses.

"He deserved what he got! I was merciful. He didn't suffer for long before I shot him. No one ever showed me any mercy!"

Madison wishes she would just tell her what her father did that was so bad, but Gina's not thinking straight right now, so she tries a different line of questioning. "Is Toby even real?"

"Of course he is! He's my son. I want him back more than anything."

Madison is both relieved and alarmed. "Then tell me what really happened. It's the only way I can help you."

The woman starts weeping, and it becomes clear she took no pleasure from killing her father. "You won't take my side. So much has happened. No one can understand. No one except Macy."

Madison frowns. "Macy? Is that Claire Barlow?"

"You know about *her*?" Gina sounds like she's disgusted with Claire. It suggests the young women aren't friends and they didn't commit this murder together.

Frustrated, Madison needs answers. "Come to the station. Or I'll come and see you if you tell me where you are. Just tell me the truth and I promise I'll do everything possible to find Toby. I won't touch another case until he's found. He'll be my one and only priority." She means it, too. She needs to get the woman psychological support and unravel this terrible mess if she's to find the infant.

Gina chokes back a sob. "I wish my husband was here to deal with all this. I miss him so much."

Madison blinks. "Your *husband*? You were married?" Gina

had told her previously that she "kind of" had a partner, but never mentioned a husband.

"He took care of everything. He loved me when no one else would."

She's piecing it together in her head, and suddenly everything snaps into place. When she realizes what Gina means, she feels overwhelming horror for the woman. "Do you mean the person who abducted you when you were a child? Did he make you marry him?"

"You make it sound so sordid." Gina's voice is hollow. "He was a good husband. I'd still be with him if he hadn't died of cancer when Toby was just six months old."

Madison closes her eyes as everything becomes clear. Gina spent so long with her captor that her situation became normal. She relied on him so heavily that she gave in and accepted it. They developed a sick, trauma-bonded relationship, and when he passed away, she was alone with their baby. "Gina, he wasn't your husband. He was your *captor*. He spent years grooming you." She thinks of the young woman's alcoholism. "Did he reward you with alcohol if you were good? If you did what he wanted?"

It takes a minute for Gina to reply, and when she does, she sounds uncertain. "No. He gave me gifts to show me how much he loved me. He'd buy treats for dessert and let me drink alcohol before and after sex in those early years, as he knew I found it difficult to be with him at first."

Madison could cry. It's a textbook case of grooming, and this woman has no idea what was happening to her. And how could she? She was a child when he took her. "He conditioned you," she says gently. "He was rewarding you for good behavior. And it's one hundred percent not your fault that you were taken in by it. Thousands of people are, because these predators are good at what they do."

"No." Gina doesn't even stop to consider that Madison could be right. "He wasn't a predator. He was my husband. And the father of my baby."

"So who is Claire?" Madison asks. "Or Macy?"

"Macy was our surrogate."

Her blood runs cold. "Your *what?*"

CHAPTER FIFTY-THREE

Madison tries to absorb the news that Toby doesn't belong to Gina. He's Claire Barlow's baby. "Is that who took him?" she says calmly, despite her heart hammering too hard. "Your surrogate?" She's beginning to realize that if Gina can pretend the young boy is hers in order to locate him, she probably lied about everything she ever told her.

"You need to find Macy and get my son back."

Softly, because Madison can't tell how stable this woman is anymore, she says, "But you just told me *Claire* is his biological mother. Did she agree to let you raise him, or was she forced to get pregnant?"

Sounding tired now, Gina says, "Her only purpose was to have our children. I've never even seen our daughter. Macy ran away before she gave birth."

Madison closes her eyes. There are *two* children involved. "What about Sofia?"

She's met with silence.

"We know that Sofia's real name was Bianca Marsh. We've found her remains. The medical examiner believes she'd carried a baby." She pauses. "Was Bianca another girl brought in to be a surrogate because you couldn't get pregnant?"

In a calm voice, Gina explains. "I preferred Sofia to Macy. She was quieter. But she didn't love her babies, so they died. We buried them on the property, a boy and a girl. Both were still-born, but their funerals were nice. Religious. Sofia said they died because they didn't want my husband as a father. It was a mean comment." Her tone is flat, as though the facts she's recounting happened in a dream or on a TV show. She's probably disassociated herself from the experience. "Sofia wanted to die, so she did. It was the kindest thing for her."

Madison rubs her forehead with her spare hand. Bianca was just fourteen when she was abducted and around seventeen or eighteen when killed. She birthed two babies during that time. Then, when she was no longer wanted by Gina's so-called husband, she was killed. Her throat is dry. How is she supposed to tell George Marsh what his daughter went through? Or about the grandchildren buried in shallow graves somewhere? She needs to find those babies and get them a proper burial.

"How much of what you told me is true?" she says wearily. "You and Toby didn't live on Brook Street, did you? There was no blonde girl in the drugstore with a little boy matching Toby's description, right?"

"No, but Macy is blonde. I wanted you to look for her."

"So there was no PI who shot himself before cancer took him? No one-night stand with a stranger, resulting in Toby's conception?" She shakes her head. "Was any of what you told me true?"

A minute ticks by before Gina responds. "I *was* drinking the night he vanished. I was upset that evening. I went to lie down. Macy brought me some vodka. I've always wondered whether she laced it with sleeping pills and that's why I slept for so long. When I woke, she had already fled with Toby."

Madison takes a deep breath. She has so many questions,

but fears Gina could hang up at any minute and then disappear for good, so she tries to concentrate on the most important ones. Gina hid the fact she was a missing person in order to get Toby back, but there's something she doesn't understand. "Why didn't you tell me about Macy so I could just look for her? Why all the lies?"

"I never knew her last name. Not her real one. And besides, if you got to her first, she'd tell you I wasn't Toby's real mother. She'd lie about me and my husband. That's why I followed you. I wanted to keep one step ahead of you, just long enough to take my baby back from her. If you find Macy before I do," she goes on, suddenly coming alive, "tell her she can keep the girl as long as I get my son back. That's fair, right? I spent six months loving him, raising him. Pouring all my hopes into him. Please make her see sense!" A sob escapes from her, and Madison can tell that during her horrific ordeal, Toby was her only ray of sunlight. Her heart aches for sixteen-year-old Amber Nelson. But that's not who she's talking to. Twenty-nine-year-old Gina Clark is the result of her suffering, and she's dangerous.

"You have to understand," Gina whispers down the line. "If I don't get him back, it means it was all for nothing. I endured years of loneliness and suffering for absolutely nothing. I can't live with that, so *please get my baby back!*" Her voice becomes shrill. She's reaching breaking point.

Madison's horrified by what Gina did to her father. And she's disgusted that she would try to take another woman's child and claim him as her own, but part of her still feels this poor woman was so badly mistreated by her captor that she's also a victim in all this. It's gut-wrenching to listen to her. She's unstable, and who wouldn't be after what she must have endured?

"You hate me now, don't you?" says Gina quietly. "I'm sad about that because I felt like we could've been friends. I *like* you. But now you want to lock me up and see me punished for what I've done."

"It's not up to me whether you get locked up," Madison says, suddenly exhausted.

"But if it was?" urges Gina.

Madison finds it difficult to respond, because the case is so complex. The perpetrator is both a killer and a victim. She swallows. "I feel like your punishment came before your crime. Being abducted and forced to live with a stranger for over a decade should be enough punishment for whatever you went on to do after, but in the eyes of the law, murder isn't acceptable, no matter what led to it."

Gina cries softly down the phone. "I never expected to turn out this way. I didn't ask for any of this."

Despite feeling terrible for her, Madison looks at the severed head and forces herself to focus, because there's a little boy's life at stake, and possibly a little girl's too. "Gina? Tell me who abducted you. Who was your husband? I need a name. It will help me find Toby." When there's no response, she tries something else. "Did he help you kill your father? Because I know you had help. I know you couldn't have done this alone."

Gina sniffs. "Within hours of my husband's death, my brother-in-law arrived to take over my care, exactly as my husband instructed him to."

Just when Madison thinks she's heard everything, Gina drops the bombshell that she never really escaped. Her captor died and left her to his brother. That must be who helped her kill her father and dump his body in the creek. Madison's knees give out at the shocking depravity Gina has endured. Even now, she's not free. She's still being held captive.

She perches on the nearby couch. Her grip on the phone tightens. "Why didn't his brother go to the police or take you home to your family once he realized you were a missing person?"

"Because I'm his sister-in-law. And he's Toby's uncle. He made a promise to his dying brother to take care of us. He let me live with him, but he's more relaxed than my husband was. I'm allowed out for short periods now, as long as I don't try to contact my so-called family. I have to sleep with him, of course, and act like his girlfriend. But he knew I'd been well trained. He knew I'd never tell anyone my real name or what happened to me. Why would I? I had nowhere to go. No one cared that I vanished."

Madison hears a car engine revving in the background and wonders where Gina is. It sounds like she's in her vehicle rather than a building, as the street noise is unmistakable.

"It was his idea to enlist your help," Gina continues. "He said the police were so dumb you'd lead us straight to Macy. That's why I've been following you: to try to figure out where she's hiding Toby. To try to beat you to him. But once I got to know you, I realized he was wrong about you. You're not dumb. You're just too busy to see what's right under your nose."

Madison takes the insults without comment. She's been listening carefully, hoping Gina would let slip the name of her dead husband or his brother, but she didn't. She was careful. "What are their names, Gina? Please let me help you. They've both done despicable things to you. You don't need to live with that man any longer. You can be free from everything that's happened. I can put you somewhere safe while we unravel everything and get justice for you."

Gina weeps down the line. "It's too late for that. You'll put me in prison. I can't live with that many people around me all day. It would kill me. I like solitude. I told you that already. That part was true. I just want my son. And once I have him back, I'm leaving Lost Creek behind for good."

The statement alarms Madison. She has to stop Gina from getting to Toby and his real mother before she does. "Your husband gave you the name Gina Clark, so I'm guessing his last name was Clark?"

Suddenly, the line goes dead, suggesting she's correct.

Madison runs out of the house, calling Sergeant Adams as she goes. When he answers, she says quickly, "Find me a list of every male from Lost Creek who died between sixteen and nineteen months ago with the last name of Clark. It's urgent." If they find him, they can trace who his brother is. She prays it's not Jerry Clark.

CHAPTER FIFTY-FOUR

Time captive: 13 years 5 months

Eugene's house has finally sold, eighteen months after his death. Having cleared most of his belongings already, she and her brother-in-law will today remove the final boxes and pieces of furniture they want to keep. It's difficult to return, as the house still smells of him. It makes her realize how much she preferred living with him to living with his brother.

Although she enjoys more freedom with her brother-in-law, she doesn't like him. He speaks about women like they're the root of all evil, and he has some nasty sexual fetishes that she has to endure. It's good that he holds down a job, unlike Eugene, which affords her some much-needed alone time, and he taught her to drive, which she's grateful for. He's instilled in her the importance of never being pulled over by the police, as she has no ID, never mind a driver's license.

They plan to skip town together once they have Toby, but she doesn't think he cares about her son. She suspects he might take the money from the sale of the house and go without her. Mainly because he's suggested their living arrangement can't go on forever. She senses that she's a burden on him, and once he's taken everything he can get from her, she'll be discarded. She doesn't know whether he'd kill her or just let her go. She's not sure she cares. Not without Toby in her life.

She has her first meeting with Detective Harper in two days, and tries to be hopeful that the woman will lead her right to her son. Then she can try to escape from her brother-in-law and raise Toby alone. She wants to give him a normal childhood. He'll be allowed to have friends over for birthday parties and spend all his time outdoors if he wants to. He'll grow up to be strong and healthy, not pale and sickly like her.

She enters Eugene's basement after finding the key to the padlock in a kitchen drawer, which is only accessible to her now because they've removed all the locks in the house, of which there were many. The new owners can't know what took place here. While her brother-in-law is focused on picking through the attic, she takes her chance to disobey her dead husband. No one has been down here since Eugene's death, and he made her promise she would never intrude on his privacy, but she has to know what he's been hiding from her.

The basement steps creak as she enters the low-ceilinged, claustrophobic space. He never fitted it out, so the timber frames are still exposed, the floor is bare concrete and there are no windows. At the bottom of the steps, she can just about stand up without her head touching the ceiling. Eugene must've had to crouch. The room is bare, with just a large chest freezer in one corner, an old leather armchair for seating, some boxes of belongings, a TV and... her bike. The one she was riding when all this began.

She steps forward and runs a hand along the red leather seat. The bike came with an uncomfortable black seat, which her dad swapped for her after she complained about it. The stickers given to her by friends are peeling away from the metal frame. Her head fills with memories of classmates, boys she had crushes on, and her mom and dad. She really had lived the perfect life until she was thirteen, when everything had changed overnight.

She takes a deep breath and opens the musty-smelling boxes. The cardboard is soft with damp and contains a bunch of VHS tapes. Her father once showed her some of these, along with a videocassette recorder to play them on. She and her mother had laughed at how old-fashioned they were. Her mom said her dad needed to throw them out and get with the times, calling him Grandpa. She smiles faintly at the memory before letting her smile falter, not trusting that it's real. Maybe it happened to a family from her imagination. They might've come to her in a dream.

She selects one tape at random to watch on the small TV with a built-in VCR underneath. The machine comes alive, eating the tape and making clunky sounds as it starts up. The TV screen awakens. The tape is deteriorating with age, but she can just make out what was recorded on it. A man is crying in his favorite armchair in the living room upstairs.

She shivers from the cold, or perhaps it's from seeing her dead husband so young and alive. She watches with interest. It becomes clear he's crying because someone has unexpectedly died.

"I should've known this would happen." His words slur into each other. "I read in a newspaper once that women are more likely to try to escape their situation when they're pregnant. It's thought the baby gives them an incentive. They realize they have something to live for." He scoffs. "Like you had nothing to live for already." He suddenly yells, "You had *me*, dammit!"

A snowstorm attacks the picture, making it difficult to see the man for a few seconds.

Her stomach flips as she watches. What is he talking about? Could he mean that time *she* tried to escape? Did he think she was pregnant? She keeps watching.

"Is that what happened, sweetie?" His tone is sympathetic now. "You thought the baby needed a better life than I could provide?"

He listens for a response. When there isn't one, he downs the liquor directly from the bottle and wipes his eyes with his spare hand. "I should be angry that you tried to take my first-born child away from me before I even met them, but I'm not. I could never get angry with you, as you well know. Hell, I let you walk all over me." He snorts affectionately at some memory the camcorder can't capture. "You know what I'm most upset about?" He doesn't wait for a response this time. "The loneliness that's waiting for me now. The long, drawn-out nights will close in on me again. The silence will scare me to the point of wanting to blow my brains out."

She feels her blood drain from her as she realizes Eugene was married before. In what appears to be a similar arrangement to their own. Except *that* woman had managed to get pregnant. The baby died with her as she tried to escape her marriage. A jealous fire rages in her belly at the thought that she wasn't Eugene's first love. He had never disclosed anything about this woman, which leaves her wondering whether she ever really knew him. Perhaps she was wrong to trust him.

Frozen to the spot, she can't feel her hands. She watches as he cries in despair. He clearly loved his first wife. Perhaps more than her. That's why he never allowed her down here. These tapes keep her memory alive. He liked spending time down here with his other woman.

She forces herself up to select a second tape from the box. She ejects the first one and pushes the new one into the dated machine with shaky hands. Eugene recorded *her* arrival here, and other milestones along the way. He'd done it with Sofia and then Macy too. Which means he likely filmed his first wife.

She needs to see who this female was. Because sometimes, in the early days, she sensed Eugene's heart belonged to another woman. She felt he was dressing her in that woman's clothes and wanted them to be the same person.

She hits play on the VCR. This one must be older, as the screen is filled with dancing white lines of static. Eventually, it clears, and a woman is standing against the front door as Eugene hands her something. Squinting at the tape, she realizes it's the wedding ring ceremony. She had gone through the same thing herself. The woman's face is blurred, but she's wearing blue jeans and a white T-shirt with a band logo on the front. The T-shirt Eugene told *her* was his favorite whenever she wore it. Now she knows why.

"I'm not marrying you," says the woman on the tape. She sounds both afraid and angry. "This means nothing."

Goosebumps break out across her entire body as she watches. She leans away from the TV, confused. Because she knows that voice. The interference clears from the screen. When she sees the woman's face, she retches so hard that vomit covers her feet. She bends over as she sees stars. Her throat burns with acid. She forces herself to look back at the screen.

The woman's eyes convey distress at her situation, and when Eugene says something the tape doesn't catch, she backs away in fear before letting him slip the ring on her finger without comment.

"No." She squeezes her eyes shut. "Please, no. That's not fair." Everything suddenly clicks into place. The shoulder-length hairstyle Eugene had forced on her. The secondhand T-shirt with the band logo she wore that was his particular favorite. How it smelled of a perfume she recognized. And why her relationship with her father deteriorated so suddenly during her teens. Why he became so strict and wouldn't let her out of his sight.

Her eyes are drawn to the chest freezer in the corner of the room. It's large enough to hold a body. And it's still plugged into the electrical outlet, which is why she can't smell anything bad.

She retches again, but only bile comes up this time. When she's done, she forces her feet to move. Wiping her mouth with one hand, she uses the other to reach for the freezer's handle. With a deep, steadying breath, she pulls the lid up.

Inside, her beautiful mother looks up at her, her face frozen in fear, her hands resting on her swollen belly. Her favorite necklace, a silver chain with a red rose pendant, sits around her neck.

"Mommy?" Amber's eyes fill with tears as she reaches out to touch the face she hasn't seen in sixteen years. Her mother vanished from their family home three years before she was abducted. "*This* is where you went?" Her voice sounds tiny, childlike.

It seems her mother only lasted a short time in captivity, just long enough to get pregnant. She had more fight than Amber ever did. And she died trying to get home to her and her father.

With one hand on her mother's belly, Amber hangs over the side of the freezer. She sobs as her fingertips quickly cool from the ice encasing her mother and her unborn sibling.

CHAPTER FIFTY-FIVE

Madison races back to the station to give an improvised press conference in an attempt to reach out to Claire Barlow. She needs to get Claire and Toby into protective custody immediately, or they risk being harmed by Gina and whoever's been helping her.

Steve meets her at the entrance and keeps pace as she heads straight to the conference room. "Kate Flynn's been calling repeatedly," he says. "Asking why there's no record of Toby Clark's disappearance from eighteen months ago."

Madison smiles faintly. She knew Kate would be on it.

"And Claire Barlow's parents had no idea their daughter was in town," he continues. "Never mind what might've really happened to her. They were both convinced she'd run away with a boy she'd been dating because the boy left town around the same time she vanished. But it was pure coincidence. They're frantic with worry about where she could be now. I told them we'll be in touch as soon as we know more."

She nods. "Claire was definitely abducted and held captive along with Amber Nelson and Bianca Marsh. I've spoken to Gina. She wants to be called Gina, not Amber, and I don't want to upset her. She admits shooting her father dead." She stops at the entrance to the conference room and takes a deep breath. "Her captor died of cancer and got his brother to take over where he left off. I suspect he's the one who dismembered Thomas Nelson's body and dumped him in the creek."

"*What?*" Steve looks horrified. "I can't even get my head around Gina being responsible for killing someone, never mind the rest of it."

"I know. It's sicker than we ever could've imagined. We need to find out who the two men are who've held her captive. Adams is working on a lead for me."

"Has Adams told you what else he's discovered?" he asks. "You're gonna be shocked."

She tries not to sigh. She could do without more revelations. "No. I need to do this before I speak with him. Give me a few minutes." She heads inside the crowded room. Steve stands at the back to watch. Madison's legs are a little shaky from an adrenaline rush as she makes her way to the front. Her palms sweat as she grips the stand in front of her. She meets Kate Flynn's eyes and smiles briefly. Kate's hyperalert, desperate to know what this is about.

A hush falls over the room.

"Okay, guys," says Madison. "Sorry for the short notice, but we're looking for someone who could be in imminent danger, so we'd appreciate it if you could make this breaking headline news." A flurry of excitement ripples through the gathered reporters and TV crews. They live for this shit.

Madison clears her throat, hoping Chief Mendes doesn't mind her taking the initiative in her absence. The chief's office is empty, the door locked. Once she's back from the hospital, she'll break the news about Officer Fuller's death to the wider team. It's going to be awful. Even Officer Kent doesn't know yet, and Madison suspects it might put the young rookie off working in law enforcement.

Movement outside the room catches her eye. Chief Mendes is back, and she's gathering officers. Madison's stomach lurches with dread.

She needs to focus. Looking directly into a camera lens, she says, "We've asked you here at short notice because there's been a development in the investigation into the missing infant Toby Clark."

"Have you found him?" asks an overexcited young reporter.

"Not yet," Madison says. "This is an appeal for Toby's *biological* mother to come forward."

Shocked, the reporters glance at each other.

"We've recently discovered that Gina Clark is going by a false name. Her real name is Amber Nelson, and she was abducted by an unknown assailant in July 2007. We're trying to apprehend Amber, and if the public sees her anywhere, she should be considered armed and dangerous, so please call us without approaching her." Madison can't believe she's saying these words. Just two days ago, she invited the woman into her home. "What we now know is that although Toby Clark did vanish eighteen months ago at age six months, he was taken by his real mother, Claire Barlow, who may be going by the name of Macy."

Some of the crowd look confused.

With a deep breath, she tries to explain. "We believe Claire and Amber were abducted by the same person and spent several years in captivity along with another young female. Amber presented herself to us as Gina Clark and told us that Toby was her missing son. It's since become evident that Claire Barlow is his biological mother, and that she is in danger." She swallows, looking directly into the lens. "Claire? If you're watching this, please contact us immediately. We can protect you and your son. Your parents..." She clears her throat. "Your parents are desperate to see you. And we know it was you who put a photograph on my car, trying to help us piece everything together. We're concerned for your safety, so please get in touch. We can pick you up from wherever you are."

Once it's clear she's finished, the reporters explode with questions, but Madison doesn't have time to answer them. She's given them enough to go on. If they want to know more, they can do their jobs.

She and Steve quickly head to their desks.

CHAPTER FIFTY-SIX

Time captive: 13 years 5 months

Gina gets out of the passenger seat, slipping into the dark evening before turning back and leaning down. "Wait here for five minutes, then you can follow me inside."

Her brother-in-law nods, remaining in the car as she hurries around the back of the house, trying not to picture her mother's frozen grimace as she goes. This morning's grim discovery in Eugene's basement was gut-wrenching and she knows she'll never forget it. She couldn't stay a second longer and had raced from the house in tears, begging her brother-in-law to take her home. She plans to enlist his help to remove the chest freezer from the house before the new people move in, and to give her mother and sibling a proper burial, but not until her father has paid for what he's done.

Ignoring all the memories she has of her family home, she's relieved to find he still leaves the back door unlocked when he's home. She creeps into the house and finds him in the dimly lit living room. He must've fallen asleep in his armchair while watching TV.

He's aged badly in her absence and is barely recognizable to her now. She tries to feel something for the man, but he sold her to Eugene, wanting her dead. That's what Eugene told her. Did he sell her mother too? Or was Rose's disappearance the catalyst for everything that followed?

She touches the rose necklace around her neck while gulping back a sob. The noise that escapes her rouses Thomas Nelson from his slumber. He looks up at her, puzzled.

"Recognize me?" she says.

Startled and clearly afraid, he slowly slips his glasses on and stares hard at her face. Within seconds, his hand shoots to his mouth, and he looks like he's about to stand and embrace her.

"No," says Gina. "Stay there."

"Amber?" The blood has drained from his face. He looks confused by her appearance after all these years. "Is that really you, or am I dreaming again?"

"It's me. Sorry to disappoint."

He's speechless for a long time as he rests a hand on his chest. His heart must be thudding as hard as hers is. "Where have you been?"

"What do you care? You wanted me dead."

His face screws up in confusion. "What are you *talking* about? I never stopped looking for you. This is a miracle!"

She's confused. He appears happy to see her.

His eyes move downward to the weapon in her outstretched hand. "I... I don't understand, honey. Why the gun? What's wrong? Why can't I come and hug you? Did the police find you?" He leans forward again, peering over her shoulder as if expecting to see the police with her.

"I loved you so much," she says, her throat thick with emotion. "When Mom was still around and before you turned mean." Her parents had a wonderful relationship filled with love and laughter. His personality changed after Rose vanished. Amber became a burden to him. They argued often.

His face is so pale she thinks he might pass out. "I know things turned bad after she disappeared, honey. I'm so sorry. I missed her so much. It was killing me that I couldn't find her. If I took it out on you, I'm sorry. But you're home now. We can start fresh, right?"

She ignores him. "I found Mom."

His mouth drops open. "I... I don't understand."

"Watch this." She pulls out Eugene's cell phone. She'd used it to record some of the footage found in his basement. She hits play and holds it out for him to see the screen. He gasps when he sees his wife being paraded on camera. He gasps again when he sees her pregnant belly. This footage was filmed just days before her death.

"What's going on?" he says angrily. Tears roll down his face. "Who did that to her? Where is she?"

When Gina doesn't reply, he yells, "Where's your mother, *dammit*!"

She realizes then that he misses Rose far more than he ever missed her. Eugene was telling the truth. Her father didn't want her.

"The man in the video had Mom. You sold her to him. He impregnated her."

Her father's jaw tightens as his throat constricts. He looks like he might vomit. "You're not making any sense, Amber. Where is she now? We need to go to the police and get this man locked up."

"He's dead."

His eyes widen in disbelief. "So Rose can come home?" Tears accumulate on his cheeks.

For a second, she almost believes he genuinely doesn't know Eugene. It makes her wonder whether Eugene abducted her mother without her father's involvement. "No," she says. "Mom's dead too. Her body's in a freezer in Eugene's basement. She died trying to escape him."

Thomas Nelson falls forward, out of the chair and onto his knees. He breaks down, hitting the floor with his fist over and over in anger. She lets him suffer before she continues.

"Look at me."

His bloodshot eyes eventually find her face.

"You let that happen to Mom. You didn't protect her."

"How could I—"

She cuts him off. "You let it happen to me too."

His face is wet and puffy. "Amber, I don't know what you mean! You snuck out of your room at night without telling me. When you didn't return home, I searched everywhere for you. I spent years searching for both of you!"

She shakes her head. "You're a liar. Eugene told me what you did."

He frowns. "Who the hell is Eugene?"

"The man on the tape."

"You spoke to your mother's abductor?"

She meets his gaze. He's either a good liar, or he *really* doesn't know Eugene. "I *lived* with Mom's abductor. He took me. He was obsessed with Mom, but when she died trying to escape from him, he needed a replacement. Mom couldn't cope. I saw it in her eyes on the videos. She wanted to escape so bad. But *I* was different. I adapted. Eventually. I'm his widow. He protected me far better than you ever did."

Her father starts heaving. She takes his arm and sits him in the armchair before pulling out a length of rope and tying it around him, securing him to the sturdy back of the chair. Still in shock, he doesn't put up a fight. From her purse, she pulls out a beautiful red rose. "Do you know what it's like to be violated? To have something forced inside you against your will?"

"Of course not, honey," he sobs. "I'm so sorry." He isn't even trying to break free. Perhaps he hasn't noticed he's bound.

"It hurts," she says, trying to keep her voice steady. "The first time Eugene tried to get me pregnant, it really hurt. I felt like I was being torn up inside. The pain lasted for days afterward." She pushes aside thoughts of her first attacker. The man who knocked her off her bike. He had hurt her even more than Eugene did, but she doesn't allow herself to think about him.

He shakes his head, pained. "If I could've taken your place, your pain, I would've done so in a heartbeat."

"It hurt the second and third time too." She continues as if he hadn't spoken. "Eugene wasn't one for foreplay. In his mind, if he was ready, I was ready." Her feelings for her husband are conflicted. Those first years were horrific. But there's no doubt she had grown to love him through necessity. She had no one else.

"You'll never know what it's like to be overpowered by a stranger and torn up inside." She steps forward. "But I thought this might give you a glimpse into the fear and the pain that Mom and I went through." She holds the rose in front of his mouth. He turns his face away, so she forces it to his lips. His eyes are filled with terror and bewilderment.

"Eat it."

"What are you talking about?"

Done with words, she shoves the rose into his mouth. He tries hard to spit it out, but she holds his mouth closed and massages his throat the way you would get a dog to swallow a pill. She allows him gasps of air, and when he starts chewing, she lets him bite the head of the rose off. He eventually swallows it, but she sees it wedged in his throat. "You're sick!" he gasps. "You need help! Let me get you help!" His eyes implore her. The lump slowly slides down his throat as he tries not to vomit it back up.

She looks at the long green stalk. It's covered in protruding thorns. They're sharp. "Open your mouth and keep it open while I force this down your throat."

"What? No way! Why are you doing this?"

"If you truly wanted to share my pain," she says, "you'd eat this to experience what I went through. You'd want to know why I'm no longer your daughter and why your wife died with another man's baby inside her."

Panicked, he squirms. "Honey, I can sympathize without eating that!"

She pulls Eugene's gun from her waistband and points it at her father's head. "Swallow the stalk without chewing, or die. It's up to you."

He stills. "You wouldn't kill me, Amber. You're my little girl."

"No. I'm Eugene's girl now." A single tear rolls down her face. She wants to go back to being Amber, but it's impossible. You can never go back. Not after trauma. It changes you. It changes the trajectory of your life. You never become the person you were supposed to be. You're denied your real life. Your personality is tinged with survival instincts and trust issues. You can never truly relax again. She thinks of poor Sofia, running away, thinking she could go back to her old life after giving birth to two dead babies under horrific circumstances. Sofia was delusional. Is *she*?

Seconds tick by, the air filled with tension. It feels like she's watching someone else torture her father. His face blurs every so often. Sometimes he's her father, sometimes he's Eugene. Doubt creeps in as she considers whether this is right. She blinks, trying to focus. Someone has to be held accountable for what happened to her, don't they?

Realizing he can't subject himself to the pain, he closes his mouth tight and shakes his head. Gina grabs his throat, squeezing it tight to make him gasp for air. With his mouth finally open, she shoves his head back and forces the stem into his throat. He gags and chokes, his eyes wide with horror. Tears of pain run down his face, as they do hers.

He retches without bringing anything up as she holds his head back by his hair, pushing the stem of the rose down as far as her hand will go without him biting her fingers off with his chewing reflex. He chokes often, and she thinks he might die, but eventually his ordeal is over.

She collapses onto the chair opposite him, muscles aching from the effort. She wipes her face and stares at the clock on the wall.

Her father gags, trying to force the stem up, which sends him into a painful coughing fit. Blood trickles down his chin. She has no idea if the rose will stay down.

"Amber?" he croaks, trying not to move his neck. "It hurts so bad."

She keeps her eyes on the clock on the wall. "My name's Gina."

"Gina, *please!*" He retches again, but the rose stays down. Probably because he's tied up and can't bend over to dislodge it.

She doesn't move. "The first time Eugene forced himself on me, it lasted nine painful minutes." The second hand seems to slow down as she watches it. She's going to make him experience that nine minutes of traumatic agony, and then she's going to shoot him dead.

Her brother-in-law enters, having waited longer than five minutes. He snaps on some latex gloves and stares at her father without comment before circling the room, seemingly looking for something valuable to steal. He stops at a framed photograph on the sideboard. It's of Amber on her bike. The photograph was taken days before she was abducted by the stranger who left her for dead.

He turns to look at her. "Hey," he says with a smile of recognition. "Your bike. Man, that was a heavy piece of crap."

Gina's heart rate quickens. Blood roars in her ears. How would *he* know her bike was heavy? The only way he could possibly know is if it was him who knocked her off it that fateful night. She stares at him as it dawns on her. It was *him* who snatched her in his truck and then threw her bike in the back, not wanting to leave any evidence behind. It was *him* who raped her, beat her and left her for dead before Eugene showed up.

Bile rises in her throat as hatred bubbles up, but she doesn't outwardly react. She glares at him, trying to keep her horror in check. Inside, she vows to kill him for what he did that night, but not before he helps her find Toby.

CHAPTER FIFTY-SEVEN

"Why do you think Claire never went to the police after she escaped with Toby?" asks Steve.

Madison has no idea, but the woman's only twenty-one and has suffered a traumatic ordeal. "Perhaps she thought Gina would track her down through us and take her son. She must've thought hiding was her safest option."

Adams stands as she approaches. He nods to the briefing room, which is filled with everyone who has yet to be told about Officer Fuller's death. "Mendes is currently breaking the news."

They watch through the glass, their thoughts with Corey's family. After a minute or so, an audible gasp comes from the room, followed by angry denials. It's gut-wrenching, but what's worse is Officer Kent's heartbroken shriek. Madison turns away, dropping into the seat at her desk.

Stella joins them with tears in her eyes. "The chief wants to have Corey's end-of-watch call today. While we're all together."

Madison closes her eyes. She's only attended one other last call, which was for Detective Don Douglas, and it was horrendous. But it's a show of respect for an officer who lost their life in the line of duty, so she knows she has to attend. They all do.

"Dina's coming in early for it." Stella squeezes Madison's shoulder before returning to her cubicle.

The door to the briefing room opens as everyone pours out. The more experienced officers, including Shelley Vickers and Gloria Williams, manage to keep it together as they pass, their eyes downcast. Officer Luis Sanchez, their youngest officer despite being here longer than the rookies, looks pissed, his eyes rubbed red. He's coming to terms with the fact that there won't be any justice for Corey, because his killer is already dead.

Officer Kent's face is wet with tears. Her expression portrays disbelief. She's probably thinking it could just as easily have been her trying to move Rob Hammond away from the construction site. The thought goes through everyone's head when an officer dies in the line of duty. How frail their existence is when working in law enforcement. Madison won't let herself think about Owen joining the force. Not right now.

Chief Mendes is the last to leave the room, switching off the light and closing the door behind her. She's spent hours at the hospital with Corey's family. Her face is drained of color, but she's stayed strong for the team. She goes straight into her office without making eye contact with anyone, and once there, she closes her door, then the blinds. She doesn't want to be disturbed.

Madison composes herself and tries to focus on the job at hand. "So what's this shocking revelation you have to tell me?" she asks Adams.

He drops his pen on his desk and takes a deep breath. "Gina's mother, Rose Nelson, disappeared when she was thirty-two years old. She was never found. Gina was only thirteen at the time."

Incredulous, Madison leans forward. "You're telling me both Gina *and* her mother vanished, what, three years apart?"

"Yep," says Adams, crossing his arms. "Her husband

reported her missing and was never considered a suspect. He had a credible alibi, and everyone in their life who Detective Ramsey spoke to said the pair were inseparable. They genuinely came across as the happiest family."

Detective John Ramsey retired years ago. Madison didn't work with him for long, which she was pleased about as they didn't get along well. She lowers her eyes. "I wonder if Gina killed her father because she felt he failed to protect her and her mother."

Steve nods. "It's a valid motive, in her eyes at least."

"Did Ramsey have any suspects for Rose's disappearance?" she asks.

Adams shrugs. "A couple of guys. One who I think needed looking at more closely, but the investigation didn't seem to delve very deeply into him as they never knew his full name."

It doesn't surprise her. Detective Ramsey worked alone as the LCPD's sole detective for part of his time here, so he would have been overworked. But she also knows from experience that he's a misogynist, and she wonders how hard he actually tried to find Rose Nelson. "Who?" she asks.

He picks up a case file from his desk and finds what he's looking for. "Twenty-nine-year-old Eugene something. Well, he was twenty-nine in 2004. Ramsey took a statement from one of Rose's co-workers who said they thought Eugene was infatuated with her as she was once kind to him in her place of work, a bank downtown. He wasn't a customer, but he'd come in every few days just to talk to her. This co-worker thought she saw Eugene watching Rose from his car one time, and Rose apparently mentioned he might have followed her home."

"So was he questioned?" she asks.

"No. Ramsey found no evidence and couldn't locate the guy as he didn't know his last name or his address, and no one took down his license plate. So he let the lead go cold."

Madison knows it's the best lead they've had so far. "See if his last name was Clark. You never know, he could be our guy."

He nods. "Got it. Oh, and I've issued a BOLO for Gina using both her names."

"This is such a mess," says Steve with a long sigh. "I mean, what do we do when we find her—arrest her or get her help?"

Madison nods. "My thoughts exactly." She's glad he has some sympathy for Gina. It would be easy to assume they're dealing with a monster, but Gina's been created by her experiences. It's unlikely she would've been capable of murder had she not been abducted and held captive for thirteen years.

"Come on," says Adams incredulously. "She *decapitated* a guy. Her own *father*, no less! She needs to be locked up for life."

Madison remains silent.

"Okay, imagine it was a guy who'd done that," he presses. "You wouldn't feel sorry for him, right?"

Steve walks back to his desk without comment.

Perhaps Adams is right. She's not sure. "Maybe." She turns to her computer. They need to focus on finding Claire Barlow and her son before Gina and her accomplice do. Within minutes, her cell phone buzzes with a message. She pulls it out of her pocket and frowns at the number on the screen. She doesn't recognize it.

It's me. I'm outside. Can we talk? N

Her heart flutters lightly with nerves. Nate's back. Earlier than Vince predicted. Maybe he couldn't wait to see her.

She's tempted to tell him she's too busy. Let him feel hurt that she can't be bothered to see him immediately. After all, he hurt her by leaving in the middle of the night. But the truth is, she needs to see a friendly face right now. It's been a crappy week that's only going to get worse.

Steve glances over at her. "Everything okay?"

She swallows. "Yeah. I need some fresh air." Standing, she adds, "I won't be long."

Her legs feel shaky as she heads to the exit.

CHAPTER FIFTY-EIGHT

Nate watches Brody sniff the outskirts of the dark parking lot as he leans on Madison's car, waiting for her to appear. Vince dropped them here, but he can't rely on people giving him rides for long. He'll need to buy a new vehicle as soon as possible. The bank canceled the cards his brother stole from him before dumping him at the church like an orphaned child, but Nate didn't bother to report his stolen Chevy to the police. Kurt can keep it for all he cares.

He thinks about the interview he gave Vince in a hotel room on the way home, and how Madison will react when she finds out. She'll probably be glad. It wasn't as difficult as he'd thought it would be, and in the end, it was a relief to get things off his chest. He got to say in no uncertain terms what he really thinks of the people who facilitated his wrongful conviction, and those who perpetuate false rumors about him even to this day. Vince needs to edit it before he releases it on his podcast, so he'll have a few days' reprieve before it goes out. He's glad it's done. It means he can truly move forward now. He's even booked a session with a therapist to help him deal with taking another person's life. He's finally realized it's time to stop punishing himself, because that also punishes Madison.

He feels more positive than when he left town earlier this week. But whether or not life can return to normal depends on how Madison feels about him.

He glances at his new cell phone, wondering if she'll leave him out here all night. Then he spots her peering out at him, reluctant to come into the cold. He straightens as the door opens.

Brody runs to her. Nate watches as the dog jumps up at her, tail wagging, ecstatic to be home.

"I know!" she says, ruffling his fur with a smile. "I told you he'd come home eventually, right?"

Brody grunts in agreement before running over to Nate.

Madison slowly approaches. She doesn't come in for a hug. Instead, she slips her hands into her jacket pocket and looks him in the eye. "You're home then." It's a statement more than a question.

He nods. "I'm so sorry, Madison. I wasn't in control of myself, and the only thing I could think of doing was getting away before I did something even more stupid." He holds his hand out to her, but she keeps hers in her pocket. Instead, Brody excitedly nuzzles it, leaving it wet with saliva before running away to chase movement in the bushes, probably a squirrel.

"I'm sorry too," she says sadly. "I should never have made you carry a weapon. I was just so afraid that you'd be hurt." Tears brim her eyes, which she lowers.

Nate pulls her in for a hug. She feels warm in his embrace. Her hair smells clean and floral. He's missed the smell of her favorite shampoo, the cheapest the store sells because she spent so long without money after her release from prison that even now she buys the basic stuff, insisting it's just as good as the expensive brands. "Don't apologize," he says into her hair. "It's all on me. Not you." He doesn't want to let go. "I've given Vince an interview and I have a therapy session booked for next week. I'm confronting my issues so this doesn't happen again."

She pulls away, surprised. "I never thought you'd talk about your ordeal on record. Are you sure that's the right thing to do?"

He shrugs. "Well, I've tried everything else and none of that's worked, so what do I have to lose, right?"

She smiles sadly. "Was it cathartic, at least?"

"It was for me, but there's some folks in Texas who'll be mad about it."

Her smile widens. "Good. They deserve it."

She finally removes her hands from her pockets, so he takes one, interlacing their fingers.

She notices his bruised knuckles and raises an eyebrow at him. "What happened here?"

He thinks of Dawn's obnoxious husband. "I was defending your honor."

She rolls her eyes. "I don't even want to know."

"So, what have I missed?" he asks.

With a deep breath, she says, "Oh, man. Where do I start? Well, Lena Scott fled in the night after revealing herself as a domestic abuser, my loving sister Angie is out of prison and wants to become BFFs, and... oh yeah, Owen's decided he wants to become a cop instead of a lawyer."

Nate's mouth drops open. "Owen wants to be a *cop*?"

"I know, right? Like I don't lose enough sleep already." She looks away. "I'm terrified, Nate, because we lost an officer in the line of duty today."

Nate squeezes her hand. "*What*? Who?"

"One of the rookies. In fact, the person who arrested you for murder last month."

"Fuller? What happened?"

As she tells him how it transpired, Nate can't get his head

around what a waste of a life it was. Fuller was an intelligent guy who took his job seriously. There's no doubt he would've quickly risen up the ranks if his life hadn't been cut short.

She sniffs. "How can I let Owen put himself in danger like that?"

He rests her hand on his chest and rubs it. "We'll make sure he finishes his degree first. But he's an adult, which means you can't stop him if that's what he wants to do. But you'll be there to watch out for him. He'll be luckier than most young cops."

The ride home from Kansas gave Nate time to think about what to do with his compensation money. He decides now to invest it where his heart is. In Madison and Owen. Or, more specifically, in the LCPD. He's already paying for the department therapist. But if he invests, they could expand their forensic team, perhaps set up a small crime lab for faster test results, as well as buying better equipment. They wouldn't be spread so thinly, and both Madison and Owen would be safer as a result.

He laughs to himself. Never in a million years did he ever think that the money he was paid as a result of his wrongful conviction and horrendous treatment at the hands of law enforcement would be spent on, well, law enforcement. The fact that he's also engaged to a detective and has a former K9 as a pet, *and* now a soon-to-be police officer for a stepson, suggests that some of the bitterness he's felt about his past and how he was mistreated is finally easing. Maybe he's not a lost cause after all.

"More importantly," he says, "I hope you told Angie to go to hell?"

She smiles sheepishly. "Not exactly. I've spoken with her a couple of times, and I think she might be capable of change since—"

"Madison, *no*." It comes out more forcefully than he

intended. "That would be like inviting the devil into your life. It would be reckless, and I won't stand by and allow Angie into our home. Imagine what you would say if I invited Father Connor over for dinner. It's madness!"

"I know, I know." She looks away, giving him the sense that she's craving family, just like he was recently.

But he learned the hard way that family can hurt you more than anyone else. And they often do, sometimes because they know they can get away with it. They know you're bound to them no matter what, so they can behave however they want unless you're brave enough to cut them out of your life. But cutting them out *does* take bravery, and it's easy to forget what they're really like and to forgive them when you shouldn't.

"Think about Owen," he says gently. "She probably just wants to get to him."

Fear crosses her face, and she quickly changes the subject. "Speaking of psycho siblings, how were your brother and sister? Pleased to see the black sheep of the family?"

He scoffs. "Let's just say we won't be inviting them to our wedding anytime soon."

She peers at him. "The wedding's back on?"

He glances at her engagement ring finger and sees it's bare. His chest tightens with dread. His leaving town must have made her doubt his feelings for her. "Of course it is. Assuming you'll still have me?"

With a deep breath, she says, "You can't leave again, Nate. That has to be the last time. I'm nobody's doormat."

He nods. "Deal. Does that mean you'll marry me?"

She pretends to think about it. "Well, I've recently been propositioned by a hot young surfer dude, so I should probably keep my options open."

He tilts her chin up and kisses her softly. "Madison? We're getting married, but let's wait until my interview is out, the interest has died down and I've been to therapy to work some stuff out. I want to be in a good place when I promise to protect you from any more hurt. Does that sound good to you?"

She nods, making his shoulders lighten with relief.

"Oh, by the way," he says, "when I checked my emails earlier, I had an invoice from Kyle Davenport, so I called him to pay for the security cameras." He pauses. "He said you don't like him very much. How come?"

She scoffs. "Poor guy. I thought he was using the cameras to watch me. You know me, suspicious of everyone. I'm probably wrong."

He smiles.

"We're having an end-of-watch call for Fuller later," she says. "Do you want to come, since you knew him?"

He suspects she's asking him to be there to support her. "Sure. How about I bring Owen too, so he can see what he's getting himself into?"

She nods. "That's actually a good idea. It might put him off, God willing."

"I'll need your car keys, though. I, er, lost my car."

"You lost your car?" She snorts as she hands him the keys to her Dodge Demon. "I can't wait to hear *that* story."

"Madison?" Steve calls to her from the door to the station. "Got a minute?" His eyes linger on Nate, but he doesn't nod in greeting. Instead, he looks a little pissed.

Nate wonders whether her new partner has been advising her against taking him back. He's always thought Steve has feelings for her, though he couldn't prove it. It's the way he's always happy to help her, even leaving his girlfriend hanging on several occasions.

"I'll be right there," she shouts over her shoulder. Turning back to Nate, she grins. "Sorry. Like I said, I'm incredibly popular these days."

He kisses her for longer than he should, not wanting to let

her go. He wants to whisk her away somewhere and have her all to himself. When she pulls away, he says, "I love you."

She blushes. She's never been good with public displays of affection. "Love you too, you weirdo." She ruffles Brody's fur as she leaves.

Nate smiles as he watches her run back into the station. He doesn't know how he got so lucky.

CHAPTER FIFTY-NINE

Madison spends the early evening desperately searching for leads that might provide a clue to where Claire Barlow could be hiding. She hasn't heard from Gina again, and the young woman isn't answering her phone. It leaves her feeling uneasy. She has no idea what Gina's next move will be, and she's already proved herself capable of murder.

Her phone rings. It's Officer Williams at the front desk. "Yeah?" she says.

"Claire Barlow is here to see you."

Madison blinks, thinking she heard wrong. "What?"

"Claire Barlow." Williams lowers her voice, adding, "She's looking a little skittish, so you might want to get out here quick."

Madison drops her phone and touches Steve's shoulder as she passes. "Claire Barlow's here! Let's go!" She races to the front of the station and enters the waiting area.

An attractive young blonde woman around five foot six is standing in front of the glass-paneled entrance, nervously bouncing her little boy on her hip.

The sight of them both makes Madison choke up with relief. Toby looks just like his photo: blond, cute and wide-eyed, though now, eighteen months older, he has more hair. He also looks healthy. It's clear his real mother has taken good care of him.

Claire eyes her fearfully as she says, "Can we move? I feel too exposed here." She glances behind her at the parking lot. She's in full view of anyone watching.

Steve opens the internal door that leads to the offices. "Come with us. We'll keep you safe."

After a second's hesitation, Claire walks ahead of him, giving Steve and Madison time to exchange a look of relief. Madison approaches Officer Williams. "For the rest of the day, no members of the public are to enter this station. Understood?"

Gloria nods. "Yes, ma'am." She walks around the desk to lock the entrance. If anyone needs help, they can call from outside.

Madison feels reassured. She follows Steve and Claire to Chief Mendes's office, where Steve knocks once.

"What is it?" says the chief without looking up.

He opens the door. "Chief, we have Claire Barlow and her son, Toby, here."

Mendes quickly gets up and approaches Claire with interest. She holds out her hand in greeting, which Claire shakes. "Good to see you safe and well." Then she smiles widely at Toby, who turns shy. "Hey, little guy. We've been looking for you."

"His name's Noah, not Toby," says Claire defensively. "And he's mine, not Gina's."

"We know he's yours," says Madison. "Don't worry, we won't let Gina get anywhere near him. Is Toby what she and his father named him?"

"Right." Claire lowers her voice, resting a hand on the boy's head. "But I never call him that. And I'll make sure he never knows who his father was."

It makes sense to Madison that she wouldn't want to burden

her son with a father like his. Something occurs to her. "I thought you had another child? A girl?"

Claire looks pained for a second. "I was pregnant when I escaped from the house, but the stress of it caused me to lose the baby. I was bleeding heavily by the side of the road and got picked up by a woman driving by. She took us to her home and let us stay with her. I told her I was fleeing an abusive boyfriend. I couldn't risk anyone knowing what really happened in case word got back to Gina."

Madison can't even begin to imagine the ordeal she's been through. "I'm so sorry for everything you've experienced. We have so many questions for you, but first, we need to find Gina and her accomplice, so I have to ask: what are the names of your captor and his brother?"

Claire shivers before responding. Her eyes are haunted as she remembers her time with them. "Eugene took us. But he's dead now. That's how I escaped. I don't know his last name."

Eugene is the name Sergeant Adams is looking into. Steve leaves to tell him they're on the right track.

"And his brother?" she presses.

Claire shakes her head. "I never met him."

Madison's shoulders slump with disappointment. Identifying him seems impossible. Her only option might be to bring all her suspects in one at a time: Kyle Davenport and his girlfriend Elaine, seemingly affable Jerry Clark, and perhaps even Stanley Smith—who she realizes now never got back to her with the details of the man he said he'd hooked up with at the time of Thomas Nelson's death.

"He was used as a threat to keep us compliant," Claire explains. "Eugene would tell us that if we misbehaved, he'd invite his brother over, implying his brother was even worse than him." Her spare hand flies to her mouth. "But who could be worse than Eugene?"

Madison doesn't know what to say. Nothing seems good

enough. When she's ready, Claire will need to talk to a trauma specialist. Perhaps her son will too.

Chief Mendes clears her throat. "While we intend to do everything we can to keep you safe, unfortunately you've joined us at a difficult time. We lost an officer today, and we're about to take a minute to remember him outside in the back lot. Most of the team will want to be present, so you'd be alone if we left you inside the station."

"It'll be safer to come with us," says Madison. "We can keep you protected. It won't last long."

Fear crosses Claire's face. "Don't leave me in here. I'd rather come with you. We'll stay quiet, right, sweetie?" She smiles at her son, who nods sleepily, resting a head on her shoulder with his tiny thumb in his mouth.

"Fine," says Mendes. "I'll gather the troops."

Madison's stomach flips with dread. This won't be easy.

CHAPTER SIXTY

It's bitterly cold outside as the team silently gathers around the cruiser that Officer Fuller last used. The driver's door is open so they can hear the radio, and perhaps picture Corey still on duty. It looks as though he's just slipped away to grab coffee. The night is clear, the stars visible. The moon casts a glow over everyone present, making them appear pale and afraid.

Alex has left Mrs. Pebbles in his office, perhaps not trusting her to behave. He stands quietly, keeping his eyes on the ground as Officer Kent approaches, her head held high, desperately trying to keep it together for the event she probably never dreamed would happen to her or Corey as they graduated from the academy. At least, not so soon.

Madison watches as Nate and Owen appear, having been let into the secure lot by Officer Sanchez. It looks like they've left Brody at home. Owen keeps his eyes lowered and stays back to avoid getting in the way. Nate approaches Madison and takes her hand, briefly squeezing it before letting go. He knows she won't want a fuss, but having him here is reassuring. They have so much to catch up on later.

Dr. Conrad Stevens arrives next, his expression somber. He

removes his hat before nodding at Chief Mendes. "My assistants are on their way." The team from the medical examiner's office may not be law enforcement, but they work closely together.

Madison sees Jeff entering the lot behind Stevens. He discreetly drops a cigarette and picks up the spent stub, then instantly pulls out another. She stares at it, suddenly craving nicotine.

Jeff briefly squeezes Skylar's shoulders affectionately as they approach. His co-worker seems upset. The pair spent time socializing with both rookies, and now they're having to care for Corey's body in the morgue. It has to be tough for them, and Skylar's pregnancy hormones will only add to the emotion of what she's about to witness.

Skylar makes a beeline for little Noah, who's sleeping against his mom's chest with his thumb still in his mouth. She quietly asks a few questions about the boy, which Claire happily answers, having spotted Skylar's bump. She even lets her hold him.

Madison smiles, thinking how no one connects faster than two mothers.

The only people left inside the station are a few officers and the dispatchers, Stella and Dina. Chief Mendes stands alone, looking downcast. Madison thinks she could do with a hug but knows it wouldn't be appropriate.

A hush falls over the crowd as they wait patiently. Madison braces herself as the cruiser's radio crackles to life.

"Attention all units," says Dina. "Clear the air for priority traffic."

A second later, they hear Stella's voice. "Dispatch calling Officer Fuller. Do you copy?"

Steve and Adams are nearby, but Madison is careful not to make eye contact with anyone.

"This is a final call for Officer Fuller." Stella's voice is even, and Madison doesn't know how she can hold it together. She thinks of the officers on patrol who will be pulled over briefly, listening in while life goes on around them.

A full minute passes in silence, where no doubt everyone wishes Officer Fuller would respond.

"No response," says Stella, followed by a pause. "Officer Corey Fuller, we thank you for your professionalism and your dedication to law enforcement. You were an excellent team member who was taken far too soon. Your dedication to service will be missed." Another pause as the crack in her voice suggests she's struggling.

Madison looks up at the stars when she continues.

"You can rest in peace, Officer Fuller. Your watch has ended. We have it from here. Dispatch out."

The radio falls silent, and Steve closes the car door.

Officer Kent loses it. She lets out long, gasping sobs as shock and grief spill out of her. Madison struggles to contain herself, but she must set a good example. The younger officers will find comfort in it. She moves over to Kent and takes her hand.

All eyes are lowered as they remember Corey and consider how his parents must be feeling right now. But something is nagging at Madison. She gets a whiff of smoke, and goosebumps break out over her arms. *Smoke*. Gina always smells of smoke. She looks up and her eyes land on Jeff. Jeff's a heavy smoker.

Her heart skips a beat as she reaches for her weapon, but Jeff steps forward and casually takes Noah from Skylar before Madison can stop him.

"What are you doing?" says Claire. She tries to grab for him, but Jeff's fast, and once he has the boy, he pushes her hard. She falls to the ground and her head hits the concrete, making her grunt in pain.

Before anyone can react, Gina Clark appears from the secure entrance, making Madison's blood run cold as she grasps what's happening.

Jeff is Eugene's brother. And he stayed at the back of the crowd to let Gina into the lot. She must have been waiting nearby. Madison doesn't remember ever knowing Jeff's last name. Or Skylar's, for that matter. There's a chance he doesn't even share Eugene's last name, to throw law enforcement off his scent in case his brother was ever revealed as a monster. She'll need to check. All of this runs through her mind while she stares in horror at Jeff and Gina. Captor and victim, working in unison to steal someone else's child.

"If anyone reaches for their guns," says Jeff, "the pregnant woman gets it." A weapon has appeared in his hand. He's aiming it at Skylar, the woman he comforted less than two minutes ago. The woman he's worked with for years. From the shock on her face, it's clear that she has no idea what's happening. What her co-worker was capable of.

Officer Sanchez lowers his hand from his hip. Madison keeps hold of her weapon. Someone has to.

She thinks back to all the interactions she's ever had with the guy, which mostly consisted of five minutes here and there during visits to the morgue. The morning they'd gone there to see Thomas Nelson's body before the autopsy, Jeff had been yawning loudly and repeatedly, saying he'd had a busy weekend. She never dreamed he'd spent it dismembering the body he'd retrieved from the refrigerator for them. And then there's the situation with Lena throwing a boot at him in anger. He implied he was ready to retaliate and said he wouldn't put up with it twice, proving he would hurt a woman. He only stopped himself that time from fear of losing his job.

And in the bar recently, he'd told them he had a needy girlfriend who he was ready to dump. He even said she was too old for him. Gina's only twenty-nine, but Jeff is clearly as sick as his brother and likes to prey on young girls. When talking about her partner, Gina had told her that men found her too much of a burden due to her anxiety. Had Jeff made her feel that way?

Madison swallows as Jeff discards his cigarette. He's smoked every time she's seen him. And although she's never witnessed Gina with a cigarette, she always carries the smell with her like an invisible blanket. She curses herself for figuring it out a second too late.

Out of the corner of her eye she notices Nate taking a step toward her. She turns to him and hisses, "*Owen.*"

He nods, understanding he needs to protect her son.

The looks on the faces of Sanchez, Adams and Steve suggest they're seconds away from pulling their weapons. Madison just has to hope no one does anything reckless.

Chief Mendes tries to gain control of the situation. "Jeff? I suggest you put that gun down immediately, or my officers will be within their rights to fire at you. You only have one weapon. We have all these." She gestures to the team, all on high alert. Conrad has silently moved aside, giving them clear shots of Jeff and Gina.

Jeff appears to find the situation amusing. "Yeah, but I'm the one holding the kid. You wanna be responsible for the death of this one *and* the expectant mother, Chief?"

Madison glances at Owen. He's standing alone behind the others, over to their left. An easy target.

Gina reaches Jeff and allows herself a brief glance at Noah, who's awake now. She takes his hand. "I'm so glad to see you, my beautiful baby boy."

"He's not yours!" yells Claire, struggling to get up. "Leave us alone! Haven't you done enough damage already?" Her entire neck is flushed red, but her face is ashen. She knows better than anyone what Gina is capable of.

Madison's mouth is bone dry. She considers shooting at Gina as a distraction, but Jeff's gun is still fixed on Skylar, so it won't achieve anything. He'll just start firing, and there's no telling how many of them he could take down before he's wounded.

"Stand still!" shouts Jeff suddenly.

Madison looks to see who he's talking to. It's Nate. He's been creeping toward Owen.

"Why are you going to that one?" asks Jeff, his interest piqued.

Gina looks Madison in the eye. "Because that's *her* son."

With blood roaring in her ears, Madison realizes they're going to target Owen.

"His life is worth more to her than Skylar's."

"Is that so?" says Jeff, smirking. He moves his aim to Owen.

Madison's legs almost give out.

CHAPTER SIXTY-ONE

Everyone stands in stunned silence, unsure how to end this devastating stand-off.

"What do you want, Gina?" says Madison, trying to sound self-assured when really she wants to beg this pair to leave her son out of it.

"I want my baby back." Gina takes Noah from Jeff, then reaches for the weapon in his hand.

Jeff looks confused for a minute before letting her take it. "Keep your aim on that one." He points to Owen.

Gina steps back from him and does as he says. But it's Jeff she addresses. "It was you who abducted me that night, wasn't it?"

Jeff finally takes his eyes off the officers and turns to look at her. "What?"

"I never knew who knocked me off my bike and spent the next five hours assaulting me," she says evenly. "Not until you recognized my bike in that photo at my dad's house."

He laughs nervously. "Yeah, so what? Eugene was following you too. He would've taken you anyway. You can't blame me for him being a creep."

She frowns, confused. "He was following me?"

"Right. He confessed everything at the hospital. Turns out he was obsessed with your mother." He smirks at her. "He told me the two years she spent with him were the best years of his life, and his time with you doesn't even come close."

Madison's heart sinks. *Eugene* took Gina's mother, Rose Nelson. Then he went after Rose's daughter, thinking he could continue what he started. She can't even begin to imagine how Gina feels. How Thomas Nelson felt losing both his wife *and* his daughter. He must've been elated when Gina turned up at his house recently, never considering she was there to kill him. She can only assume that Eugene Clark brainwashed Gina into thinking her father was somehow responsible for her situation.

"You're lying," says Gina calmly. "Eugene loved me. What we had was real. I wasn't just second best."

Jeff continues. "He told me that when she tried to escape from him, he caught up with her and pushed her too hard, causing her death. It was an accident. He was devastated. Just telling me about it made him cry. Once she was gone, his obsession turned to you." He scoffs as if it's funny. "Sick bastard. He'd been watching you for weeks, waiting to pounce. He thought I didn't know about his obsession with you, but I did. That's why I was waiting for you that night you were at your friend's house. I wanted to beat him to it." His eyes darken. It's clear he feels no remorse. "Besides, what did you expect would happen riding along the road at midnight all on your own? If you ask me, you *wanted* to be picked up by someone. You were the easiest prey I ever had. *You* put yourself in that situation, not me. And I think you enjoyed it."

Madison shudders. She had no idea what this asshole was capable of, and it sounds like Gina wasn't his first victim. He needs life without parole.

"I had no idea Eugene kept girls as pets, though. Not until he was dying in the hospital."

Madison glances at Gina and can see what's coming by the look on her face. It's eerily calm, suggesting she's planning revenge. "Gina?" she says. "Stay focused. You have Toby now. You can leave without hurting anyone else."

"His name's not Toby, it's *Noah!*" screams Claire, agitated.

Being the closest to her, Chief Mendes whispers something into her ear. She'll be trying to reassure Claire that they'll get her son back, but they need to do so carefully as the situation is precarious. No one wants to upset Gina right now.

"That means Eugene lied to me about my dad," says Gina, the cogs visibly turning for her. "He said my dad sold me to him. That he wanted me dead."

"That's not true," says Steve from beside Madison. "Your father did everything he could to find you. We've read the case file, including all his statements to the police. He never stopped looking for you or your mother."

Gina looks at Jeff, distraught. "So I killed my dad for *nothing*? And I lived with Eugene thinking he rescued me when all along he was just as bad as you."

Jeff laughs mockingly. "So what? It's done now. What's meek little Amber Nelson going to do about it?"

Madison shudders. She wants to shoot the asshole herself, so she can only imagine what Gina's thinking. Her grip on her weapon tightens, but her arms are tiring from holding it level for so long. Gina is still aiming her weapon at Owen. Surely she wouldn't take her anger out on him instead of Jeff? "Gina. If you put the gun down, we can take Jeff into custody. He'll pay for what he did to you."

"No way," says Jeff. "I'm skipping town. *Alone.* She's been dragging me down for eighteen long months." He takes a step toward Gina. "Give me the gun."

Gina moves back, her eyes laser-focused on him. "You're forgetting something," she says evenly. "I'm not Amber Nelson anymore. I'm Gina Clark. I'm what you and Eugene made me.

And while it's true that Amber was meek and wouldn't hurt a fly, Gina's capable of murder."

In a heartbeat, she shifts her aim from Owen to Jeff and puts two bullets through this crotch. He screams like a wild animal, his shrill shrieks echoing into the night sky. Blood seeps through his blue jeans and his hands seem to want to cup himself but the wound is too painful to touch.

The gunshots make everyone jump. Officer Sanchez takes the opportunity to shoot at Gina, but his shot narrowly misses.

"No!" yells Madison as everyone else present pulls their weapons. Her heart is in her mouth, thinking of the consequences of gunshots around Noah and her own son. "Don't fire near the boy!"

Claire is sobbing beside them, dreading poor Noah being caught in the crossfire.

Gina has already aimed her weapon at Owen again, and everyone goes still. Except Jeff, who's writhing on the ground. His face has broken into a sweat, and blood is fast draining from him.

"Can we help him?" Steve asks Gina, wanting to administer first aid.

"No," she says. "No one helped me when I was in pain. Let's see how he feels."

It soon becomes clear that no amount of first aid would have helped Jeff, because he quickly goes still, as a puddle of shiny liquid spreads underneath him.

Gina doesn't care. She glances at the whimpering child in her arm. "Don't cry, sweetie. You're back with Mommy now."

Noah looks for his real mother and holds his hands out toward Claire, desperately squirming away from Gina.

Her face clouds over. She gets the boy's attention. "No, not her. *I'm* your mommy, Toby. You must remember? You love me, right?"

Noah shakes his head and his cries grow louder.

Madison can well imagine how heartbreaking this is for her. "Gina? Please lower your weapon. You're scaring Toby, and I know you don't want to hurt him, right? You have to protect him, and that means letting him go to Macy." She uses their alternate names because Gina has never really left the house she was held captive in. Not mentally. She's still living in that world, identifying with that woman instead of the woman she could have been if Jeff hadn't snatched her the night before she turned sixteen.

Gina's expression turns dark. She looks at Madison. "If you insist on taking my son away from me, I'll take yours away from you." Without warning, she fires a shot at Owen.

He drops to the ground quicker than Nate can reach him.

Madison's heart stops beating. The world stops turning.

She lowers her weapon, overwhelmed with hopelessness. Everything she does day in and day out to keep the people of Lost Creek safe is meaningless if she can't even protect her own son. Nothing will ever matter to her again. Not if Owen's dead.

Blood roars in her ears. She can't even find the energy to blink. Her throat seizes as she pictures the day Owen was born. The happiness that overwhelmed her when the midwife placed him in her arms, and his tiny hand grasped her index finger. She knew she'd spend the rest of her life fighting to look after him. But she hadn't anticipated the terrible period they would spend apart. The fact they were able to reconnect over the last eighteen months kept her alive when she had nothing else to live for. So if he dies now, what was it all for?

She tries to take a deep breath to avoid passing out.

Then her eyes refocus. The scene erupts into chaos around her. Conrad is forcefully removing the toddler from Gina. Steve is cuffing Gina's hands behind her back. She's crying. She looks remorseful now, but the damage is done.

Sergeant Adams crouches over Jeff, looking for signs of life.

He gets on the radio to dispatch, requesting multiple ambulances at the station immediately, but it's too late for Jeff.

Is it too late for Owen?

Chief Mendes pulls the weapon out of Madison's hand in case she decides to retaliate.

She sees it, she hears it, but she doesn't feel as if she's present.

She forces her legs to take her to where Owen is sprawled on the ground. Nate has taken his jacket off and laid it over her son. The closer she gets, the more of his head she can see. And eventually, his face. Although drained of blood and visibly shaking all over, Owen is alive.

"Come on, guys," he says with a nervous laugh. "I'm fine." He isn't smiling. He's in pain.

Madison searches for the wound with her eyes. There must be one, as he's not getting up.

Nate's kneeling over him. He sits back on his heels as he looks up at her, and grabs her clammy hand in his, which is slick with blood.

She can't breathe. This is her son's blood.

"The bullet skimmed his torso," says Nate. "He's losing blood, but he should be fine as long as the EMTs arrive fast."

Owen finally smiles up at her, and all she sees is the face of her little boy. "Don't worry, Mom. I'm fine."

Officer Sanchez tries to lighten the mood as he applies pressure to the wound. "Women love guys who've taken bullets. You're going to be a babe magnet, my friend."

Owen's teeth are chattering with shock, but he forces a laugh. "I'm joining the police academy. I want to be a cop."

Sanchez glances up at Madison, surprised, and no doubt curious for her reaction.

Madison turns away from everyone and breaks down so hard her knees hit the ground painfully.

She hears Owen tell her team behind her that his mom's

always overly dramatic, but no one laughs. Because they understand what she's going through. If Owen really does become a cop and one day has a family of his own, he'll understand it too.

Nate approaches. He crouches down to hug her as she lets out her relief that Owen's alive, and her fear over what could happen to him in the future. She can't stop trembling. She's also thinking of Amber Nelson, and struggling to see Gina as that poor girl. Amber deserved so much better. So did Rose Nelson, Bianca Marsh and Claire Barlow.

When she finally stops crying, Nate wipes away her tears with his sleeve. "Owen's going to be fine. So are they." He nods to Claire, who has Noah back in her arms and is kissing him all over his wet face. Despite what she's been through tonight, her expression is lighter. She knows that all the threats against her and her son, from Eugene, Jeff and Gina, are now over. With Gina in custody, Claire can finally reunite with her parents and give Noah the life he deserves, surrounded by doting grandparents and extended family.

Madison looks up at Nate. "If Owen makes it through the academy and joins the department, you need to as well. I'll petition for Mendes to hire you as a cold case consultant. You've helped us on so many cases already that she can't really say no, right? That way, Owen will have two of us nearby at all times. Because we need to keep him safe, Nate." She implores him with her eyes. "Will you help me keep him safe?"

He pushes a strand of her loose hair behind her ear. "Will I help protect my wife and son from danger?" He nods. "Seems like a no-brainer to me."

Madison's eyes brim with tears. He may not be Owen's biological father, but he's better than that. He loves her son voluntarily. She swallows back a sob as she realizes she's going to have to finally accept her little boy has become a young man. The thought terrifies her, but at least he has her and Nate in his life to help guide him.

A LETTER FROM WENDY

Thank you for reading *The Crying Girls*, book eight in the Detective Madison Harper series.

You can follow along with the journey by signing up to my newsletter here, and by following me on Facebook. This means you'll be alerted as soon as the next book in the series is available.

www.bookouture.com/wendy-dranfield

I suspect long-term readers of the series may have missed Nate working closely with Madison in this installment, but you'll understand from everything he's been through that there was no way he could take a person's life in the previous book (*Grave Mountain*) without any repercussions to his mental health. As much as he and Madison deserve to live happily ever after, their story has to be realistic. Nate is a man with morals, and taking someone else's life obviously triggered something in him that he needed to deal with before he can be the husband Madison deserves.

And with that, you are cordially invited to the wedding of Madison Harper and Nate Monroe, which will take place in Lost Creek, Colorado, in book nine! I think it's about time they put the past behind them and had some happiness in their lives. I'm sure you'll agree!

Anyone starting the series with this book who would like to understand what triggered Nate to go downhill, you'll find the answers in the previous book. But to understand his time on death row, and how his and Madison's relationship started, you'll need to read the books in order, starting with *Shadow Falls*. Writing a series is a balancing act of providing new and exciting plots for continuing readers while touching on what has already happened in the series for people joining it part-way through. Personally, I can't read a series out of order, but that's just me!

If you enjoyed this book, please leave a rating or review (no matter how brief) on Amazon. This helps it to stand out among the thousands of books published each week, allowing it to reach more readers and ensuring the series continues.

Thanks for reading.

Wendy

www.wendydranfield.co.uk

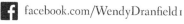 facebook.com/WendyDranfield1

ACKNOWLEDGMENTS

Thank you to the readers who have followed me from the beginning of my career and cheer me on with each new book. Also to the advance readers and book bloggers who review my books with so much enthusiasm. I love reading your reviews.

As always, thank you to everyone at Bookouture who worked on my latest book.

And finally, a special thanks to my wonderful husband, the reader of all my first drafts. He always suspects every single character of being the bad guy, and gets it wrong every single time!

PUBLISHING TEAM

Turning a manuscript into a book requires the efforts of many people. The publishing team at Bookouture would like to acknowledge everyone who contributed to this publication.

Audio
Alba Proko
Melissa Tran
Sinead O'Connor

Commercial
Lauren Morrissette
Hannah Richmond
Imogen Allport

Cover design
The Brewster Project

Data and analysis
Mark Alder
Mohamed Bussuri

Editorial
Jessie Botterill
Ria Clare

Made in the USA
Monee, IL
03 October 2024